Mudwoman

NOVELS BY JOYCE CAROL OATES

With Shuddering Fall
(*1964*)

A Garden of Earthly
Delights (*1967*)

Expensive People (*1968*)

them (*1969*)

Wonderland (*1971*)

Do with Me
What You Will (*1973*)

The Assassins (*1975*)

Childwold (*1976*)

Son of the Morning (*1978*)

Unholy Loves (*1979*)

Bellefleur (*1980*)

Angel of Light (*1981*)

A Bloodsmoor Romance
(*1982*)

Mysteries of Winterthurn
(*1984*)

Solstice (*1985*)

Marya: A Life (*1986*)

You Must Remember This
(*1987*)

American Appetites (*1989*)

Because It Is Bitter, and
Because It Is My Heart
(*1990*)

Black Water (*1992*)

Foxfire: Confessions of a
Girl Gang (*1993*)

What I Lived For (*1994*)

Zombie (*1995*)

We Were the Mulvaneys
(*1996*)

Man Crazy (*1997*)

My Heart Laid Bare (*1998*)

Broke Heart Blues (*1999*)

Blonde (*2000*)

Middle Age: A Romance
(*2001*)

I'll Take You There (*2002*)

The Tattooed Girl (*2003*)

The Falls (*2004*)

Missing Mom (*2005*)

Black Girl / White Girl
(*2006*)

The Gravedigger's
Daughter (*2007*)

My Sister, My Love (*2008*)

Little Bird of Heaven
(*2009*)

Mudwoman

Joyce Carol Oates

HARPER LUXE

An Imprint of HarperCollinsPublishers

"Mudgirl in the Land of Moriah. April 1965" and "Mudgirl Saved by the King of the Crows. April 1965" were first published in *Boulevard*, 2010, 2011.

FIRST HARPERLUXE EDITION

HarperLuxe™ is a trademark of HarperCollins Publishers

Library of Congress Cataloging-in-Publication Data is available upon request.

ISBN: 978-0-06-210726-8

12 13 14 ID/RRD 10 9 8 7 6 5 4 3 2 1

For Charlie Gross,
my husband and
first reader

What is man? A ball of snakes.
FRIEDRICH NIETZSCHE,
Thus Spake Zarathustra

Here the frailest leaves of me and yet
my strongest lasting,
Here I shade and hide my thoughts,
I myself do not expose them,
And yet they expose me more than all my other poems.
WALT WHITMAN,
"Here the Frailest Leaves of Me"

Time is a way of preventing all things
from happening at once.
ANDRE LITOVIK,
"The Evolving Universe: Origin, Age & Fate"

Mudwoman

Mudgirl in the Land of Moriah.

You must be readied, the woman said.

Readied was not a word the child comprehended. In the woman's voice *readied* was a word of calm and stillness like water glittering in the mudflats beside the Black Snake River the child would think were the scales of a giant snake if you were so close to the snake you could not actually see it.

For this was the land of Moriah, the woman was saying. This place they had come to in the night that was the place promised to them where their enemies had no dominion over them and where no one knew them or had even glimpsed them.

The woman spoke in the voice of calm still flat glittering water and her words were evenly enunciated as if the speaker were translating blindly as she spoke and the words from which she translated were oddly shaped and fitted haphazardly into her larynx: they would give her pain, but she was no stranger to pain, and had learned to find a secret happiness in pain, too wonderful to risk by acknowledging it.

He is saying to us, to trust Him. In all that is done, to trust Him.

Out of the canvas bag in which, these several days and nights on the meandering road north out of Star Lake she'd carried what was needed to bring them into the land of Moriah safely, the woman took the shears.

In her exhausted sleep the child had been hearing the cries of crows like scissors snipping the air in the mudflats beside the Black Snake River.

In sleep smelling the sharp brackish odor of still water and of rich dark earth and broken and rotted things in the earth.

A day and a night on the road beside the old canal and another day and this night that wasn't yet dawn at the edge of the mudflats.

Trust Him. This is in His hands.

And the woman's voice that was not the woman's familiar hoarse and strained voice but this voice of detachment and wonder in the face of something that has gone well when it was not expected, or was not expected quite so soon.

If it is wrong for any of this to be done, He will send an angel of the Lord as He sent to Abraham to spare his son Isaac and also to Hagar, that her son was given back his life in the wilderness of Beersheba.

In her stubby fingers that were chafed and bled easily after three months of the gritty-green lye-soap that was the only soap available in the county detention facility the woman wielded the large tarnished seamstress's shears to cut the child's badly matted hair. And with these stubby fingers tugging at the hair, in sticky clumps and snarls the child's fine fawn-colored hair that had become "nasty" and "smelly" and "crawling with lice."

Be still! Be good! You are being readied for the Lord.

For our enemies will take you from me, if you are not readied.

For God has guided us to the land of Moriah. His promise is no one will take any child from her lawful mother in this place.

And the giant shears clipped and snipped and clattered merrily. You could tell that the giant shears took pride in shearing off the child's befouled hair that was disgusting in the sight of God. Teasingly close to the

4 · JOYCE CAROL OATES

girl's tender ears the giant shears came, and the child
shuddered, and squirmed, and whimpered, and wept;
and the woman had no choice but to slap the child's
face, not hard, but hard enough to calm her, as often the
woman did; hard enough to make the child go very still
the way even a baby rabbit will go still in the cunning
of terror; and then, when the child's hair lay in wan
spent curls on the mud-stained floor, the woman drew
a razor blade over the child's head—a blade clutched
between her fingers, tightly—causing the blade to
scrape against the child's hair-stubbled scalp and now
the child flinched and whimpered louder and began to
struggle—and with a curse the woman dropped the
razor blade which was badly tarnished and covered
with hairs and the woman kicked it aside with a harsh
startled laugh as if in wishing to rid the child of her
snarly dirty hair that was shameful in the eyes of God
the woman had gone too far, and had been made to
recognize her error.

For it was wrong of her to curse—*God damn!*

To take the name of the Lord in vain—*God damn!*

For in the Herkimer County detention facility the
woman had taken a vow of silence in defiance of her
enemies and she had taken a vow of utter obedience to
the Lord God and these several weeks following her
release, until now she had not betrayed this vow.

Not even in the Herkimer County family court. Not even when the judge spoke sharply to her, to speak—to make a plea of *guilty, not guilty.*

Not even when the threat was that the children would be taken forcibly from her. The children—the sisters—who were five and three—would be wards of the county and would be placed with a foster family and not even then would the woman speak for God suffused her with His strength in the very face of her enemies.

And so the woman took up a smaller scissors, out of the canvas bag, to clip the child's fingernails so short the tender flesh beneath the nails began to bleed. Though the child was frightened she managed to hold herself still except for shivering as the baby rabbit will hold itself still in the desperate hope that is most powerful in living creatures, our deepest expectation in the face of all evidence refuting it, that the terrible danger will pass.

For—maybe—this was a *game?* What the spike-haired man called a *game?* Secret from the woman was the little cherry pie—sweet cherry pie in a wax-paper package small enough to fit into the palm of the spike-haired man's hand—so delicious, the child devoured it greedily and quickly before it might be shared by another. There was *splash-splash* which was bathing the child in the claw-footed tub while the woman slept in the next room on the bare mattress on the floor her limbs sprawled as if she'd fallen from a height onto her back moaning in her sleep and waking in a paroxysm of coughing as if she were coughing out her very guts. Bathing the child who had not been bathed in many days and mixed with the bathing was the *game of tickle*. So carefully!—as if she were a breakable porcelain doll and not a tough durable rubber doll like Dolly you'd just bang around, let fall onto the floor and kick out of your way if she was in your way—and so quietly!—the spike-haired man carried the child into the bathroom and to the claw-footed tub that was the size of a trough for animals to drink from and in the bathroom with the door shut—forcibly—for the door was warped and the bolt could not be slid in place—the spike-haired man stripped the child's soiled pajamas from her and set her—again so carefully!—a forefinger pressed to his lips to indicate how carefully and without noise this must be—set her into the tub—into the water that sprang from the faucet tinged with rust and was only lukewarm and there were few soap bubbles except when the spike-haired man rubbed his hands vigorously together with the bar of nice-smelling Ivory soap between his palms and lathered the suds on the child's squirmy little pale body like something soft prized out of its shell in what was the *game of tickle—the secret game of tickle;* and amid the splashing soon the water cooled and had to be replenished from the faucet—but the faucet made a groaning sound as if in protest and the spike-haired man pressed his forefinger against his lips pursed like a TV clown's lips and his raggedy eyebrows lifted to make the child laugh—or, if not laugh, to make the child cease squirming, struggling—for the *game of tickle* was very *ticklish!*—the spike-haired man laughed a near-soundless hissing laugh and soon after lapsed into an open-mouthed doze having lost the energy that rippled through him like electricity through a coil and the child waited until the spike-haired man was snoring half-sitting half-lying on the puddled floor of the bathroom with his back against the wall and water-droplets glistening in the dense wiry steel-colored hairs on his chest and on the soft flaccid folds of his belly and groin and when finally in the early evening when the spike-haired man awakened—and when the woman sprawled on the mattress in the adjacent room awakened—the child had climbed out of the tub naked and shivering and her skin puckered and white like the skin of a defeathered chicken and for a long time the woman and the spike-haired man searched for her until she was discovered clutching at her ugly bareheaded rubber doll curled up like a stepped-on little worm in skeins of cobweb and dustballs beneath the cellar stairs.

Hide-and-seek! Hide-and-seek and the spike-haired man was the one to find her!

For what were the actions of adults except *games,* and variants of *games.* The child was given to know that a *game* would come to an end unlike other actions that were *not-games* and could not be ended but sprawled on and on like a highway or a railroad track or the river rushing beneath the loose-fitting planks of the bridge near the house in which she and the woman had lived with the spike-haired man before the *trouble.*

This is not hurting you! You will defame God if you make such a fuss.

The woman's voice was not so calm now but raw-sounding like something that has been broken and gives pain. And the woman's fingers on the child were harder, and the broken and uneven nails were sharp as a cat's claws digging into the child's flesh.

The child's tender scalp was bleeding. The hairs remaining were stubbled. Amid the remaining sticky strands of hair haphazardly cut and partly shaved were tiny frantic lice. By this time the child's soiled clothes had been removed, wadded into a ball and kicked aside. It was a tar paper cabin the woman had discovered in the underbrush between the road and the towpath. The sign from God directing her to this abandoned place had been a weatherworn toppled-over cross at the roadside that was in fact a mileage marker so faded you could not make out the words or the numerals but the woman had seen M O R I A H.

In this foul place where they had slept wrapped in the woman's rumpled and stained coat there was no possibility of bathing the child. Nor would there have been time to bathe the child, for God was growing impatient now it was dawn which was why the woman's hands fumbled and her lips moved in prayer. The sky was growing lighter like a great eye opening and in most of the sky that you could see were clouds massed and dense like chunks of concrete.

Except at the tree line on the farther side of the mudflats where the sun rose.

Except if you stared hard enough you could see that the concrete clouds were melting away and the sky was layered in translucent faint-red clouds like veins in a great translucent heart that was the awakening of God to the new dawn in the land of Moriah.

In the car the woman had said *I will know when I see. My trust is in the Lord.*

The woman said *Except for the Lord, everything is finished.*

The woman was not speaking to the child for it was not her practice to speak to the child even when they were alone. And when they were in the presence of others, the woman had ceased speaking at all and it was the impression of those others who had no prior knowledge of the woman that she was both mute and deaf and very likely had been born so.

In the presence of others the woman had learned to shrink inside her clothing that hung loosely on her for at the time of her pregnancies she had been ashamed and fearful of the eyes of strangers moving on her like X-rays and so she had acquired men's clothing that hid her body—though around her neck in a loose knot, for her throat was often painful, and she feared strep throat, was a scarf of some shiny crinkly purple material she had found discarded.

The child was naked inside the paper nightgown. The child was bleeding from her razor-lacerated scalp in a dozen tiny wounds and shivering and naked inside the pale green paper nightgown faintly stamped HERKIMER CO. DETENTION that had been cut by the giant shears to reduce its length if not its width so that the paper nightgown came to just the child's skinny ankles.

A paper gown to be tracked to the Herkimer County medical unit attached to the women's detention home.

In the rear seat of the rattling rusted Plymouth which was the spike-haired man's sole legacy was the child's rubber doll. *Dolly* was the name of the doll that had been her sister's and was now hers. Dolly's face was soiled and her eyes had ceased to see. Dolly's small mouth was a pucker in the grim rubber flesh. And Dolly too was near-bald, only patches of curly fair hair remaining where you could see how the sad feathery fawn-colored hairs had been glued to the rubber scalp.

Seventy miles north of Star Lake as remote to the woman and the child as the farther, eclipsed half of the moon, the shadowed mudflats beside the river.

So meandering and twisting were the mountain roads, a journey of merely seventy miles had required days, for the woman feared to drive the rattling automobile at any speed beyond thirty. And urgent to her too, that her obedience to God was manifest in this slowness and in this deliberateness like one who can only read by drawing his forefinger beneath each letter of each word to be enunciated aloud.

The child did not fret. But the woman believed, in her heart the child did fret for both the children were rebellious. No comb could be forced through such snarled hair.

In harsh jeering cries the crows reviled God.

Jeering demanding to know as the (female, middle-aged) judge had demanded to know why these children have been found filthy and partly clothed pawing through a Dumpster behind the Shop-Rite scavenging for food like stray dogs or wild creatures shrinking in the beam of a flashlight. And the elder of the sisters clutching at the hand of the younger and would not let go.

And how does the mother explain and how does the mother plead.

Proudly the woman stood and her chin uplifted and eyes shut against the Whore of Babylon there in black robes but a lurid lipstick-mouth and plucked eyebrows like arched insect wings. No more would the woman *plead* than fall to her knees before this whorish vision.

The children had been taken from her and placed in temporary custody of the county. But the will of God was such, all that was rightfully the woman's was restored to her, in time.

In all those weeks, months—the woman had never weakened in her faith that all that was hers, would be restored to her.

And now at dawn the sky in the east was ever-shifting, expanding. The gray concrete-sky that is the world-bereft-of-God was retreating. Almost you could see angels of wrath in these broken clouds. Glittering light in the stagnant strips of water of the mudflats of the hue of watery blood. Less than a half mile from the Black Snake River in a desolate area of northeastern Beechum County in the foothills of the Adirondacks, where the hand of God had guided her. Here were the remains of an abandoned mill, an unpaved road and rotted debris amid tall snakelike marsh grasses that shivered and whispered in the wind. Exposed roots of trees and collapsed and rotting tree trunks bearing the whorled and affrighted faces of the damned. And what beauty in such forlorn places, Mudgirl would cherish through her life. For we most cherish those places to which we have been brought to die but have not died. No smells more pungent than the sharp muck-smell of the mudflats where the brackish river water seeps and is trapped and stagnant with algae the bright vivid green of Crayola. Vast unfathomable acres of mud-flats amid cattails, jimsonweed and scattered litter of old tires, boots, torn clothing, broken umbrellas and rotted newspapers, abandoned stoves, refrigerators with doors flung open like empty arms. Seeing a small squat refrigerator tossed on its side in the mud the child thought *She will put us inside that one.*

But something was wrong with this. The thought came a second time, to correct—*She has put us inside that one. She has shut the door.*

There came a frenzy of crows, red-winged black-birds, starlings, as if the child had spoken aloud and said a forbidden thing.

The woman cried shaking her fist at the birds, God will curse you!

The raucous accusing cries grew louder. More black-feathered birds appeared, spreading their great wings. They settled in the skeletal trees fierce and clattering. The woman cried, cursed and spat and yet the bird-shrieks continued and the child was given to know that the birds had come for *her.*

These were sent by Satan, the woman said.

It was time, the woman said. A day and a night and another day and now the night had become dawn of the new day and it was time and so despite the shriek-ing birds the woman half-walked half-carried the child in the torn paper nightgown in the direction of the ruined mill. Pulling at the child so that the child's thin pale arm felt as if it were about to be wrenched out of its socket.

The woman made her way beyond the ruined mill which smelled richly of something sweetly rancid and fermented and into an area of broken bricks and rotted lumber fallen amid rich dark muddy soil and spiky weeds grown to the height of children. In her haste she startled a long black snake sleeping in the rotted lumber but the snake refused to crawl away rapidly instead moving slowly and sinuously out of sight in defiance of the intruder. At first the woman paused— the woman stared—for the woman was awaiting an angel of God to appear to her—but the sinuous black-glittering snake was no angel of God and in a fury of hurt, disappointment and determination the woman cried, Satan go back to hell where you came from but already in insolent triumph the snake had vanished into the underbrush.

The child had ceased whimpering, for the woman had forbade her. The child barefoot and naked inside the rumpled and torn pale green paper gown faintly stamped HERKIMER CO. DETENTION. The child's legs were very thin and stippled with insect bites and of these bites many were bleeding, or had only recently ceased bleeding. The child's head near-bald, stubbled and bleeding and the eyes dazed, uncomprehending. At the end of a lane leading to the canal towpath was a spit of land gleaming with mud the hue of baby shit and tinged with a sulfurous yellow: and the smell was the smell of baby shit for here were many things rotted and gone. Faint mists rose from the interior of the marsh like the exhaled breaths of dying things. The child began to cry helplessly. As the woman hauled her along the land-spit the child began to struggle but could not prevail. The child was weak from malnutrition yet still the child could not have prevailed for the woman was strong and the strength of God flowed through her being like a bright blinding beacon. Light flared off the woman's face, she had never been so certain of herself and so joyous in certainty as now. For knowing now that the angel of God would not appear to her as the angel of God had appeared to both Abraham and Hagar who had borne Abraham's child and had been cast into the wilderness by Abraham with the child to die of thirst.

And this was not the first time the angel of God had been withheld from her. But it would be the last time.

With a bitter laugh the woman said, Here, I am returning her to You. As You have bade me, so I am returning her to You.

First, Dolly: the woman pried Dolly from the child's fingers and tossed Dolly out into the mud.

Here! Here is the first of them.

The woman spoke happily, harshly. The rubber doll lay astonished in the mud below.

Next, the child: the woman seized the child in her arms to push her off the spit of land and into the mud—the child clutched at her only now daring to cry *Momma! Momma!*—the woman pried the child's fingers loose and pushed, shoved, kicked the child down the steep incline into the flat glistening mud below close by the ugly rubber doll and there the child flailed her thin naked limbs, on her belly now and her small astonished face in the mud so the cry *Momma* was muffled and on the bank above the woman fumbled for something—a broken tree limb—to swing at the child for God is a merciful God and would not wish the child to suffer but the woman could not reach the child and so in frustration threw the limb down at the child for all the woman's calmness had vanished and she was now panting, breathless and half-sobbing and by this time though the ugly rubber doll remained where it had fallen on the surface of the mud the agitated child was being sucked down into the mud, a chilly bubbly mud that would warm but grudgingly with the sun, a mud that filled the child's mouth, and a mud that filled the child's eyes, and a mud that filled the child's ears, until at last there was no one on the spit of land above the mudflat to observe her struggle and no sound but the cries of the affronted crows.

Mudwoman's Journey.
The Black River Café.

October 2002

Readied. She believed yes, she was.

She was not one to be taken by surprise.

"Carlos, stop! Please. Let me out here."

In the rearview mirror the driver's eyes moved onto her, startled.

"Ma'am? Here?"

"I mean—Carlos—I'd like to stop for just a minute. Stretch my legs."

This was so awkwardly phrased, and so seemingly fraudulent—*stretch my legs*!

Politely the driver protested: "Ma'am—it's less than an hour to Ithaca."

He was regarding her with a look of mild alarm in the rearview mirror. Very much, she disliked being observed in that mirror.

"Please just park on the shoulder of the road, Carlos. I won't be a minute."

Now she did speak sharply.

Though continuing to smile of course. For it was unavoidable, in this new phase of her life she was being observed.

The bridge!

She had never seen the bridge before, she was sure. And yet—how familiar it was to her.

It was not a distinguished or even an unusual bridge but an old-style truss bridge of the 1930s, with a single span: wrought-iron girders marked with elaborate encrustations of rust like ancient and unreadable hieroglyphics. Already M.R. knew, without needing to see, that the bridge was bare planking and would rattle beneath crossing vehicles; all of the bridge would vibrate finely, like a great tuning fork.

Like the bridges of M.R.'s memory, this bridge had been built high above the stream below, which was a small river, or a creek, that flooded its banks after rainstorms. To cross the bridge you had to ascend a steep paved ramp. Both the bridge and the ramp were narrower by several inches than the two-lane state highway that led to the bridge and so in its approach to the bridge the road conspicuously narrowed and the shoulder was sharply attenuated. All this happened without warning—you had to know the bridge, not to blunder onto it when a large vehicle like a van or a truck was crossing.

There was no shoulder here upon which to park safely, at least not a vehicle the size of the Lincoln Town Car, but canny Carlos had discovered an unpaved service lane at the foot of the bridge ramp, that led to the bank of the stream. The lane was rutted, muddy. In a swath of underbrush the limousine came to a jolting stop only a few yards from rushing water.

Some subtle way in which the driver both obeyed his impulsive employer, and resisted her, made M.R.'s heart quicken in opposition to him. Clearly Carlos understood that this was an imprudent stop to have made, within an hour of their destination; the very alacrity with which he'd driven the shiny black limousine off the road and into underbrush was a rebuke to her, who had issued a command to him.

"Carlos, thank you. I won't be a—a minute . . ."

Won't be a minute. Like *stretch my legs* this phrase sounded in her ears forced and alien to her, as if another spoke through her mouth, and M.R. was the ventriloquist's dummy.

Quickly before Carlos could climb out of the car to open the door for her, M.R. opened the door for herself. She couldn't seem to accustom herself to being treated with such deference and formality!—it wasn't M.R.'s nature.

M.R., whom excessive attention and even moderate flattery embarrassed terribly; as if, by instinct, she understood the mockery that underscores formality.

"I'll be right back! I promise."

She spoke cheerily, gaily. M.R. couldn't bear for any employee—any member of her staff—to feel uncomfortable in her presence.

As, teaching, when she'd approach a seminar room hearing the voices and laughter of the students inside, she'd hesitate to intrude—to evoke an abrupt and too-respectful silence.

Her power over others was that they *liked* her. Such *liking* could only be volitional, free choice.

She was walking along the embankment thinking these thoughts. By degrees the rushing water drowned out her thoughts—hypnotic, just slightly edgy. There is always a gravitational pull toward water: to rushing water. One is drawn *forward*, one is drawn *in*.

Now. Here. Come. It is time. . . .

She smiled hearing voices in the water. The illusion of voices in the water.

But here was an impediment: the bank was tangled with briars, vines. An agonized twisting of something resembling guts. It wasn't a good idea for M.R. to be walking in her charcoal-gray woolen trousers and her pinching-new Italian shoes.

Yet if you looked closely, with a child's eye, you could discern a faint trail amid the underbrush. Children, fishermen. Obviously, people made their way along the stream, sometimes.

A nameless stream—creek, or river. Seemingly shallow, yet wide. A sprawl of boulders, flat shale-like rock. Froth of the hue and seeming substance of the most *nouveau* of *haute cuisine*—foam-food, pureed and juiced, all substance leached from it, terrible food! Tasteless and unsatisfying and yet M.R. had been several times obliged to admire it, dining at the Manhattan homes of one or another of the University's wealthy trustees, who kept in their employ full-time chefs.

The creek, or river, was much smaller than the Black Snake River that flowed south and west out of the southern Adirondacks, traversing Beechum County at a diagonal—the river of M.R.'s childhood. Yet—here was the identical river-smell. If M.R. shut her eyes and inhaled deeply, she was *there*.

Here was an odor of something brackish and just slightly sour—rancid / rotted—decaying leaves—rich damp dark earth that sank beneath her heels as she made her way along the bank, shading her eyes against the watery glitter like tinfoil.

Mingled with the river-smell was an odor of something burning, like rubber. Smoldering tires, garbage. A wet-feather smell. But faint enough that it wasn't unpleasant.

All that M.R. could see—on the farther bank of the stream—was a wall of dark-brick buildings with only a few windows on each floor; and beyond the windows, nothing visible. High on the sides of the buildings were advertisements—product names and pictures of— faces? human figures?—eroded by time and now indecipherable, lost to all meaning.

" 'Mohawk Meats and Poultry.' "

The words came to her. The memory was random, and fleeting.

" 'Boudreau Women's Gloves and Hosiery.' "

But that had been Carthage, long ago. These ghost-signs, M.R. could not read at all.

Carlos was surely correct, they weren't far from the small city of Ithaca—which meant the vast sprawling spectacular campus of Cornell University where M.R. had been an undergraduate twenty years before and had graduated summa cum laude, in another lifetime. Yet she had no idea of the name of this small town or where exactly they were except south and west of Ithaca in the glacier-ravaged countryside of Tompkins County.

It was a bright chilly October day. It was a day splotched with sumac like bursts of flame.

The not-very-prosperous small town of faded-brick storefronts and cracked sidewalks reminded M.R. of the small city in which she'd grown up in Beechum County in the foothills of the southern Adirondacks. Vaguely she was thinking *I should have planned to visit them. It has been so long.*

Her father lived there still—in Carthage.

She had not told Konrad Neukirchen that she would be spending three nights within a hundred miles of Carthage since virtually every minute of the conference would be filled with appointments, engagements, panels, talks—and yet more people would request time with M.R., once the conference began. She had not wanted to disappoint her father, who'd always been so proud of her.

Her father, and also her mother of course. Both the Neukirchens: Konrad and Agatha.

How painful it was to M.R., to disappoint others! Her elders, who'd invested so much in her. Their love for her was a heavy cloak upon her shoulders, like one of those lead-shield cloaks laid upon you in the dentist's office to shield you from X-rays—you were grateful for the cloak but more grateful when it was removed.

Far rather would M.R. be disappointed by others, than to be the agent of disappointment herself. For

M.R. could forgive—readily; she was very good at for-giveness.

She was very good at forgetting, also. To forget is the very principle of forgiveness.

Perhaps it was a Quaker principle, or ought to have been, which she'd inherited from her parents: *forget, forgive.*

Boldly now she walked on the bank of the nameless river amid broken things. An observer on the bridge some distance away would have been surprised to see her: a well-dressed woman, alone, in this place so im-practical for walking, amid a slovenly sort of quasi-wilderness. M.R. was a tall woman whom an erect backbone and held-high head made taller—a woman of youthful middle-age with an appealingly girlish face—fleshy, flush-cheeked. Her eyes were both shy and quick-darting, assessing. In fact the eyes were a falcon's eyes, in a girl's face.

How strange she felt in this place! The glittery light—lights—reflected in the swift-running water seemed to suffuse her heart. She felt both exhila-rated and apprehensive, as if she were approaching danger. Not a visible danger perhaps. Yet she must go forward.

This was a common feeling of course. Common to all who inhabit a "public" role. She would be addressing an audience in which there was sure to be some opposition to her prepared words.

Her keynote address, upon which she'd worked intermittently, for weeks, was only to be twenty minutes long: "The Role of the University in an Era of 'Patriotism.'" This was the first time that M. R. Neukirchen had been invited to address the National Conference of the prestigious American Association of Learned Societies. There would be hostile questions put to her at the conclusion of her talk, she supposed. At her own University where the faculty so supported her liberal position, yet there were dissenting voices from the right. But overwhelmingly her audience that evening would support her, she was sure.

It would be thrilling—to speak to this distinguished group, and to make an impression on them. Somehow it had happened, the shy schoolgirl had become, with the passage of not so many years, an impassioned and effective public speaker—a Valkyrie of a figure— fiercely articulate, intense. You could see that she *cared so much*—almost, at moments, M.R. quivered with feeling, as if about to stammer.

Audiences were transfixed by her, in the narrow and rarified academic world in which she dwelt.

I am baring my soul to you. I care so deeply!

Often she felt faint, beforehand. A turmoil in her stomach as if she might be physically ill.

The way an actor might feel, stepping into a magisterial role. The way an athlete might feel, on the cusp of a great triumph—or loss.

Her (secret) lover had once assured her *It isn't panic you feel, Meredith. It isn't even fear. It's excitement: anticipation.*

Her (secret) lover was a brilliant but not entirely reliable man, an astronomer/cosmologist happiest in the depths of the Universe. Andre Litovik's travels took him into extragalactic space far from M.R. yet he, too, was proud of her, and did love her in his way. So she wished to believe.

They saw each other infrequently. They did not even communicate often, for Andre was negligent about answering e-mail. Yet, they thought of each other continuously—or so M.R. wished to believe.

Possibly unwisely, given the dense underbrush here, M.R. was approaching the bridge from beneath. She'd been correct: the floor was planking—you could see sunlight through the cracks—as vehicles passed, the plank floor rattled. A pickup truck, several cars—the bridge was so narrow, traffic slowed to five miles an hour.

She'd learned to drive over such a bridge. Long ago.

She felt the old frisson of dread—a visceral unease she experienced now mainly when flying in turbulent weather—*Return to your seats please, fasten your seat belts please, the captain has requested you return to your seats please.*

At such times the terrible thought came to her: *To die among strangers! To die in flaming wreckage.*

Such curious, uncharacteristic thoughts M. R. Neukirchen hid from those who knew her intimately. But there was no one really, who knew M. R. Neukirchen intimately.

In a way it was strange to her, this curious fact: she had not (yet) died.

As the pre-Socratics pondered *Why is there something and not rather nothing?*—so M.R. pondered *Why am I here, and not rather—nowhere?*

A purely intellectual speculation, this was. M.R.'s professional philosophizing wasn't tainted by the merely personal.

Yet, these questions were strange, and wonderful. Not an hour of her life when she did not give thanks.

M.R. had been an *only child.* An entire psychology has been devised involving the *only child,* a variant of the *first-born.*

The *only child* is not inevitably the *first-born,* however. The *only child* may be the survivor.

The *only child* is more likely to be gifted than a child with numerous siblings. Obviously, the *only child* is likely to be lonely.

Self-reliant, self-sufficient. "Creative."

Did M.R. believe in such theories? Or did she believe, for this was closer to her personal experience, that personalities are distinct, individual and unique, and unfathomable—in terms of influences and causality, inexplicable?

She'd been trained as a philosopher, she had a Ph.D. in European philosophy from one of the great philosophy departments in the English-speaking world. Yet she'd taken graduate courses in cognitive psychology, neuroscience, international law. She'd participated in bioethics colloquia. She'd published a frequently anthologized essay titled "How Do You Know What You 'Know': Skepticism as Moral Imperative." As the president of a distinguished research university in which theories of every sort were devised, debated, maintained, and defended—an abundance like a spring field blooming and buzzing with a profusion of life—M.R. wasn't obliged to believe but she was obliged to take seriously, to respect.

My dream is to be—of service! I want to do good.

She was quite serious. She was wholly without irony.

The Convent Street bridge, in Carthage. Of course, that was the bridge she was trying to recall.

And other bridges, other waterways, streams—M.R. couldn't quite recall.

In a kind of trance she was staring, smiling. As a child, she'd learned quickly. Of all human reflexes, the most valuable.

The river was a fast shallow stream on which boulders emerged like bleached bone. Fallen tree limbs lay in the water sunken and rotted and on these mud turtles basked in the October sun, motionless as creatures carved of stone. M.R. knew from her rural childhood that if you approached these turtles, even at a distance they would arouse themselves, waken and slip into the water; seemingly asleep, in reptilian stillness, they were yet highly alert, vigilant.

A memory came to her of boys who'd caught a mud turtle, shouting and flinging the poor creature down onto the rocks, dropping rocks on it, cracking its shell. . . .

Why would you do such a thing? Why kill . . . ?

It was a question no one asked. You would not ask. You would be ridiculed, if you asked.

She had failed to defend the poor turtle against the boys. She'd been too young—very young. The boys had been older. Always there were too many of them— the enemy.

These small failures, long ago. No one knew now. No one who knew her now. If she'd tried to tell them they would stare at her, uncomprehending. *Are you serious? You can't be serious.*

Certainly she was serious: a serious woman. The first female president of the University.

Not that *femaleness* was an issue, it was not.

Without hesitation M.R. would claim, and in interviews would elaborate, that not once in her professional career, nor in her years as a student, had she been discriminated against, as a woman.

It was the truth, as M.R. knew it. She was not one to lodge complaints or to speak in disdain, hurt, or reproach.

What was that—something moving upstream? A child wading? But the air was too cold for wading and the figure too white: a snowy egret.

Beautiful long-legged bird searching for fish in the swift shallow water. M.R. watched it for several seconds—such stillness! Such patience.

At last, as if uneasy with M.R.'s presence, the egret seemed to shake itself, lifted its wide wings, and flew away.

Nearby but invisible were birds—jays, crows. Raucous cries of crows.

Quickly M.R. turned away. The harsh-clawing sound of a crow's cry was disturbing to her.

"Oh!"—in her eagerness to leave this place she'd turned her ankle, or nearly.

She should not have stopped to walk here, Carlos was right to disapprove. Now her heels sank in the soft mucky earth. So clumsy!

As a young athlete M.R. had been quick on her feet for a girl of her height and ("Amazonian") body-type but soon after her teens she'd begun to lose this reflexive speed, the hand-eye coordination an athlete takes for granted until it begins to abandon her.

"Ma'am? Let me help you."

Ma'am. What a rebuke to her foolishness!

Carlos had approached to stand just a few feet away. M.R. didn't want to think that her driver had been watching her, protectively, all along.

"I'm all right, Carlos, thank you. I think. . . ."

But M.R. was limping, in pain. It was a quick stabbing pain she hoped would fade within a few minutes but she hadn't much choice except to lean on Carlos's arm as they made their way back to the car, along the faint path through the underbrush.

Her heart was beating rapidly, strangely. The birds' cries—the crows' cries—were both jeering and beautiful: strange wild cries of yearning, summons.

But what was this?—something stuck to the bottom of one of her shoes. The newly purchased Italian black-leather shoes she'd felt obliged to buy, several times more expensive than any other shoes M.R. had ever purchased.

And on her trouser cuffs—briars, burrs.

And what was in her hair?—she hoped it wasn't bird droppings from the underside of that damned bridge.

"Excuse me, ma'am . . ."

"Thanks, Carlos! I'm fine."

"Ma'am, wait . . ."

Gallant Carlos stooped to detach whatever it was stuck to M.R.'s shoe. M.R. had been trying to kick it free without exactly seeing it, and without allowing Carlos to see it; yet of course, Carlos had seen. How ridiculous this was! She was chagrined, embarrassed. The last thing she wanted was her uniformed Hispanic driver stooping at her feet but of course Carlos insisted upon doing just this, deftly he detached whatever had been stuck to the sole of her shoe and flicked it into the underbrush and when M.R. asked what it was he said quietly not meeting her eye:

"Nothing, ma'am. It's gone."

It was October 2002. In the U.S. capital, war was being readied.

If objects pass into the space "neglected" after brain damage, they disappear. If the right brain is injured, the deficit will manifest itself in the left visual field.

The paradox is: how do we know what we can't know when it does not appear to us.

How do we know what we have failed to see because we have failed to see it, thus cannot know that we have failed to see it.

Unless—the shadow of what-is-not-seen can be seen by us.

A wide-winged shadow swiftly passing across the surface of Earth.

In the late night—her brain too excited for sleep—she'd been working on a philosophy paper—a problem in epistemology. *How do we know what we cannot know: what are the perimeters of "knowing". . .*

As a university president she'd vowed she would *keep up* with her field—after this first, inaugural year as president she would resume teaching a graduate seminar in philosophy/ethics each semester. All problems of philosophy seemed to her essentially problems of epistemology. But of course these were problems in perception: neuropsychology.

The leap from a problem in epistemology/neuropsychology to politics—this was risky.

For had not Nietzsche observed—*Madness in individuals is rare but in nations, common.*

Yet she would make this leap, she thought—for this evening was her great opportunity. Her audience at the conference would be approximately fifteen hundred individuals—professors, scholars, archivists, research scientists, university and college administrators, journalists, editors of learned journals and university presses. A writer for the *Chronicle of Higher Education* was scheduled to interview M. R. Neukirchen the following morning, and a reporter for the *New York Times Education Supplement* was eager to meet with her. A shortened version of "The Role of the University in an Era of 'Patriotism'" would be published as an Op-Ed piece in the *New York Times*. M. R. Neukirchen was a new president of an "historic" university that had not even admitted women until the 1970s and so boldly in her keynote address she would speak of the unspeakable: the cynical plot being contrived in the U.S. capital to authorize the president to employ "military force" against a Middle Eastern country demonized as an "enemy"—an "enemy of democracy." She would find a way to speak of such things in her presentation—it would not be difficult—in addressing the issue of the Patriot Act, the need for vigilance against government surveillance, detention of "terrorist suspects"—the terrible example of Vietnam.

But this was too emotional—was it? Yet she could not speak coolly, she dared not speak ironically. In her radiant Valkyrie mode, irony was not possible.

She would call her lover in Cambridge, Massachusetts—to ask of him *Should I? Dare I? Or is this a mistake?*

For she had not made any mistakes, yet. She had not made any mistakes of significance, in her role as *higher educator.*

She should call him, or perhaps another friend—though it was difficult for M.R., to betray weaknesses to her friends who looked to her for—uplift, encouragement, good cheer, optimism. . . .

She should not behave rashly, she should not give an impression of being *political, partisan.* Her original intention for the address was to consider John Dewey's classic *Democracy and Education* in twenty-first-century terms.

She was an idealist. She could not take seriously any principle of moral behavior that was not a principle for all—universally. She could not believe that "relativism" was any sort of morality except the morality of expediency. But of course as an educator, she was sometimes obliged to be pragmatic: expedient.

Education floats upon the economy, and the good-will of the people.

Even private institutions are hostages to the economy, and the good—enlightened—will of the people.

She would call her (secret) lover when she arrived at the conference center hotel. Just to ask *What do you advise? Do you think I am risking too much?*

Just to ask *Do you love me? Do you even think of me? Do you remember me—when I am not with you?*

It was M.R.'s practice to start a project early—in this case, months early—when she'd first been invited to give the keynote address at the conference, back in April—and to write, rewrite, revise and rewrite through a succession of drafts until her words were finely honed and shimmering—invincible as a shield. A twenty-minute presentation, brilliant in concision and emphasis, would be far more effective than a fifty-minute presentation. And it would be M.R.'s strategy, too, to end early—just slightly early. She would aim for eighteen minutes. To take her audience off guard, to end on a dramatic note . . .

Madness in individuals is rare but in nations, common.

Unless: this was too dire, too smugly "prophetic"? Unless: this would strike a wrong note?

"Carlos! Please put the radio on, will you? I think the dial is set—NPR."

It was noon: news. But not good news.

In the backseat of the limousine M.R. listened. How credulous the media had become since the terrorist attacks of 9/11, how uncritical the reporting—it made her ill, it made her want to weep in frustration and anger, the callow voice of the defense secretary of the United

States warning of *weapons of mass destruction believed to be stored in readiness for attack by the Iraqi dictator Saddam Hussein . . . Biological warfare, nuclear warfare, threat to U.S. democracy, global catastrophe.*

"What do you think, Carlos? Is this ridiculous? 'Fanning the flames' . . ."

"Don't know, ma'am. It's a bad thing."

Guardedly Carlos replied. What Carlos felt in his heart, Carlos was not likely to reveal.

"I think you said—you served in Vietnam. . . ."

Fanning the flames. Served in Vietnam. How clumsy her stock phrases, like ill-fitting prostheses.

It hadn't been Carlos, but one of her assistants who'd mentioned to M.R. that Carlos had been in the Vietnam War and had "some sort of medal—'Purple Heart' "— of which he never spoke. And reluctantly now Carlos responded:

"Ma'am, yes."

In the rearview mirror she saw his forehead crease. He was a handsome man, or had been—olive-dark skin, a swath of silver hair at his forehead. His lips moved but all she could really hear was *ma'am.*

She was feeling edgy, agitated. They were nearing Ithaca—at last.

"I wish you wouldn't call me 'ma'am,' Carlos! It makes me feel—like a spinster of a bygone era."

She'd meant to change the subject and to change the tone of their exchange but the humor in her remark seemed to be lost as often, when she spoke to Carlos, and others on her staff, the good humor for which M. R. Neukirchen was known among her colleagues seemed to be lost and she drew blank expressions from them.

"Sorry, ma'am."

Carlos stiffened, realizing what he'd said. Surely his face went hot with embarrassment.

Yet—she knew!—it wasn't reasonable for M.R. to expect her driver to address her in some other way— as *President Neukirchen* for instance. If he did he stumbled over the awkward words—*Pres'dent New-kirtch-n.*

She'd asked Carlos to call her "M.R."—as most of her University colleagues did—but he had not, ever. Nor had anyone on her staff. This was strange to her, disconcerting, for M.R. prided herself on her lack of pretension, her *friendliness.*

Her predecessor had insisted that everyone call him by his first name—"Leander." He'd been an enormously popular president though not, in his final years, a very productive or even a very attentive president; like a grandfather clock winding down, M.R. had thought. He'd spent most of his time away from campus and among wealthy donors—as house guest, traveling companion, speaker to alumni groups. As a once-noted historian he'd seen his prize territory—Civil War and Reconstruction—so transformed by the inroads of feminist, African American studies, and Marxist scholarship as to be unrecognizable to him, and impossible for him to re-enter, like a door that has locked behind you, once you have stepped through. An individual of such absolute vanity, he wished to be perceived as totally without vanity—just a "common man." Though Leander Huddle had accumulated a small fortune—reputedly, somewhere near ten million dollars—by way of his University salary and its perquisites and investments in his trustee-friends' businesses.

M.R.'s presidency would be very different!

Of course, M.R. was not going to invest money in any businesses owned by trustees. M.R. was not going to accumulate a small fortune through her University connections. M.R. would establish a scholarship financed—(secretly)—by her own salary. . . .

It will be change—radical change!—that works through me.

Neukirchen will be but the agent. Invisible!

She did have radical ideas for the University. She did want to reform its "historic" (i.e., Caucasian-patriarchal/hierarchical) structure and she did want to hire more women and minority faculty, and above all, she wanted to implement a new tuition/scholarship policy that would transform the student body within a few years. At the present time an uncomfortably high percentage of undergraduates were the sons and daughters of the most wealthy economic class, as well as University "legacies"—(that is, the children of alumni); there were scholarships for "poor" students, that constituted a small percentage; but the children of middle-income parents constituted a precarious 5 percent of admissions . . . M.R. intended to increase these, considerably.

For M. R. Neukirchen was herself the daughter of "middle-income" parents, who could never have afforded to send her to this Ivy League university.

Of course, M. R. Neukirchen would not appear *radical*, but rather *sensible, pragmatic and timely*.

She'd assembled an excellent team of assistants and aides. And an excellent staff. Immediately when she'd been named president, she'd begun recruiting the very best people she could; she'd kept on only a few key individuals on Leander's staff.

At all public occasions, in all her public pronouncements, M. R. Neukirchen stressed that the presidency of the University was a "team effort"—publicly she thanked her team, and she thanked individuals. She was the most generous of presidents—she would take blame for mistakes but share credit for successes. (Of course, no mistakes of any consequence had yet been made since M.R. had taken over the office.) To all whom she met in her official capacity she appealed in her eager earnest somewhat breathless manner that masked her intelligence—as it masked her willfulness; sometimes, in an excess of feeling, this new president of the University was known to clasp hands in hers, that were unusually large strong warm hands.

It was the influence of her mother Agatha. As Agatha had also influenced M.R. to *keep a cheerful heart, and keep busy.*

As both Agatha and Konrad were likely to say, as Quakers—*I hope.*

For it was Quaker custom to say, not *I think* or *I know* or *This is the way it must be* but more provisionally, and more tenderly—*I hope.*

"Yes. I hope."

In the front seat the radio voice was loud enough to obscure whatever it was M.R. had said. And Carlos was just slightly hard of hearing.

"You can turn off the radio, please, Carlos. Thanks."

Since the incident at the bridge there was a palpable stiffness between them. No one has more of a sense of propriety than an older staffer, or a servant—one who has been in the employ of a predecessor, and can't help but compare his present employer with this predecessor. And M.R. was only just acquiring a way of talking to subordinates that wasn't formal yet wasn't inappropriately informal; a way of *giving orders* that didn't sound aggressive, coercive. Even the word *Please* felt coercive to her. When you said *Please* to those who, like Carlos, had no option but to obey, what were you really saying?

And she wondered was the driver thinking now *It isn't the same, driving for a woman. Not this woman.*

She wondered was he thinking *She is alone too much. You begin to behave strangely when you are alone too much—your brain never clicks off.*

The desk clerk frowned into the computer.

" 'M. R. Neukirchen' "—the name sounded, on his lips, faintly improbable, comical—"yesss—we have your reservation, Mz. Neukirchen—for two nights. But I'm afraid—the suite isn't quite ready. The maid is just finishing up. . . ."

Even after the unscheduled stop, she'd arrived early!

She hadn't even instructed Carlos to drive past her old residence Balch Hall—for which she felt a stab of nostalgia.

Not for the naïve girl she'd been as an undergraduate, nor even for the several quite nice roommates she'd had—(like herself, scholarship girls)—but for the thrilling experience of discovering, for the first time, the *livingness* of the intellectual enterprise, that had been, to her, the daughter of bookish parents, previously confined to books.

M.R. told the desk clerk that that was fine. She could wait. Of course. There was no problem.

" . . . no more than ten or fifteen minutes, Mz. Neukirchen. You can check in now, and wait in our library-lounge, and I will call you."

"Thank you! This is ideal."

Smile! Win more flies with honey than with vinegar Agatha would advise though this was not why, in fact, Agatha smiled so frequently, and so genuinely. And there was Konrad's dry rebuttal, with a wink of the eye for their young impressionable daughter.

Sure thing! If it's flies you want.

The library-lounge was an attractive wood-paneled room where M.R. could spread her things out on an oak table and continue to work.

Always it is a good thing: to arrive early.

The impulsive stop in the nameless little town by the nameless little creek or river hadn't been a blunder after all—only just a curious episode in M.R.'s (private) life, to be forgotten.

Arrive early. Bring work.

She'd begun to acquire a reputation for being the most astonishing zealot of *work*.

It was known, M.R. was very bright—very earnest, idealistic—but it had not been quite known, how hard M.R. was willing to *work*.

For this brief trip, she'd brought along enough work for several days. And, of course, she would be in constant communication with Salvager Hall—the president's team of aides, assistants, secretarial staff. In a constant stream e-mail messages came to her as president of the University, and these she dealt with both expeditiously and with an air of schoolgirl pleasure so it was known, and it would become more widely known, that M.R. never failed to include personal queries and remarks in her e-mail messages, she was irrepressibly *friendly*.

For we love our work. No more potent narcotic than work!

And M.R.'s administrative work was very different from her work as a writer/philosopher—administration is the skillful organizing of others, its center of gravity is *exterior;* all that matters, all that is significant, urgent—profound—is *exterior.*

"I want to be 'of service.' I do not want to be 'served.'"

This too was a legacy of the Neukirchens. For the Quaker, the commonweal outweighs the merely personal.

Critically now M.R. was re-examining her address—
"The Role of the University in an Era of 'Patriotism' "—
even as she found herself distracted by a memory of the
bridge and the sharp water-smells—the mysterious
faded lettering on the dark-brick building on the farther
bank.

In the lobby, uplifted voices. Her fellow conferees
were arriving.

She felt a stirring of apprehension, excitement. For
soon, her anonymity would vanish.

The desk clerk had no idea who she was—(this was a
relief!)—but others would know her, recognize her. This
past year M. R. Neukirchen had become renowned in
academic circles. She could not but think her elevation
very unnerving, and very strange—accidental, really.

*God has chosen you, dear Merry! God is a principle
in the universe for good, and God has chosen you to
implement His work.*

In emotional moments her mother spoke like this—
warmly, earnestly. It was something of a small shock
to M.R. to realize that Agatha probably did believe in
such a personal destiny for her daughter.

Another time M.R. leafed through the conference
program—to check her name, to see if it was really there.

The program was a large glossy-white booklet
with gilt letters on its cover: *Fiftieth Annual National*

Conference of the American Association of Learned Societies. October 11–13, 2002. The conference was scheduled to begin with a 5:30 P.M. reception at which M.R. and other speakers were to be honored. Dinner was at 7 P.M. and at 8 P.M. the keynote speaker was listed—*M. R. Neukirchen.*

She'd given many talks, of course. Many lectures, speeches—presentations—but mostly in her academic field, philosophy. It was an honor for her to have been invited to speak to this organization, not the largest but the most distinguished of American intellectual/ academic societies, for membership was limited and selective.

M.R. had herself been inducted into the organization young—not yet thirty, and an associate professor of philosophy at the University.

"Oh! Damn."

She'd discovered mud on the cuffs of her trousers, and in the creases of her shoes. Irritably she brushed at the stains, that were still damp.

She touched her hair discovering something cobwebby-sticky in her hair, that must have sifted down from the wrought-iron bridge.

Fortunately, she'd brought other clothes to the conference. She would wash her face—check her hair— change quickly once she was given her room.

She had good clothes to wear, this evening. Since she'd become president of the University her female staffers had seen to it that M.R. looked "stylish"—her assistant Audrey Myles had insisted upon taking M.R. to New York City to shop and they'd come back with a chic Chanel-imitation Champagne-colored wool suit— with a skirt—by an American designer. And Audrey had convinced M.R. to buy handsome new shoes as well, with a one-inch heel—bringing M.R.'s height to a teetering five feet ten and a half inches.

At such a height, you could not hide. You had best imagine yourself as a prow on a ship—a brave Amazon girl-warrior with breastplates, spear uplifted in her right hand.

Her astronomer-lover, when he'd first sighted her on a street in Cambridge, Massachusetts, years before, had described her in his way. He'd claimed to have fallen in love with her, in this first sighting. And her hair in a tight-woven braid hanging down between her shoulder blades like a glittery bronze-brown snake.

Since she'd risen in administration at the University, M.R. had long since gotten rid of the girl-scholar braid. As she'd tried to rid herself of a naive sentimentality about the sort of love her astronomer-lover could provide her. Now her hair was cropped short, trimmed and styled by a New York City hairdresser, at Audrey's insistence: it was dense, springy, no longer golden brown but the ambiguous hue of a winter-ravaged field threaded with metallic-gray hairs that glittered like filaments.

In official biographies, M. R. Neukirchen was forty-one years old in September 2002. And looking much younger.

As a little girl she'd seen her birth certificate. Her parents had shown her. A document stamped with the heraldic New York State gold seal stating her birth date, her name—her names.

Our secret you need to tell no one.

Our secret, God has blessed our family.

She was "Merry" then—"Meredith Ruth Neukirchen." Her birthday was September 21. A very nice time of year, the Neukirchens believed: a prelude to the beautiful season of autumn. Which was why they'd chosen it for her.

Which was why she often forgot her birthday, and was surprised when others reminded her.

She hadn't minded not being beautiful, as a girl in Carthage, New York. She'd learned to be objective about such matters. There were those who liked her well enough—who loved her, in a way—for her fierce wide smile that resembled a grimace of pain, and her stoicism in the face of actual pain or discomfort; she'd had to laugh seeing her picture in local papers, the expression of longing in her face that was so scrubbed-looking plain it might have been a boy's face and not that of a young woman of eighteen:

MEREDITH RUTH NEUKIRCHEN, CLASS OF '79 VALEDICTORIAN CARTHAGE HIGH SCHOOL.

It had been the kind of upstate New York, small-city school in which, as in a drain, the least-qualified and -inspired teachers wound up, bemused and stoical and resigned; there had been several teachers who'd seen in Meredith something promising, even exciting—but only one who had inspired her, though not to emulate him personally. And when poor Meredith—"Merry"—hadn't even been asked to the senior prom, though she'd been not only valedictorian of her graduating class but also its vice president, one of the women teachers had consoled her—"You'll just have to make your way somehow else, Meredith"—with fumbling directness though meaning to be kind.

Not as a woman, and not sexual.

Somehow else.

Soon after the senior prom to which M.R. had not been invited, M.R.'s prettiest girl-classmates were married, and pregnant; pregnant, and married. Some were soon divorced, and became "single mothers"— a very different domestic destiny from the one they'd envisioned for themselves.

Very few of M.R.'s classmates, female or male, went on to college. Very few achieved what one might call careers. Of her graduating class of 118 students very few left Carthage or Beechum County or the southern Adirondacks, where the economy had been severely depressed for decades.

One of those regions in America, M.R. had said, trying to describe her background to her astronomer-lover who traveled more frequently to Europe than to the rural interior of the United States, where poverty has become a natural resource: social workers, welfare workers, community-medical workers, public defenders, prison and psychiatric hospital staffers, family court officials—all thrived in such barren soil. Only fleetingly had M.R. considered returning, as an educator—once she'd left, she had scarcely looked back.

Don't forget us, Meredith! Come visit, stay a while . . .
We love our Merry.

M.R. had pushed her laptop aside and was examining road maps, laid out on a table in the library-lounge for hotel guests.

Particularly M.R. was intrigued by a detailed map of Tompkins County. She hoped to determine where she'd asked Carlos to stop. South and west of Ithaca were small towns—Edensville, Burnt Ridge, Shedd—but none appeared to be the town M.R. was looking for. With her forefinger M.R. traced a thin curvy blue stream—this must be the river, or the creek—south of Ithaca; but there was only a tiny dot on that stream as of a settlement too minuscule to be named, or extinct.

"Why is this important? It is not important."

She whispered aloud. She was puzzled by her disappointment.

Abruptly the map ended at the northern border of Tompkins County but there were maps of adjoining New York State counties; there was a road map of New York State that M.R. eagerly unfolded, with no hope that she could fold it neatly back up again. Some crucial genetic component was missing in M.R., she could never fold road maps neatly back up again once she unfolded them. . . .

In the Neukirchen household, Konrad had been the one to carefully, painstakingly re-fold maps. Agatha had been totally incapable, vexed and anxious.

It feels like some kind of trick. It can't be done!

M.R. saw: to the north and east of Tompkins County was Cortland County—beyond Cortland, Madison—then Herkimer, so curiously elongated among other, chunkier counties; beyond Herkimer, in the Adirondacks, the largest and least populated county in New York State, Beechum.

At the northwestern edge of Beechum County, the city of Carthage.

How many miles was it? How far could she drive, on a whim? It looked like less than two hundred miles, to the southernmost curve of the Black Snake River in Beechum County. Which computed to about three hours if she drove at sixty miles an hour. Of course, she wouldn't have to drive as far as Carthage; she could simply drive, with no particular destination, see how far she got after two hours—then turn, and drive back.

How quickly her heart was beating!

M.R. calculated: it was just 1:08 P.M. She'd been waiting for her hotel room for nearly twenty minutes. Surely in another few minutes, the desk clerk would summon her, and she could check into the room?

The reception began at 5:30 P.M.—but no one would be on time. And then, at about 6 P.M., everyone would arrive at once, the room would be crammed with people, no one would notice if M.R. arrived late. Dinner was more essential of course since M.R. was seated at the speakers' table—that wasn't until 7 P.M. And of course, the *keynote address* at 8 P.M. . . .

There was time—or was there? Her brain balked at calculations like a faulty machine.

"Absurd. No. Just *stop*."

The spell was broken by the cell phone ringing at M.R.'s elbow. The first stirring notes of Mozart's *Eine Kleine Nachtmusik*.

M.R. saw that the caller ID was UNIVERSITY—meaning the president's office. Of course, they were waiting to hear from her there.

"Yes, I've arrived. Everything is fine. In a few minutes I'll be checked in. And Carlos is on his way back home."

It was a fact: Carlos had departed. M.R. had thanked him and dismissed him. Late in the afternoon of the third day of the conference Carlos would return, to drive M.R. back to the University.

Of course, M.R. had suggested that Carlos stay the night—this night—at the hotel—at the University's expense—to avoid the strain of driving a second five-hour stretch in a single day. But Carlos politely demurred: Carlos didn't seem to care much for this well-intentioned suggestion.

It was a relief Carlos had left, M.R. thought. The driver had lingered in the lobby for a while as if uncertain whether to leave his distinguished passenger before she'd actually been summoned to her hotel room; he'd insisted upon carrying her suitcase into the hotel for her—this lightweight roller-suitcase M.R. could handle for herself and in fact preferred to handle herself, for she rested her heavy handbag on it as she rolled it along; but Carlos couldn't bear the possibility of being observed—by other drivers?—in the mildest dereliction of his duty.

"Ma'am? Should I wait with you?"

"Carlos, thank you! But no. Of course not."

"But if you need . . ."

"Carlos, really! The hotel has my reservation, obviously. It will be just another few minutes, I'm sure."

Still he'd hesitated. M.R. couldn't determine if it was professional courtesy or whether this dignified gentleman in his early sixties was truly concerned for her—perhaps it was both; he told her please call him on her cell phone if she needed anything, he would return to Ithaca as quickly as possible. But finally he'd left.

M.R. thought *Of course. His life is elsewhere. His life is not driving a car for me.*

Questioned afterward Carlos Lopes would say *I asked her if I should stay—her room wasn't ready yet in the hotel—she said no, I should leave—she was working in a room off the lobby—I said maybe she would need me like if they didn't have a room for her and I could drive her to some other hotel and she laughed and said no Carlos! That is very kind of you but no—of course there will be a room.*

As the desk clerk would say *Her room was ready for her at about 1:15 P.M. She was gracious about waiting, she said it was no trouble. But then a few minutes later she called the front desk—I spoke with her—she asked about a car rental recommendation. Sometime after that she must have left the hotel. Nobody would've seen her, the lobby was so crowded. Her room was empty at 8:30 P.M. when some people from the conference asked us to open it. There was no* DO NOT DISTURB *sign on the door. The lights were off. Her suitcase was on the bed opened but mostly unpacked and her laptop was on the bed, not opened. There weren't any signs of anybody breaking into the room or anything disturbed and there was no note left behind.*

By 2 P.M. she was in the rental car driving north of Ithaca.

Her lungs swelled with—relief? Exultation?

She'd told no one where she was going or even that she was going—somewhere.

Of course, M.R. was paying for the compact Toyota with her personal credit card.

Of course, M.R. knew that her behavior was impulsive but reasoned that since she'd arrived early at the conference, in fact hours before the conference officially began, this interlude—before 6 P.M., or 6:30 P.M.—was a sort of free fall, like gravity-less space.

Once she'd asked her (secret) lover how an astronomer can bear the silence and vastness of the sky which is unbroken/unending/unfathomable and which yields nothing remotely *human* in fact rather makes a mockery of *human* and he'd said—*But darling! That is what draws the astronomer to his subject: silence, vastness.*

Driving north to Beechum County she was driving into what felt like silence. For she'd left the radio off, and the wind whining and whistling at all the windows drained away all sound as in a vacuum leaving her brain blank.

Ancient time her lover called the sky without end *predating every civilization on Earth that believed it was the be-all and end-all of Earth.*

She'd resolved to drive for just an hour and a half in one direction. Three hours away would return her to the hotel by 5 P.M. and well in time to change and prepare for the reception.

Except the driving was wind-buffeted. She'd rented a small car.

Not so very practical for driving at a relatively high speed on the interstate flanked and overtaken by tractor-trailers.

In high school driver's education class, M.R. had been an exemplary student. Aged sixteen she'd learned to parallel park with such skill, her teacher used her as a model for other students. Approvingly he'd said of her *Meredith handles a car like a man.*

Remembering how when she'd first begun driving she'd felt dizzy with excitement, happiness. That thrill of sheer power in the way the vehicle leaps when you press down on the gas pedal, turns when you turn the steering wheel, slows and stops when you *brake.*

Remembering how she'd thought *This is something men know. A girl has to discover.*

" 'Just to stretch my legs.' No other reason."

She laughed. Her laughter was hopeful. A thin dew of fever-dreams on her forehead, oily and prickling in her armpits. And some sort of snarl in her hair. As if in the night she'd been dreaming of—something like this.

She would have time to shower before the reception—wouldn't she? Change into her chic presidential clothes.

As a girl—a big husky girl—a girl-athlete—M.R. had sweated like any boy, sweat-rivulets running down her sides, a torment at the nape of her neck beneath the bushy-springy hair. And in her crotch—a snaggle of even denser hair, exerting a sort of appalled fascination to the bearer—who was "Meredith"—in dread of this snaggle of hair being somehow known by others; as there were years—middle school, high school—of anxiety that her body would *smell* in such a way to be detected by others.

Of course, it had. Many times probably. For what could a husky girl *do?* Warm airless classroom-hours, sturdy thighs sticking/slapping together if you were not very careful.

As on certain days of the month, anxiety rose like the red column of mercury in a thermometer, in heat.

Having her period. Poor Meredith!

Everything shows in her face. Funny!

Early that morning before Carlos arrived—for M.R. had slept only intermittently through the night—she'd showered, of course, shampooed her hair. So long ago, seemed like another day.

And so another shower, back at the hotel. When she returned.

On the interstate M.R. was making good time in the compact little vehicle. Her speed held steady at just above sixty miles an hour which was a safe speed, even a cautious speed amid so many larger vehicles hurtling past her in the left lane as if with snorts of derision.

But—the beauty of this landscape! It required going away, and returning, to truly see it.

Farmland, hills. Wide swaths of farmland—corn-fields, wheat—now harvested—rising in hills to the horizon. She caught her breath—those flame-flashes of sumac dark-red, fiery-orange by the roadside—amid darker evergreens, deciduous trees whose leaves hadn't—yet—begun to die.

Already she was beyond Bone Plain Road, Frozen Ocean State Park. Passing signs for Boontown,

Forestport, Poland and Cold Brook—names not yet familiar to her from her girlhood in Beechum County.

These precious hours! If her parents knew, they'd have wanted to see her—they'd have been willing to drive to Ithaca for the evening.

They'd have wanted to hear her *keynote address.* For they were so very proud of her. And they loved her. And saw so little of her since she'd left Carthage on that remarkable scholarship to Cornell, it must have perplexed them.

"I should have. Why didn't I!"

It was as if M.R. had not thought of the possibility at all. As if a part of her brain had ceased functioning.

That peculiar sort of blindness/amnesia in which objects simply vanish as they pass into the area monitored by the damaged brain. Not that one forgets but that experience itself has been blocked.

Now that M.R. had assistants, it was no trouble to make such arrangements. At the hotel, for instance. Or, if the conference hotel was booked solid, at another local hotel. Audrey would have been delighted to book a room for M.R.'s parents.

M.R.'s lover had heard her speak in public several times. He'd been surprised—impressed—by her ease before a large audience, when M.R. was so frequently uneasy in his company.

Well, not uneasy—excited. M.R. was frequently so *excited* in his company.

She couldn't bring herself to confess to her (secret) lover that intimacy with him was so precious to her, it was a strain to which she hadn't yet become accustomed. She'd said with a smile *No speaker makes eye contact with his audience. The larger the audience, the easier. That is the secret.*

Her lover imagined her a far more composed and self-reliant individual than she was. It had long been a fiction of their relationship, that M.R. didn't "need" a man in her life; she was of a *newer, more liberated generation*—for her lover was her senior by fourteen years, and often remarked upon this fact as if to absolve himself of any candidacy as the husband of a girl "so young." Also, Andre was enmeshed in a painful marriage he liked to describe as resembling Laocoön and sons in the coils of the terrible sea-serpents.

M.R. laughed aloud. For Andre Litovik was so very funny, you might forget that his humor frequently masked a truth or a motive not-so-funny.

"Oh—God . . ."

Powerful air-suction from a passing/speeding trailer-truck made M.R.'s compact vehicle shudder. The trucker must have been driving at eighty miles an hour. M.R. braked her car, alarmed and frightened.

She'd been daydreaming, and not concentrating on her driving. She'd felt her mind *drift.*

Better to exit the interstate onto a state highway. This was safer, if slower. Through acres of steeply hilly farmland she drove into Cortland County, and she drove into Madison County, and she drove into Herkimer County and into the foothills of the Adirondacks and at last into Beechum County where mountain peaks covered in evergreens stretched hazy and sawtoothed to the horizon like receding and diminishing dreams.

She'd planned to drive north for only an hour and a half before turning around but decided now that a few minutes more—a few miles more—would do no harm.

Wherever she found herself at—4:30 P.M.?—she would stop at once, turn her car around and head back to Ithaca.

This was likely the first time in months that no one on M.R.'s staff knew where she was, at such an hour of a weekday. No friends knew, no colleagues. M.R. had passed into the blind side of the brain, she'd become invisible.

Was this a good thing, or—not so good? Both her parents had praised her as a girl for her maturity, her sense of "responsibility." But this was something different, a mere interlude.

This was something different: no one would ever know.

She'd turned off her cell phone. More practical to take messages and answer them in sequence.

And what relief, to have left her laptop behind on the hotel bed! She was attached to the thing like a co-lostomy bag. Her senses reacted in panic if it appeared to be malfunctioning for just a few minutes. A flurry of e-mails buzzing in her wake like angry bees.

Belatedly M.R. remembered—she was supposed to meet with a prominent educator now chairing a national committee on bioethics who'd been asked to invite M.R. to join the committee. This was a commit-tee M.R. wanted to join—nothing seemed to her more crucial than establishing guidelines on bioethics—yet somehow, she'd forgotten. In her haste to rent a car and drive up into Beechum County, she'd forgotten. And M.R. had scheduled their meeting-time herself—just before the reception, at 5 P.M.

She might have called the man to postpone their meeting to the next day but she didn't have his cell phone number. Nor did she want to call her assistant Audrey to place the call for her for Audrey would naturally inquire where M.R. was and M.R. could not possibly tell her—"Just crossing the Black Snake River, up in Beechum County."

Audrey would have been speechless. Audrey would have thought that M.R. must be joking.

Now in Beechum County M.R. switched on the car radio. She hoped to tune in to a Watertown station—WWTX. Once an NPR affiliate but now M.R. couldn't locate it on the dial only just deafening patches of rock music and advertisements—the detritus of America.

On one FM station there appeared to be news—*news from Washington*—but static swept it away like ribald laughter.

News from Washington—but the U.S. Congress wouldn't yet be voting on the war resolution, would it? This was too soon. There had to be days yet of debate.

M.R. couldn't quite believe that legislators in Washington would authorize the bellicose Republican president to wage war against Iraq—this would be madness! The U.S. hadn't entirely recovered from the debacle of the Vietnam War of which little ambiguity remained—the war had been a terrible mistake. Still, excited war rumors in the media—even the more liberal media like the *New York Times*—flared and rippled like wildfire in dried brush. There was a terrible *thrillingness* to the possibility of war.

It was astonishing how effectively the administration had lied to convince the majority of the American public that there was a direct link between Iraq and the terrorist attacks of 9/11. For since that catastrophic episode a near-palpable toxic-cloud was accumulating over the country, a gradual darkening of logic—an impatience with logic.

Madness! M.R. could not think of it without beginning to tremble.

She was an ethicist: a professional. It was criminal, it was self-destructive, it was cruel, stupid, quixotic—unethical: waging war on such flimsy pretexts.

What was the appeal of war?—the appeal of a paroxysm of sustained and collective violence repeated endlessly, from the earliest prehistory until the present time? It was not enough to say *Men are bred to war, men are warriors—men must perform their role as warriors.* It was not enough to say *Humankind is self-destructive, damned. Of all the species, damned.*

As a liberal, as an educator, M.R. did not believe in such primitive determinism. She did not believe in *genetic determinism* at all.

Very likely she had young relatives scattered through Beechum County who were in the National Guard or in a branch of the armed services. Some might even now be stationed in the Middle East awaiting deployment to battle, as in the Gulf War of some years ago. Like the more southern Appalachian region Beechum County was the sort of economically depressed rural-America that provided fodder for the military machine.

M.R.'s immediate family—Agatha and Konrad—were Quakers, if not "active" in the nearest Friends' congregation, which was some distance from Carthage. ("Too lazy to drive," Konrad said. "You can 'Quaker' at any time and any place.") None of the other Neukirchens were Quakers and certainly none were pacifists like Konrad who'd been granted the status of conscientious objector during the Korean War and instead of being incarcerated in a federal prison was allowed to work in a VA hospital in Baltimore.

Konrad was a kindly man, short and squat as a fireplug and fierce in declaring that if somehow he'd found himself in the army—in combat—he could never fire at any "enemy." He could not even hold a gun, point a gun at anyone.

M.R. smiled, recalling her father. She was recalling Konrad not as he was at the present time—an aging ailing man—but as he'd been in her earliest memories, in the mid- and late 1960s.

The one thing they can't make you do is kill another person. They can't even make you hate another person.

There was a sign—CARTHAGE 78 MILES. But M.R. could not drive to Carthage today.

Uneasily she was thinking—is it time to turn back? Some instinct kept her from checking the time. . . .

How strange she was feeling! This sensation she'd felt as a girl inching out—with other, older children— onto the frozen river; so darkly swift-flowing a river, like a black snake with glittering scales, that water froze only at shore and continued to rush along at the center of the stream.

Unmistakably, there was a thrill to this. Daring and reckless the older boys crept out onto the ice, toward the unfrozen center. Younger children stayed behind out of timidity.

You must not let them entice you, Meredith! If you are injured they will run away and abandon you for that is their kind—they are cruel, can't help themselves for their God is a God of conquest and wrath and not a God of love.

There was a dislike, a resentment of Meredith's parents—not to their faces but behind their backs—for Konrad's unmanly pacifism. For Beechum County was a gun culture. Hunters, warriors.

M.R. felt a mild headache coming on. She hadn't eaten since early that morning and then at her desk at home, answering e-mails.

Solitary mealtimes are not very pleasurable. Solitary mealtimes are best avoided.

The deficiency of philosophy is that it has no stomach, no guts. In all of classic philosophy not a single pulsebeat of *feeling*.

Oh why hadn't she invited Agatha and Konrad to Ithaca for this evening! It would have been so easy to have done, and would have meant so much to them.

M.R. loved her parents but often seemed to forget them. Like clouds sailing overhead, they were—snowy-white clouds of surpassing and unearthly beauty at which no one thinks to look.

"I will do better. I will try harder. I hope they will forget me."

She meant *forgive* of course. Not *forget*.

In fact she was—just now—crossing the Black Snake River. The wrought-iron truss bridge vibrated beneath the lightweight Toyota. The river was thirty or more feet below the bridge, rushing like something demented. Wheels—spirals—of light—like defects in the eye. You could imagine a giant serpent in that molten liquid—lifting its head, tawny eyes and fanged jaws.

Look again, the serpent has vanished beneath the water's surface.

Farther to the west, at Carthage, in layers of crusted shale there were fossils M.R. had searched for, as a girl. Ancient crustaceans, long-extinct fish. Her biology teacher had sent her out: he'd identified the fossils for her. M.R. had drawn them in her notebook, with particular care.

A string of A-pluses attached to *Meredith Neukirchen* like a comet's long tail.

Here the river's shore was less rocky, more marshy. The river did not appear to be the river of her girlhood and yet—it was strangely familiar to her, like the serpent's head.

Off the bridge ramp was a sign for RAPIDS—5 MILES. SLABTOWN—11 MILES. RIVIERE-DU-LOUP—18 MILES. In the near distance Mount Moriah—one of the highest peaks in the southern Adirondacks—and beyond, shadowy peaks whose names M.R. couldn't recall with certainty: Mount Provenance, Mount Hammer? Mount Marcy? It was geology—nineteenth-century geology— that had first shaken the Christian creation-myth so deeply entrenched in Europe, and in the blood-steeped soil of Europe, you would never think it might be extirpated like rotted roots; eruptions of human certainty like eruptions of volcanic lava scouring everything in its path. For what was the earth but a mass of roiling lava—not a "created" thing at all.

Within a few decades, the old faith was shaken utterly. All was devastation.

Except, as Nietzsche so shrewdly observed, the devastation was ignored. Denied. Knowledge of Earth's position in the universe had entered the blind-visual field of neglect.

She would not be a party to such denial, such blindness. *She,* empowered as the first woman president of a great university, would speak the truth as she saw it.

For in her vanity she wished to align herself with the great truth-tellers—not with those who spoke to placate.

In high school M.R. had been drawn to geology as to other sciences but in subsequent years her passion for the abstract—for philosophy—"ethics"—had driven out the hard concrete names like irreducible ores—*igneous, sedimentary, metamorphic.*

Science is another name for God-seeking, the Neukirchens had assured her. Their Quaker faith was so very wide, vast, all-encompassing—a Sargasso Sea without boundaries and without a Savior.

M.R. dared not glance at the dashboard clock. It was time for her to turn back, she knew.

She was passing trailer villages, small asphalt-sided houses, semi-abandoned farmhouses and barns. She was passing the Old Dutch Road—was this familiar?—and the Sandusky Road. The narrow Black River Road curved dangerously close to the river. On that side, the shoulder had been eaten away by erosion. On the farther shore was a curious steep step-ladder-like hill or small mountain near-bare of vegetation from which gigantic boulders seem to have loosed and fallen into the river. There was the look of an ancient landscape shaken, broken. Yet a powerful beauty in these broken shapes.

A sharp pain struck between her shoulder blades like a stinging insect for she'd been tensing up, driving. Leaning forward gripping the steering wheel in both hands as if fearing the wheel might get away from her.

He'd said to her—her (secret) lover—*Eternity hasn't a damn thing to do with time*—but he'd been joking, he had not meant to be cruel or mocking and she had kissed his mouth, daring to kiss his mouth that was only just barely hers to kiss.

More mysteriously he'd said *Earth-time is a way of preventing everything happening at once.*

Did he mean—what? M.R. wasn't sure.

Telling a story, you must lay out "events"—in a chronological sequence. Or rather, you must establish a chronological sequence, so that you know what your story is, and can "tell" it.

Only in time, calendar-time and clock-time, is there chronology. Otherwise—an entire life is but a nanosecond, as swiftly ended as it began, and everything has happened at once.

Possibly, this was what Andre meant. His field was galaxy evolution and star formation in galaxies—his boyhood obsession had been a hope of "mapping" the Universe.

M.R. had had few lovers—very few. For men were not naturally—she supposed, *sexually*—attracted to her. Her weakness was for men of exceptional intellect—at least, intelligence greater than her own. So that she would not be required to mask her own.

The sorrow was, such men seemed to have been, through her life, invariably older than she. And some of them cynical. And some worn like old gloves, scuffed boots. Most were married and some twice- or even thrice-married.

She did want to be married! One day.

She did want to marry Andre Litovik.

He'd tried to discourage her from accepting the presidency of the University. She'd had a sense that he was fearing his girl-Amazon might drift from him after all.

If truly he loved her—he'd have been hopeful for her, proud of her.

Or maybe: even an exceptional man has difficulty feeling pride in an exceptional woman.

M.R. tried to determine where she was. Ever more uneasily she was conscious of time passing.

Ready you must be readied. It is time.

A sign for SPRAGG 7 MILES. SLABTOWN 13 MILES. A sign for Star Lake, in the opposite direction—66 MILES.

Spragg—Slabtown—Star Lake. M.R. had heard of Star Lake, she thought—but not the others, so oddly named.

Abruptly then she came to a barrier in the road.

DETOUR

ROAD OUT NEXT 3 MILES

You could see how beyond the barrier a stretch of road had collapsed into the Black Snake River. Quickly M.R. braked the Toyota to a stop—the earth-slide was shocking to see, like a physical deformity.

"Oh! Damn."

She was disappointed—this would slow her down.

She was thinking how swiftly it must have happened: the road caving in beneath a moving vehicle, a car, a truck—a school bus?—plunging into the river, trapped and terrified and no one to witness the horror. Not likely that the road had simply collapsed beneath its own weight.

Death by (sheer) accident. Surely this was the most merciful of deaths!

Death at the hands of another: the cruelest.

Death by the hands of another *who is known to you, close as a heartbeat:* the very cruelest.

By the look of the fallen-away road, vines and briars growing in cracks, a tangle of sumac and stunted trees, the river road had not collapsed recently. Beechum County had no money for the repair of so remote a road: the detour had become perpetual.

Like a curious child—for one is always drawn to DETOUR as to NO TRESPASSING: DANGER—M.R. turned her car onto a narrow side road: Mill Run. Though of course, the sensible thing would be to turn back.

Was Mill Run even paved? Or covered in gravel, that had long since worn away? The single-lane road led into the countryside that appeared to be low-lying, marshy; no farmland here but a sort of no-man's-land, uninhabited.

At a careful speed M.R. drove along the rutted road. She was a good driver—intent upon avoiding potholes. She knew how a tire can be torn by a sudden sharp declivity; she could not risk a flat tire at this time.

M.R. was one who'd learned to change tires, as a girl. There was the sense that M.R. had better learn to fend for herself.

In fact there had been inhabitants along the Mill Run Road, and not too long ago—an abandoned house, set back in a field like a gaunt and etiolated elder; a

Sunoco station amid a junked-car lot, that appeared to be closed; and an adjoining café where a faded sign rattled in the wind—BLACK RIVER CAFÉ.

Both the Sunoco station and the café were boarded up. Just outside the café was a pickup truck shorn of wheels. M.R. might have turned into the parking lot here but—so strangely—found herself continuing forward as if drawn by an irresistible momentum.

She was smiling—was she? Her brain, ordinarily so active, hyperactive as a hive of shaken hornets, was struck blank in anticipation.

In hilly countryside, foothills and densely wooded mountains, you can see the sky only in patches—M.R. had glimpses of a vague blurred blue and twists of cloud like soiled bandages. She was driving in odd rushes and jolts pressing her foot on the gas pedal and releasing it—she was hoping not to be surprised by whatever lay ahead and yet, she was surprised—shocked: "Oh God!"

For there was a child lying at the side of the road—a small figure lying at the side of the road broken, discarded. The Toyota veered, plunged off the road into a ditch.

Unthinking M.R. turned the wheel to avoid the child. There came a sickening thud, the jolt of the vehicle at a sharp angle in the ditch—the front left wheel and the rear left wheel.

So quickly it had happened! M.R.'s heart lurched in her chest. She fumbled to open the door, and to extract herself from the seat belt. The car engine was still on—a violent peeping had begun. She'd thought it had been a child at the roadside but of course—she saw now—it was a doll.

Mill Run Road. Once, there must have been a mill of some sort in this vicinity. Now, all was wilderness. Or had reverted to wilderness. The road was a sort of open landfill used for dumping—in the ditch was a mangled and filthy mattress, a refrigerator with a door agape like a mouth, broken plastic toys, a man's boot.

Grunting with effort M.R. managed to climb—to crawl—out of the Toyota. Then she had to lean back inside, to turn off the ignition—a wild thought came to her, the car might explode. Her fingers fumbled the keys—the keys fell onto the car floor.

She saw—it wasn't a doll either at the roadside, only just a child's clothing stiff with filth. A faded-pink sweater and on its front tiny embroidered roses.

And a child's sneaker. So small!

Tangled with the child's sweater was something white, cotton—underpants?—stiff with mud, stained. And socks, white cotton socks. And in the underbrush nearby the remains of a kitchen table with a simulated-maple Formica top. Rural America, filling up with trash.

An entire household dumped out on the Mill Run Road! Not a happy story.

M.R. stooped to inspect the refrigerator. Of course it was empty—the shelves were rusted, badly battered. There was a smell. A sensation of such unease—oppression—came over her, she had to turn away.

"And now—what?"

She could call AAA—her cell phone was in the car. But probably she could maneuver the Toyota out of the ditch herself for the ditch wasn't very deep.

Except—what time was it?

Staring at her watch. Trying to calculate. Was it already past 4:30 P.M.—nearly 5 P.M.? This was unexpectedly late! Mid-October and the sun slanting in the sky and dusk coming on.

This side of the Black Snake River were stretches of marshland, mudflats. She'd been smelling mud. You could see that the river often overran its banks here. There was a harsh brackish smell as of rancid water and rotted things.

Staring at her watch which was a small elegant gold watch inscribed with the name and heraldic insignia of a New England liberal arts college for women. It had been given to M.R. to commemorate her having received from the college an honorary doctorate in humane letters and shortly thereafter, an invitation to interview for its presidency. She'd been thirty-six at the time. She'd been dean of the faculty at the University at the time. Graciously she'd declined. She did not say *I am so grateful but no—it isn't likely that I would accept a position at a women's college.*

Or—*It isn't likely that I would accept a position at any university other than a major research university. That is not M. R. Neukirchen's plan.*

Amid the cast-off household litter was a strip of rotted tarpaulin.

M.R. pulled it loose, dragged it to the Toyota to place beneath the wheels on the driver's side, that were mired in mud. This was good! This was good luck! Awkwardly then she crawled back into the badly tilted car, located the keys on the floor mat, and managed to start the engine—eased the car forward a few inches, let it rock back; eased it again forward, and let it rock back; at first the wheels spun, then began to take hold. The car moved, jerked spasmodically; in another minute or two she would have eased the Toyota back up onto the road except—the rotted tarpaulin must have given way, the wheels spun frantically.

"God *damn.*"

M.R. reached for the cell phone, that had fallen to the floor. Tried to call AAA but the phone was unreceptive.

If only she'd thought to call her assistant a half hour ago—the cell phone might have worked then. Just to allow the (anxious?) young woman to know *I may be late for the reception. A few minutes late. But I will not be late for the dinner. I will not be late for my talk of course.*

She would have spoken to Audrey in her usual bright brisk manner that did not invite interruptions. It was a bright brisk manner that did not invite murmurs of commiseration. She would have said, if Audrey had expressed concern for her, *Of course, I'm fine! Good-bye for now.*

She was hiking along the road with the cell phone in her hand. Repeatedly she tried to activate it but the damned thing remained dead.

Useless plastic, dead!

If she ascended to higher ground? Would the phone be more likely to work? Or—was this a ridiculous notion, desperate?

"I am not desperate. Not yet."

Amid the mudflats was a sort of peninsula, a spit of land raised about three feet, very likely man-made, like a dam; M.R. climbed up onto it. She was a strong woman, her legs and thighs were hard with muscle beneath the soft, just slightly flabby female flesh; she made an effort to swim, hike, run, walk—she "worked out"

in the University gym; still, she quickly became breathless, panting. For there was something very oppressive
about this place—the acres of mudflats, the smell. Even
on raised ground she was walking in mud—her nice
shoes, mud-splattered. Her feet were wet.

She thought *I must turn back. As soon as I can.*

She thought *I will know what to do—this can be
made right.*

Staring at her watch trying to calculate but her
mind wasn't working with its usual efficiency. And her
eyes—was something wrong with her eyes?

The reception would begin at—was it 6 P.M.? But
M.R. wouldn't need to arrive promptly at 6 P.M. M.R.
wouldn't have to attend the reception at all. Such events
were hardly crucial. And the dinner—was the dinner
at 7:30 P.M.? She would hurry to the table which would
be the head table in the enormous banquet room—she
would murmur an apology—she could explain that
she'd had to drive somewhere, unavoidably—her car
had broken down returning.

Stress, overwork the doctor had told her. Hours
at the computer and when she glanced up her vision
was distorted and she had to blink, squint to bring the
world into some sort of focus.

How faraway that world—there could be no direct
route to that world, from the Mill Run Road.

A crouched figure. Bearded face, astonished eyes. Slung over his shoulder a half-dozen animal traps. With a gloved hand prodding at—whatever it was in the mud.

"Hello? Is someone . . . ?"

She was making her way along the edge of a makeshift dam. It was a dam comprised of boulders and rocks and it had acquired over the years a sort of mortar of broken and rotted tree limbs and even animal carcasses and skeletons. Everywhere the mudflats stretched, everywhere cattails and rushes grew in profusion. There were trees choked with vines. Dead trees, hollow treetrunks. The pond was covered in algae bright-green as neon that looked as if it were quivering with microscopic life and where the water was clear the pebble-sky was reflected like darting eyes. She was staring at the farther shore where she'd seen something move— she thought she'd seen something move. A flurry of dragonflies, flash of birds' wings. Bursts of autumn foliage like strokes of paint and deciduous trees looking flat as cutouts. She waited and saw nothing. And in the mudflats stretching on all sides nothing except cattails, rushes stirred by the wind.

She was thinking of something her (secret) lover had once said—*There is no truth except perspective. There are no truths except relations.* She had seemed to know what he'd meant at the time—he'd meant something matter-of-fact yet intimate, even sexual; she was quick to agree with whatever her lover said in the hope that someday, sometime she would see how self-evident it was and how crucial for her to have agreed at the time.

Thinking *There is a position, a perspective here. This spit of land upon which I can walk, stand; from which I can see that I am already returned to my other life, I have not been harmed and will have begun to forget.*

Thinking *This is all past, in some future time. I will look back, I will have walked right out of it. I will have begun to forget.*

The spit of land—a kind of raised peninsula—the ruin of an old mill. In the tall spiky weeds remnants of lumber. Shattered concrete blocks. She was limping—she'd turned her ankle. She was very tired. She had not slept for a very long time. In the president's house she was so lonely! Her (secret) lover had not come to visit her. Her (secret) lover had not come to visit her since she'd moved into the president's house and there was no plan for him to visit—yet.

In the president's house which was an historic landmark dating to Colonial times M.R. had her own private quarters on the second floor. Still, the bed in which she slept in the president's house was an antique four-poster bed of the 1870s and it was not a bed M.R. would have chosen for herself though it was not so uncomfortable a bed that M.R. wished to have it moved out and another bed moved in.

For his back, Andre required a hard mattress. At least, the mattress in M.R.'s bed was that.

At the end of the peninsula there was—nothing. Mudflats, desiccated trees. In the Adirondacks, acid rain had been falling for years—parts of the vast forest were dying.

"Hello?"

Strange to be calling out when clearly no one was there to hear. M.R.'s uplifted hand in a ghost-greeting.

He'd been a trapper—the bearded man. Hauling cruel-jawed iron traps over his shoulder. Muskrats, rabbits. Squirrels. His prey was small furry creatures. Hideous deaths in the iron traps, you did not want to think about it.

Hey! Little girl—?

She turned back. Nothing lay ahead.

Retracing her steps. Her footprints in the mud. Like a drunken person, unsteady on her feet. She was feeling oddly excited. Despite her tiredness, excited.

She returned to the littered roadway—there, the child's clothing she'd mistaken so foolishly for a doll, or a child. There, the Toyota at its sharp tilt in the ditch.

Within minutes a tow truck could haul it out, if she could contact a garage—so far as she could see the vehicle hadn't been seriously damaged.

Possibly, M.R. wouldn't need to report the accident to the rental company. For it had not been an "accident" really—no other vehicle had been involved.

She walked on, not certain where she was headed. The sky was darkening to dusk. Shadows lifted from the earth. She saw lights ahead—lights?—the gas station, the café—to her surprise and relief, these appeared to be open.

There was a crunch of gravel. A vehicle was just departing, in the other direction. Other vehicles were parked in the lot. In the café were lights, voices.

M.R. couldn't believe her good luck! She would have liked to cry with sheer relief. Yet a part of her brain thinking calmly *Of course. This has happened before. You will know what to do.*

At a gas pump stood an attendant in soiled bib overalls, shirtless, watching her approach. He was a fattish man with snarled hair, a sly fox-face, watching her approach. Uneasily M.R. wondered—would the attendant speak to her, or would she speak to him, first? She was trying not to limp. Her leather shoes were hurting her feet. She didn't want a stranger's sympathy, still less a stranger's curiosity.

"Ma'am! Somethin' happen to ya car?"

There was a smirking sort of sympathy here. M.R. felt her face heat with blood.

She explained that her car had broken down about a mile away. That is—her car was partway in a ditch. Apologetically she said: "I could almost get it out by myself—the ditch isn't deep. But . . ."

How pathetic this sounded! No wonder the attendant stared at her rudely.

"Ma'am—you look familiar. You're from around here?"

"No. I'm not."

"Yes, I know you, ma'am. Your face."

M.R. laughed, annoyed. "I don't think so. No."

Now came the sly fox-smile. "You're from right around here, ma'am, eh? Hey sure—I know you."

"What do you mean? You know—me? My name?"

"Kraeck. That your name?"

" 'Kraeck.' I don't think so."

"You look like her."

M.R. didn't care for this exchange. The attendant was a large burly man of late middle age. His manner was both familiar and threatening. He was approaching M.R. as if to get a better look at her and M.R. instinctively stepped back and there came to her a sensation of alarm, arousal—she steeled herself for the man's touch—he would grip her face in his roughened hands, to peer at her.

"You sure do look like someone I know. I mean—used to know."

M.R. smiled. M.R. was annoyed but M.R. knew to smile. Reasonably she said: "I don't think so, really. I live hundreds of miles away."

"Kraeck was her name. You look like her—them."

"Yes—you said. But . . ."

Kraeck. She had never heard it before. What a singularly ugly name!

M.R. might have told the man that she'd been born in Carthage, in fact—maybe somehow he'd known her, he'd seen her, in Carthage. Maybe that was an explanation. There was a considerable difference between the small city of Carthage and this desolate part of the Adirondacks. But M.R. was reluctant to speak with this disagreeable individual any more than she had to speak with him for she could see that he was listening keenly to her voice, he'd detected her upstate New York accent M.R. had hoped she'd overcome, that so resembled his own.

"Excuse me . . ."

Badly M.R. had to use a restroom. She left the fox-faced attendant staring rudely at her and climbed the steps to the café.

It was wonderful how the sign that had appeared so faded, derelict, was now lighted: BLACK RIVER CAFÉ.

Inside was a long counter, or a bar—several men standing at the bar—a number of tables of which less than half were occupied—winking lights: neon advertisements for beer, ale. The air was hazy with smoke. A TV above the bar, quick-darting images like fish. M.R. wiped at her eyes for there was a blurred look to the interior of the Black River Café as if it had been hastily assembled. Windows with glass that appeared to be opaque. Pictures, glossy magazine cutouts on the walls that were in fact blank. From the TV came a high-pitched percussive sort of music like wind chimes, amplified. M.R. was smelling something rich, yeasty, wonderful—baking bread? Pie? Homemade pie? Her mouth flooded with saliva, she was weak with hunger.

"Ma'am! Come in here. You look cold. Hungry."

Out of the kitchen came a heavyset woman with a large round muffin-face creased in a smile. She wore a man's red-plaid flannel shirt and brown corduroy slacks and over this a stained gingham apron. She was holding the kitchen door open, for M.R. to join her.

"Ma'am—mind if I say—you lookin' like you had some kind a shock. You better come here."

M.R. smiled, uncertainly. With a touch of her warm hand the heavyset woman drew M.R. forward as the men at the bar stared frankly.

Maybe—they liked what they saw. They approved of the girl-Amazon in city clothes, disheveled.

The woman was as tall as M.R.—in fact taller. Her hair was knotted and coiled about her head—a wan, faded gold like retreating sunshine. Her wide-set eyes were lighted like coins. And that wide, wet smile.

"Good you got here, ma'am. Out on that road after dark—you'd get lost fast."

"Oh yes! Thank you."

M.R. was dazed with gratitude. She felt like a drowning swimmer who has been hauled ashore.

In the kitchen, M.R. was given a chair to sit in. It was a familiar chair, this was comforting. The paint worn in a certain pattern on the back—the wicker seat beginning to buckle. And just in time for her knees had become weak.

Another comfort, the smell of baked goods. Simmering food, some kind of stew, on the stove. Like a sudden flame a frantic hunger was released in M.R.

"Hel-lo! Wel-come!"

"Ma'am! Wel-come."

There were others in the kitchen, warmly greeting M.R. She could not see their faces clearly but believed that they were relatives of the older woman.

There came a bowl of dark glistening soup, placed steaming before M.R. She supposed it was some kind of beef soup, or lamb—mutton?—globules of grease on the surface but M.R. was too hungry to be repelled. Her lips were soon coated with grease, there was no napkin with which she might wipe her face. She'd become so civilized, it was awkward for her to eat without a napkin in her lap—but there were no napkins here.

"Good, eh? More?"

Yes, it was good. Yes, M.R. would have more.

She was seated at a familiar table—Formica-topped, simulated maple, with battered legs. The air in the kitchen was warm, close, humid. On the gas-burner stove were many pots and pans. On another table were fresh-baked muffins, whole grain bread, pies. These were pies with thick crusts and sugary-gluey insides. Apple pies, cherry pies.

A bottle of beer. Bottles of beer. A hand lifted the bottle, poured the foaming dark liquid into a glass. M.R. drank.

So thirsty! So hungry! Her eyes welled with tears of childish gratitude.

The heavyset woman served her. The heavyset woman had enormous breasts to her waist. The heavyset woman had a coarse flushed skin and sympathetic eyes. Her crown of braids made her appear regal yet you knew—you could not coerce this woman.

When others—men, boys—tried to push into the kitchen to peer at M.R. in her rumpled and mud-stained clothes, the heavyset woman shooed them away. Laughing saying, Yall go away get the hell out noner your business here.

M.R. was eating so greedily, soup spilled onto the front of her jacket.

Her hands shook. Beer in her nostrils making her cough, choke.

She'd had too much to drink, and to eat. Too quickly. Laughing became coughing and coughing became choking and the heavyset woman thumped her between the shoulder blades with a fist.

It was the TV—or, a jukebox—loud percussive music. She could not hear the music, so loud. Something was entering her—lights?—like glinting blades. She wasn't drunk but a wild drunken elation swept over her, she was so very grateful trying to explain to the heavyset woman that she had never tasted food so wonderful.

Thinking *I have never been so happy.*

For it was revealed to M.R. that there were such places—(secret) places—to which she could retreat. (Secret) places not known even to her that would comfort her in times of danger. A sudden expansion of being as if something had gotten inside her tight-braided brain and pumped air and light into it—fire, wind—laughter—music.

Hel-lo. Hel-lo. Hel-lo!

Don't I know you?

Hey sure—sure I do. And you know me.

Feeling so very relieved. So very happy. A warmth spread in her heart. Clumsily M.R. tried to stand, to step into the embrace of the heavyset woman—press her face against the woman's large warm spongy breasts and hide inside the warm spongy fleshy arms.

You know—you are safe here.

Waiting for you—here.

Jewell!—*Jedina.* We are waiting for you—here.

Yet there was something wrong for the heavyset woman hadn't embraced her as M.R. had expected—instead the heavyset woman pushed M.R. away as you might push away an importunate child not in anger or annoyance or even impatience but simply because at that moment the importunate child isn't wanted. There was a rebuke here, M.R. did not want to consider. She was thinking *I must pay. I must leave a tip. None of this can be free.* She was fumbling with her wallet—she'd misplaced her leather handbag but somehow, she had her wallet. And she was trying to see her watch.

The numerals were blurred. In fact there were no hands on the watch-face to indicate the time. Let me see that, ma'am. Deftly the watch was removed from her wrist—she wanted to protest but could not. And her wallet—her wallet was taken from her. In its place she was given something to drink that was burning-hot. Was it whiskey? Not beer but whiskey? Her throat burned, her eyes smarted with tears. That'll speak to you, ma'am, eh?—a man's voice, bemused. There was laughter in the café—the laughter of men, boys—not mocking laughter—(she wanted to think)—but genial laughter—for they'd pushed into the kitchen after all.

Ma'am where're you from?—for her voice so resembles theirs. Ma'am where're you going?—for despite her clothes she's one of them, their staring eyes can see.

Her heavy head is resting on her crossed arms. And the side of her face against the sticky tabletop. So strange that her breasts hang loose to be crushed against the tabletop. The rude laughter has faded. So tired! Her eyes are shut, she is sinking, falling. There's a scraping of chair legs against the floor that sound unfriendly. A hand, or a fist, lightly taps her shoulder.

"Ma'am. We're closing now."

Mudgirl Saved by the King of the Crows.

April 1965

In Beechum County it would be told—told and retold—how Mudgirl was saved by the King of the Crows.

How in the vast mudflats beside the Black Snake River in that desolate region of the southern Adirondacks there were a thousand crows and of these thousand crows the largest and fiercest and most sleek-black-feathered was the King of the Crows.

How the King of the Crows had observed the cruel behavior of the woman half-dragging half-carrying a weeping child out into the mudflats to be thrown down into the mud soft-sinking as quicksand and left the child alone there to die in that terrible place.

And the King of the Crows flew overhead in vehement protest flapping his wide wings and shrieking at the retreating woman now shielding her face with her arms against the wrath of the King of the Crows in pursuit of her like some ancient heraldic bird-beast in the service of a savage God.

How in the mists of dawn less than a mile from the place where the child had been abandoned to die there was a trapper making the rounds of his traps along the Black Snake River and it was this trapper whom the King of the Crows summoned to save the child lying stunned in shock and barely breathing in the mudflat like discarded trash.

Come! S'ttisss!

Suttis Coldham making the rounds of the Coldham traps as near to dawn as he could before predators—coyotes, black bears, bobcats—tore their prey from the jaws of the traps and devoured them alive weakened and unable to defend themselves.

Beaver, muskrat, mink, fox and lynx and raccoons the Coldhams trapped in all seasons. What was *legal* or *not-legal*—what was listed as *endangered*—did not count much with the Coldhams. For in this desolate region of Beechum County in the craggy foothills of the Adirondacks there were likely to be fewer human beings per acre than there were bobcats—the bobcat being the shyest and most solitary of Adirondack creatures.

The Coldhams were an old family in Beechum County having settled in pre-Revolutionary times in the area of Rockfield in the Black Snake River but scattered now as far south as Star Lake, and beyond. In Suttis's immediate family there were five sons and of these sons Suttis was the youngest and the most bad-luck-prone of the generally luckless Coldham family as Suttis was the one for whom Amos Coldham the father had the least hope. As if there hadn't been enough brains left for poor Suttis, by the time Suttis came along.

Saying with a sour look in his face—Like you're shake-shake-shaking brains out of some damn bottle—like a ketchup bottle—and by the time it came to Suttis's turn there just ain't enough brains left in the bottle.

Saying—Wallop the fuckin' bottle with your hand won't do no fuckin' good—the brains is all used up.

So it would be told that the solitary trapper who rescued Mudgirl from her imminent death in the mudflats beside the Black Snake River had but the mind of a child of eleven or twelve and nowhere near the mind of an adult man of twenty-nine which was Suttis's age on this April morning in 1965.

So it would be told, where another trapper would have ignored the shrieking of the King of the Crows or worse yet taken shots with a .22 rifle to bring down the

King of the Crows, Suttis Coldham knew at once that he was being summoned by the King of the Crows for some special purpose.

For several times in his life it had happened to Suttis when Suttis was alone and apart from the scrutiny of others that creatures singled him out to address him.

The first—a screech owl out behind the back pasture when Suttis had been a young boy. Spoke his name *SSSuttisss* all hissing syllables so the soft hairs on his neck stood on end and staring up—upward—up to the very top of the ruin of a dead oak trunk where the owl was perched utterly motionless except for its feathers rippling in the wind and its eyes glaring like gasoline flame seeing how the owl knew *him*—a spindly-limbed boy twenty feet below gaping and grimacing and struck dumb hearing *SSSuttisss* and seeing that look in the owl's eyes of such significance, it could not have been named except the knowledge was imparted—*You are Suttis, and you are known.*

Not until years later came another creature to address Suttis and this a deer—a doe—while Suttis was hunting with his father and brothers and Suttis was left behind stumbling and uncertain and out of nowhere amid the pine woods there appeared the doe about fifty feet away—a doe with two just-born fawns—pausing to stare at Suttis wide-eyed not in fright but with a sort of surprised recognition even as Suttis lifted his rifle to fire with a rapidly beating heart and a very dry mouth—*Suttis! SuttisSuttisSuttis!*—words sounding inside his own head like a radio switched on so Suttis was given to know that it was the doe's thoughts sent to him in some way like vibrations in water and he'd understood that he was not to fire his rifle, and he did not fire his rifle.

And most recent in January 1965 making early-morning rounds of the traps, God damn Suttis's brothers sending Suttis out on a morning when none of them would have gone outdoors to freeze his ass but there's Suttis stumbling in thigh-high snow, shuddering in fuckin' freezing wind and half the traps covered in snow and inaccessible and finally he'd located one—one!—a mile or more from home—not what he'd expected in this frozen-over wet-land place which was muskrat or beaver or maybe raccoon but instead it was a bobcat—a thin whistle through the gap in Suttis's front teeth for Suttis had not ever trapped a bobcat before in his life for bobcats are too elusive—too cunning—but here a captive young one looked to be a six-to-eight-months-old kitten its left rear leg caught in a long spring trap panicked and panting licking at the wet-blooded trapped leg with frantic motions of its pink tongue and pausing now to stare up at Suttis in a look both pleading and reproachful, accusatory—it was a female cat, Suttis seemed to know—beautiful tawny eyes with black vertical slits fixed upon Suttis Coldham who was marveling he'd never seen such a creature in his life, silver-tipped fur, stripes and spots in the fur of the hue of burnished mahogany, tufted ears, long tremulous whiskers, and those tawny eyes fixed upon him as Suttis stood crouched a few feet away hearing in the bobcat's quick-panting breath what sounded like *Suttis! Suttis don't you know who I am* and drawn closer risking the bobcat's talon-claws and astonished now seeing that these were the eyes of his Coldham grandmother who'd died at Christmas in her eighty-ninth year but now the grandmother was a young girl as Suttis had never known her and somehow—Suttis could have no idea how—gazing at him out of the bobcat's eyes and even as the bobcat's teeth were bared in a panicked snarl clearly Suttis was made to hear his girl-grandmother's chiding voice *Suttis! O Suttis you know who I am—you know you do!*

Not for an instant did Suttis doubt that the bobcat was his Coldham grandmother, or his Coldham grandmother had become the bobcat—or was using the bobcat to communicate with Suttis knowing that Suttis was headed in this direction—no more could Suttis have explained these bizarre and improbable circumstances than he could have explained the "algebra equations" the teacher had chalked on the blackboard of the one-room school he'd attended sporadically for eight mostly futile years even as he had not the slightest doubt that the "algebra equations" were real enough, or real in some way that excluded Suttis Coldham; and so Suttis stooped hurriedly to pry open the spring-trap fumbling to release the injured left rear leg of the bobcat kitten murmuring to placate the spirit of his girl-grandmother who both was and was not the elderly woman he'd known and called *Gran'maw* and the bobcat bared her teeth, snarled and hissed and squirmed and clawed at his hands in leather gloves shredding the gloves but leaving Suttis's hands mostly unscathed and raking his face only thinly across his right cheek and in the next instant the bobcat kitten was running—limping, but running—on three swift legs disappearing into the snow-laden larch woods with no more sound than a startled indrawn breath and leaving behind nothing but a scattering of cat feces and patches of blood-splattered silver-tipped fur in the ugly serrated jaws of the trap and a sibilant murmur *S'ttus! God bless.*

And now it was the King of the Crows summoning Suttis Coldham unmistakably—*SSS'ttissss! SSS'ttiss!*

Suttis froze in his tracks. Suttis stood like one impaled. Suttis could not hide his eyes and refuse to see.

Suttis could not press his hands over his ears and refuse
to hear.

SSS'ttisss come here! Here!

The King of the Crows was the largest crow Suttis
had ever seen. His feathers were the sleekest and black-
est and his wingspread as wide as any hawk's and his
yellow eyes glared in urgency and indignation. Like a
hunted creature Suttis made his way along the river-
bank, as the King of the Crows shrieked in his wake,
flying from tree to tree behind him as if in pursuit. For
it would not be true as Suttis would claim that he had
followed the King of the Crows to the child abandoned
to die in the mudflat but rather that the King of the
Crows had driven Suttis as a dog might drive cattle.
Suttis could not hide, could not escape from the King
of the Crows for he knew that the King of the Crows
would pursue him back to the Coldham farm and would
never cease harassing and berating him for having disobeyed him.

Suttis stumbled and staggered along a three-foot-
high embankment that jutted out into the vast mudflat. Not long ago the last of the winter snows had
melted and the mudflat was puddled with water, as
the Black Snake River was swollen and muddy and
swift-rushing south out of the mountains. Everywhere was a buzzing-thrumming-teeming of new life,

and the rapacity of new life: blackflies, wasps, gnats. Suttis swatted at the air about his head, a cloud of new-hatched mosquitoes. Underfoot was the ruin of a road. Ahead was the ruin of a mill. Suttis knew the mudflats—the Coldhams hunted and trapped here— but Suttis had no clear idea what the purpose of the mill might have been at one time, or who might have owned it. His grandfather would know, or his father. His older brothers maybe. The ways of adults seemed to him remote and inaccessible and so their names were blurred and of little consequence to him as to any child.

Come here! Come here S'ttis come here!

SSS'ttisss! Here!

On the narrowing embankment Suttis moved with caution. The King of the Crows had so distracted him, he'd left his trapping gear behind—the burlap sack which bore the limp broken bloodied bodies of several dead creatures—but still he had his knife, sheathed in his jacket which was Amos Coldham's Army-issue jacket of a long-ago wartime, badly stained and frayed at the cuffs. On his head he wore a knit cap, pulled down onto his narrow forehead; on his lower body, khaki workpants; on his feet, rubber boots from Sears, Roebuck. Passing now the part-collapsed mill with its roof covered in moss that made him uneasy to see—

any building, however in ruins, Suttis Coldham was in-clined to think that something might be hiding inside, observing him.

In the mountains, you might be observed by a man with a rifle, at some distance. You would never know how you were viewed in a stranger's rifle-scope even as the stranger pulled the trigger and for what reason?—as the Coldhams liked to say *For the hell of it.*

Suttis cringed, worried that he was being observed and not by just the King of the Crows. Entering now into a force field of some other consciousness that drew him irresistibly.

Broken things in the winter-ravaged grasses, rotted planks, chunks of concrete, a man's single boot. A shredded tractor tire, strips of plastic. In the vast mud-flat tracks ran in all directions with a look of frenzied determination—animal tracks, bird tracks—and on the embankment, what Suttis identified as *human-being footprints.*

Suttis's eye that gazed upon so much without recog-nition, still less interest, for instance all printed mate-rials, seized at once upon the *human-being footprints* on the embankment which Suttis knew to be, without taking time to think, not the footprints of his brothers or any other trapper or hunter but *female footprints.*

Suttis knew, just knew: *female*. Not even the boot-prints of a young boy. Just *female* boot-prints.

There were other prints, too—mixed with the *female*. Possibly a child. Suttis knew without calculating, with just-seeing.

Not that these tracks were clear—they were not clear. But Suttis understood that they were fresh for no other tracks covered them.

What was this! Suttis whistled through the gap in his front teeth.

A piece of cloth—a scarf—of some crinkly purple material, Suttis snatched up and quickly shoved into his pocket.

SSS'ttisss! Here!

Atop a skeletal larch the King of the Crows spread his wings. The King of the Crows did not like it that Suttis had paused to pick up the crinkly-purple scarf. For the King of the Crows had flown ahead of Suttis, to bade him to hurry to that point, to see.

And now Suttis saw—about twelve feet from the base of the embankment, amid a tangle of rushes—a doll?

A child's rubber doll, badly battered, hairless, un-clothed and its coloring mostly flaked off—too light to sink in the mud and so it was floating on the surface in a way to cause Suttis's heart to trip even as he told himself *Damn thing's only a doll.*

Was he being mocked? Had the King of the Crows led him so far, to rescue a mere *doll?*

Suttis drew nearer and now—he saw the second figure, a few yards from the first. And this, too, had to be a doll—though larger than an ordinary doll—discarded in this desolate place like garbage or trash.

Pulses beat in his head like spoons against some wooden vessel. A doll! A doll! This had to be a doll, like the other.

As so much was tossed away into the Black Snake mudflats that were an inland sea of cast-off human things of all kinds. Here you could find articles of clothing, boots and shoes, broken crockery, plastic toys, even shower curtains opaque and stained as polyurethane shrouds. Once, Suttis had found a pair of jaws in the mud—plastic teeth—he'd thought were dentures but had had to have been Hallowe'en teeth and another time the wheel-less chassis of a baby buggy filled with mud like a gaping mouth. Mostly these cast-off things accumulated at the edge of the mudflat where borne by flooding water they caught in exposed roots amid the debris of winter storms, the skeletons of small drowned creatures and the mummified fur-remnants with blind pecked-out eyes like gargoyles fallen from unknown and unnameable cathedrals while farther out in the mudflats such objects were likely to sink and be sub-merged in mud.

Lurid tales were told in Beechum County of all that was "lost"—discarded and buried and forgotten—in the mudflats.

Bodies of the hated and reviled. Bodies of "enemies."

Humped outlines of dead logs in the mudflat like drowsing crocodiles.

Cries of smaller birds silenced by the furious shriek-ing of crows.

Was this a doll, so large? It looked to be the size of a small child—Suttis had no clear idea how old—two years? Three?

Weak-kneed Suttis approached the very edge of the bank.

The King of the Crows shook his wings, jeering, impatient.

SSS'ttisss! Here!

The King of the Crows was very near to speaking, now. Human speech the great bird could utter, that Suttis could not stop his ears from hearing.

As the wide black-feathered wings of the King of the Crows fluttered wind and shadows across Suttis's slow-blinking eyes.

"Jesus!"

A little girl, Suttis thought, but—dead?

Her head was bare as if shaved—so small! So sad!

Nothing so sad as a child's bare head when the head has been shaved for lice or the poor thin hair has fallen out from sickness and it seemed to Suttis, this had happened to him, too. Many years ago when he'd been a small child.

Lice, they'd said. Shaved his head and cut his scalp with the razor cursing him as if the lice were Suttis's fault and then they swabbed the cuts with kerosene, like flames too excruciating to be registered or gauged or even recalled except now obliquely, dimly.

Poor little girl! Suttis had no doubt, she was dead.

Maybe it was lice, they'd punished her for. Suttis could understand that. The small face was bruised, the mouth and eyes swollen and darkened. Blood-splotches on the face like tears and what was black on them, a buzzing blackness, was flies.

Only the head and torso were clearly visible, the lower body had sunk into the mud, and the legs. One of the arms was near-visible. Suttis stared and stared and Suttis moved his lips in a numbed and affrighted prayer not knowing what he was saying but only as he'd been taught *Our Father who art in heaven hallowed be thy name bless us O Lord for these our gifts and help us all*

*the days of our lives O Lord thy will be done on earth
as it is in heaven! Amen.*

Suttis had seen many dead things and was not uncomfortable with a dead thing for then you know, it is
dead and cannot hurt you. Only a fool would lay his
bare hand upon a "dead" raccoon or possum and that
fool would likely lose his hand in a frantic rake of sharp
curved claws and a slash of razor-teeth.

A dead thing is a safe thing and only bad if it has
started to rot.

The poor little girl in the mudflat had started to
rot—had she? For something smelled so very bad,
Suttis's nostrils shut tight.

It was a wild extravagant prayer of Suttis Coldham,
he'd never have believed he could utter:

God don't let her be dead. God help her be alive.

For cunning Suttis knew: a dead child could mean
that Suttis would be in trouble. As an older boy he'd
been beaten for staring at children in a wrong way,
or a way deemed wrong by others, by the children's
mothers for instance who were likely to be his Coldham relatives—sisters, cousins, young aunts. Staring
at his baby nieces and nephews when they were being
bathed in the very presence of their young mothers
and such a look in Suttis's face, of tenderness mixed
with brute yearning, Suttis had somehow done wrong

in utter innocence and been slapped and kicked-at and run out of the house and in his wake the cry *Nasty thing! Pre-vert! Get to hell out nasty pre-vert Sut-tis shame!*

And so now if this little girl is naked Suttis will turn and run—but it looks as if on what he can see of the little body is a nightgown—torn and grimy but a nightgown—isn't it?—for which Suttis is damned grateful.

The King of the Crows has been screaming for Suttis to bring the little girl to shore. In a crouch half-shutting his eyes groping for something—a long stick, a pole—a piece of lumber—with which to prod the body loose.

Suttis has it!—a part-rotted plank, about five feet long. When he leans out to poke at the doll-figure in the mud he sees—thinks he sees—one of the swollen eyelids flutter—the little fish-mouth gasping for breath—and he's stricken, paralyzed—*The little girl is alive!*

A terrifying sight, a living child—part-sunken in mud, a glint of iridescent insects about her face—has to be flies—suddenly Suttis is panicked, scrabbling on hands and knees to escape this terrible vision, moaning, gibbering as the King of the Crows berates him from a perch overhead and like a frenzied calf Suttis blunders into a maze of vines, a noose of vines catches him around the neck and near-garrots him the shock of it bringing him to his senses so chastened like a calf swatted with a stiff hunk of rope he turns to crawl back to the edge of the embankment. There is no escaping the fact that Suttis will have to wade into the mudflat to rescue the girl as he has been bidden.

At least, the sharp stink of the mud has abated, in Suttis's nostrils. The most readily adapted of all senses, smell: almost, Suttis will find the mud-stink pleasurable, by the time he has dislodged and lifted the mud-child in his arms to haul back to shore.

Suttis slip-slides down the bank, into the mud. Makes his way to the mud-child lifting his booted feet as high as he can as the mud suck-suck-sucks at him as in a mockery of wet kisses. Above the mud-child is a cloud, a haze of insects—flies, mosquitoes. Suttis brushes them away with a curse. He's shy about touching her—at first. He tugs at her arm. Her exposed shoulder, her left arm. She's a very little girl—the age of his youngest niece Suttis thinks except the little nieces and nephews grow so quickly, he can't keep them straight—can't keep their names straight. Lifting this one from the mud requires strength.

Crouched over her, grunting. He's in mud nearly to his knees—steadily sinking. Rushes slap against his face, thinly scratching his cheeks. Mosquitoes buzz in his ears. A wild sensation as of elation sweeps over him—*You are in the right place at the right time and no other place and no other time will ever be so right for you again in your life.*

"Hey! Gotcha now. Gonna be okay."

Suttis's voice is raw as a voice unused for years. As it is rare for Suttis to be addressed with anything other than impatience, contempt, or anger so it is rare for Suttis to speak, and yet more rare for Suttis to speak so excitedly.

The part-conscious child tries to open her eyes. The right eye is swollen shut but the left eye opens—just barely—there's a flutter of eyelashes—and the little fish-mouth is pursed to breathe, to breathe and to whimper as if wakening to life as Suttis carries her to shore stumbling and grunting and at the embankment lays her carefully down and climbs up out of the mud and removes his khaki jacket to wrap her in, clumsily; seeing that she is near-naked, in what appears to be the remnants of a torn paper nightgown all matted with mud, slick and glistening with mud and there is mud caked on the child's shaved head amid sores, scabs, bruises and so little evidence of hair, no one could have said what color the child's hair is.

"Hey! You're gonna be okay. S'ttis's got you now."

Such pity mixed with hope Suttis feels, he has rarely felt in his life. Carrying the whimpering mud-child wrapped in his jacket, in his arms back along the embankment and to the road and along the road three miles to the small riverside town called Rapids murmuring to the shivering mud-child in the tone of one of his young-mother sisters or cousins—not actual words which Suttis can't recall but the tone of the words—soothing, comforting—for in his heart it will seem a certainty that the King of the Crows had chosen Suttis Coldham to rescue the mud-child not because Suttis Coldham happened to be close by but because of all men, Suttis Coldham was singled out for the task.

He was the chosen one. Suttis Coldham, that nobody gave a God damn for, before. Without him, the child would not be rescued.

Somewhere between the mudflats and the small town called Rapids, the King of the Crows has vanished.

The sign is RAPIDS POP. 370. Suttis sees this, every time Suttis thinks there's too many people here he couldn't count by name. Nor any of the Coldhams could. Not by a long shot.

First he's seen here is by a farmer in a pickup truck braking to a stop and in the truck-bed a loud-barking dog. And out of the Gulf gas station several men—he thinks he maybe knows, or should know their faces, or their names—come running astonished and appalled.

Suttis Coldham, Amos Coldham's son. Never grew up right in his mind, poor bastard.

Now more of them come running to Suttis in the road. Suttis carrying the little mudgirl wrapped in a muddied jacket in his arms, in the road.

A little girl utterly unknown to them, the child of strangers—so young!—*covered in mud*?

Amid the excitement Suttis backs off dazed, confused. Trying to explain—stammering—the King of the Crows that called to him when he was checking his traps on the river . . . First he'd seen a doll, old rubber doll in the mudflat—then he'd looked up and seen . . .

Quickly the barely breathing mud-child is removed from Suttis's arms. There are women now—women's voices shrill and indignant. The child is borne to the nearest house to be undressed, examined, gently bathed and dressed in clean clothing and in the roadway Suttis feels the loss—the mud-child was *his*. And now—the mud-child has been taken from him.

Harshly Suttis is being asked where did he find the child? Who is the child? Where are her parents? Her mother? What has happened to her?

So hard Suttis is trying to speak, the words come out choked and stammering.

Soon, a Beechum County sheriff's vehicle arrives braking to a stop.

In the roadway Suttis Coldham stands shivering in shirtsleeves, trousers muddied to the thighs and mud-splotches on his arms, face. Suttis has a narrow weasel-face like something pinched in a vise and a melted-away chin exposing front teeth and the gap between teeth near-wide enough to be a missing tooth and Suttis is dazed and excited and trembling and talking—never in his life has Suttis been so *important*—never drawn so much *attention*—like someone on TV. So many people surrounding him, so suddenly!—and so many questions . . .

Rare for Suttis to speak more than a few words and these quick-mumbled words to a family member and so Suttis has no way of measuring speech—a cascade of words spills from his lips—but Suttis knows very few words and so must repeat his words nor does Suttis know how to stop talking, once he has begun—like running-sliding down a steep incline, once you start you can't stop. Lucky for Suttis one of the onlookers is a Coldham cousin who identifies him—insists that if Suttis says he found the child in the mudflat, that is where Suttis found the child—for Suttis isn't one who would take a child—Suttis is *simple and honest as a child himself and would never do harm, not ever to anyone—Suttis always tells the truth.*

In a Beechum County sheriff's vehicle the nameless little girl is taken to the hospital sixty miles away in

Carthage where it is determined that she is suffering from pneumonia, malnutrition, lacerations and bruising, shock. For some weeks it isn't certain that the little girl will survive and during these weeks, and for some time to follow, the little girl is mute as if her vocal cords have been severed to render her speechless.

Beaver, muskrat, mink, fox and lynx and raccoons he trapped in all seasons. How many beautiful furred creatures wounded, mangled and killed in the Coldham traps, and their pelts sold by Suttis's father. And it is the child in the mudflat Suttis Coldham will recall and cherish through his life.

In bed in his twitchy sleep cherishing the crinkly-purple scarf he'd found on the embankment, still bearing a residue of dirt though he'd washed it with care and smoothed it with the edge of his hand to place beneath the flat sweat-soaked pillow, in secret.

Mudwoman Confronts an Enemy. Mudwoman's Triumph.

March 2003

Must ready yourself. Hurry!

But there was no way she could ready herself for this.

"I don't wish to accuse anyone."

His name was Alexander Stirk. He was twenty years old. Formally and bravely he spoke. For his small prim child's mouth had been kicked, torn and bloodied. His remaining good eye—the other was swollen shut, grotesquely bruised like a rotted fruit—was fixed on M.R. with hypnotic intensity as if daring her to look away.

"Though I have, as you know, President Neukirchen—numerous enemies here on campus."

President Neukirchen. With such exaggerated respect this name was uttered, M.R. felt a tinge of unease—*Is he mocking me?*

M.R. decided no, that wasn't possible. Alexander Stirk could not mistake M.R.'s attentiveness to him for anything other than *sympathy.*

His head was partly bandaged, with the look of a turban gone askew. His wire-rimmed glasses were crooked on his nose because of the bandage and the left lens had a hairline crack. In the thin reproachful voice of one accusing an elder of an obscure hurt he spoke calmly, deliberately. For he had a genuine grievance, he'd been martyred for his beliefs. He'd hobbled into the president's office using a single aluminum crutch that was leaning now against the front corner of the president's desk in a pose of nonchalance.

M.R.'s heart went out to Stirk—he was so *small.*

"That is—President Neukirchen—there are many individuals among both the undergraduate and the graduate student body—and faculty members as well— who have defined themselves as 'enemies' specifically of Alexander Stirk as well as 'enemies' of the conservative movement on campus. You know their names by now, or should—Professor Kroll has seen to that, I think."

Kroll. M.R. smiled just a little harder, feeling blood rush into her face.

"Of these self-defined 'enemies' I'm not able to judge how many would actually wish 'Alexander Stirk' harm, apart from the usual verbal abuse. And how many, among these, would be actively involved in actually harming me."

Stirk smiled with disarming candor. Or seeming candor. M.R. smiled more painfully.

She'd invited Stirk to her office, to speak with her in private. She wanted the young man to know how concerned she was for him, and how outraged on his behalf. She wanted the young man to know that, as the president of the University, she was *on his side.*

The assault had taken place on the University campus just two nights before, at approximately 11:40 P.M. Returning—alone—for Alexander Stirk was frequently alone—to his Harrow Hall residence, Stirk had been accosted on a dimly lit walkway beside the chapel by several individuals—seemingly fellow undergraduates; in his confusion and terror he hadn't seen their faces clearly—not clearly enough to identify—but he'd heard crude jeering voices—"fag"—"Fascist-fag"—as he was being clumsily shoved and slammed against the brick wall of the chapel—nose bloodied, right eye socket cracked, lacerations to his mouth, left ankle sprained when he was thrown to the ground. So forcibly was Stirk's backpack wrenched from his shoulders, his left shoulder had been nearly dislocated, and was badly bruised; the backpack's contents were dumped on the ground—leaflets bearing the heraldic fierce-eyed American eagle of the YAF—(Young Americans for Freedom)—to be scattered and blown about across the snow-stubbled chapel green.

Evidently, campus security hadn't been aware of the fracas. No one seemed to have come to Stirk's aid even after he'd been left semiconscious on the ground. M.R. found this difficult to believe, or to comprehend—but Stirk insisted. And it was wisest at this point not to challenge him.

For already, Stirk had been interviewed by the campus newspaper in a florid front-page story. Bitterly he'd complained of "unconscionable treatment"—that several witnesses to the attack, in the vicinity of the chapel, had ignored his cries for help as if knowing that the victim was *him.*

Alexander Stirk had a certain reputation at the University, for his outspoken conservative views. He had a weekly half-hour program on the campus radio station—*Headshots*—and a biweekly opinion column in the campus newspaper—"Stirk Strikes." He was a senior majoring in politics and social psychology, from Jacksonville, Florida; he was an honors student, an officer in the local chapter of the YAF and an activist member of the University's Religious Life Council. When high-profile liberal speakers like

Noam Chomsky spoke at the University, Stirk and a boisterous band of confederates were invariably seen picketing the lecture hall before the lecture and, during the lecture, interrupting the speaker with heckling questions. Stirk's particular concern seemed to be, oddly for a young man, abortion: he was resolutely opposed to abortion in any and all forms and particularly opposed to any government funding of abortion.

But he was also opposed to free condoms, contraception, "sex education" in public schools.

It was so, evidently—Stirk had roused angry opposition on the campus including a barrage of "threatening" e-mails, of which he'd turned over some to authorities. He'd been, by his account, "insulted"—"called names"—told to "shut the fuck up"; but until the other evening he'd never been physically assaulted. Now, he said, he was "seriously frightened" for his life.

At this, Stirk's voice quavered. Beneath the supercilious pose—the posturing of a very bright undergraduate whose command of language was indeed impressive—there did seem to be a frightened boy.

Warmly M.R. assured Alexander Stirk—he had nothing to fear!

University proctors had been assigned to his floor in Harrow Hall and would escort him to classes if he wished. Whenever he wanted to go anywhere after dark—a proctor would accompany him.

And whoever had assaulted him would be apprehended and expelled from the University—"This, I promise."

"President Neukirchen, thank you! I would like to believe you."

Stirk spoke with the mildest of smiles—unless it was a smirk. M.R. had the uneasy sensation that the young man who'd limped into her office was addressing an audience not visibly present, like a highly self-conscious actor in a film. There came—and went—and again came—that sly smirk of a smile, too fleeting to be clearly identified. For his meeting with President Neukirchen Stirk wore a dark green corduroy sport coat with leather buttons, that appeared to be a size or two too large; he wore a white cotton shirt buttoned to the throat, and flannel trousers with a distinct crease. Except for the luridly swollen eye and mouth, Stirk gave the appearance of a pert, bright, precocious child, long the favorite of his elders. Almost, you would think that his feet—small prim feet, in white ankle-high sneakers—didn't quite touch the floor.

How strange Stirk seemed to M.R.! Not so much in himself as in her intense feeling for him, that was quite unlike any sensation she'd ever experienced, she was

sure, in this high-ceilinged office with its dark walnut
wainscoting, dour hardwood floors and somber lighting grudgingly emitted from a half-dozen tall narrow
windows. The president's office on the first floor of
"historic" Salvager Hall—old, elegantly heavy black-
leather furnishings, massive eighteenth-century cherrywood desk, Travertine marble fireplace and shining
brass andirons and built-in shelves floor-to-ceiling
with books—rare books—books long unread, un-
touched—behind shining glass doors—had the air of
a museum-room, perfectly preserved. Visitors to this
office were suitably impressed, even wealthy graduates, donors—the portrait over the fireplace mantel, of
a soberly frowning if just slightly rubefacient bewigged
eighteenth-century gentleman bore so close a resemblance to Benjamin Franklin that visitors invariably in-
quired, and M.R. was obliged to explain that Ezechiel
Charters, the founder of the University—that is, the
Presbyterian minister founder of the seminary, in 1761,
that would one day be the University—had been in fact
a contemporary of Franklin's, but hardly a friend.

Reverend Ezechiel Charters had been something of
a Tory, in the tumultuous years preceding the Revolu-
tion. His fate at the hands of a mob of local patriots
would have been lethal except for a "divine intervention" as it was believed to be—the noose meant to

strangle him broke—and so Reverend Charters lived to become a Federalist, like so many of his Tory countrymen.

A Federalist and something of a "liberal"—so the founding-legend of the University would have it.

But twenty-year-old Alexander Stirk hadn't been impressed by all this history. Brashly he'd limped into the president's office on his single, clattering crutch, lowered himself with conspicuous care into the chair facing the president's desk, glanced about squinting and smirking as if the anemic light from the high windows hurt his battered eyes, and murmured:

"Well! This is an unexpected honor, President Neukirchen." If he'd been speaking ironically, President Neukirchen, in the way of those elders who surround the just-slightly-insolent young, hadn't seemed to register the irony.

For M.R. was strangely—powerfully—struck by the boy. There was something pious and stunted and yet poignant about him, even the near-insolence of his face, as if, unwitting, he was the bearer of an undiagnosed illness.

"The police were asking—could I identify my assailants?—and I told them I didn't think so, I was jumped from behind and didn't see faces clearly. I heard voices—but. . . ."

M.R. had questions to ask of Stirk, but did not interrupt as he continued his account of the assault. She was thinking that most of the individuals who came to her office to sit in the heavy black leather chair facing her desk wanted something of her—wanted something from her—or had a grievance to make to her—or of her—as president of the University; most of them, M.R. would have to disappoint in some way, but in no way that might be interpreted as indifferent. Uncaring. For it was M. R. Neukirchen's (possible) weakness as an administrator—she *did care.*

She was not a Quaker. Not a practicing Quaker. But the benign Quaker selflessness—the concern for "clearness"—and for the commonweal above the individual—had long ago suffused her soul.

All that matters—really matters—is to do well by others. At the very least, to do no harm.

And so, M.R. didn't want to question the injured boy too closely, nor even to interview him as the police had done in the ER; she didn't see her role, at this critical time, as anything other than supportive, consoling.

Almost as soon as the news had been released, bulletin e-mails sent to all University faculty and staff, there'd been, among the more skeptical left-wing faculty, some doubt of Stirk's veracity. And among students who knew Stirk, who weren't sympathetic with his politics, there was more than just some doubt.

But M.R. who was known on campus as *the students' friend* did not align herself with these.

And it was so—seeing Stirk up close, the boy's very real and obviously painful injuries including a broken eye socket, M.R. wasn't inclined to be skeptical.

Or, rather—she'd learned such a technique, from her first years as an administrator—her skepticism was lightly repelled, suspended, like a balloon that has been given a tap, to propel it into a farther corner of the room.

"Of course, the University is going to investigate the assault. I've named an emergency committee, and I will be ex officio. Whoever did this terrible thing to you will be apprehended and expelled, I promise."

Stirk laughed. The wounded little mouth twisted into a kind of polite sneer.

"Better yet, President Neukirchen, the township police will investigate. Whoever attacked me committed a *felony*, not a campus misdemeanor. There will be *arrests*—not mere *expulsions*." The thin boyish voice deepened again, with a kind of suppressed exaltation. "There will be *lawsuits*."

Lawsuits was uttered in a way to make an administrator shudder. But President Neukirchen did not overtly react.

M.R. had been vaguely aware, before the assault, of the controversial undergraduate—at least, the name "Stirk." In recent months she'd been made aware of the conservative movement on campus, that had been gathering strength and influence since the terrorist attacks of 9/11 to the very eve, in early March, of a "military action" against Iraq, expected to be ordered by the president of the United States within a few days.

It couldn't be an accident, Alexander Stirk had declared himself passionately in favor of war against Iraq, as against all "enemies of Christian democracy." A wish to wage war as a religious crusade was a part of the conservative campaign for a stricter personal morality.

Before every war in American history there'd been a similar campaign in the public press—often, demonic and degrading political cartoons depicting the "enemy" as subhuman, bestial. The campaign against Saddam Hussein had been relentlessly waged since October, mounting to a fever pitch on twenty-four-hour cable news programs in recent weeks—Fox, CNN. It was a farcical sort of tragedy that the murder-minded Republican administration led by Cheney and Rumsfeld had its ideal foil in the murder-minded Iraqi dictator Saddam Hussein. Except that hundreds of thousands of innocent individuals might die, these deranged adversaries deserved one another.

Disturbing to realize that the conservative student movement was steadily gaining ground on American campuses in these early years of the twenty-first century. Even at older, more historically distinguished private universities like this one, that were traditionally liberal-minded.

In the hostile vocabulary of Alexander Stirk and his compatriots—*leftist-leaning.*

"I told the township officers, and I will go on record telling you, President Neukirchen—I don't feel that I should try to identify my assailants even if I have some idea who some of them are." Stirk paused to remove a handkerchief from his coat pocket which he unfolded and dabbed against his injured eye, in which lustrous tears welled. He spoke with exaggerated care as if not wanting to be misunderstood.

It was clear to M.R.—unmistakably!—that Stirk was speaking with an air of adolescent sarcasm, perhaps hoping to provoke her.

It hadn't happened often, in M.R.'s university career, that students had spoken disrespectfully to her. Perhaps in fact no student ever had—until now. And so she wasn't accustomed to the experience—wasn't sure how to react, or whether to react. In her chest she felt a sharp little pang of—was it hurt? disappointment? chagrin? Was it *anger?* That Alexander Stirk whom she'd hoped to befriend was not so very charmed by President Neukirchen.

Yet more daringly—provocatively—Stirk was saying: "Frankly I can tell you—as I am sure you would hardly repeat it—President Neukirchen—when I was attacked, I had blurred impressions of faces—and maybe—an impression of just one face—or more than one—belonging to a light-skinned 'person of color.'" Stirk paused to let this riposte sink in, with a look both grave and reproachful. Then as if he and President Neukirchen were in complete agreement on some issue of surpassing delicacy he continued, piously: "But—as a Christian—a Catholic—and a libertarian—on principle I don't believe that it is just—as in *justice*—to risk accusing an innocent individual even if it means letting the guilty go free. That isn't a principle that makes sense to pro-abortion people—who grant no value whatever to nascent human life—but it's a principle greatly cherished by the YAF."

Pro-abortion? Nascent human life? What this had to do with Stirk being assaulted, M.R. didn't quite know. But she knew enough not to rise to this bait.

"Well. After I'd been knocked to the ground, kicked and humiliated and threatened—'You don't shut the fuck up, you're dead meat, fag'"—Stirk's boyish voice assumed a deeper and coarser tone, reiterating these crude words—"still no one came to my aid. Within seconds all witnesses fled the scene—laughing—I could hear them laughing—and by the time some Good Samaritan alerted a campus security cop in the office behind Salvager Hall, I'd managed to get to my feet and stagger out to the street—*off campus*—a passing motorist saw me, and took pity on me."

Passing motorist. The phrase struck M.R. oddly.

Like one who has told a story many times, though in fact Stirk could not have told this story many times, the bruised and battered undergraduate related how he'd been helped into the vehicle of the *passing motorist* and driven to the local hospital ER—"This citizen didn't worry about the inside of his car getting bloodied, thank God"—where he was X-rayed and treated for his injuries and township police officers were called— "Since this wasn't an accident, but a vicious attack"— and came to interview him; when he was feeling a little stronger Stirk called Professor Kroll, his politics adviser, also faculty adviser for the local chapter of the Young Americans for Freedom, at whose house Stirk had been before the assault.

Strange, M.R. thought, that Stirk hadn't called his family in Jacksonville. Stirk had been adamant, the dean of students was not to contact them without his permission.

Where once the university was legally held to be in loco parentis, now the university was forbidden to assume any sort of parental responsibility not specifically granted by the individual student.

Where once the university was likely to be sued for failure to behave like a protective parent, now the university was likely to be sued for behaving like a protective parent, against even the wishes of an eighteen-year-old freshman.

"Y'know what Professor Kroll's first words were to me, President Neukirchen?—'So it's started, then. Our war.' "

Our war! How like Oliver Kroll this was—to make of the private something political. To make of the painfully specific something emblematic, impersonal. For *our war* meant a division of campus and nationalist loyalties as it meant *our war* soon to be launched in Iraq.

Somehow, campus politics had become embroiled with such issues as abortion, sexual promiscuity and drunkenness on campus; patriotism was measured by the fervor with which one argued for "closed borders"— "War on Terror"—the need for "military action" in the Middle East. M.R. had followed relatively little of this at the University for she'd been busy with other, seemingly more pressing matters.

Proudly Stirk was telling President Neukirchen that, though it was after midnight by the time he'd called him, Oliver Kroll came at once to the ER. There, Professor Kroll had been "astonished" to see Stirk's injuries—"disgusted"—"furious." Professor Kroll had insisted upon speaking with township police officers, informing them of threats he'd personally seen that Stirk had received from "radical-left sources" at the University, in protest of Stirk's outspoken views on politics and morality. More specifically, in the week prior to the assault, Stirk had addressed in both his radio program and in his newspaper column a "truly despicable, unspeakable" situation that had transpired at the University—the "open secret" that an undergraduate girl had had a third-trimester abortion in a Planned Parenthood clinic in Philadelphia. Stirk had slyly—dangerously—come very close to "naming names, placing blame"—and for this, he'd received a fresh barrage of "hate mail" and "threats."

M.R. had been dismayed when one of her staff members brought the student newspaper to her, to show her Stirk's column rife with innuendos and accusations like a tabloid gossip column. Though the student paper was overall a politically liberal publication, yet its editors believed in "diversity of expression"— "controversy." There had not been any attempt to censor or even to influence student publications at the University for at least fifty years—such publications were self-determined by students. M.R., like most faculty members, had only a vague awareness of the politically conservative/born-again Christian coalition at the University, that sought converts for its cause. The coalition was a minority of students, probably less than 5 percent of the student body, yet it had become a highly vocal and impassioned minority at odds with the predominant liberal atmosphere, and it didn't help the situation that certain of the Christian students, like Alexander Stirk, seemed to be courting martyrdom— at least, the public attention accruing to martyrdom.

Especially, M.R. had been disturbed by the bluntness of the column "Stirk Strikes" with its provocative title "Free (For Who?) Choice" and, in boldface type, the mocking rhyme in the first paragraph:

FREE CHOICE IS A LIE!
NOBODY'S BABY WANTS TO DIE!

Unbidden the thought came to M.R.—*My mother wanted me to die.*

But how ugly this was, and in the student newspaper! No wonder Stirk had drawn what he claimed to be hate e-mail. No wonder there were undergraduates who resented him, mocked him. If Stirk were gay—as it appeared to be Stirk was—this "gayness" had nothing to do with his conservative beliefs, in fact would seem to be in opposition to conventional conservatism—which would have made of Alexander Stirk an unusual individual, perhaps, and a brave one. But in these issues which roused emotion like a dust storm, there was no time for nuance or subtleties; no time to consider paradoxes of personality.

Distressing to M.R. and her (liberal-minded) colleagues, that campus conservatives, in mimicry of conservatives through America since the triumphant Reagan years, were inclined to forgo subtleties. Their strategies of opposition were adversarial, confrontational—ugly. Their strategies were, as they put it, to go *for the jugular.*

When M.R. had first known Oliver Kroll, when she'd first come to teach moral philosophy at the University, Kroll had been less passionately involved in the conservative movement; M.R. had read Kroll's essays on the history of American libertarianism, published in such prestigious journals as *American Political Philosophy,* and been impressed. For here was a perspective very different from her own, intelligently if not persuasively argued. M.R. had never felt comfortable with Kroll—for both political and personal reasons—but she'd admired his work and, to a degree, painful now to recall, they'd been friends—or more than friends, for a brief while; since that time, Kroll had become a (well-paid) consultant for the Republican administration in Washington and had become closely aligned with the University's most famous—or notorious—conservative spokesman, G. Leddy Heidemann, an authority on "fundamentalist Islam" who was rumored to be intimately involved with (secret) preparations for the Iraqi invasion, a confidant of Defense Secretary Donald Rumsfeld. Both Kroll and Heidemann were much disliked at the University by a majority of their colleagues but they had a following among a number of students, primarily undergraduates.

M.R. found all this disturbing, and distasteful—like any administrator she feared for her authority even as she believed herself the very sort of administrator who cared little for "authority"—it was M. R. Neukirchen's specialness that made her an effective president, an air of open-minded friendliness to all.

Yet it was upsetting to her that in growing quarters in the public media as on her very campus, the word *liberal* had become a sort of comic obscenity, not to be murmured without a smirk.

Like "pointy-headed intellectual"—the crude, coarse smear-phrase that had been used to discredit Adlai Stevenson in the ill-fated 1956 presidential election. How to defend oneself against such a—charge? Even to attempt to refute it was to be sullied by it, an object of ridicule.

"So, President Neukirchen—"

In his mock-reproachful pious-accusing voice Stirk continued his account of the assault and its aftermath. For twenty minutes he'd been speaking virtually non-stop as if declaiming his plight to a vast TV audience among which M.R. was a single listener. With remarkable brazenness—as if he understood how he was intimidating the president of the University—he paused to touch a forefinger to his lips.

"I wonder, President Neukirchen—have you ever listened to my radio broadcast—*Headshots*?"

"I'm afraid I have not."

"But I think—I hope—you've seen my column in the campus paper—'Stirk Strikes'?"

"Yes. I've seen that."

"The columns are posted online, too. So my 'kingdom' is not just of this campus."

Stirk was speaking in his radio voice, M.R. supposed—a forced-baritone that belied the small-boned and seemingly muscleless body. *How small. How easily he could be hurt.*

Stirk's bandaged head—the markedly narrow forehead that looked as if it had been pinched together in a vise, and the weak, melted-away chin . . . The eyes were Stirk's most attractive feature despite being blackened and bruised and M.R. saw in them both insolence and yearning, desperation.

Love me! Love me and help me please God.

The plea that would never be voiced.

Without his pose of arrogance, as without his clothes, how defenseless Stirk would be! A sexless little figure, utterly vulnerable. M.R. imagined him as a young adolescent, or as a child—intimidated by bigger boys, made to feel inferior, contemptible. In the world in which she'd grown up, in upstate New York south of the Adirondacks, a boy like Alexander Stirk wouldn't have had a chance.

It seemed touching to her, a gesture of sheer courage, or bravado—to have proclaimed himself so openly "gay." Except Stirk's "gayness" seemed also a kind of guise, or ruse; a provocation and a mask to hide behind.

Stirk was revealing now to M.R. that he had a list of names which he hadn't yet given to the police—a list that Professor Kroll had helped him prepare—"Not just students but faculty, too. Some surprising names." He intended to give this list to the University committee investigating the assault—but he wasn't sure "just yet" about giving the list to the police.

What was wonderful about the assault—ironically!—was that he'd been receiving so much support from people "all over the country"—"an outpouring of sympathy and outrage." Within the past day or so he'd had offers from "world-class" attorneys offering to represent him in lawsuits against his assailants and against the University for having failed to protect him. . . . The *Washington Times*, the Young America Foundation, the cable Fox News had contacted him requesting interviews. . . .

M.R. winced to hear this. Of course—the conservative media would leap at the opportunity to interview one of their martyred own.

Sobering to consider how an incident on the University campus so very quickly made its way into a global consciousness—"cyberspace"—to be replicated—amplified—thousands of times! M.R. was beginning to feel faint. For this was shaping up to be the sort of campus controversy, swirling out of control like sewage rising in a flash flood, M.R. knew she must avoid; M.R. had assumed she could, with goodwill, common sense, hard work and *sincerity* avoid. Hadn't she assumed that, if she met with the stricken boy personally, and alone—that would make a difference?

Leonard Lockhardt and other staffers had strongly suggested to M.R. that she not meet with Alexander

Stirk alone—but M.R. had insisted: she wasn't the sort of university president to distance herself from individual students, she was precisely the sort of administrator known to care for individuals. She'd expected that speaking with Stirk calmly, in private, she could reach out to him, and understand him; she could—oh, was this mere vanity?—naïveté?—*impress him with her sincerity, and win his trust.*

Make her his friend.

The call had come late the other night—very late—2 A.M.—when M.R. had only just gone to bed and lay sleepless amid the thrumming of her brain like a hive of bees—sleepless alone in the president's bed in the president's bedroom in the president's house which was an "historic" building in the older, "historic" part of the University campus—she had only just left her home office, only just shut down her computer for the night and hoped to sleep a few hours at least before waking at 7 A.M. for a long day—all weekdays were long days—to be navigated with zest, with optimism, with hope—like a ski slope, a very long ski slope, the bottom of which wasn't in sight from the top.

Nothing so beautiful and so thrilling as downhill skiing—if you have the skill.

The ringing phone, at 2 A.M.—precisely, 2:04 A.M.— and M.R. had answered it with apprehension, for of course it could be only bad news at such an hour—a call to the president's unlisted, private line—a number which few individuals knew—the urgent voice of the University's head of security informing her of this shocking news. . . .

Oh God! Is he—how badly is he hurt?

Is it known who attacked him? Were they—students?

It would seem to M.R. that a bright, blinding light had suffused the room, and the nighttime landscape outside the window. Immediately she'd been wide awake—hyper-awake. She would be on, or near, the phone for hours.

Thinking *What folly this is! I am not prepared for this.*

Yet she would persevere. She would do what she could. Vastly relieved that the boy wasn't critically—seriously—injured; impulsively deciding to drive to the hospital, to see him, at 6:20 A.M. in a wet wind-driven snow.

The hospital was a little more than a mile away from the president's house. The last time M.R. had driven there, she'd visited an older colleague, a woman who'd had breast cancer surgery.

Before that, a male colleague, not older, who'd had prostate cancer surgery.

Both individuals had recovered, or so M.R. was given to believe.

She would tell no one at the University about this reckless pre-dawn act—no one on her staff, no confidante or friend. Certainly not the University counsel who urged caution in all matters that might involve publicity. And certainly not her (secret) lover for whom the entire adventure of M.R.'s University presidency was an improbable phantasmagoria, tinged with folly, vanity, naïveté.

Why this was, M.R. wasn't so sure. Maybe because the presidency, beyond even M. R. Neukirchen's brilliant academic career, was so very alien to him and so excluded him.

In a haze of excitement fueled by the insomniac stress of the past several hours M.R. drove to the hospital and parked at the brightly lighted emergency room at the rear and hurried inside breathless and apprehensive—a tall anxious-eyed woman asking if a young University student named Alexander Stirk was still there, and could she see him . . .

By this time, Stirk had been discharged. He'd left the hospital in the company of an individual M.R. had to assume was Oliver Kroll.

"Oh, I see! And is he—how is he?"

A young Indian doctor regarded M.R. with quizzical eyes. Who was this woman? What relationship to Stirk?

M.R. introduced herself. Seeing in the doctor's startled gaze that yes, it was something of an incident in
itself, something to be remarked upon, spoken of, that
the president of the University had hurried to the ER
before dawn to see the badly beaten undergraduate.

With a polite smile the doctor told M.R. that Alexander Stirk had been considered well enough to leave
the ER and he would tell her what he wanted her to
know of his medical condition—best to inquire of him.

M.R. went away rebuked. M.R. went away *relieved*.

For it had been a rash act, to drive to the hospital.
She wondered if it had been a foolish act.

The University counsel Leonard Lockhardt would
have disapproved. This canny individual whom President Neukirchen had inherited from her canny predecessor and whose general advice to the new University
president was *caution*.

*These are litigious times, keep in mind! And this
University is known to be very wealthy.*

But Leonard Lockhardt would never know that
M.R. had driven to the hospital before dawn. No one
would ever know, including Alexander Stirk.

Naturally Lockhardt advised M.R. not to meet
with the excitable young man in private. M.R. insisted
she would meet with Stirk in private. Lockhardt had
cautioned M.R. not to "seem to be taking sides—

prematurely"—and M.R. said that of course she would
be very careful about what she said. Most of all she
wanted simply to speak to the boy, to console him. For
he'd suffered a terrible shock—whether his account of
the assault was entirely true, he had been injured. It
was M.R.'s wish to console him and she believed it was
her duty to console him—as a University student, Stirk
was *her student.*

And so M.R. took care not to suggest that she didn't
believe Stirk's story or that in any way she wished to
defend the University that had, by his account, failed to
protect him.

Grimly Stirk was saying that his enemies would be
accusing him of fabricating the very attack they'd made
on him. They'd threatened him, with worse harm.

"—think that they can intimidate me—silence me.
But they will be very surprised when—"

M.R. perceived a deep hurt in the stricken boy—a
woundedness like spiritual anguish. For he'd been insulted, and the insult wasn't recent.

Difficult to believe that this was a twenty-year-old
and not a boy of fifteen, or younger; seen from a short
distance, Stirk more resembled a girl than a boy. He
could have been no more than five feet two inches tall
and could not have weighed more than 110 pounds.
How painful to have made his way in school, being so

very bright—aggressively bright—and in so undersized a body; how painful his early years must have
been, in grade school, and middle school. Even at the
University, with its rigorous academic standards, sports
were a passion in some quarters; the old eating clubs
and "secret societies" still dominated undergraduate
social life. . . . And there was the sexual element: in
adolescence, the predominant element.

Though it hadn't been in M. R. Neukirchen at that
age! And so perhaps sexual longing was not so predominant in this boy, either.

Sexual feeling—"desire"—had not seemed nearly so
natural in M.R. as in an adolescent, as other sorts of
desire.

It did seem that Stirk's grievances against the University were long-standing—since his arrival as a freshman. What had "come to a head" the other night had
been "long building, like an abscess"—the "hostility,
hatred" of his enemies—their "jealousy" of his position on campus and "leftist-liberal resentment" of the
conservative coalition on campus, which was gaining
in numbers steadily. M.R. was determined to listen to
Stirk without interrupting him or challenging him but
was having a difficult time following his reasoning, or
his charges—the connection between the undergraduate woman who'd (allegedly) arranged for a late-term

abortion and other (alleged) incidents at the University and the local chapter of the Young Americans for Freedom—and Alexander Stirk—wasn't clear; very likely, there were relationships among certain of these undergraduates of which no one had spoken yet, that hadn't only to do with their contrasting politics.

Stirk said he was seriously considering "granting" interviews, and of course he intended to write about the incident, not just for the campus newspaper but also on the Internet and elsewhere—even against the advice of Professor Kroll. It seemed crucial to him—before it was "too late" and "something worse" happened to him—to "expose to the media" the "hostile leftist environment" of the University. . . .

Now M.R. did interrupt. Though she tried to speak evenly.

Saying she didn't think it was a very good idea to go to the media so quickly, while the assault was being investigated by the police and the University committee—

"Are you threatening to censor me, President Neukirchen? Shut me up?—so that I don't embarrass you?"

Eagerly Stirk spoke, as if he'd been waiting for M.R.'s objection. His good eye shone with a sort of sick, thrilled elation and his knees trembled and quaked in sideways movements like those of a hyperkinetic child who has been sitting restrained for too long.

"Alexander, of course not. You are free to write about this—to write about anything—of course—but—"

"But—what?"

Calmly M.R. continued. Calmly if a bit tightly she smiled. In the Quaker Meeting the ideal is *clearness— clarity*—out of confusion and dissension an *infusion of the Light* will prevail. Without ever having quite examined her beliefs M.R. seemed to believe this, or wished to believe it.

Not in her analytical/skeptical mode as an academic philosopher but in her mode as professor/president, she wished to believe in a vision of humankind as evolving toward light, truth, compassion like a gigantic flower opening—otherwise, one's compassion, like one's na-ïveté, was an embarrassment.

"—for the present time, while the investigations are going on—isn't it wiser just to wait? It really isn't a good idea, as you must know—to write something prematurely. Especially if you don't want to tell your family— they would surely discover it, and be upset. . . ."

Stirk shifted excitedly in his chair. As if M.R. had tossed a lighted match onto flammable material, immediately Stirk began speaking in a rapid stammer. "So this meeting is about—censorship! Censoring me! Threatening me with telling my family—worrying my family! Like—like this is—blackmail! Trying to censor the voice of the conservative movement on this campus! Already the leftist-liberals control the media—already you control the majority of universities—now, you are putting pressure to silence—censor—a victim— Trying to censor me—with the pretense of 'helping' me. . . ."

"Alexander, please! There's no need to raise your voice. I am just pointing out that—"

" 'Pointing out that'—vicious, immoral behavior is condoned on this campus—sexual promiscuity, drunkenness—infanticide—but revealing to the media what has happened to me—is 'not a good idea'?"

Stirk's voice was raised. Stirk was both incensed and gloating. M.R. was stunned by the sudden outburst.

"Are you—recording this? Our conversation? Is that what you are doing?" Suddenly M.R. knew this must be so.

But Stirk shook his head quickly—no. As if M.R. had leaned across the desk to touch him—to touch him improperly—he recoiled in his seat with a look of childish guilt, insolence. "No, I am not. I am—not— 'recording'—our conversation, President Neukirchen. Maybe you'd like to—frisk me? Call in your security cops—maybe a—strip search?"

Laughing Stirk lurched to his feet. In the commotion the aluminum crutch clattered to the floor and

Stirk snatched it up as if in fear it might be taken from him. Astonished and mortified M.R. understood that, of course, this devious young man had been recording their conversation. Some sort of recording device was in a pocket of that bulky corduroy jacket.

Probably, Oliver Kroll had encouraged him. For this was *our war,* an early skirmish.

M.R.'s face flushed with heat. She hoped she had not spoken recklessly—said something incriminating—during the course of their conversation. In a mild panic she wondered—could her remarks to Alexander Stirk be broadcast, posted on the Web? Without her permission? Weren't there laws regulating unauthorized tapings of private conversations? Was this in fact a private conversation? Had the University president a reasonable expectation of privacy, in such an exchange with a student? Her heart was beating painfully and her face throbbed with heat as if she'd been slapped.

Stirk said impudently, "And what if it is being recorded, President Neukirchen? I'm only trying to protect myself—no one can expect fair treatment—'justice'—from their enemies. I will have to build my case using the weapons I can."

M.R. was on her feet behind the massive presidential desk. M.R. who had never been known to raise her voice, to betray upset or agitation, still less anger or dislike, staring at the smirking boy as if she'd have liked now to hit him.

"You weren't really 'attacked'—were you? You've fabricated the entire incident—you injured yourself—filed a false report to the police—"

Hotly Stirk protested: "I *did not.* How dare you—insult me—slander me! How dare you accuse me of—'fabricating'—"

"Well—did you? You *did.*"

Never once in this austere presidential office—not once in her months—years—at the University—had M. R. Neukirchen spoken in so uncalculated a voice, with such vehemence; never once had her face betrayed any emotion so extreme as annoyance, still less dislike, repugnance. The effect upon Stirk was immediate—his pinched little boy's face contorted with rage and in a sudden tantrum he overturned the chair in which he'd been sitting.

M.R. cried angrily, "Stop! Stop that! You aren't a child!"

M.R. cringed as Stirk lifted the crutch to strike at the desk, or at her—he swept a stack of documents onto the floor—a small ceramic bowl containing pens, paper clips—M.R. tried to grab the crutch, to wrench it from Stirk's fingers—Stirk gave a loud yelp as if she'd struck him—a yelp as of surprised pain—"Hey! Jesus!

What're you doing—that *hurts*"—for the benefit of the
recording device in his corduroy jacket.

"But I didn't—I didn't—"

"Didn't what, President Neukirchen? Hit me? You
didn't—hit me?"

As M.R. stared in astonishment the gloating boy
stuck his tongue out at her. His tongue! Within these
swift and irretrievable seconds the conversation M.R.
had believed so forthright had shifted to farce, and
President Neukirchen was the butt of the farce. Quivering with mischief Stirk fitted the crutch into his armpit
and turned to limp out of the office just as the door
was being opened by the president's secretary whom
he pushed aside with the crutch, laughing—"Here's a
witness! Another female! Expect a subpoena, lady!"

Limping noisily and conspicuously through the
president's outer office Alexander Stirk departed historic Salvager Hall like a sequence of mallet strokes
against a just barely unyielding hardwood floor.

So it would be shortly charged: not only had M. R.
Neukirchen tried to "censor" Alexander Stirk, the
woman had actually—in some sort of "scuffle" in the
president's office—struck him.

In some versions of the lurid story, she'd struck him
with the injured undergraduate's very crutch.

Should have known. Hadn't she been warned.

This is a war. There are enemies.

Her heart beat in her ears. Barely she could hear the man addressing her, in an air of scarcely concealed exasperation.

Lockhardt had been chief counsel for the University for more than thirty years. Presidents of the University had inherited him as they'd inherited the presidential office itself—its austere furnishings and leather-bound books, the portrait of grim Reverend Charters above the fireplace mantel. Lockhardt's manner was unapologetically patrician—he had virtually no presence in the consciousness of the University faculty but his presence was essential to the board of trustees who looked to him as the president's key adviser, beside whom the president could seem but a temporary and expedient hireling.

Before taking office M.R. had imagined that she might encourage Leonard Lockhardt to retire and in his place she'd hire a younger attorney of her own generation and liberal convictions but as soon as she'd become president M.R. had known how she needed the man, his experience, his influence with trustees and "major" donors. He'd graduated from the University with a degree in classics in 1955 and he'd gone to Harvard Law and like most graduates of his generation he'd been opposed to the appointment of a female president at the University, though M.R. wasn't supposed to know this.

He was a bachelor. His long lean cheeks were clean-shaven and he exuded an airy sexless good cheer in all weathers. He wore suits tailored for him in Bond Street, London, long-sleeved linen and cotton shirts, bow ties. *Can't trust a man who wears a bow tie* M.R.'s father Konrad Neukirchen used to say but M.R. had no choice, she had to trust her chief legal counsel whose thinning silvery hair was styled in swirls like wings rising from his high forehead. In the lapel of Leonard Lockhardt's pinstriped suit was the small gold coiled-snake insignia of the University's most selective eating club, to which he'd belonged as an undergraduate and which had barred from membership all categories of individuals except heterosexual Caucasian-Christian males from "good" families until, begrudgingly, the mid–1980s.

M.R. had hoped to become so friendly with Lockhardt, she could suggest to him in the most casual of ways that it wasn't a good idea to continue to wear that particular eating-club pin at the University and Lockhardt would understand and cease to wear it at such times. But this intimacy hadn't yet happened and by late winter of 2003 M.R. had come to understand that very likely, it would not happen.

Gradually and in his gentlemanly manner Lockhardt had become adjusted to the female president.
He was not the sort of civic-minded individual who
bears grudges—as soon as M. R. Neukirchen had been
chosen by a majority of the trustees as the most exemplary of all candidates for the presidency despite her
relative inexperience, Lockhardt was committed to her.
He had come to like her as a person, whom he called
"Meredith"—for "M.R." seemed silly and pretentious
to him, inappropriate for a female—and to admire
her style of leadership which was perilously close to
no style at all—just the woman's unfettered personality. Neukirchen was guileless, zealous, far more intelligent and sharp-witted than she appeared. Shrewdly
he'd sized her up as an indefatigable workhorse—one
to be exploited. That the University had inaugurated
its first female president in nearly 250 years was a glo-
rious banner unfurled and flapping in the wind for all
to behold.

And so Leonard Lockhardt was anxious on Neukirchen's behalf, and on behalf of the University,
which he loved. When M.R. had had her "accident"
in October—en route to deliver a keynote address at
a convening of the American Association of Learned
Societies at Cornell University—when she'd failed to
show up at the banquet hall, and had gone missing

overnight, to the great alarm of her colleagues, friends, and the conference organizers—it had been Leonard Lockhardt who'd explained the situation to the trustees and assured them that M.R. hadn't behaved in a way at all irresponsible or eccentric, whatever he'd privately thought.

To M.R. he'd been politely solicitous. He had not asked her, as others had not, why she'd been driving—alone—in a rented car—in rural Beechum County so far from Ithaca, New York—and not even near Carthage, which was her hometown; why she'd departed the Cornell hotel without informing anyone, even her assistant who'd been desperate—frantic—for hours when M.R.'s whereabouts were unknown. He hadn't told her as perhaps he might have that she'd behaved not only irresponsibly and in an eccentric fashion but dangerously. *You might have died there. Disappeared. Who would have known?*

Instead Lockhardt had told M.R. that she had been "very lucky" not to have been seriously injured "in such a remote setting"—and that in the future, should she decide to drive somewhere alone, she should leave word with her staff.

M.R. replied that she believed she had left word with her assistant—a phone call, or an e-mail. She was sure.

Of that afternoon in October in Beechum County M.R. had a confused recollection. All that had happened she both recalled with painful exactitude and yet could not grasp that it had happened to *her*.

Or maybe—she couldn't remember. Waking with a pounding head, a bloodied face, near-smothered by the exploded air bag and near-strangled by the safety harness—a stranger stooping above the car overturned in a ditch calling to her *Hello? Hello? Hello? Are you— alive?*

Lockhardt hadn't pressed the issue of October 2002. Whatever he thought of M.R.'s utterly inexplicable behavior, whatever trustees of the University thought, or M.R.'s staff, or those faculty members who knew of her failure to deliver the keynote address at the conference in Ithaca—that period of some eighteen hours when M. R. Neukirchen seemed to have vanished—Leonard Lockhardt had not elaborated. His manner was discreet, diplomatic; he did not question motives, or even curious behavior, except as these threatened to erupt into public matters involving the University.

Now, regarding the alleged assault of the undergraduate Alexander Stirk, Lockhardt most dreaded a highly publicized lawsuit in which his superior skills would not prevail. For it was a new era, this era of "diversity"—it was not Leonard Lockhardt's era. The

University was no longer his University. The lawsuit was coming, he knew—or some similar disaster.

"Yes, you warned me, Leonard. But—I had to try, you know."

"Had to try! Try what?"

"To communicate with Alexander Stirk. To show him that he could trust me."

"Of course he could trust you. But you couldn't trust *him.*"

Of all of her staff it was Leonard Lockhardt who could speak most forcibly to M.R. and it was Leonard Lockhardt whose good opinion M.R. craved. Sensing how Lockhardt would have preferred her predecessor in her place, who'd been a consummate politician, and no naïve female idealist to be manipulated by an undergraduate.

"Oh, Leonard. Do you think I've made a terrible— irrevocable—mistake?"

And she had not told Lockhardt—she would tell no one, for pride would not allow this—how, on the way out of her office, the smirking little bastard had stuck his tongue out at her.

Andre. I have to speak with you. I know that this is a difficult time for you—I'd hoped to have heard from you by now—but—something has happened here, at

the University—I will explain. . . . I need to know—
have I made a terrible—irrevocable—mistake. . . .
Will you call me back Andre please.

Pausing before adding, with a breathless little laugh
Love you so much dear Andre!

For it was possible for M.R. to utter such words
at such a time. At the very end of a brief phone message, in a voice of girlish exuberance—a kind of giddy
drunkenness—what could not be bluntly, unequivo-
cally stated

Love you Andre so much. You must know.

And never with the mildest hint of reproach, or
hurt—or desperation—*Love you so much Andre do*
you love me?

Still less would M.R. dare to leave a message of
unfettered emotion, yearning—*Andre, when will you*
come see me again? Why don't you call me? What is
happening in your life? I feel so distant from you . . . I
am so utterly lonely here. . . .

Between them from the first—M.R. had been
twenty-three, Andre Litovik thirty-seven—this had
been the (unstated) agreement, the bond. M.R. would
love Andre Litovik more than he loved her because
M.R.'s capacity for love was greater than his as M.R.'s
capacity for sympathy, patience, generosity and civility was far greater than his. *I can love enough for us*

both. I will! M.R. had thought in the early years of their (secret) relationship but now she wasn't so certain she could continue to retain the strength of her old loyalty.

Loyalty: naïveté.

And yet: loyalty.

But as soon as Alexander Stirk departed, and M.R. was alone again in her office stunned, humiliated, hurt—the adrenaline rush of anger had quickly subsided—she called her lover in Cambridge, Massachusetts, on her cell phone.

A (secret) call. No one among the president's staff must know.

M. R. Neukirchen's (secret) life. M. R. Neukirchen's (unacknowledged) life.

No one knew, among her wide circle of friends, acquaintances, colleagues—that M.R. had been involved with a man, a married man, since graduate school in Cambridge. So many years! And so faithful to this man, who had—very likely—not been altogether faithful to her.

As long as I know that I am the one he loves. To the extent to which he can love anyone.

As no one knew how lonely M.R. was. Amid the busyness of her professional life like a sequence of blinding lights rudely shone into her eyes this loneliness persisted.

She could confide in no one, of course. In this exalted position so many of her colleagues envied.

In the president's house, in which she was a perpetual guest. As in the four-poster brass bed to which Andre Litovik had come not once in the months since her inauguration, to sleep with her.

In fact Andre had visited the University twice in those months. He'd come for M.R.'s inauguration in April and in November he'd returned to give a lecture for the astronomy/astrophysics department and at that time M.R. had hosted a dinner in his honor at the president's house. But he hadn't wanted to stay overnight in this house though it was understood—it seemed to be understood—that M.R. and Andre Litovik were "old friends" from her Cambridge days.

M.R. had invited him of course—but she hadn't pressed him.

There are guest rooms here. We have at least one guest a week, often more. You would not be—it would not seem. . . .

She'd meant, it would not have seemed suspicious.

He'd told her no. He'd been adamant, not very gracious. He had seemed almost to dislike her, so emphatically he spoke declining her invitation.

Still, they'd managed to spend some time alone together on that occasion—but not in the president's house, and not in the president's bed.

M.R. understood—of course. It would be folly, it would be the most careless of blunders, to arouse suspicion. At least at this time while M.R. was president of the University and Andre Litovik was—still—married.

Look, darling: I'm so proud of you. Don't risk your reputation. Someday—soon—we'll work this out. But not—not just yet.

He'd gripped her hands in his, tightly. He had appealed to her to believe him and so she had believed him.

Yet, he'd been eager to return home. For always—at home—there was a family crisis—which Andre must mediate.

Of all men of her acquaintance M.R. had never known anyone so personally *persuasive* as Andre Litovik— whether the public man, or the private man. Waking from sleep he was, in an instant, fully awake—warm, suffused with energy, thrumming like a hive of bees.

And the big fist of a heart quick-beating inside the barrel-chest yet calm, Olympian and bemused.

If a heart can be Olympian and bemused, Andre Litovik's was that heart.

"Please call me. Please—I need to speak to you. . . ."

The most piteous appeals are those we make in utter solitude, no one to hear. The objects of our appeals distant, oblivious.

It seemed to be so—Andre was proud of her, now. He admired successful women—in particular, academic and intellectual women—he'd married a brilliant young Russian-born translator and Slavic studies post-doc at Harvard and very likely he'd been involved with a number of other women before meeting M.R.—(and after?).

He hadn't wanted her to become president of the University. He'd been frankly astonished that among several very strong candidates, M.R. had been chosen.

M.R. had not said to him *You could dissuade me, if you wanted to. If you wanted to badly enough.*

For maybe this wasn't true. Maybe—M.R. contemplated the possibility—she did prefer the public position, the opportunity to *serve, to lead, to hold in the Light*—to a more private life.

At any rate, she'd accepted the offer of the board of trustees of the University. Leonard Lockhardt had drawn up her contract. The faculty of the University overwhelmingly approved of Neukirchen for the presidency—this had been crucial to M.R.'s acceptance. Never had she felt so—*vindicated.*

Almost, you might say—*loved.*

For this was the high point of Mudwoman's life—to be *admired, loved.*

The phone rang: 9:09 P.M.

Not the president's phone but M.R.'s cell phone for which very few people had the number.

She saw—the caller ID wasn't LITOVIK.

She pushed the little phone away, she had no desire to answer it.

She'd fallen asleep at her desk. The massive cherrywood desk with its numerous deep drawers. Folded her arms on the desktop and laid her head on her arms and drifted into an exhausted sleep. For the day—this ignominious day!—had begun so long before, in the dark preceding dawn.

FREE CHOICE IS A LIE!
NOBODY'S BABY WANTS TO DIE!

Salvager Hall was empty and darkened except for the president's office where a single desk lamp was lighted. Three floors deserted as a stage set from which actors have departed. The new female president had a plucky-loyal staff to work closely with her and to defend her against her critics and detractors while conferring worriedly among themselves *Is something wrong with M.R.? Is she—ill? She seems to be making mistakes—misjudgments. . . . Since the accident in October . . .*

"No. I can make things right again."

The cell phone had ceased ringing. Then, within seconds it rang again—the opening bars of *Eine Kleine Nachtmusik.*

M.R.'s (secret) lover had bought her the cell phone. So that she could call him, and he could call her. That had been years before in an earlier and more idyllic phase of their friendship.

It was not Andre. In the caller ID window was KROLL.

She was appalled, that Oliver Kroll would be calling her at such a time. And on her cell phone, not the president's phone. She wouldn't have thought that Kroll had her number or that he would dare to call her, after what had happened that afternoon.

For M.R. had no doubt, Oliver Kroll had conspired with Stirk to record their conversation. *This is war. Our war has begun.*

They would gloat together. They would play the tape, and laugh at her.

And now—Kroll was calling *her.*

M.R. felt a swirl of nausea. She was not so strong as people thought—even Leonard Lockhardt who'd come to know her painfully well misjudged her as a stronger woman than she was.

Remarkable woman. Such enthusiasm!

A natural-born leader.

She'd been in hiding. She'd been eating at her desk. The remains of M.R.'s supper on a greasy paper napkin: dry pita bread, strips of lettuce like confetti, "grilled" vegetables dry and tasteless as wood chips and a can of Diet Coke.

She'd canceled her dinner for that evening—she'd needed to be alone. As president of the University M. R. Neukirchen was scheduled for luncheons, receptions, dinners through the semester virtually day following day.

And such a friendly—accessible—person . . . So sympathetic, and so informed . . .

Such energy!

What comfort in being alone—at last. No one to observe the wounded "leader."

The little phone ceased ringing. After a brief wait M.R. checked her messages hoping that Kroll hadn't left a message but that—somehow—Andre had left a message instead.

Thinking *Love is a sickness for which the only cure is love.*

Of course—there was Kroll's unmistakable voice. M.R. steeled herself for irony/mockery which was the politics professor's usual style but this was very different.

"Hello? It's Oliver—Kroll. . . ." Haltingly Kroll spoke like one uncertain of his way. M.R. could hear his breath close against the mouthpiece. "I'm calling to say—to explain—I hope you don't think that I had anything to do with . . . I don't know what Alexander told you or hinted at but—it wasn't—it isn't—so . . . *I did not have anything to do with him recording your conversation.* . . . If I'd known what the hell he'd intended, I would have tried to dissuade him." Kroll's voice was strained, urgent. This was hardly a message M.R. might have expected from Oliver Kroll and so she listened surprised and fascinated. "He's a—an—excitable young man . . . He's brilliant but—obviously troubled. . . . Some things have come to light, Meredith, he's told me about—just tonight—that will have to be revealed tomorrow, to the township police, to the security office, and to you. . . . Could you call me? Regardless of how late it is, call me? It would be better if we could talk, before. . . . Please call me at—" Hurriedly Kroll gave his number, and repeated it, though he'd have known that M.R. already had the number in her cell phone memory. He was breathing—panting—as if about to say more but broke the connection instead.

Meredith he'd called her. Beyond that, M.R. scarcely heard.

How they'd met, M.R. could not clearly recall. How they'd parted, M.R. hoped to forget.

It had been a time when M.R.'s (secret) lover had abandoned her.

Sent her into exile she'd joked. Sadly joked.

Somewhere in the hinterland of north central New Jersey he'd sent her—this prestigious Ivy League university floating like an improbable island of academic excellence amid vestiges of quaint-Colonial American history and a hilly-rolling ultra-affluent rural/suburban landscape which, until M.R. was invited to be interviewed for a position in the philosophy department, she had not visited and had not envisioned. Reporting back to her lover *This can't be a real place! It is too perfect.*

She hadn't quite been willing to think that Andre Litovik wanted her—hoped her to be—*gone.*

Not *permanently gone*—only just a respectable distance from Cambridge, Massachusetts. From his house on Tremont Street, and his household. From his family.

Nor had she been willing to think that really it was a good idea—a very good idea—for M.R. to leave the force field of her lover, a gravitational pull roughly equivalent to that of the planet Jupiter. With her instinct for self-effacement M.R. had planned to seek a teaching position in the Boston area, to be near Andre, at one or another far less distinguished university or college, which would have fatally sabotaged her career at the start; with her Harvard Ph.D. and early, much-admired publications in moral philosophy, ethics, and aesthetics, M. R. Neukirchen had been an extremely attractive candidate, and *female.*

At a time when institutions of higher education were scrambling to hire *blacks, minorities, females* as (belated, partial) restitution for several thousand years of bigotry.

So, M.R. had accepted a position at the University— an assistant professorship in one of the top-ranking philosophy departments in the United States. Where a decade before an individual with even her outstanding qualifications, handicapped by her sex, would have been summarily dismissed from consideration, at this time, in the 1980s, the combination of such outstanding qualifications and *femaleness* was irresistible. *A consolation prize* M.R. remarked to her (secret) lover—*but more a prize than a consolation.*

Did M.R. mean to be witty? (Andre couldn't see her face—M.R. couldn't see his—they were speaking on the phone.) Andre chose to think yes, and laughed.

Dear Meredith! You will outgrow me.

Once, in a similarly philosophical mood, Andre had begun to say *You will outlive me . . .* but his voice trailed off. Mortality was too real an issue to Andre Litovik, to be joked about with his much-younger lover.

(*Lover!* What an archaic-sounding word, M.R. thought. It hardly seemed a word that might be applied to *her.*)

And so it happened, M.R. was exiled from Cambridge, Massachusetts, and moved to the hills of north central New Jersey in the late summer of 1986. A very young and "inexperienced"—(i.e., sexually)—twenty-five-year-old wondering if her life had ended, or was only just set to begin.

It did feel like exile—a surreal sort of afterlife—at this University like Harvard University sequestered from the outer world by a wall—(in this case a ten-foot wrought-iron fence with medieval-looking gates)—yet wholly unlike Harvard in other, more essential ways—missing the urban busyness of Cambridge, a sense of life lived at a pitch just slightly higher than normal; a life lived, for all its desperation, at the white-hot *core.*

You weren't happy here, darling. You weren't happy with me.

So her lover told her.

Wittily M.R. protested *But happiness is so— ordinary! Like not dreaming so you can avoid the risk of nightmares.*

They kept in touch—of course. If M.R. called Andre and left a message, Andre would call back within an hour, a day, two days. . . . It was not so frequent that Andre called M.R.

Despite her fear of abandonment Andre did not abandon her, entirely. For he was her lover who was the first man M.R. had ever loved and he'd promised, he would never cease to *think of her*. Like a theory of God as pure consciousness suffusing all sentient beings in the universe, binding them together inviolably.

No one knew of their (secret) relationship. No one must know!

(But surely—many knew? Over the years, in Cambridge, Massachusetts. And at the University? M.R. was uneasy when women friends hinted of their concern for her—*You must find someone who is free to commit himself to you. You must not let that man exploit you. . . .*)

Alone M.R. lived in faculty housing overlooking a small lake upon which the University crew teams rowed. Alone she was wakened by the sound of shouted commands careening across the glassy water like steel blades. At a distance—given a harsh impatient twang by distance—the crew coaches' voices reminded her of her lover's voice.

Alone, alone! It is a fact, you hear most acutely and you see and think most acutely, when you are alone.

Hurriedly then on such mornings M.R. dressed and—yet more alone—went outside to run along Echo Lake on wood chip paths in the damp air that smelled of pine needles. Alone, alone! But there is happiness in *alone*, if you believe that you have chosen it.

And here was a prevailing strangeness: no matter that the previous night had been a miserable night beset by jeering dreams like the flinging of mud into a smiling face—the particular insult of mud in eyelashes, mouth—mud unwittingly breathed in, in nostrils—yet there was always for the dreamer-who-has-wakened the adventure of the new day—the new week, the new month, the new semester—beside which the tangled and smutty old narrative of the past had no more substance than a tabula rasa—a reflecting surface of some cheap metal that reflected nothing.

With running M.R.'s legs grew stronger, springier—her thoughts were revived, and began to whip in the wind like festive flags—in her head that otherwise would have swarmed like a hornet's nest with unwanted, impractical, and despairing thoughts she quite deftly prepared essays, conference papers, lectures for her courses—she'd been given the responsibility of "Ancient and Medieval Philosophy" and "Moral Philosophy: An Introduction"—like gigantic albatrosses these courses might have hung about her neck except M. R. Neukirchen rose to the challenge of revamping them, reconstituting them as subjects of such inherent and timely interest, enrollment in each rose dramatically, in the moral philosophy course in particular where the enrollment had to be capped at three hundred fifty. This, within two years of M.R.'s arrival at the University.

Alone in the University-owned house on Echo Lake M.R. lived so much more intensely than her colleagues who were married. Alone M.R. lived so much more intensely than if she'd lived with another. For *aloneness* is the great fecundity of the mind, if it is not the destruction of the mind.

M.R. published philosophical papers in prominent journals—more impressively, M.R. read her colleagues' papers in prominent journals. (If they published books, M.R. bought their books!) The discipline of philosophy is a discipline of *thinking.* That one might combine *thinking* with *doing*—and with *doing publicly well*—is something of an anomaly, like a giraffe that might also, beyond its giraffeness, plow a field with its hooves, or a tractor that might play Beethoven. M.R. exhibited a naïve willingness to be a good citizen—in academic circles, a rare and heedless action akin to smearing one's naked body with honey in some outdoor setting—and so she was asked to chair committees, and to help organize conferences, and to advise students—a task that is endless since the supply of students is infinite.

She was asked to review graduate applications—hundreds of graduate applications for fewer than twenty positions—and to rank them, for her colleagues' perusal. She was soon a favorite dissertation committee member for she read each of her colleagues' students' dissertations as thoroughly as if it were her own student's dissertation, and far more thoroughly than her colleagues had time to read it; if there were small errors, or enormous egregious errors, no one would be mortified by overlooking them—for M.R. would ferret them out.

She could be relied upon to correct misspellings, grammar. She could be relied upon to console students on the verge of breakdowns. She could be relied upon to write letters of recommendation when her colleagues had not time. Of course she was a workhorse—but an uncomplaining workhorse—with the Harvard degree, and publications, something of a Thoroughbred-workhorse.

Within a few years M.R. was promoted to the rank of associate professor, with tenure; by then she'd been an (unpaid) assistant to the philosophy department chair, soon to be appointed acting chair and eventually, in her eighth year at the University, departmental chair. She was an associate of the Renaissance Studies Program, the Program for the Study of Women and Gender, the Ethics and Human Values Institute. She was director of the Council of the Humanities. She was a faculty adviser for the University film series. She was one of several (female) faculty advisers for the local chapter of the Association for the Advancement of Women in Mathematics, Philosophy, and the Physical Sciences. She was an editorial adviser of the *Journal of Contemporary Philosophy*, the *Journal of Women in Philosophy*, *Studies in Ethics*. She wrote for the *Chronicle of Higher Education* and the *New York Review of Books*. She chaired the University's most powerful committee—the president's advisory committee on appointments and advancements. She was named "special assistant" to the dean of the faculty and when the dean retired, she was appointed to take his place. Soon then in the spring of 2001 she was appointed to the presidential search committee—that is, the committee to seek a new president following Leander's retirement; after a few meetings of this committee, her fellow members met without her knowledge and named "M. R. Neukirchen" their first-choice candidate, to be presented to the board of trustees.

Her life flashing before her eyes—so swiftly all this seemed to have happened.

Because Andre didn't want me.

———

Mill Run was the name of the road. No choice but to turn onto Mill Run.

For the Black River Road had collapsed into the riverbed like a toothless mouth and desperately/recklessly she'd turned onto the narrow unpaved detour-road though knowing—with a part of her mind absolutely knowing—that if she didn't turn back immediately she would be late for the event that evening in Ithaca; she would be late, very late, for the occasion when M. R. Neukirchen was to be elevated above a banquet room of onlookers.

Readied. You must be readied.

And where is the Angel of the Lord, to save you?

Taking a turn—a tight turn—carelessly and recklessly and half-sobbing beforehand as if knowing what would happen—knowing what would not-happen: her speech, the applause—suddenly she found herself in the skidding and then overturned Toyota in the ditch beside the detour-road tangled and part-strangled in the safety belt too dazed now to sob or cry aloud for help she saw her life flash before her swift and airy and of no more consequence than a trout-fly cast upon a glittering but shallow stream.

Waking then hours later—was this *waking*?—chill sunshine and a taste of brackish blood in her mouth

and blood-mucus crusting her nose and a stranger's
face—a stranger's staring eyes—*H'lo! Hey! Ma'am—
you alive?*

That was how it was: what had happened.

What had happened, that M.R. knew.

*Life flashing before her. Rewinding, and the trout-
fly another time cast out onto the glittering stream.*

It was a season in M.R.'s life before she'd lost faith in
herself as a woman.

Yet still in this new place—so unlike Cambridge,
she ached with homesickness—through the first year,
and through the second year, and into the third year of
her exile—M.R. often saw, or imagined she saw, her
lover at a distance crossing a street, or on a staircase,
or amid a clutch of students on a campus walkway. Her
first reaction was something like panic—*He's here! But
why didn't he tell me. . . .* When M.R. stopped dead in
her tracks as if she'd been shot—causing companions
to regard her with surprise—she would recover, she
would laugh in embarrassment, rebuke herself *No.
This is madness.*

There were several University colleagues—middle-
aged, grizzle-haired, thick-necked and barrel-chested
and moving with a swaggering sort of gait to compensate

for painful knees, hips, spines—M.R. learned to recognize and avoid. She did not tell Andre of such sightings: he'd have laughed at her. He had little patience for weakness in others, as in himself.

Nor did she tell him about Oliver Kroll. She'd reasoned that the friendship between Kroll and her—if "friendship" was the correct term—wasn't significant enough to warrant mentioning. And for the brief while she'd fantasized that she might come to feel deeply for Kroll, or to feel something at all like emotion, she hadn't wanted to confide in Andre who would have been annoyed, hurt—or worse, amused.

If you love another man more than you love me— that can't be helped. And maybe it is a good idea, darling—you must know.

She could not risk it! She had not once said anything to Andre Litovik that had not rebounded back upon her in a way to confound her. For her (secret) lover was the only individual in her (adult) life whose reactions she could not predict.

It was at a public lecture—"The Politicized Republic"—that M.R. became aware of Kroll seated in front of her, across an aisle; he seemed to be impatient with the speaker, shaking his head, irritably shifting his shoulders, sighing audibly; for it was true that the speaker had a slow grave platitudinous manner, that tested one's resilience; by his remarks during the question period following the lecture, M.R. gathered that her disgruntled colleague was a "libertarian"—an "economic libertarian"—who didn't think much of the speaker's "quasi-Utilitarian welfare-state" politics.

This was Oliver Kroll: Professor of Politics. M.R. knew the name—knew that Kroll was a friend, if not a protégé, of the more renowned—more notorious— G. Leddy Heidemann who'd been a consultant for the last several Republican administrations, a "personal friend" of Ronald Reagan as he would be one day a "personal friend" of Vice President Cheney. Kroll, whose field was political theory, was said to be associated with the Cato Institute which was rumored to be funded by the CIA—(only a rumor! M.R. hoped to keep an open mind). Kroll had a blade-sharp face, a spade-shaped dark beard, a permanent crease between his eyebrows and a head that looked stylishly shaved, and not (merely) bald. Unlike M.R.'s lover who looked as if he'd dressed hurriedly in the dark, with a contempt for the very act of dressing, as for the ritual of grooming, Kroll looked like a man who took time selecting his clothes, with a predilection for sweater-vests, sharp-creased trousers, camel's-hair sport coats and silk neckties. His face was clean-shaven above the spade-shaped beard and the spade-shaped beard was meticulously trimmed.

At the reception following the lecture Kroll made his way to M.R. and introduced himself in a manner that suggested an oddly engaging sort of intimacy—as if they'd met before, and there was some sort of rapport between them. M.R. was intimidated by Kroll's severe—savage—critique of the lecturer, whom he accused of "willful ignorance" in the matter of global economics; she was impressed with the passion with which Kroll spoke, as if the issue that seemed so abstract to her, as to others in the audience, was personally meaningful to him. She was yet more impressed that Kroll seemed to be familiar with her work, at least several articles she'd recently published in philosophical journals and essay-reviews in the *New York Review* on such subjects as Spinoza, John Stuart Mill, Mary Wollstonecraft's *A Vindication of the Rights of Women,* Shelley's *Frankenstein.*

In the *Journal of Philosophical Inquiry* M. R. Neukirchen had published an article provocatively titled " 'I Have Lost My Soul': Possible Ontological Meanings" and this Oliver Kroll singled out for particular admiration.

"We think alike—to a degree. I mean—our mode of inquiry."

Kroll gazed at M.R. with unexpected warmth. His eyes were dark, rather small—he had a habit of squinting. Except for the crease between his eyebrows, the severe blade-face relaxed just slightly.

"Of course, I'm not a philosopher—'M.R.' I'm not trained in 'theory of mind.' But I appreciated the subtlety of your argument. You seem to me quite right—there is no 'I' in consciousness—only just consciousness. And so—no 'I' can possess a 'soul'—even if there were a 'soul.' " Kroll frowned thoughtfully. He did seem to be pressing close to M.R. and in the exigency of the moment she felt confused, off balance—it wasn't that often that a man looked at her in such a way. "The entire concept of 'soul'—that's another category of, what d'you call it—'ontological being.' "

" 'Ontological actuality.' "

So solemnly M.R. spoke, both she and Kroll laughed.

Of course, these terms were ridiculous—M.R. understood. She was trained in a certain Anglo-subspecies of contemporary philosophy which meant that she'd acquired a particular, highly specialized vocabulary—like learning a language to which virtually no one else had access. Professors in other fields, including more traditional fields of philosophy, could not know what M.R. meant—the very concept "meant" was believed to be ambiguous.

"I don't always write in an analytical mode," M.R. said. "That was really just for the *Journal of Philosophical Inquiry.*"

Almost, she had to force herself to recall what she'd said. For each of her essays she had cultivated a voice distinct and appropriate to the subject of the piece, as to the publication and its (presumed) audience. Like an actor who expresses herself exclusively through scripts—in the "voices" of others—M.R. had no "voice" of her own—or so she believed.

It was philosophical truth M.R. pursued, not an expression of self—"truth" elusive as a butterfly blown and tattered in the wind.

Kroll was saying, in that self-critical tone that suggests a childlike pleasure in the very flaws of the self, that everything he wrote was recognizably *his.* He could not vary his writing style, no more than he could vary his speaking style. He could not vary his fundamental, unshakable, and to him self-evident *beliefs.* Of course, as an intellectual, as a professor of political theory who might lecture on the Enlightenment and the anti-Enlightenment within the space of a few hours, or on such disparate figures as Plato and Machiavelli, Descartes and Hobbes, Malthus and Hume and Jeremy Bentham and John Stuart Mill—"Even the Nazi apologist Heidegger"—he was trained to present differing points of view but he could hardly take these viewpoints seriously; especially among his colleagues and contemporaries he couldn't but think that people whose opinions differed from his own were being dishonest, hypocritical: "What they *say* is for *saying's* sake. What they *do* is for their own sake." Kroll had been involved in the Libertarian Party, for instance, in the 1980s, but he'd soon dropped out. He hated it that in recent decades libertarianism had become fragmented, contentious, anarchic—his was a specific sort of economic-philosophical libertarianism, in opposition to "conservatism."

Kroll uttered the word *conservatism* with such disdain, M.R. had to smile. She asked what was libertarianism—for very likely, in Kroll's specific terms, she had no idea.

" 'Libertarianism'—'liberty.' It's the belief that the highest value is 'liberty'—the most that the state should do for its citizens is to assure their liberty. All the rest is—detritus."

Kroll spoke passionately. M.R. had the idea that he'd said these words, biting, succinct, provoking, many times.

She had the idea that Kroll expected her to react, to protest. *Oh but what of—the poor, the ill, the disenfranchised . . . What of taxes for education, highways, water purification, health care . . .*

Kroll was standing close, as M.R. tried unobtrusively to step back.

A faint scent as of something sulfurous and mint-y lifted from the man's heated skin. M.R. saw others in the room glancing at Kroll, and at her. She understood that Oliver Kroll had a certain reputation at the University—he was combative, contentious, admired but not well liked. In any faculty gathering there are sharp glittery swords, kitchen knives, a preponderance of bread knives—dull, dutiful, inclined to envy. Kroll was one of the sharp glittery swords you could cut your fingers on, if you came too near.

Except, strangely and unexpectedly, Kroll seemed to like M. R. Neukirchen. He seemed to like her very much. He was saying, " 'M.R.'—what I find fascinating in your work—the work of yours I've read—is that no one would know, or guess, that you are a woman. Your perspective is—wholly objective."

M.R. said that that was her intention, her hope—"That's why I use just initials—'M.R.' "

Had she explained this to anyone else, except Andre? Or—had Andre been the one to suggest it, somewhat playfully?

She said, "I don't see what sex—gender—has to do with writing, or teaching."

"Of course! Of course not. You're absolutely right."

Kroll spoke adamantly, like one conferring a blessing. M.R. felt how such words would dazzle students who would both fear and adore him.

"Ideally, we might all wear masks. Those large masks Greek actors used. We might walk on stilts—to give ourselves height."

M.R. laughed. He was teasing her, was he—it was good for M.R. to be teased, who took herself too seriously.

When you are alone, you take yourself *too seriously*. That is the terrible risk of *alone*.

"And what does 'M.R.' stand for?"

Reluctantly M.R. told Kroll: " 'Meredith Ruth.' "

" 'Meredith Ruth'—Neukirchen." Kroll pronounced the names carefully. "And what were you called as a girl?"

"I was called—'Meredith.' "

"Not 'Merry'?"

"Yes, in fact—my mother called me 'Merry.' Some of my high school friends—'Merry.' " M.R. spoke slowly. Until this moment, she had not remembered "Merry."

" 'Merry'! That would be a sort of burden, I suppose. 'Merry'—unless it was mistaken for 'Mary'—yes?"

M.R. could not think of a reply. Was any of this true? Or did it simply seem plausible as truth?

She was finding it difficult to breathe. This man—
she'd forgotten his name, for the moment—seemed to
be sucking away her breath.

She could not bear another intrusion in her life. Another change in her life.

She'd begun to perspire, Kroll's attention felt hot to
her like a light shining into her face, onto her exposed
skin. Her armpits itched, miserably.

Go away. Let me go. Leave me alone please.

Yet it flattered M.R., that the glaring expression
Kroll had turned upon the lecturer only a short while
ago seemed to have vanished. Like a belligerent dog
that has ceased barking, Kroll seemed transformed,
even charming.

To his students, charismatic. Perhaps. The force of
one who believes passionately in something and with
yet more passion can denounce other points of view.

If Kroll sensed M.R.'s discomfort, he gave no sign. It
was like an aggressive male to not-see, or to ignore, discomfort in another. M.R. was reminded of how Andre
too frequently questioned her—almost, interrogated
her. It was Andre Litovik's professorial style—the
Socratic method. Yet it was Andre's intimate style as
well for he insisted that his close questioning of M.R.
was a sign of respect—most people, Andre hadn't the
slightest interest in questioning—but M.R. found such

attention exhausting; she couldn't but think that there was an air of mockery in it. How much more productive, the Quaker method of silence—silence among individuals—until one is moved to speak; but Andre wouldn't have had the patience for it.

Against the grain of her temperament, M.R. had become something of a public speaker. Unexpectedly in her early twenties she'd discovered that she was a natural teacher—she felt an ease at the front of a classroom not unlike the ease of slipping into a warm bath. Yet more comfortable she felt at the front of a lecture hall, or on a stage, with space between herself and an audience. When scrutiny is abstract, anonymous!

Not one of you knows who I am. But what I will tell you, you will believe.

"'Meredith'—or should I say 'M.R.'?—would you like to have dinner sometime?"

"Dinner? I—"

"Tonight? Now?"

"I don't think—this isn't—"

"Tomorrow night? Or—when?"

Kroll had followed M.R. out of the reception room, and into a high-ceilinged front foyer. And from the foyer, down the steps of the building which was one of the old historic buildings on the University campus, originally designed to resemble a Greek temple.

She'd meant to discreetly retreat—escape. But he'd followed her of course. Spangled late-afternoon sunshine and dappled light filtered through the leaves of those tall thick-trunked trees with peeling bark—sycamores?—the season was early autumn. And a sound of fevered adolescent shouts, careening Frisbees on the green. How easy the lives of others appear, seen from a little distance! There was no reason that her own life could not be easy as well, seen from a little distance.

Though she was eager to escape from the aggressive man with the spade-shaped beard—eager to return to her refuge overlooking the glassy lake—she was thinking—conceding—that Kroll's presence did excite her, in a way; his attention, like a beacon of light shone in her startled face, was both disconcerting and flattering. And she was lonely—beyond the protective boundaries of her work: her work that was words; walls, barriers, concentric circles of words like the rings of Saturn.

Thinking—conceding—that Andre wasn't likely to telephone her that evening.

Nor would Andre e-mail M.R.: fearing an *e-mail trail* his suspicious wife might discover.

Kroll had called her *Merry.* No one had called her *Merry* in decades. She felt a thrill of—was it hope? Reckless hope? Thinking *I must make my own life, apart from Andre. I know this.*

Kroll told M.R. that they'd met before—in fact, several times at the University.

"Not very flattering, 'M.R.'—you don't remember me." Kroll's smile was tight with an expression M.R. could not have named and his eyes were narrowed as if he too were staring into a bright blinding light.

And so M.R. had to protest of course she remembered him—she thought. And she'd had to say yes. She would like to have dinner with Oliver Kroll— sometime.

"Tomorrow?"

This was the fall of 1990. They would see each other for no more than six weeks but these were intense weeks for M.R. Initially Kroll was warmly friendly, or gave that impression—he took M.R. to dinner, to movies and University events and art museums— when M.R. offered to pay for her ticket to a Cézanne exhibit at the Philadelphia Museum of Art to which Kroll drove them on Sunday afternoon in October— (in a sleek low-slung vehicle M.R. discovered was a Jaguar XK coupe, cobalt-blue, with a speedometer astonishingly equipped to measure 250 mph)—Kroll brushed aside the suggestion with a brusque sweep of his hand and a tight little smile. Was this a re- buke? Had she offended him? Or had her offer been too hesitant, and seemingly insincere? M.R.'s (secret) lover was the sort of man to fling down bills and loose change—bills of all denominations, change that included pennies—onto tables and counters with the lavish air of a king; no one dared defy Andre Litovik and offer to pay instead, or as well as Andre; no one who wanted to be his friend dared resist Andre's promiscuous generosity which M.R. had come to assume was a quintessentially masculine trait. Kroll too exhibited an adversarial air when taking out his wallet, bills or credit cards—the knife-crease between his eyebrows deepened. In a restaurant near the University where they'd met another couple for dinner, when M.R. offered to pay for her meal Kroll had said to her in an undertone, rather sharply, "Another time, thank you."

She saw that she'd wounded Kroll, in the presence of the other couple who were old friends of his, from the University. He would not glance at her and for some minutes would not speak to her, as if she'd ceased to exist though seated close beside him in a booth.

That Kroll was proud, and vain—so easily wounded—was touching to M.R. For Kroll was an attractive man, or nearly—except for his sharp-chiseled features that seemed always about to stiffen guardedly and the fleeting quasi-smile on his lips that seemed always about to turn downward, in irony.

And M.R. began to see too that, in the eyes of Kroll's friends, a middle-aged couple named Steigman, she and Kroll were a couple of some undefined sort—friends? companions? *Lovers?* The possibility was unnerving to M.R., like staring at an object rolling to the edge of a precipice—and over.

In a mirror against a farther wall in the candlelit restaurant, M.R. saw their booth—two couples, four glimmering pale faces—you could just barely distinguish Kroll from his colleague-friend and you could just barely distinguish M.R. from the other woman. The thought came to her *But why not? A couple like any other.*

At this time M.R. was still a very young-looking woman—in her thirtieth year, with the ruddy cheeks of a girl hockey player, a flushed and breathless look, very appealing; her hair was a fair, burnished brown, with streaks of silver, a thick mane she'd tamed and braided into a single plait that fell between her shoulder blades. She had so little sense of herself as a physical being—let alone an aesthetic object in another's eyes—she'd been deeply embarrassed when Kroll told her that he'd been initially drawn to her not just because of her "exemplary" written work but because she reminded him of a portrait by Joshua Reynolds—"*Jane, Countess of Harrington*—I saw it in an exhibit at the British Museum,

I think. Years ago when I was a post-doc at Oxford but I still remember it—the effect of the portrait—her . . ." Squinty-eyed Kroll was smiling at M.R. in a way to make her uneasy. Her face warmed with blood—she blushed so readily!

How Andre Litovik would have laughed at this. How droll and foolish, like one of those mawkishly tender scenes in a Chekhov play that take on a bitter irony, as the play evolves.

Of course, M.R. sought out the Reynolds portrait in a book of color plates in the University art library— she was stunned to see that yes, the young woman so lovingly painted by Sir Joshua Reynolds in 1775 did bear some slight resemblance to M. R. Neukirchen— except the woman in the painting was far more beautiful than M.R., her skin creamy-pale, flawless. What was most striking about the portrait of Jane, Countess of Harrington was the aura of confidence it exuded— not merely the figure of the beautifully composed young noblewoman, her slender face seen just slightly in profile so that her elegantly long nose was outlined, but an air of ontological entitlement as different from M.R.'s sense of being in the world as if she and "Jane, Countess of Harrington" were of two distinct species.

Being in the world. Either you believed that you were entitled, or you were not.

Between one and none there gapes an infinity. How alone Friedrich Nietzsche had to be, to know this!

M.R. laughed—did Oliver Kroll see her this way? Or was this the man's fantasy, impressed upon M. R. Neukirchen from Carthage, New York?

This season in M.R.'s life before she lost faith in herself as a woman.

This season when M.R. approached the edge of the precipice, in fascinated dread.

They were not lovers—exactly. But they were rapidly becoming more than friends.

There was this—unexpected!—romantic side to Kroll.

He brought her flowers: a large pale-blue hydrangea in a clay pot. Then, each time he visited her, he looked for the hydrangea—he examined the soil with a forefinger, to see if it was damp—that is, if M.R. had remembered to water it.

"So beautiful!"—M.R. stared at the flowers that looked strangely artificial as if they'd been dyed, or were made of a crinkly sort of paper.

He brought her a glossy reproduction of Joshua Reynolds's *Jane, Countess of Harrington*—poster-sized. He expected M.R. to have it framed and hung on a wall in her house and when M.R. didn't have the poster framed within a week or two he became angry with her—"If you don't want the portrait, give it back. You aren't obliged to keep it." M.R. was stunned by his reaction and quickly apologized—her Quaker instincts led her to apologize for wrongs not her own, to minimize conflict; she had the poster framed, at some expense, and she hung it prominently on a wall in her small living room, displacing other, smaller works of art which she preferred.

(She couldn't bring herself to look often at the portrait—Jane, Countess of Harrington was too coolly beautiful and so extravagantly dressed, her mere image on the wall was a rebuke to earthly/fleshy/damp-eyed M.R.) And each time Kroll came to the house he gazed at the portrait on the wall as at an old friend; M.R. had placed the poster just slightly high, so that you looked up at the Countess's creamy-pale face.

"It's a beautiful poster," M.R. said, awkwardly. "I mean—the portrait is beautiful. Reynolds painted so many—masterpieces. . . ."

Staring at the countess on the wall, Kroll seemed scarcely to hear M.R.

Kroll swam several times a week—early—in the University pool.

Kroll invited M.R. to come with him—he'd been inviting her for weeks—and at last M.R. said yes, yes she would join him; she had not wanted to say yes yet she'd heard herself say yes, she heard the eagerness in her voice for it was distressing—shameful—how M.R. was beginning to fear being alone, now that Oliver Kroll had intruded into her life.

She did not want the man in her life, yet she had allowed the man in her life. And now by degrees she could not bear losing the man, whom she had allowed in her life.

She didn't want to be with him, really—she was awkward in his company, always anxious, unsettled. Especially she didn't want to swim in the University pool at the desperate hour of 7 A.M. yet there she was lowering herself into the lapping aqua water that felt unnaturally soft, dizzy from the smell of chlorine, bizarre thoughts like sea serpents assailing her as she swam laps—arm over arm, Australian crawl, eyes fluttering shut—*Will we be married? Is that what will happen? Is that why I am here?* On the mosaic ceiling of the University pool and on the upper walls were rippling reflections like quivering nerves. The smell of chlorine and the echo-chamber of the pool reminded her of high school in Carthage which caught at her heart, this was not a memory M.R. wished to revive in her new life. Especially she dreaded the isolation of the swimmer, amid propelled and splashing figures yet she was isolated, always one is isolated in the water where thoughts await like froth on the surface of the water that smelled like chemicals. *It will happen, then. The man makes a claim.*

She had only to not-resist. She felt a thrill of excitement, a childish vindication like one who has tightened a noose around her neck ever tighter, tighter—if her (secret) lover would not leave his wife for her, another man would claim her; M.R. could not resist this other man if only to demonstrate her ability to love another man—wasn't this proof?

M.R. had never asked Andre Litovik to leave his wife for her. For *her*—that would not have seemed possible.

The wife, like the son, was unwell. Though Andre did not speak in such clinical terms, scarcely did he speak of his "difficult"—"temperamental"—wife at all, Meredith surmised that the wife suffered from something resembling bipolar disorder.

A very fashionable malady, in intellectual circles.

For the son, there was no diagnosis that Andre Litovik would accept.

M.R. shuddered to think—*If something should happen to the son. To either of them. And Andre were—free . . .*

She would know, then: if he loved her.

Or, rather: she could not deceive herself about knowing, in such circumstances.

Thinking of these matters, that were disturbing to her, yet familiar-disturbing, like snarls in her hair when she'd been a girl, that no amount of combing seemed to dispel for long, M.R. was swimming quite capably—vehemently. Despite her self-consciousness she was a quite good swimmer. She'd been a high school athlete—though not on the girls' swimming team, for she'd been too self-conscious about her solid, flat-breasted body in a clinging swimsuit, for all to see—and retained still a young athlete's coordination. To Oliver Kroll's surprise M.R. was swimming laps nearly as well as he did—and Oliver had happened to mention that, as a Yale undergraduate, he was told he might have been a candidate for the Olympic swim team if he'd had time to train—"Of course, that was a long time ago."

Olympics? Swim team? M.R. wondered how this could be. Of course, she said nothing.

Kroll was impressed by M.R.'s swimming. His eyes on her body—the unflattering single-piece swimsuit of some polyester fabric resembling a thin sort of reptile hide; the fleshy dimpled thighs that seemed to explode out of the suit, the small high hard breasts, shapely upper arms—Kroll gazed at her blinking. "Hey. 'Meredith.' You're beautiful."

Even at such a time, meaning to flatter, Kroll could not speak without sounding ironic, insincere.

In embarrassment M.R. laughed, turning away. She'd managed to push—shove—her thick hair up inside a rubber bathing cap that felt distended, like an encephalitic brain. She was not beautiful and was made uneasy by the claim—she had no wish to try to live up to such a claim.

What a farce! Masquerade . . .

Kroll never swam less than a mile, he'd said. For the sake of his back. When at last he climbed out of the pool M.R. saw how water streamed from his hard-muscled legs; the long dark hairs of his legs flat against his pale skin, glistening with moisture. She saw the just slightly flabby flesh at his waist, the bulge of his groin, and the antic hairs of his thighs that descended from it. . . . She felt an unexpected tenderness for the man: his maleness.

At a short distance of fifteen or twenty feet, M.R. liked Kroll best. She felt her heart expand with an emotion she could not have named—not love, not sexual desire, but a wish to touch, and to protect; a wish to *console*. She thought there could be nothing more tender between a man and a woman, than this wish to *console*.

It was missing from her relationship with Andre. He did not ever think to *console* her.

He did not ever think that M.R. was anyone other than *a strapping young Amazon* who did not require such coddling.

Nor would Andre have wished M.R. to console *him*.

Kroll saw M.R. gazing at him—(though she was not thinking of him but of the other, her astronomer-lover)—and smiled, tentatively. There was a leap of sexual interest between them—suddenly.

M.R. knew, from her limited experience with men, which was more or less her experience with her long-married astronomer-lover, that a man is very easily flattered, sexually; as a man is very easily satisfied, sexually. As in a droll but unsettling Magritte painting the man's squinty eyes were mimicked—mirrored—in the small nubby nipples of his flat male breasts which she wanted, impulsively, to touch—to stroke. To kiss?

He'd been married before—"Too young."

He'd been divorced—"Not so young."

Divorced now for eleven years. And no children—"Fortunately."

"Why 'fortunately'?"

"Because we'd still be married now, possibly. And I wouldn't have met you."

Offhandedly Kroll spoke. It was left to the woman—to M.R.—to speculate whether he spoke sincerely, or just offhandedly.

He wasn't emotionally involved with his ex-wife, Kroll said. But he had no interest in talking about her, or his "failed" marriage. Nor did Kroll ask M.R. about former lovers, or if she'd been married.

That day he'd been lecturing on Hobbes. Theories of humankind as machines lacking free will, "soul." He quite liked Hobbes's famous—infamous—aphorism: *Life is nasty, brutish, and short.* You could see that Kroll liked this aphorism as it applied to others, unlike himself.

Kroll said: "If man is a machine, man can be manipulated. For his own good, man can be manipulated. You've said you aren't religious, Meredith? But what do you believe?"

"I'm—not sure what I believe."

She told Kroll that her parents were Quakers but that she was not a Quaker though she respected the religion for its civility, sanity.

"Quakers value the commonweal over the individual—that isn't very American. We are a nation of individuals."

Kroll, the libertarian, disagreed: "All nations are nations of individuals—unless they're nations of ants."

He'd discovered an article that M.R. had published in *Ethics*—"Kant's Moral Imperative and 'Right to Life'"—he'd thought it was a very interesting essay, and wondered why M.R. had not mentioned it to him, or given him an offprint.

M.R. said she'd meant to mention it to him. She was intending to give him an offprint.

M.R. said she'd thought of the article as an exercise, or an experiment—"I was exploring the problem as it might be explored from various ethical viewpoints. But I don't 'believe' the conclusion—necessarily."

"You don't 'believe' the conclusion? Then—why did you write the article?"

"Because I was exploring ethical issues. I was not arguing for one side or another."

"And what is the purpose of that? 'Exploring'?"

"That is—philosophy. There is a 'philosophy of ethics'—as there is a 'philosophy of physics'—or a 'philosophy of law.'"

"But there is 'ethics' too—primarily. Isn't there?"

"'Primarily'?—I'm not sure."

"In politics, that's all there is—sides. The quest for power—and then, the determination to keep it."

"Power! Not only does power 'corrupt,' power 'blinds.' If it's truth that is the goal, power is a disability."

M.R. protested: philosophy could be approached as a series of problems for which there were no specific answers. Questions, and not answers. Many of her colleagues were exploring such problems, some of them were exploring metaphysical "counter-worlds"—in the pursuit of abstract truth.

"And what is a 'counter-world'? What I think it is?" Kroll smiled, vastly amused.

"A counter-world is a possibility of a—a world . . . A universe. . . ."

"Bullshit, darling." Crudely Kroll laughed, like one who wants you to know you haven't put anything over on him. "This 'right-to-life' movement—let's say in America, right now—you are either for it, or against it. You are either pro-abortion, or anti-abortion."

"Not *pro*-abortion but *pro*-choice. The issue is— *pro*-choice."

"Your article suggests that you are not *pro*-choice—if I understand it correctly. Kant's 'moral imperative'—we should never act unless our actions constitute a principle for all other human beings—if you take that as an ideal, you can hardly be *pro*-choice for you'd have wanted, in your own case, to be born—not aborted. Yes?"

"But I don't take it as an 'ideal'—only as a philo-sophical proposition."

"Have you ever been pregnant, Meredith?"

The question came so abruptly, M.R. hadn't time to be shocked, or insulted. Not very convincingly she stammered, "N-no."

"No? Well. You don't have a perspective, then. Maybe that's why you're irresolute."

" 'Irresolution' isn't the—the issue. I mean, 'irresolution' isn't the precise term. . . ."

" 'Objectivity' then? In ethical matters, as in political matters, there is no 'objectivity.' "

Still Kroll smiled, amused. M.R. tried to explain that, in an experiment, the experimenter doesn't know what the results of the experiment will be, beforehand. In philosophy, if one is exploring the possibilities of a position. . . . Kroll brushed aside her faltering words like one brushing away gnats.

"Bullshit, darling. And you know it."

M.R. thought she would not see Kroll again. In the wake of his presence she was unsettled, often sleepless. She didn't want this intimacy. Yet then, when he called her, she heard her eager voice say *yes*.

The pale-blue hydrangea had faded, died. M.R. worried that she'd forgotten to water it—unless she'd over-watered it. She hurried to a florist's to buy a replacement, the identical shade of blue. She reasoned that Kroll couldn't have told the difference even if he'd been suspicious, which he was not. He continued to check the soil with his forefinger.

———

In late October, M.R. invited Kroll to dinner at her house.

The first time she'd prepared a meal for any man except Andre Litovik—(but not, for Andre, in this house)—and she'd felt an illicit sort of excitement purchasing groceries in the better of the local food stores pushing a cart amid other women who were very likely wives, mothers, lovers—*women* caught up in the drama of lives with *men*.

Which maybe she'd envied, in the past. A life entwined with another's life, however unpredictable.

For Kroll was unpredictable. Kroll was a man of moods. Often Kroll was impatient, obscurely discontented. Half-consciously he deflected her questions to him—what was wrong?—was he upset?—and at times, if she touched his arm, he seemed to shrink from her. Often to M.R. he seemed to be bringing—as in an embrace out of which clumsy objects were spilling, falling and shattering—a mysterious residue of irritation, annoyance, barely suppressed fury that had little to do with her.

Except of course she was *the woman*.

If she'd felt envy for the role of *woman* that envy dissolved now into an excited apprehension/anxiety, for Oliver Kroll was not easy to please, and the ways in which he might be displeased, or disappointed, were largely unpredictable. For dinner that evening Kroll brought a bottle of French wine—M.R. supposed it was expensive red wine, though she knew little of wine; she drank less than a half-glass, and distractedly, which must have annoyed Kroll for he lapsed into a brooding sort of silence. When M.R. asked him what was wrong he said, with a twist of a smile, "What d'you mean— 'what's wrong'?—nothing is wrong, with me."

He had a way of staring at her—coldly, without evident recognition. While M.R. smiled a strained hopeful girl-smile—wondering if the effort, the continued effort, was worth it.

With Andre, moods were all, also. But Andre's moods tended to be capacious, magnanimous—wind blowing through a house, flinging open French windows, slamming doors—a rattling bustle on all sides. Kroll's moods were tightly executed like a man opening an umbrella in a cramped space.

Near the end of an evening, Kroll might say suddenly that he had to leave—he had work to do. Quickly he was on his feet, rattling car keys in his hand and eager to go. At such a moment he might hold M.R.'s hand, stroke her arm—he might kiss her. M.R. allowed herself to be kissed and M.R. kissed the man in return, as if with feeling. Well, in fact—*with feeling.*

For she did feel an attraction to Oliver Kroll—she thought she did.

She would allow him to make love to her—would she?—if she could bear it. She would allow this, it had to be done. For it wasn't a normal relationship between adults, female and male, if there was no *lovemaking*— or some gesture in that direction.

M.R.'s adoration of her (secret) lover was unquestioning, an adoration of his soul. As the soul was inhabited inside the body, M.R. might adore the body as well.

Kroll was a different matter, very different from Andre. She had no sense of Kroll's soul—it might have been teaspoon-sized, or the size and width of a tongue depressor. If M.R. made love with him, he wouldn't have known how *not-there* she was in his arms; he hadn't the perspicacity to sense the woman's detachment from him, as a physical being. It was Kroll's own sensations Kroll monitored—the other, the woman, scarcely existed for him.

Often M.R. imagined that Kroll would simply cease to call her—abruptly, one day, whatever he'd felt for her, whatever fantasy-net he'd cast over her, in thrall to stately *Jane, Countess of Harrington* in a fond memory of his youth in England—and she would never hear from him again. That seemed to her utterly plausible, even probable, for Kroll spoke casually—disparagingly—of old, ex-friends, colleagues and "aging protégés" he'd outgrown. As soon as Kroll lost interest in a person, that person ceased to exist for him. Surely, M.R. was forewarned?

And on those warmer companionable evenings when she did feel attracted to Oliver Kroll, her feelings for her (secret) lover intervened, as a strong radio frequency will drown out a weaker. *Am I going to be married? Is that possible?*—M.R. smiled at the astonishing thought.

An elderly woman who'd died when M.R. had been a schoolgirl, in Carthage. And her body not found for several weeks. The horror of such loneliness—aloneness. At the time no one had wished to speak of the woman or give her a name except M.R.'s mother Agatha who'd been appalled, guilt-stricken though the woman had lived several blocks away, and neither of the Neukirchens had known her.

Repeatedly Agatha had said to M.R. *What a terrible thing! Terrible—just terrible. . . . We could have helped that poor woman. We should have known.*

It was distressing to M.R.—"Meredith"—that her mother who was normally so calm should speak in this way; her mother Agatha who took care not to say upsetting things, especially to children. Her mother who hadn't seemed to believe, in the way of Quaker idealism, in the reality of evil.

If we could make amends! Oh how—how can we make amends. . . .

With other members of the Quaker congregation, Agatha and Meredith began visiting elderly, isolated individuals in the area. They'd brought food, blankets and bedding, clothing. They'd brought household tools, to make repairs. Where serious repairs were needed, Konrad had come with them. Until now, M.R. had forgotten these well-intentioned but awkward visits that had continued at irregular intervals through her senior year of high school. She'd felt enormous sympathy for the elderly women—for those visited happened to be exclusively women—but the visits had been ordeals to her, exhausting. Her face had ached with smiling. Her nostrils had pinched at rancid odors. Where Agatha and the other Quakers had seemed to draw a sort of radiant strength from the visits, M.R. had found them upsetting. Never had the horror of loneliness—aloneness—been so real to her: stark as a mirror reflecting her own face.

I can love him, then. I will!

That final time, Kroll came to dinner at M.R.'s house.

It was early winter. They were seeing each other several times a week. M.R. had learned to navigate

Kroll's moods like a skier on a tricky slope. There had been intimacies between them—wordless, just slightly clumsy—like a wayward vehicle out of control on a steep slope, and no one at the wheel.

M.R. supposed that, like herself, Kroll was starved for affection—for an affirmation of his existence.

And there was the issue of the man's *maleness*—like a spinning saw, you dared not touch, yet were drawn to touch, fascinated.

That evening M.R. awaited Kroll's arrival apprehensively. She'd carefully prepared a meal, she'd bought wine of the sort Kroll seemed to favor, and hard crusty French bread; she'd watered the hydrangea plant with the pale-blue crinkly petals which was, like its predecessor, beginning to fade despite her best efforts. Yet she wasn't prepared for a stab of emotion when Kroll stepped into the house and greeted her so warmly, avidly—taking hold of her shoulders and kissing her mouth, prodding her teeth with his tongue in a manner both playful and passionate. "Hello hello hello! Darling!"—Kroll was in an exuberant mood.

Though M.R. wished to kiss Kroll in turn—wished to kiss him avidly, and her arms tightening around him—yet she stiffened involuntarily, just perceptibly, as if someone had whispered to her: *No!*

Kroll dropped his hands from M.R.'s shoulders and stepped back, frowning. It was a moment like stumbling in a dream—a misstep off a curb, or down a flight of stairs—and no turning back. M.R. heard herself stammering, "Oliver, I'm afraid—I should tell you . . ."

"Tell me—what?"

"I've liked—loved—our evenings together. Especially—lately. But I don't want to mislead you, Oliver, I'm . . . there is. . . ."

Coldly Kroll stared at M.R. He wasn't going to make this easy for her. His face was darkening beet-red with resentful blood and the corners of his mouth tightened.

" . . . someone in my life. I mean, before I came here—there was someone. I really can't claim"—M.R. was laughing, lifting her hands in a gesture of helplessness—"that this person is a serious, permanent part of my life, I mean from his perspective. But . . ."

"But you are 'involved' with him—or is it her?"

" 'Her'?" M.R. smiled uncertainly. "No—'him.' "

" 'Him.' " Kroll smirked.

He would never forgive her, she knew.

"You might have indicated this a little earlier, yes?"

Kroll laughed mirthlessly. The spade-shaped beard seemed to bristle with hostility. He was very angry with her, M.R. saw. When she touched his wrist with her fingers, he thrust her away.

"You might have indicated weeks ago. For instance—"

M.R. was stunned. Kroll was itemizing events he'd taken her to, dinners, drives into the countryside—of course, how could she have failed to understand! How insensitive she'd been.

"You allowed me to pay for your tickets each time we went out—and some of those tickets aren't cheap. You allowed me to pay for most of our dinners. It may be that my salary at the University is higher than yours but you are entirely financially independent, you have no obvious dependents, while I—I have obligations." Kroll's voice trailed off, he'd begun to be embarrassed by the vehemence of his words.

Obligations?—M.R. had no idea what Kroll meant. Another time she tried to touch Kroll's arm and another time he rebuffed her. She said, faltering, "I—I'm so sorry. I've behaved unconscionably. I don't know why—I think—I think that—this isn't any sort of defense, just a clumsy explanation—that I thought you might be offended if I offered to pay—as I'd offered to pay the first time we went out. And a few other times—in fact I think I did pay—a few times. I'd thought—there are men who. . . ."

"Well, yes—'there are men who'—plenty of men who will pay for women for whom they have strong feelings, and who reciprocate those feelings. But our situation isn't—wasn't—that sort of situation, was it? And you knew this from the start."

"But I didn't—I didn't know— I mean, I didn't—"

She was a woman of thirty: hardly a girl. And she'd been involved with Andre Litovik for many years—at least, at a distance. Yet she knew little more of the ways of the world than a girl of fifteen might have known, when M.R. had been a girl of fifteen: she could not imagine herself as an *active agent* in a relationship with a man, only as *passive*. She had no *ease* with men; she could never gauge what a man might be thinking, or planning; in a conversation the man was likely to be dominant, but in the way in which a large vessel floats in water; you can guide the vessel by subtle movements of your hands even as the proprietor of the vessel believes that he is the one who is steering.

Seeing that M.R. was so genuinely stricken with repentance, Kroll relented just slightly, like one withdrawing a dagger slowly, instead of twisting it. Coolly he said, "I wouldn't have mentioned any of this except. . . . It's God-damned annoying when. . . . Women make as much money as men, and yet . . . women expect men to pay for them. . . ."

"But I—I did make dinner for you, Oliver—didn't I? Several times?"

"Dinner at home is something different. Of course you would *make dinner* for a friend and not expect to be paid for it, I hope."

M.R. saw that everything she said was misunderstood by this angry man buzzing and thrumming like a wasp. "Then—it's hopeless. If I make dinner for you in this house, it's only what's expected. When you take me out, I should pay for my own meal."

She stammered in confusion and hurt. She had not experienced such hostility as an adult, even when Andre had spoken harshly to her; she had no defense against what she perceived to be sheer dislike, repugnance.

Meanly Kroll persisted, like a pit bull that has closed its teeth around something living and must shake, shake, shake it to death: "And you never offer to drive. You could drive—but you take it for granted, I will drive. My car is no more suited for—for driving— than yours." Kroll's face was beet-red in indignation, he seemed scarcely to know what he was saying. Such loathing of her, she'd never guessed at, in the man's eyes!

Yet Kroll continued, with the air of one who has been grievously mistreated. His manner was professorial, even lawyerly—he was drawing up a devastating brief against her, who had so wounded him. For now it developed that, on one of their recent evenings,

Kroll had scraped the right rear fender of his Jaguar, backing out of a tight parking space—this, too, was a grievance lodged against M.R. who listened stunned, baffled; she'd never known any man who expected a woman to drive a vehicle instead of him—except on long journeys perhaps; her father had always driven when he and her mother were together; no adult male in Carthage, in M.R.'s memory, would have wished to surrender a steering wheel to any woman—this would have signaled incapacity, illness. And Andre Litovik, of course, would not have allowed anyone else to drive any vehicle in which he was a passenger, certainly not a woman.

Faintly M.R. protested: "I can only say—I didn't know. I am so very sorry. You'd seemed to enjoy—your beautiful car. Maybe you should have suggested. . . ."

"I did. More than once."

"You did—?"

M.R. was sure that Kroll had not made any such suggestion. Most evenings Kroll drove to M.R.'s house to pick her up; occasionally, it was more convenient for M.R. to drive to Kroll's house, after her day at the University, or to meet him in town. When M.R. drove to meet Kroll she was often late—some strange spell overtook her, slowing her as if a narcotic had entered her veins; she who was compulsively early for most engagements, found herself leaving at the last possible minute to meet Kroll, or after the last minute.

Oliver Kroll was somewhat vain of the sporty cobalt-blue Jaguar and certainly wouldn't have wanted to drive anywhere in M.R.'s very ordinary American compact car with the ridiculous name "Saturn"—(ridiculous to Kroll who teased M.R. about the fact that M.R. hadn't been able to identify the brand name of her own car, she'd hurriedly purchased as "pre-owned" several years before)—still less would he have consented to allow M.R. to drive the Jaguar. Yet this new grievance was deeply wounding to him, as extreme as the first grievance and a confirmation of it.

As Kroll raged M.R. tried to compute: how much did she owe this angry man? For certainly she owed Oliver Kroll something, she saw that now; she'd failed to behave equitably with him, she'd behaved shamefully and obliviously. . . . Kroll lived several miles from M.R.'s little house on Echo Lake: three miles, each way? Multiplied—how many times? (How many times had they gone out together? M.R. could not think.) Gasoline, wear and tear on the Jaguar, Kroll's valuable time spent driving? M.R. was hot with shame, seeing such loathing in the face of a man she'd imagined had cared for her.

Loved her! What a farce. ❧

M.R. excused herself and hurried to another room to locate her checkbook in a desk drawer for—how much?—what was a reasonable sum?—her head felt as if it were inside a clanging bell. . . . Seeing then that the name she'd written in haste was misspelled she began another check, made out not to *Krull* but *Kroll;* she feared insulting Kroll but very likely by this time the man was beyond being insulted by M.R.: he loathed her, he wanted his money from her! Naïvely M.R. was hoping that some tattered remnant of their relationship might be salved if M.R. could manage to behave as a man might, reasonably and without an excess of emotion.

She returned to Kroll, with the check. Kroll was standing in front of the Reynolds portrait, staring without seeming to see it; his face was still very red. Profusely M.R. apologized. "Oliver, I'm so sorry! I hope you can forgive me. I hope you won't think ill of me. I'm just—I was just—I think I am just"—wanting to say *naïve* but correcting herself, seeing Kroll's look of contempt—"stupid. Unthinking."

M.R. held out the check to him. She saw that Kroll wanted to take the check even as he was insulted by the offer—for of course Kroll wished to maintain the dignity of a gentleman for whom such grubby issues

are trivial even as he wanted the woman to abase herself before him, to explain and apologize and repay
him. He took the check from her, frowning—"This is
too much."

She'd made out the check for $350. She'd calculated
that she might owe Kroll half that amount, and giving
him $350 allowed a margin of error.

"Please, Oliver. Just take it."

She tried to speak calmly. She was feeling sick, as if
she'd been kicked in the stomach. With the look as of
one confronted by a bad odor Kroll folded the check
and shoved it into his coat pocket as if he were doing
M.R. a favor.

"Well. Let's eat."

M.R. could not believe these words. *Eat?* Kroll
wanted her to serve dinner to him after all this, that he
might *eat?*

He was making an effort to smile. His eyes were
narrowed, wary. He had no clear idea how far he'd
gone—what he had said, that might be irrevocable.

"I don't think so, Oliver. After—this—I'm not
hungry. I don't feel well. I think that you should leave."

"Leave? Now that we've straightened this out?"

Kroll seemed genuinely surprised. He had looked
at her as if he loathed her, he had drawn up his case
brilliantly and irrevocably against her, and now he

expected to behave as if nothing had passed between them?

M.R. said: "Yes. I think you should leave."

Now a deeper woundedness seeped into Kroll's face. Now his mouth worked inside the spade-shaped beard, in fury. M.R. backed away from him. She was frightened of him. He might explode at any moment, he might lay his hands on her. . . .

She meant to move past him, into another room, but Kroll blocked her way. His face was livid with dislike. But if he hated her—why didn't he leave?

"I think, Oliver, you had better leave. I've repaid you, I hope. If it isn't enough, please let me know—I will be happy to pay you more."

She was desperate now to be rid of him. The fury in the man's face was terrifying.

It may have been a mistake to turn her back on Kroll—M.R. ran to open the front door and he gripped her shoulder, her arm—with a little cry of surprise and pain, she wrenched away—"Please. Please leave. I want to be alone." She was close to fainting, she dared not allow Kroll to see how agitated he had made her, how weakened.

He gripped her again—her arm, her wrist. And again M.R. pulled away.

Kroll tried to smile—protesting he'd only just arrived—he'd had something to tell her and he'd told her—he didn't want to leave, just yet—but M.R. was unable to look at him, only wanting him gone.

"Please. Please leave."

"I think you're making a mistake, Meredith."

But he was very angry, his voice quavered. M.R. could feel how he would have liked to take hold of her, and shake-shake-shake her into submission.

Such shame—she'd so miscalculated the man's feelings for her—she had thought he'd *cared for her*—and in an instant, all that had vanished. He might have taken a knife to the portrait-poster on the wall, slashing beautiful Jane, Countess of Harrington, to shreds.

Indignant Kroll stepped outside. The check was in his hand again—M.R. saw that his hand shook. She thought *He will tear it into shreds, he will scatter them on the walk.*

Instead, Kroll returned the check to his pocket. Without a backward glance he made his way to the curb and to the low-slung car with the scratched right-rear fender that required you to bend, to bow as you climbed into it, and M.R. watched through a window not daring to breathe as the car jerked from the curb, and away.

Like a drunken woman M.R. made her way into her bedroom and fell onto the bed where she lay sick, sickened in her soul for hours through the long night too shocked to fully comprehend what had happened: how the man had revealed himself to her, his dislike of her, his fury.

A phone rang, rang—she pressed her hands over her ears.

If he returned! If he made his way into the house!

Not out of love for her—but out of wounded pride. He would revenge himself upon her, if he could.

Her shoulder ached where he'd gripped her, her arm would bruise from his hard angry fingers. It was shame more than fear, that paralyzed her. Black brackish water gathered at the back of her mouth. She was in terror of being violently sick, choking on her vomit and so they would find her as they'd found the elderly woman in Carthage, partly decomposed, rancid with decay, alone.

Scarcely breathing for her ribs had been broken and the mud-muck stinking in her nostrils, in her mouth, the very lashes of her eyes stuck together.

Die why don't you. Mudgirl, garbage-girl—die.

In time she would think almost calmly, wryly—he wasn't the first man to break her heart.

He wasn't the crucial man to break her heart.

He was *a man* in her life. Not *the man.*

"Meredith!"

She called him as he'd requested on this evening in March 2003, he'd answered on the first ring.

There was an unnerving intimacy in the man's voice, after so many years—"Meredith! Thanks for calling."

Asking if he could come to see her, he had something urgent to tell her. M.R. hesitated a moment—it was a perceptible moment, Oliver Kroll would register it—before saying yes.

"Yes of course."

It was news of Alexander Stirk, and could not be good news.

And so Oliver Kroll came to the president's house, at midnight. This interminable day, that had begun long ago in a kind of innocence! M.R. opened the front door for him, before he rang the bell. The old intimacy between them was such, neither could quite bear to shake the other's hand.

An observer, watching, would conclude from this—there was a mysterious bond between them.

"Strange to be here. At this hour."

Kroll might have added *And alone.*

For very few people came to the president's house individually. It was not the sort of residence—it had not the sort of *atmosphere*—to which individuals came, as friends. Oliver Kroll had in fact been a guest at Charters

House more than once since M.R. had become president of the University, but always in the company of others: formal receptions, dinners for distinguished speakers.

Amid this company of others, he and M.R. were obliged to acknowledge each other only formally, politely.

She had never been able to forget that look of hatred in the man's face. That loathing for *the woman,* as she saw it. In Oliver Kroll's TV personality, the dry, droll, sarcastic wit, the caustic asides and sneering twist of his lips, the dismissive of *liberal, "left-wing"* as contemptible, if not traitorous—she felt it yet more powerfully, and she could not bear it.

Tonight, Kroll looked older, strained—the jaunty public manner was subdued. His beard was still trimmed to resemble a sharp-edged spade but it was threaded now with gray and there were bumps and shallows in the hairless scalp. M.R. wondered—was this the man who'd so intimidated her?—frightened her? At the University, Oliver Kroll was one of the enemy—a cadre of highly vocal conservative faculty members who voted in a block at meetings, in opposition to many of M. R. Neukirchen's proposals. These faculty members were all male—all "white"—they were all above the rank of assistant professor. (Not that it mattered greatly—the liberal faculty at the University so outnumbered the conservatives in matters of voting.) M.R. was inclined to believe that, if Kroll hadn't encouraged the undergraduate *Stirk* to tape their conversation, one of his conservative colleagues had.

In the decade since Kroll had departed M.R.'s life, he'd become a yet more controversial campus figure. Since the advent of the George W. Bush administration and the triumph of conservative politics in America, Kroll had joined his older colleague/mentor G. Leddy Heidemann as a White House consultant. Where Heidemann was noted in the press as the Middle East adviser to the secretary of defense—the "architect"/"moral conscience" of the wars in Iraq and Afghanistan—Kroll's influence was domestic, and more general. As a political theorist Oliver Kroll was frequently invited to appear on television—Sunday morning news commentary, CNN and Fox News. In the hectic days following the terrorist attacks on the World Trade Center in the fall of 2001, both Kroll and Heidemann had appeared frequently on television. And now in March 2003 on the eve of the invasion of Iraq the pro-war propaganda had escalated—*This is a crusade. This is not "diplomacy by other means." The time for diplomacy is past. There can be no "diplomacy" with evil.*

Rarely did M.R. watch these political discussion programs, they so upset her. And hearing her

University colleagues say such things—warmongering, pseudo-"patriotic," shameful—she hurriedly switched off the TV.

As a successor to Heidemann, Oliver Kroll became faculty adviser for the local chapter of the Young Americans for Freedom. He campaigned for funds to bring to the campus controversial conservative speakers and activists; at a teach-in on the subject of potential war in the Middle East, organized by liberal faculty members, Kroll had led the opposition of conservative professors and students who'd picketed the event and asked heckling questions of the speakers. Since October, when the U.S. Congress had voted by a considerable majority to authorize the president to use "military force" against Iraq, there had come to be an increasingly fevered and divisive political atmosphere on campus, as throughout the country. As president of this distinguished university M.R. could not become involved in political arguments, which were often embittered, angry and intolerant; she'd stayed away from the teach-in, and wrote an editorial for the campus newspaper pleading for civility. It had been told to her—she'd been warned, by Leonard Lockhardt—that an educator of her stature was required to be above the "fracas." There were conservative members of the University's board of trustees and there were—of course—

numerous conservative donors, who tracked the record of the University president in the media, closely. Even in small gatherings M.R. had learned to be reticent about her personal feelings—her predilection for liberal causes, on principle; she dared not joke, and she avoided all occasions for irony, which were occasions for ambiguity. Quickly she'd learned that a public position puts one in hostage: the first freedom you surrender is the freedom to speak impulsively, from the heart.

Initially, M.R.'s admirers had liked her *outspokenness*—that was a kind of professional naïveté. But now, months into the presidency, she was expected to behave more circumspectly.

Even with her closest friends she'd become guarded. And Andre.

She could not fully trust even him—her lover—not to repeat remarks she made, and distort them.

It had been sheerly good luck, that M.R. hadn't had an opportunity to deliver the fiery anti-war speech she'd planned at the Society of Learned Societies conference. Sheerly good luck, her rented car had skidded and overturned in a ditch in a desolate region of Beechum County.

The talk, at which she'd labored for so long, had been laced with irony like a toxic filigree. Irony wasn't M.R.'s characteristic mode of speech and not one recommended for a university president who depended upon the goodwill of the academic community to persevere. Leonard Lockhardt, who'd read M.R.'s speech after she'd failed to deliver it, had been surprised and disapproving. (And Lockhardt was himself an old-style liberal, who'd come of age politically in the era of Lyndon Johnson and the Great Society.) If she'd given that speech, and if it had been published, or made its way onto the Internet—what a blunder, for a president in her first year in office!

Yes; better that M.R. had had her mysterious "accident" and disappeared from view for an interlude of more than twelve hours, never satisfactorily explained.

"Has your staff gone home for the night? This place is enormous . . . It must be like living in a museum. . . ."

Kroll spoke lightly, distractedly. It was clear that he was upset—his small squinty eyes glanced about, his mouth was fixed in a tight little smile.

He didn't seem to hear M.R.'s offer to take his coat—in fact, a suede jacket—streaked and darkened with melting snow—nor did M.R. repeat the offer.

"No. I don't 'live' here. I have a private apartment— you could call it an apartment—on the second floor."

Just to set Kroll straight. *Private.*

She'd led her visitor along the dimly lighted front hall to the wood-paneled library at the rear of the house. Most of the house was darkened—in the large

public rooms opening off the hall were antique furnishings, carpets, chandeliers just barely visible.

In the library, there was a faint chill moonlit glisten
to the dark-polished hardwood floor. Beyond latticed
windows which by day overlooked a flagstone terrace, a landscaped English garden and a long sweep of
lawn there was darkness, oblivion. M.R. switched on
the overhead light—lights. A massive chandelier and
smaller wall-lamps. Leather chairs, sofas, small tables
were revealed in arrangements like giant chess pieces
on the brink of being played.

"Please sit down. Here."

She had not called him *Oliver.* Her throat shut
against the name she could not bring herself to utter.

They sat by a massive pale-marble fireplace inscribed with the stirring words MAGNA EST VERITAS
ET PRAEVALET. The fireplace was at least five feet in
height, six feet in width, with brass andirons, perfectly
positioned birch logs and not a trace of ashes. M.R.
could not recall a fire in this fireplace, nor had she
ever sat like this, with any visitor, in front of the fireplace. Like so much else in the University the library
was named for a wealthy donor and was lined floor-to-
ceiling with books in handsome leather-bound editions
at which no one ever glanced though there were rare
first editions on the shelves.

The thought came to her, a mocking sort of thought—*If we'd been married. Where would we live? Here?*

Uncannily—as if he'd been reading her thoughts, or had sensed the drift of her thoughts—Kroll asked if M.R. still had her place on the lake.

For a moment M.R. seemed not to know what Kroll meant, then she said no, she'd only rented the house.

There was more to explain perhaps but M.R. had no wish to pursue a personal conversation with Oliver Kroll.

"That was—is—a quite nice house."

Kroll's tone was wistful, subdued. If Kroll expected M.R. to reply to this offhand remark, he was mistaken.

M.R. was thinking of how she'd removed the Joshua Reynolds portrait from the wall, and disposed of it in the trash. The pale-blue hydrangea had died a natural death.

Kroll had called her, left messages. M.R. hadn't answered. He'd sent e-mails, which she'd deleted without reading. No more! She wasn't so naïve she would give the man the opportunity to hurt her again.

Abruptly then Kroll had ceased trying to contact her. Out of spite perhaps he'd cashed the check for $350 as out of spite—perhaps—he'd taken up so publicly the conservative cause he'd scorned years before. In rebuke of M. R. Neukirchen and other campus liberals whom he held in such contempt.

Unless—this was more likely—M.R. had nothing to do with her former lover's political pronouncements, as she'd had nothing to do with his life for the past decade.

As if reluctantly—for there was no escaping the subject that had propelled him here—Kroll asked if M.R. had heard anything further from Alexander Stirk and M.R. said guardedly that if Kroll meant since the report of the assault, and since her meeting with him in her office, no she had not.

"Alexander has asked me not to 'make it public'—he's going to do that himself. But I wanted to tell you tonight, I thought you should know."

"Know—what?"

"It turns out he'd done something like this before—that is, he'd accused classmates of attacking him, at his prep school in Connecticut. The Griffith School—you didn't know?"

M.R. stammered no. Of course—she had not known.

"Alexander is a very bright boy. But obviously he's troubled. He's had some sort of crisis since I'd known him—since he was my student two years ago. It's related to his being 'gay'—being 'conservative' on this campus—but also to his family, his father. He'd been sent to the Griffith School where his father had gone and he hadn't been able to adjust, he said—he'd been 'persecuted' by other students, and his teachers hadn't seemed to be sympathetic—so—he'd sent threatening e-mails to himself, he'd put a sign on the door of his room—'Die Fag!' He trashed his room, mangled his books. It sounds as if he had a nervous breakdown, by his account. Anyway, he was discovered to be fabricating the 'persecution'—at least, its outward signs. He was suspended from Griffith and required to have psychotherapy before he was allowed back and when he applied here, all this was expunged from his record. He was very emotional confessing all this to me, tonight—he says he is 'so ashamed'—his former roommates are 'outing' him online—'exposing' him to the media, since they'd found out about the alleged assault here." Kroll spoke rapidly and flatly with an air of detachment—if he was upset, he didn't want to reveal it.

"But—does this mean he fabricated the assault, too?"

"He claims no. He claims that the 'assault' really happened."

M.R. had been listening in astonishment. If the assault had been fabricated—as she'd suspected—was this good news? Good for the University, at least?

"When Alexander came into my office hobbling on his damned crutch—just a few hours ago—he said, in this sick-guilty voice, 'I have something to tell you, Professor Kroll'—and I said, 'You made it up, didn't you? The assault.' He looked at me as if I'd kicked him—'Noooo I didn't make that up. They tried to kill me—that happened. But I did make up—something else.' So he told me about the Griffith School, and his former roommates going online, he was crying, almost hysterical, but he swore that the assault the other night was 'real'—he was worried now that no one would believe him. This news about Griffith just about knocked me out of my chair—I was stunned. Of course I didn't tell Alexander—the township police have already been suspicious of his story. They were questioning me pretty frankly—'Does this kid have a history of making false accusations?' 'How well do you know this kid?' Anything to do with 'gay issues'—cops are suspicious and definitely not sympathetic. Alexander has been changing his account of what happened to him, evidently. The cops think that his injuries may be 'self-inflicted'—they didn't buy his story of witnesses walking away. And when he called me from the hospital, and I came over, there were things that didn't make sense to me—but I didn't want to seem suspicious of him, he did appear to have been hurt and obviously he was very upset. Now, I don't know what to think. Or rather, I know what to think—but I don't want to turn against him, he'll have no one. His father is a wealthy businessman he claims is a friend of Jeb Bush. His friends here—he doesn't have many—are going to feel betrayed. In the YAF, they'll feel that he's a traitor. They won't be sympathetic with some fucked-up kid having a mental breakdown and going online with it." Kroll laughed harshly. M.R. could see that he was deeply moved, and repelled; it was his sympathy for the stricken and now accursed Alexander Stirk that repelled him.

In a grim sneering voice Kroll said that Stirk had asked him to write letters of recommendation for him, for law school—"Of course I did. And very 'positive' letters, too! Now, I feel like an utter asshole. And he's fucked—or will be, if it comes out he's lying—again."

M.R. passed a hand over her eyes. She should have felt relief but she registered only a dull shock as of gunfire muffled by distance. "But this is terrible—he's unwell. He needs help. . . ."

"He's beyond help, if he's lying about the 'assault.' You don't fuck with the police—they'll charge him with filing a false report."

Kroll spoke with grim satisfaction. M.R. saw that the man cared for his own position, his own reputation and pride, and not so much for the welfare of his student.

"Now, no one will believe him—about anything. Anyone could hurt him." Strange for M.R. to make such an observation, at such a time. But Kroll took no notice.

"I asked the police about that—if it turns out he's lying. Any kind of 'gay' issue to them—they said—'raises flags.'"

Raises flags. M.R. had a vision of flags tattered and weatherworn whipping in a hostile wind.

She thought that Kroll might leave now: this was a natural time for Kroll to leave.

Or, she might offer Kroll a drink, belatedly. She might invite the man to remove his suede jacket that must be unpleasantly damp, and heavy, and warm.

Kroll was staring into the shadowy interior of the massive pale-marble fireplace. Beyond the gleaming brass andirons there was—nothing.

Kroll began to speak, at times brokenly, of Alexander Stirk. He'd been drawn to the boy when Stirk was a sophomore enrolled in Kroll's honors seminar in political theory—he'd been impressed by the boy's passionately written essays and after-class discussions. Here was a purely—precociously—*intellectual* undergraduate of a kind rarely encountered even at the University, where admission requirements were famously high. That Alexander was so boyishly eager, so (evidently) sexless, or asexual, yet at the same time so (seemingly) "gay"—(a term Kroll found particularly offensive)— was just one aspect of his uniqueness; one facet of his woundedness and pain, and of his virtuoso manipulation of his woundedness and pain. Kroll thought it was courageous of Stirk to turn his "gayness" inside out, so to speak—to make of it part of his identity, not a part to be hidden. Among conservatives, of course "gayness"— "homosexuality"—is an issue—in the Catholic church, to which Stirk belonged, it was particularly an issue. "It's as if Alexander chose to make *gayness* a weapon to bludgeon his enemies—his 'liberal' enemies—and also his father. Yet—the kid wants to impress his father, too. He was always inviting me to visit him—to meet his father. The political is always personal, in adolescents."

M.R. was thinking *In a counter-world this boy is our son. Misbegotten and wayward, because we abandoned him.*

An utterly absurd thought! So swiftly it passed through M.R.'s brain like a short piece of string through the eye of a needle, and was lost.

"Is there any truth to the rumor—the ugly rumor— Alexander hinted at in his newspaper column—that a woman student had had a very late-term abortion?"

"Yes, of course. In everything Alexander has said there is a residue—some residue—of truth."

They lapsed into an uncomfortable silence. To avoid looking at each other, they stared into the fireplace that contained no fire, nor even the memory of a fire.

"If I hadn't behaved so stupidly . . . "

Kroll's voice trailed off. M.R. wasn't going to finish his sentence for him.

Was he thinking—they might be together, now? Might have been together, as a couple, for the past decade? Was this possible? Could this ever have been possible? And if possible, would M.R. be residing in this museum-mansion, with Professor Kroll as a husband?

Not very likely. This was a *counter-world* impossible to imagine.

M. R. Neukirchen had been—until just recently, at least—a highly successful administrator precisely because she hadn't been married, hadn't had a family to distract her, or a domestic life of any scale—loneliness had galvanized her, and a fierce unswerving wish to *go forward* as along a very narrow plank over a raging river.

Maybe she'd fallen in love with Andre Litovik, as the unattainable male. Maybe, her (secret) lover was the prime mover of M.R.'s adult life.

Remembering how, removing the portrait of Jane, Countess of Harrington from her wall in the rented house, removing the poster from the expensive frame, she'd crumpled and torn it, and felt a surge of relief and elation—then, suddenly, sorrow.

Something had clawed at her chest. Had she loved Kroll despite all her resistance? Or had her feeling for him been, from the start, sheer desperation?

"Of course, if that had been—you wouldn't be here in this house, Meredith. Probably."

Kroll spoke dryly, with his TV air of bemusement. It was a tone cultivated to maintain the demeanor of control as the spiky-sharp beard was a disguise that both hid and protected the vulnerable face beneath.

With a sound between a grunt and a sigh Kroll heaved himself to his feet. He'd gained weight, even his close-shaven head looked thicker, more solid. As if his back had stiffened, and was giving him pain, he stretched his arms, and yawned, somewhat boorishly—as if in mockery of their former intimacy.

"Well! Tomorrow all this will be out, I hope. Or most of it."

M.R. was still sitting, rather stunned. She would be sleepless most of the night, considering what Kroll had been kind enough to tell her.

For he'd come to her, and he'd informed her—he'd had her best interests in mind. That Professor Kroll was M.R.'s political adversary did not preclude his behaving gallantly toward her.

"Oliver, thank you so much! This can't have been easy for you."

It was M.R.'s presidential voice, warmly bright, earnest. If there was more to be said, this voice would not speak it.

M.R. led her midnight visitor to the front door. Retracing their steps along the long somber hallway where underfoot was an Oriental-carpet runner and overhead lights that cast unflattering shadows downward onto their faces rendering them masklike with exaggerated eye sockets, brackets beside mouths. In the foyer a spectacular Irish-crystal chandelier was still on, as if for a festive occasion that had gone wrong. And the outside light, that M.R. had hurried to switch on just before Kroll drove up to park in the circular drive just beyond the front steps.

"Well—Meredith. Good night."

"Good night! And again—thank you so much."

In the effort of opening the door, M.R. was spared having to look into the man's face—his eyes. She held the door open for her departing visitor, a massive antique-oak door with a wrought-iron eagle knocker which all who entered Charters House paused to admire, though Kroll took no notice of it. He had only to step outside and M.R. would shut and lock the door behind him.

Kroll stepped outside. Snow fell thinly, wetly. There was a sharp fresh smell as of marrow spilled from bone, unexpectedly moist and cleansing and this seemed to M.R. the very smell of late-night, solitude and deserted streets and large stone houses emptied of all inhabitants save one.

M.R. didn't watch Kroll stride to his car, drive away. She'd switched off the outside light even as he was switching on his car headlights.

He could still come back. A pretext of more to say, or . . .

Upstairs in her private quarters preparing for bed—at last—M.R. would wonder suddenly—did he still drive that low-slung sleek luxury car—what was it called—*Jaguar?* She had not noticed.

Mudgirl Reclaimed.
Mudgirl Renamed.

April–May 1965

In the hilly countryside south and west of the Adirondacks in Herkimer and Beechum counties quickly the grim news spread: one of the little Kraeck girls had been found in the mudflats by the Black Snake River abandoned by her mother and left to die.

No it could be no accident. No one would leave a child by chance. Not thrown into the mudflats and her battered little doll beside her . . .

For they'd seen on TV news a photograph of the *unidentified child approximately three years of age* in the hospital at Carthage.

Even with a crude-shaved head, bruised face, swollen and mournful eyes the child was recognized by residents of Star Lake who'd known the mother Marit Kraeck—had to be the younger girl, they thought.

Unless it was the elder, the five-year-old, emaciated, near-death and speechless as if the rapacious mud had sucked away her breath.

Not until the child was *found* had it been known that the child was *lost*.

As decades later she would propose a teasing proposition at a philosophy colloquium *If words cease to exist do their meanings cease to exist too?*

If names are nullified are the named nullified—or, renamed, reconstituted?

Excited calls were placed to the county sheriff's office. Residents of Star Lake reported that the Kraeck woman hadn't been seen in or around Star Lake for at least a week and the picture of the little girl on TV— the one found in the mudflats—could have been either of the little Kraeck girls.

And there was the stammering young man—a trapper along the Black Snake River—who'd found and rescued the girl—interviewed on local TV a dozen times and one of these times standing on the embankment above the mudflat to which he'd brought sheriff's deputies to show them exactly where he'd found the little girl in the mud—as well as the rubber doll he'd described, that was still there in a tangle of mud and rushes.

And so on TV the shocking sight of this naked and hairless castaway doll revealed there in the rushes like a castaway child.

The Kraeck girls were Jewell and Jedina.

There was no known father, or fathers. There were none to come forward to claim the little girl in the hospital at Carthage.

Neither girl had gone to any school. No birth certificates or any documents pertaining to them could be discovered in either Herkimer or Beechum counties or, in time, in any county in New York State. Star Lake neighbors testified as to their probable ages.

When finally after several weeks in the hospital the little girl regained her ability to speak—in a hoarse whisper at first, comprehensible only to the nurses who most cared for her—she would say that she was *Jewell.*

She did not seem to know her last name. But she knew that she was not *Jedina,* but *Jewell.*

Of *Jedina,* she did not speak. Of *Jedina,* she could not be coaxed to speak.

Nor of her mother, she could not be coaxed to speak.

So terribly emaciated, near death. And her head shaved and stippled with bruises, scabs.

Yet insisting yes she was *Jewell.*

Her injured eyes blinking up from the small battered face both fear and in steely resolution *Not Jedina but Jewell.*

Jewell. Jewell!

Of *Jedina* truly the child seemed to know nothing. Of *Jedina* the child would never speak for words had been taken from her, and her mouth filled with mud.

And so it was, the surviving girl was noted to be *Jewell Kraeck.* The birth date for *Jewell Kraeck* was believed to be 1960 but this could not be official for no official certificate seemed to exist.

Naturally then it was wondered where was the other sister—whose name was *Jedina*?

And where was their mother *Marit Kraeck*?

The mudflats beside the Black Snake River were searched by rescue workers. The desolate countryside of northern Beechum County, hills of shattered shale, glacial rock-ruins, beech forests part collapsed as by a mysterious plague and their exposed roots gnarled as arthritic fingers—fleetingly these images appeared on TV news, sometimes from the aerial perspective of a helicopter and at such times the rapid-gliding shadow of the helicopter was observed on the ground below like that of a gigantic predator-bird.

And there was long-armed gangling *Suttis Coldham* staring into the TV camera licking his lips trying for Christ sake not to succumb to a stammer like a man trying to contain a large writhing snake encased inside his body saying—insisting—"There was just— the one little girl in the mud. There was just the one.

If there'd been two I'd seen two but—*there was just one.*"

Residents of Star Lake and vicinity who knew Marit Kraeck—only just slightly, for Marit Kraeck shunned her neighbors and any who made inquiries of her, as she feared and despised all individuals associated with the county or the state or any government or government service whether named to her or not or actual or only just imagined—these women—for nearly all were women—believed that the county ought to have done more than just food stamps for the poor mother and her little daughters. In Sparta she'd lived for a while at Lake Clear Junction and then at Star Lake she'd arrived with a spiky-haired long-distance trucker a dozen years older than she was who liked to laugh and his gums wetly bared when he laughed—*Vietnam vet* this man identified himself—rank of *corporal* and his first name *Toby,* or *Tyrell*— "shrapnel" in his legs he'd said and a "steel plate" in his head he'd joked about so you could not know if the *ex-corporal* was serious or not-serious and both of them heavy drinkers living together in a run-down place outside town until the *ex-corporal* disappeared then it began to seem that Marit Kraeck was excessively religious—"troubled" and "not right in her head"—initially she'd gone to several churches in the Star Lake area then finally just to the Methodist church—Sunday morning, Wednesday evening prayer service—and there was some incident at Star Lake Methodist involving Marit Kraeck and the minister of the church having to call the sheriff's office to deal with the angry woman threatening him or threatening to harm herself in his presence. And there was Marit Kraeck arrested for impaired driving, public drunkenness and resisting arrest and so sentenced to a term in the women's house of detention and subsequently released on parole and for the past fifteen months living in a squalid little rented house not much larger than a packing crate with a sequence of men taking advantage of her and at last—again—the *ex-corporal* Toby, or Tyrell the long-distance trucker who seemed to have returned to her before shortly again departing for— Florida?—and Marit Kraeck had gone with him.

And the little girls, it was supposed. Gone with the adults to Florida.

After the girl believed to be *Jewell* was discovered in the mudflat and at the time of the search for the girl believed to be *Jedina* it was revealed that the run-down place Marit Kraeck had lived in down behind the Gulf station on the highway had virtually every square inch of its walls covered in some kind of religious picture, or crucifix—carved-wood crucifixes, gold-foil crucifixes, aluminum-wrap crucifixes, crucifixes of plastic

threaded with tinsel, a two-foot crucifix of crudely crocheted white lace—but no heat except a wood-burning
stove crammed with ashes and debris and turned-off
electricity and strips of soiled polyurethane over loose-
fitting windows, slapping in the wind like flayed skin.

Wherever Marit Kraeck had gone she'd left no discernible trace. The battered old Dodge she was seen to
drive had vanished also. And now there was the child in
the hospital at Carthage and no one to visit her or take
crucial notice of her except Herkimer County Family
Services which would place her in a foster home in the
Carthage area.

And so the question was everywhere asked in the
spring of 1965 in upstate New York south and west of
the Adirondacks—*Where is the lost little girl Jedina
Kraeck?*

Mudwoman Fallen. Mudwoman Arisen. Mudwoman in the Days of Shock and Awe.

March 2003–April 2003

Readied! She was.

In her sleep, still alive.

In astonished silence she fell. So suddenly she'd missed a step. So suddenly she hadn't time to draw breath, to scream. Nor was there purpose in screaming—or in breathing—for there was no one in the vast darkened house to hear her.

On the stairs she fell. Not on the staircase at the front of the house but on the steep narrow tight-curving staircase at the rear of the house that had been the servants' staircase in long-ago days when a staff of servants had lived in Charters House.

Striking the side of her head on the rungs of the railing, and her mouth. Striking her right shoulder.

Something liquid and scalding splashed on her fingers, her exposed right forearm as she fell and continued to fall slip-sliding down the steps that were carpeted—but meagerly carpeted, with inches of exposed wood painted gray, ugly and unyielding—the side of her skull, the undersides of both elbows and the underside of her jaw striking these steps in rapid succession *one-two-three* and a sharp blow like a kick in her ribs and still she could not scream for the breath was struck from her though at last there came grunts, sobs of surprise, pain, humiliation—*Alone. Alone—like this.*

It was 1:06 A.M. of March 22, 2003. In the early days of the Iraqi invasion—the days of Shock and Awe.

And in the aftermath of Alexander Stirk's (attempted) suicide.

In her public appearances the University president spoke very carefully of course. She did not discuss "sensitive" University matters—(like Stirk)—and she did not speak openly of politics. Though she was always being questioned on these subjects, she did not declare herself publicly as strongly opposed to the President and his war. Since taking office she'd been cautioned. And she'd learned. Belatedly she'd learned: impulsiveness/impetuousness in a chief administrator is not a desirable trait. Rashness is not a desirable trait. To speak plainly, frankly—to speak one's heart—is only possible when one is a private figure, not the representative of an institution. And so her anger, alarm, despair at the bellicose idiocy of the government smoldered beneath her bright animated public words. And her fury at the Bush administration's cynical exploitation of a fear of "terrorist attacks" in the wake of 9/11—all that her Quaker parents had imbued in her, to abhor and to resist. And so if she alluded to *This terrible news, this latest crisis* it was strictly in private, among people she knew felt exactly as she did.

Or, more daringly, she might allude to *This new war! This death-knell for education* . . .

Maybe—maybe in her speech to the Chicago alumni organization earlier that day—she'd uttered such words. But not from the podium, only afterward, among individuals she knew to be fervent *anti-war*.

In the country, in these early days of the Iraqi invasion, division between *pro-war, anti-war* was fierce and irreconcilable.

As fierce and irreconcilable as *pro-life, pro-choice.*

About which the University president had better not speak openly, either.

And so in Chicago, as in Minneapolis—in Cleveland, in Columbus, in Milwaukee—in Seattle, in Portland— anywhere it was the University president's duty to address University alumni groups as she did frequently through the academic year on the subject "The University in the Twenty-first Century: Challenges and Opportunities" M. R. Neukirchen was passionate on issues involving the University and issues involving education; her manner was unfailingly upbeat, optimistic; of course she smiled often, if not continuously; her face ached, so many smiles!—as, at commencement when she shook hands with each graduating senior and with the families of each graduating senior, her hand ached and throbbed. *This is my role: to bring happiness to others. If I am strong enough!*

She was remembering now, with a tinge of dismay—self-rebuke—how her voice had quavered at the podium—though she'd continued smiling, and would not have seemed, to a neutral observer, to have lost any fraction of her composure. No one had asked a political question, all questions were about the University and one of these—she'd been prepared of course, she had known this might be imminent—had been asked point-blank about Alexander Stirk—"Is the University liable, d'you think?"

It was not a hostile question. It was not even a challenging question. It was a quite natural question from a friendly older man, a Chicago alum-donor who'd endowed a professorship in economics at the University and had been negotiating with the University director of strategic partnerships and planning to endow an entire program in computational economics.

"The University is not liable, we think."

M.R. spoke carefully. M.R. was not smiling now but utterly earnest, a sharp vertical line between her brows.

"Leonard Lockhardt—our chief counsel—thinks we are not. But of course—it's a terrible thing, a"—M.R. paused, fingers gripping the edges of the podium from beneath, invisible to her audience. There came a roaring in her ears as of a distant landslide—"a tragedy."

In the elegant dining room of the University Club with its high, ornamental ceiling and silk-wallpaper walls and crystal chandeliers (unlighted, for the sunshine falling from the sharp-blue sky above windswept Lake Michigan was so powerful, no artificial light was required) amid a tinkling of china cups, coffee spoons and a sound of china and cutlery being cleared deftly away by white-uniformed servants bred for such deftness—the syllables *tragedy* sounded strangely, like the syllables of an archaic gray-cobwebbed word.

Tragedy. Trag-ed-y.

" . . . no one could have anticipated."

Friendly-faced and yet affable, the gentleman spoke with just a hint of a steely edge. And his features that had seemed Midwest-generic like those of the older gentlemen of Norman Rockwell's folksy paintings acquired a sudden sharpness.

"Except it's in the damn newspapers. In the Goddamn media—'cyberspace.' And that's a space where they don't print retractions."

Light laughter spread across the gathering like ripples on a shallow and sequestered pond. M.R. was conscious of her unnatural grip on the edge of the podium and made an effort to relax her fingers one by one.

Discreetly then the subject was changed. Another luncheon guest raised his hand to proffer a question to M.R. in the way of a pitcher pitching underhanded to a disabled batter.

Always end on an upbeat note.

Education is the—(hope? instrument? promise?) of the future. Education is—the future.

And education at the University—the vanguard of the future.

It had been a highly successful visit to Chicago arranged by the alumni organization of greater Chicago and the University's alumni-liaison staff. In attendance were eighty-four University alums of widely divergent ages—the oldest, class of 1952, the youngest, class of 1998—of which more than two-thirds were established donors to the University. The occasion was luncheon at the University Club with "remarks" by President

Neukirchen and two associates—the University vice president for campus life, an energetic young woman with flame-colored hair, and the vice president for development, who exuded an air of brisk and capable authority, like an Ivy League scoutmaster. When M.R. returned to her seat at the head table with her arms folded tight across her quick-beating heart almost immediately she ceased to actively listen: her warm-flushed face continued to exude light, but it was a fading light.

I am so ashamed.

I am sick with shame.

No—I am triumphant. I will prevail.

It was so. Despite Alexander Stirk, yet the president of the University had prevailed. More or less.

The University was one of the great clipper ships of lore, the *Cutty Sark* of universities—a majestic artifact of a long-ago era, miraculously intact, invisibly empowered by engines to withstand storms at sea that would shatter lesser vessels.

On the schedule printed for her, M.R. could now cross out *Chicago.*

A downward arrow through the heart of *Chicago.*

Her assistant had booked her for a 3:40 P.M. plane out of Chicago. Of course, she'd lost an hour, and more than an hour with flight delays, returning to the East.

From Philadelphia airport to the "historic" president's house at the edge of the University campus, an hour and forty minutes by car.

Carlos was no longer M.R.'s personal driver: now, a younger, unfailingly cheerful black man named Evander. He was twenty-six years old and had come with his parents to the U.S. when he was a baby, from "D.R."—Dominican Republic.

M.R. was very fond of Evander who chattered at her like a six-foot shiny-black parrot that did not expect her to listen attentively, still less to reply. It was true, Evander called M.R. "ma'am"—occasionally, with touching awkwardness, "Mz. Neukit'chen"—but M.R. was relaxed with Evander in the driver's seat of the Lincoln Town Car for Evander had not worked for M.R.'s predecessor and so had no notions of what a University president might/might not do. And M.R. liked it that Evander wore his thick black hair in astonishing snakelike coils that stuck out from his head as if greased.

"My wonderful driver, with dreadlocks."

(Was this condescending? Was this racist?)

M.R. knew about Evander's young wife, his twin daughters Starr and Serena. She knew that Evander planned to study computer science at the Hunterdon County Community College in a few years.

If M.R. chose to carry her own bags, wheel her own lightweight suitcase along briskly through the airport, Evander observed her bemused and not, like prim Carlos, with disapproval. It had become something of a joke—long-limbed Evander in his dark driver's uniform pretending to have to trot to keep up with M.R. "Man, ma'am—you *fast*."

Rarely now, M.R. saw Carlos Lopes. He was semiretired, worked only part-time, the senior driver on the president's staff and the one entrusted to pick up VIP visitors at the airport and drive them about during their stays at the University. If Carlos was hurt by having been replaced by dreadlock-sporting Evander—M.R. had no reason to know.

Oh God! Don't let there be anything broken. . . .

And she was alone in the darkened house: she'd sent her housekeeper home early.

Of course, she hadn't wanted her very nice housekeeper/cook to prepare a meal for her when M.R. could so easily prepare a meal for herself, if she'd wished.

"A night alone!"—she'd felt almost giddy.

Returning from Chicago late, and after dark. For flying east out of daylight, you are flying into night. And how swiftly night comes on, like an eclipse.

As soon as she'd left Chicago—as soon as she'd left the University Club and her marvelous hosts—as soon as she'd slumped into the limousine in which she was driven to the airport, she'd felt exhausted. Now her smile could be shut off, like a high-wattage lightbulb. Now her manikin-posture could relax, like a sock puppet minus fingers. Crudely she thought—or, rather, the crude thought came to her—*How much money did we make today in Chicago? Might it be— millions?*

She'd connected with what-was-his-name—Ainscott. He'd liked her, she'd seen with relief—those frank blue eyes, hair trimmed short as a Marine's and it was said of Ainscott that the man was worth more than one hundred million dollars he'd made in—was it *junk bonds?—hedge funds?*—he'd graduated from the University in 1959—and if he'd been opposed to a woman for the University presidency, he'd been gentlemanly enough to support M. R. Neukirchen as soon as she'd taken office.

A flood of protest mail had come to the University alumni magazine, when M.R.'s name was first released to the media. And some of these letters were cruel, cutting, unapologetically sexist. M.R. had insisted upon seeing them—all of them—and M.R. had replied personally to each of the letters, by hand.

Her staff had been astonished. Never had any president of the University taken on such a task but M.R. was conscious—(was this M.R.'s vanity?)—that her presidency was significant in the history of the University and that it was her privilege to define herself to her detractors, whom she could not bear to on their own terms as *enemies.*

It was her Quaker instinct. Silence, stillness. At the core of the storm, stillness. To strike a blow even in defense of oneself is to provoke another blow, and yet another. The folly of war is that it can have no natural end except in the extinction of an entire people. She would be a Child of the Light, if she was worthy.

But returning from Chicago she'd made the error of not going immediately to bed. Or, at least to undress, to lie in bed and watch TV—(for M.R. did sometimes watch late-night TV—the parody-news programs that were her students' favorite programs, reruns of PBS documentaries, classic films, foreign films—she would watch for a while until her eyes glazed over and sleep came to her quick and lovely like a great lapping tongue). Instead, she'd gone to her desk, and to her computer—always there was a phalanx of e-mail messages for her to answer and now in the aftermath of Alexander Stirk. . . .

To her housekeeper she'd insisted she wasn't hungry. But nearing 1 A.M., she'd become ravenously hungry.

Since becoming University president, M.R. rarely ate an evening meal alone; yet more rarely was she able to retire to her upstairs apartment in Charters House by 9 P.M. She might have scheduled an engagement for that evening—for there were numerous obligations for the University president, awaiting her—but her assistant had told her sharply *No!*—the luncheon in Chicago was enough for that day.

They were concerned for her, she knew. Her staffers—her loyal supporters. There was a fierce protective loyalty among M. R. Neukirchen's assistants in Salvager Hall.

Poor M.R.! She's taking this so personally.

What d'you mean? She hasn't stumbled yet.

They were shielding her—were they? There must have been many telephone calls—e-mails to the Office of the President of the University—which M.R. would never receive. And the "media"—Internet, cyberspace—*cesspoolspace*—swirling with news of Alexander Stirk.

At 12:50 A.M. after a very long day there came M.R. in wool socks, jeans and a University sweatshirt descending the narrow circular staircase at the rear of the house, to which she'd become so accustomed after nine months that she could have navigated it in the dark. And in the high-ceilinged and cheerless kitchen she'd rummaged through cupboards to find a can of Campbell's chicken-lentil soup which she'd poured into a bowl, mixed with water and set in the microwave oven for four minutes. And in the massive refrigerator that smelled just slightly of rancid butter she located several hunks of cheese, expensive imported cheeses left over from a recent reception, and there was a quarter-loaf of just slightly stale French bread. And in another cupboard, a box of just slightly stale crackers. And there was a quart bottle of seltzer water, just slightly flat. These M.R. placed on a tray to carry upstairs to her bedroom on the second floor, while the soup was rotating in the microwave. She could not have said why she hadn't waited for the damned soup, maybe in fact— yes, probably—she'd forgotten the soup; her brain was always thrumming, like a machine that has been left on while its master has gone away, and so becomes overheated in the futility of mere effort; but it wasn't *here and now* of which M.R. was thinking but *there and then:* a stray memory of an evening with her (secret) lover years ago in Cambridge when he'd dropped in to see her—late—and they'd made love—more accurately, given the degree of energy, enthusiasm, and physical prowess Andre Litovik brought to such endeavors, he'd made love to M.R.—and afterward dazed with hunger they'd staggered about M.R.'s cramped little kitchen and Andre flung together a midnight meal—coarse scrambled eggs, pita bread—a bottle of red wine he'd brought with him for rarely did Andre Litovik venture into M. R. Neukirchen's little flat without bringing his favorite red wine with him. . . .

M.R. smiled, recalling. And Andre's way of saying good-bye that roused her from melancholy—*Hey. I'm only going away so I can come back.*

This was true. And then, it was less true.

M.R. had not quite realized how, as University president, she would be traveling quite so much. *Going away so I can come back.*

But there was so little for her to come back to— here. A temporary residence—if she were president of the University for ten years, still the residence would be temporary; even her private quarters, comfortably messy, were not *hers.*

At the end of her term as president, then. She would acquire a more permanent residence. She and Andre, perhaps.

For a moment she had to think—where had she been that day? Of course—Chicago. An early flight out of Philadelphia, and home in the early evening. The visit had "gone well" yet had left her so drained of energy, it seemed now to have occurred several days before, on the farther side of an abyss.

Her next alumni visit was Atlanta—she would fly out on Monday morning.

And then Gainesville, and Miami.

A tinge of alarm: Florida was the Stirks' home state.

Jacksonville, where Alexander's parents lived.

"Oh why didn't he—like me! I was his friend."

In the room that was M.R.'s bedroom she'd set down the tray on a table. There were piles of books on the table, papers and documents and her laptop computer. In transit the quart bottle of seltzer had toppled over, and was leaking all over the tray, and now onto the table, and the floor; clumsily M.R. soaked up the spillage with the single paper napkin she'd brought with her upstairs. Such random incidents of physical clumsiness had come to characterize M.R.'s life ever more frequently in recent years. Where as a gangling-tall adolescent she'd been a quite surprisingly well-coordinated athlete—basketball, volleyball, field hockey—now in her early forties she seemed always to be spilling things, or dropping things, or colliding with things—at a semi-formal dinner the previous year while reaching over the table to shake hands with another guest in her impulsive-friendly manner somehow M.R. had nearly set her hair afire by leaning too close to a lighted candle—what a flurry of excitement!—another guest had quickly slapped her hair between his hands, to put out the sparks; M.R.'s hair had actually been singed, and emitted a smell of scorch; it was so ridiculous and embarrassing an episode, M.R. had laughed; but others had been concerned for her—"It isn't funny really, you might have been badly burnt"—as for an overgrown child that has injured herself unwittingly.

This too would pass into legend, M.R. supposed. In those rarified quarters in which M. R. Neukirchen was known.

When she was alone M.R. retreated to this room. It wasn't a very good idea to eat meals here—she hadn't gotten around to bringing in the sort of table at which she might eat comfortably, or at least not awkwardly; for everything seemed *temporary* to her, here; and all that was *merely personal* seemed petty. In her zeal to appear—to be—selfless, M.R. took a sort of childish vanity in the fact—for yes, it was a fact—reflected in the eyes of her admiring staffers—that she not only didn't care much for her personal comfort, but she was also scarcely aware of her personal comfort.

Though M.R. resided in one of the most beautiful of "historic" private houses in all of New Jersey, she hadn't the slightest interest in eating in the massive dining room alone, or in the sepulchral kitchen; less frequently than she'd planned, she did invite close friends among the faculty to have dinner with her—an "early evening" as M.R. called it—meaning that her guests should leave at about 9:30 P.M.; if she'd had a more luxuriant imagination, and cared more for such things, she might light a fire in the pale-marble fireplace in the library, and eat there, if only from a tray; she might read while she ate; it was an old pleasure now nearly lost to her, to read while she ate; her (secret) lover was always reading while he ate, even when she'd been with him, sometimes; he'd claimed that he and his wife Erika rarely ate meals together any longer, and if they did, Erika usually switched on the TV; but when M.R. ate her hurried meals alone, she often ate, or tried to eat, while working at her computer, looking through papers, taking notes.

This terrible thing that had happened to Stirk. That Stirk had done to himself.

He would never recover. He was in a coma, paralyzed. The ugly term—"brain-dead."

He could not breathe for himself—a machine would breathe for him, *in perpetuity*. For his parents were devout Catholics, never would they direct Alexander Stirk's doctors to cease treatment.

Something to be grateful for, Leonard Lockhardt had said with a pained smile—"If he dies, that ratchets it up. From 'criminal negligence' to 'wrongful death.'"

Not good to think such thoughts! M.R. felt faint, from hunger, anxiety—"I should eat."

She'd left something behind—down in the kitchen—what was it?—yes, in the microwave—a bowl of soup.

Quickly descending the back staircase in her slippery wool socks, for she'd kicked off her tight shoes as soon as she'd arrived home, and put on these socks which were in fact hiking socks Andre had purchased for her from L.L. Bean in the days when they'd hiked together—not often, but a few times. And in the kitchen—oh! this depressing kitchen!—a place of pure utility like the kitchen of a hotel with a magnetized overhead rack of large, razor-sharp and mean-looking chef's knives and a massive Sub-Zero refrigerator and freezer and a steel stove with a dozen burners—space geared for the preparation and serving of large quantities of food—here there was the microwave, that had switched itself off. A smell of hot soup—hot chicken-lentil soup—made M.R. faint with hunger.

Except: there was something wrong—was there?

To her annoyance M.R. saw—at the far end of the hallway beyond the butler's pantry, that opened off the kitchen, the door to the basement appeared to be ajar, again.

One of the household staff must have left it ajar. M.R. went to shut it, firmly.

A faint odor of chill, damp—unmistakable.

M.R. had only once ventured into the basement of Charters House and had no wish to return. She'd descended into a nether region of dank smells, gritty concrete floors, melancholy exiled furniture draped in shroudlike sheets and at the rear of the laundry room a deep, ancient sink with corroded faucets like something in a slaughterhouse, that smelled, if but faintly, of its original function. A moment of horror had come over her—sympathy for the Charters House staff that, through centuries, as in an endless procession of Hades, had had to toil in such conditions, for niggardly wages.

In this vast old house there were rooms on the third floor—"guest rooms" as they were vaguely called—which M.R. had not yet seen, and had little interest in seeing.

As a child, perhaps—she'd have been curious. Prowling about in adult habitations: the Skedd house—"foster home"—where little Jewell had had a bed, or rather a cot, in a row of three cots for three little girls on the second floor.

But Jewell had never gone into the basement. "Cellar"—it was called.

She didn't think so. Some of the other children, the older children—maybe. But not Jewell.

Thorns in her throat, the child must have swallowed. Just the broken bits of thorns, that scratched the inside of her throat. And mud—black mud. She'd choked on mud. This would prevent Jewell from crying for help if ever she needed to cry for help so Jewell was not likely to venture into forbidden parts of the Skedd house voluntarily.

And here, in Charters House, M.R. had presented herself to the housekeeper Mildred as having no interest in venturing into the cellar—as if she hadn't already visited it; and Mildred had mildly objected that the basement wasn't such a bad place once you were used to it, laundry was done there, sorting clothes and ironing, apart from the furnaces and water heaters there were mostly stored things, old furniture, china, boxes and crates that hadn't been open in decades—or longer.

"Not for me—I hate basements!" M.R. said with a shudder.

So much of what M.R. uttered, in this phase of her life, had an exclamatory air, and was accompanied by a smile, as if when she wasn't M. R. Neukirchen speaking seriously and profoundly she was an actress in a musical comedy—one who evoked indulgent smiles, like Ethel Merman.

Mildred laughed, as if M.R. had indeed meant to be amusing.

"Well—there's some of us can't avoid basements, Mz. Neukirchen."

If this was a rebuke, it was a very tactful rebuke.

For M.R. was not living in a house but *residing in a residence*—the distinction should have been clear.

It was now, M.R. made a tactical error.

Distracted by such thoughts, M.R. made a near-fatal error.

Afterward she would be unable to comprehend why she'd behaved as irrationally as she had—why, removing the very hot soup bowl from the microwave, she hadn't simply placed it on another tray, to carry upstairs. For there were many trays at her disposal, in the kitchen. And it would not have seemed frivolous for M.R. to take a second tray—there was no one to observe!

Yet somehow—her hands now shaking, for she was ravenously hungry—M.R. chose to carry the very hot soup bowl upstairs without a tray, gripping it—she'd thought, firmly—not with the thicker pot holders, which had seemed to her too thick, and clumsy—but with the thinner pot holders; though almost immediately realizing that the bowl was too hot, the pot holders not thick enough to prevent her fingers from being burnt, yet—stubbornly—M.R. did not turn back—

(for she wasn't one to make a fuss! in any gathering you could count on her not to make a fuss like other children)—and ascending the stairs holding the very hot soup bowl between her (barely protected) hands she gave a little cry of dismay, self-disgust, surprise, pain as the bowl slipped from her grip—her fingers were being burnt, she'd had no choice but to let the bowl go—*Oh oh oh oh*—once the cry erupted from her throat like the cry of a small bird that is being crushed to death, that has but one instant to cry before it is crushed to death, M.R. could not speak—her throat seemed to shut—in astonished silence she missed a step, she fell, very hard she fell, clumsily and stupidly and in a paroxysm of sudden sharp pain—pains—for she'd struck her head a numbing blow against the rungs of the railing, and her mouth—the underside of her jaw and her soft opened mouth striking the steps— several steps in rapid succession—and now there came scalding liquid onto her fingers, her wrists—a sharp blow like a kick in her ribs and her suddenly useless legs twisted beneath her so that she continued to fall, to slip-slide down the steps, and to fall—helplessly, absurdly—sprawling on the staircase that twisted like a corkscrew unable to speak aloud, unable to call for help—desperately telling herself *I am all right, I am not—seriously injured.*

When you are struck down so suddenly—there is an air, almost a conviction, of disbelief.

That which *has happened, could not have happened.*

As the child had lain helpless in the mud. Mudgirl, tossed away into the mud like the naked and battered little mud-doll.

That which *has happened, could not have not-happened.*

In philosophy, there have arisen counter-worlds, to accommodate the imagined-but-unlived possibilities of this world.

She had written of these worlds. Her colleagues had written of these worlds. Not a one of them believed in these worlds that were "real" but not "actual"—or "actual" but not "real."

There are subjects that philosophy cannot approach. There are subjects so bared, so exposed—the antic beating heart, which no words can encase.

She lay without daring to move, sprawled on the steps. Trying to recover her breath. Her heart that was a kite blown high into the treetops, fluttering and thrashing. And her bones—her legs, arms—were any of her bones broken? Her head had been struck—hard—against the rungs of the railing.

"I didn't 'lose consciousness.' I'm sure I did not."

She was explaining to someone: a doctor. His face was young and unclear as if incompletely formed.

This supercilious stranger would pass judgment on her neurological condition, shining a pencil-thin beam of light into her defenseless eyes.

He would pass judgment on her spiritual condition, shining a pencil-thin beam of light into her eyes.

If the pupil of her eye did not respond—there was neurological damage.

Spiritual damage would be more difficult to detect.

She was certain she hadn't been *concussed*. That was crucial.

The boy—Stirk—had been *concussed*. That is, he'd lost consciousness from a blow or blows to the head. And that was crucial.

Of course you're all right, Meredith! Count to sixty and then—get up! As if nothing has happened.

So Agatha advised. Agatha who had little patience for self-pity, whining, and evil.

M.R. began counting. But soon the counting became confused with the more erratic beating of her heart and the blood-pulse in her ears that frightened her, for it meant that the pressure of her blood was high, a pounding against a thin membrane that might burst.

She must see a doctor, soon. She'd been so very busy, she had several times postponed her yearly examination.

The physical ignominy and discomfort of the pelvic exam—during which M.R. was determined to carry on a bright brisk stoic conversation with the very nice (woman) gynecologist.

No time! No time! No time for her meager *self.*

No one loves a weak, needy child. No one loves a weak, needy, homely child.

In the Skedds' house, she had known: who could possibly love Mudgirl? Only an Angel of the Lord could save her.

About her on the steps the soup was still dripping! What had smelled delicious in the kitchen now just smelled—badly.

She'd been so very hungry, now all hunger had vanished. Her body was livened with adrenaline like an electric current. So stupid of her to have grasped a bowl scalding-hot from the microwave, thinking to carry it all the way upstairs without adequate protection for her fingers—now, Mildred would discover the stained carpet.

Canny Mildred would deduce something of what had happened in the night. Without her staffs—household, administrative—M. R. Neukirchen was helpless as a child.

But here was a new surprise, a shock—blood.

Was she—bleeding?

In amazement M.R. touched her throbbing face and her fingers came away bloodied—why this was so unexpected, she could not have said. Yet it seemed to her a fresh rebuke, a threat to her precarious well-being. For it seemed that M.R. was bleeding not just from her mouth, where her teeth had pierced the soft inside of her lips, but from a cut in her forehead as well.

Head wounds can bleed copiously. Capillaries close beneath the surface of the (thin, vulnerable) skin. Oh, Mildred would see this evidence!

Stand! Get up! A towel to stop the bleeding—paper towels. No one will know.

M.R. was chiding herself for she was so very disgusted with herself.

She was chiding *him.*

He'd tried to hang himself—had he? Tried, and failed.

After the fraudulent claim of being assaulted, who would believe him?

Desperate measures propel desperate people. *She* was not desperate, she had never wished to harm herself.

Where others wish to harm us, we have little need to harm ourselves.

Maybe it was her sickness-with-guilt that had caused her after all to harm herself. For the boy was her responsibility, or had been. And she had failed.

"It can't be my fault. He is not my—fault."

Yet her voice wavered, uncertain.

It had to be so: the boy had parents, a father. It had come to light that the father had spoken harshly with the son in a series of telephone calls in the wake of the alleged assault. For, from the first, Mr. Stirk had not given much credence to his troubled son's most recent accusation of having been harassed, threatened and attacked.

Mr. Stirk had not been nearly so sympathetic as the University president, in fact.

Or so the rumor was. M.R. was loathe to listen to rumors. You found yourself wanting to believe the worst, to alleviate your responsibility.

Trembling with the strain of lifting her suddenly-heavy body graceless as a bag of peat moss yet M.R. managed to haul herself erect, panting. A premonition of age—old age—this terrible heaviness of being.

"Oh! Oh God."

She was whimpering with pain, and ignominy. She'd forgotten that her face was bleeding, here was fresh blood smeared on her fingers. Something about the basement door—another time, it had been left ajar. She could not think that it was left ajar to annoy her, this was an absurd reasoning.

Her sweatshirt, jeans, even her woolen socks smelled of soup—stank of soup. How nauseating, the odor!

Never again could she bear the smell of chicken-lentil soup, the very thought of it made her want to gag.

Strange that her face was still bleeding. More seriously than she'd wished to believe. Not the mouth-wound, on the inside of her (swelling) lip, but the head-wound. Oh God—if she needed stitches!

Andre would know what to do. Andre Litovik, master of emergencies.

Especially, Andre was skilled in dealing with emergencies which he himself provoked.

In daily life Andre prevaricated and drifted like a man in a canoe who has neglected to bring a paddle with him. In the accelerations of daily life, Andre became suddenly aroused, capable.

It was not the fault of daily life, Andre conceded, that it lacked sufficient coherence and predictability for one of Andre Litovik's scientific temperament, still he'd fled from the daily-ness of life into the chill of interstellar space.

He would console M.R: *Don't catastrophize!*

Many times he had consoled M.R. Often, he'd consoled her for the harm he had done her, always inadvertently.

He would point out an advantage of living alone: no one knows of the diminished and ludicrous individuals we are, when we are alone.

No one knows of our desperation. When we are alone.

From a distance, we all appear poised. Where our *appearance* has intervened in the face of our *being*.

Yet: if M.R. had been seriously injured, her skull fractured for instance, no one would have known until morning.

If she'd broken her neck. Her back. If—just maybe— she had *died*.

And then, what a commotion! What an alarm!

If she'd been seriously hurt and needed help she'd have had to crawl—to drag herself—back downstairs to the kitchen, to call 911.

In the kitchen, reaching for the phone that was on the wall. How many seconds of excruciating pain, reaching for the plastic phone on the wall. And if she'd managed to contact 911—an ambulance would have rushed up the drive of "historic" Charters House in a flurry of swirling red lights, siren alerting everyone within earshot—what shame!

She fell on the stairs? Neukirchen? Drunk?

No—worse.

Worse how?

She's losing it.

M.R. was standing, leaning heavily onto the railing that seemed to her now rather loose, wobbly. The bleeding from her forehead continued, she'd been wiping it on the sleeve of her University sweatshirt. Her ribs hurt, her right ankle was numb with pain, her head, her jaws, her mouth—blood beat frantically in her ears—her heartbeat was still rapid and arrhythmic—the kite thrashing in the wind, tangled in tree limbs. Yet she would retake control, like seizing a steering wheel that has begun to spin—*You have been spared this time. You will survive!*

At the foot of the spiral stairs, still gripping the railing M.R. took a deep—cautious—breath preparatory to making her way back into the kitchen where she would press paper towels against her bleeding face— she would try to wash at the sink—cold water might staunch the bleeding and countermand the swelling— for already her mouth felt as if she'd been bitten by an adder. Determined as Agatha insisting that if one *holds in the Light* one will prevail against confusion, ignorance, evil *Of course you are all right. You would not have been spared otherwise* even as a giddy black mist rose before her as if taunting her and in horror she saw the boy—as vividly as if he stood before her, as he'd stood before her leaning on his crutch in her office— the boy with the doomed eyes—the boy with the moist pink tongue aimed at M.R.'s heart.

Didn't what, President Neukirchen? Hit me?

He wasn't dead. Though he had tried to die.

A terrible death, he had tried to die.

Out of despair, shame—spite. Out of spite this wish to confound his enemies. And his own family, perhaps.

In the crazed week following his claim of being assaulted on the University campus by a gang of fellow students Alexander Stirk had been interviewed on cable news programs—the "Stirk case" had flashed about the Internet like something radioactive—each issue of the University newspaper had devoted a sizable portion of the front page to developments in the "Stirk case" with the barely restrained hysteria of a tabloid publication. The admission that Stirk had lied about having been harassed at his prep school several years before—an admission Stirk made to township police on the third day after the claim of the attack, for he'd had no alternative by this time—had been greeted with dismay by Stirk's supporters, and gratification by his detractors; police officers refused to discuss the case with the media yet it quickly became known that the police investigation had become an investigation largely of Stirk himself.

Abruptly then most of the conservative commentators who'd supported Alexander Stirk in the interests of excoriating the liberal University publicly repudiated him; his undergraduate friends in the YAF were quoted in the University newspaper as feeling "betrayed" by him and "disgusted" by him; his professors, among them Oliver Kroll, could not be reached for comment or could only say tersely that they were "reserving judgment" until the case was resolved.

Through this, stubbornly and defiantly Alexander Stirk continued to insist that he had been assaulted, exactly as he'd claimed; though it was true that he'd lied about the previous harassment, *he was not lying now.* It was a new claim of Stirk's, reported to M.R. by one of her assistants, that the male undergraduates who'd attacked him had known about the incident at Stirk's prep school, and had acted with the cynical assumption that they could do "anything" to him—"with impunity"—since he wouldn't be believed when he accused them.

Now anyone could hurt him. It was an observation M.R. had had herself.

In making the claim, however, Alexander Stirk was behaving recklessly—defiantly. Yet, you had almost to admire his brashness.

For the twenty-year-old understood, as M.R. in her early forties couldn't allow herself to even consider, that in this era of the Internet, in this season in which the use of deadly force against a quasi-"enemy" was presented to the credulous public as a media event titled, like the newest multi-million-dollar Hollywood blockbuster film, *Shock and Awe*—it didn't seem to matter much what had *truly happened* but what might be *believed to have happened* by a sizable number of people.

In polls, American citizens debated the merits of the exciting new war in Iraq, and the older, less-exciting war in Afghanistan. In polls, it seemed to be determined that the United States was fighting the terrorist forces—the very individuals—who'd brought about the catastrophe of 9/11. Whether this was *historical fact* was not so relevant, if the majority of American citizens believed it.

Stirk had lied to her—he'd looked her in the eye, and lied. And she'd wanted to believe. For it was a belief in her own powers of persuasion—a vindication of the light-within which was M.R.'s deepest self—in which she'd wanted to believe.

Alexander Stirk's on-campus case fell under the commingled jurisdiction of the dean of undergraduate students, the director of campus security and public safety, the director of counseling and psychological services, and the University's legal counsel. All of these parties had reported to M.R. their strong conviction that Alexander Stirk should withdraw from the University for an indeterminate amount of time pending the outcome of the investigation—his presence in Harrow Hall was a distraction to the other students, and a continual burden to the University, that was obliged to provide "security" for him when he ventured out of his room; he'd ceased attending classes; he didn't appear to have recovered from his injuries, but refused to seek any further medical treatment. Stirk, however, refused to "retreat"—refused to be "banished"—in interviews he spoke of remaining in "the very bastion of the enemy, to fight for justice."

After the embarrassment of their confrontation in M.R.'s office in Salvager Hall—(selected details of which had been spilled out into cyberspace like malignant spores)—M.R. knew to maintain a dignified reserve about the Stirk case. The University president was stoic, uncomplaining; even privately she refrained from commenting on it, still less publicly; she didn't need to be cautioned by the University's legal counsel to say nothing. Even to Leonard Lockhardt in the privacy of her office she was reticent, circumspect; even to Leonard who believed, as nearly everyone did now, that the assault was a hoax, and Stirk a shameless liar, M.R. said—"Yes, but we can't assume that we *know*. Even now. We must wait until the investigation is concluded."

This was on a Wednesday evening. Abruptly then the next morning it was revealed—by Alexander Stirk, in one of several interviews with the township police, that yes, he had "exaggerated" the attack, a little.

What had really happened, Stirk confessed, was that he'd been "verbally—maliciously—assaulted" by fellow students, many times during the past year but each time more "threateningly"—until, the other evening, when "homophobe enemies of the YAF" had cornered him on campus and said such things to him as "Die, fag!"—he'd run from them, and they'd laughed at him, and when he was alone "something snapped"—without knowing what he was doing Stirk began to strike his head against a wall, repeatedly—he'd injured himself as in their hearts his enemies had wanted to injure him. . . . With this admission, Stirk withdrew the charge he'd made to the police, but with this admission, Stirk had made himself vulnerable to arrest by the police for having filed a false criminal complaint; now, too, the University ruled that his case would be considered by the University disciplinary committee, and in the interim, he was being asked to leave campus—he was now "suspended." His parents flew up to meet with him, in preparation for bringing him back home to Jacksonville, Florida, for at last Stirk had agreed that he would vacate his room; he would leave the University; but after his parents met with him in Harrow Hall for several hours, and returned to a local inn for the night, Stirk tried to strangle himself in haste, and naïvely—he flung a nylon cord over a closet door, secured one end around the doorknob and fashioned a noose of the other end, but he'd miscalculated the length of the rope and the distance he was to fall with the noose tightening around his neck; once he'd kicked away a chair, he didn't fall heavily enough or far enough to break his neck, or even to strangle himself, for the tips of his toes had touched the floor, horribly; it was estimated that Stirk must have suffered excruciatingly for many minutes until he lost consciousness. On his CD player, Beethoven's stridently ecstatic "Ode to Joy" played repeatedly through the night.

By the time the boy was discovered early the next morning—his distraught parents had insisted that security officers remove the door to his room when he failed to open it for them—Stirk's brain had been so deprived of oxygen, and for so long, he'd suffered irreversible brain damage.

His final e-mail, sent to a vast contingent of recipients, consisted of just two terse lines:

VENGEANCE IS MINE SAITH THE LORD
JUSTICE WILL PREVAILL

Of course she was all right. *She* would persevere.

The boy—Stirk—was on life-support system at the University of Pennsylvania medical school hospital.

His condition could not change except to deteriorate by slow or quick degrees.

There would be a lawsuit—inevitably. The University had been forewarned.

It was days later, now—nearly two weeks. Since news of Stirk's attempted suicide had come to M.R., an early-morning call from the University director of security.

Tried to kill himself! Hang himself! And his parents had discovered him . . .

M.R. had been stunned to hear the news. How desperate Alexander Stirk must have been, beneath his bravado! And how he must have suffered.

And his parents, now. The suffering would not soon end.

Soon then, Leonard Lockhardt came to meet with M.R. in the privacy of the president's office. Already an onslaught of ringing phones, demands of the media for interviews, the president's staff under duress, grim-faced and uncertain. The University attorney appeared to have dressed in haste—and to have shaved in haste—stubble glittered on the underside of the long jaw. Lockhardt was trembling with indignation over the latest outrage committed by the "God-damned miserable boy"—the nightmare of "ugly publicity" that would follow—"To think he tried to hang himself in Harrow House! Nothing like this has ever happened in Harrow House."

John Harrow, for which the "historic" stone residence was named, had been a fellow patriot and trusted aide of General George Washington in the Revolutionary War. M.R. waited for Lockhardt to mention this fact—but instead, Lockhardt continued, incensed, "The University's worst scandal in more than two hundred years."

"It isn't a 'scandal,' Leonard—it's a tragedy."

"A tragedy for who? The boy? His parents? *Us?*"

Lockhardt spoke harshly. The patrician face was stiff with dislike—M.R. had to wonder if it was dislike of her which gentlemanly Lockhardt wasn't troubling any longer to disguise.

"This is the fault of Admissions! How did this disturbed, sick, conniving young person ever slip through! *We* should sue his prep school—they expunged that incident from their records. And his letters of recommendation—lies! I tried to warn you, Meredith—we should have done all we could to get rid of Stirk as soon as he confessed he'd made up his story to the police. We should have expelled him immediately before he did harm to himself or some innocent person—in fact, he could have attacked you, in this very room."

The Stirk case had exhausted Leonard Lockhardt, and had seemed to coarsen him. As he ranted M.R.

pressed her fingertips to her temples, hating to hear what the man was saying. He was right of course— Leonard Lockhardt was always right. What excellent legal advice, what common sense the attorney had provided, which M.R. had chosen to ignore—she wasn't sure why.

Why her motives, in the face of Stirk's insolence— disrespect.

Why her motives, when Stirk so clearly viewed her as an enemy.

Before leaving M.R.'s office, Lockhardt said, as if casually, but with that look of disdain, that he was thinking of retiring.

Not immediately, Lockhardt hastened to add. He wouldn't abandon the University until the Stirk case was resolved—that is, the lawsuit—but soon then afterward.

M.R. felt as if she'd been kicked—a kick to the belly that wasn't so painful as she might have expected.

"Retiring! It will be the end of an era."

If Lockhardt had expected M.R. to protest, he must have been disappointed. For M.R. spoke with an air of startled-smiling-stoic resignation—M.R. would not protest at all.

They shook hands in parting. It was customary for M.R. to shake hands with the University's chief counsel. But how chill the man's hand was this morning,

how lacking in strength! Usually, you had to steel yourself to shake hands with Leonard Lockhardt.

"You know that I care for you, Meredith—as a
person, I mean. And as an administrator—you've
had—you have—great promise. . . ."

Lockhardt's voice trailed off, he'd turned away even
as M.R.'s secretary was approaching her with an air of
urgency.

*A tragedy, disguised as a farce. And we are all players
in the farce.*

She'd made her way along the dim-lit back hallway
and into the chill utilitarian kitchen. Already she was
feeling better—stronger. In the kitchen she ran cold
water to wash her throbbing face. She rinsed her
bloodied mouth and with paper towels staunched the
bleeding from her forehead. She brought upstairs an
ice bag, to press against her alarmingly swollen mouth.

For a long time upstairs she showered in water as hot
as she could bear until she was satisfied she'd removed all
traces of—whatever it was—that had gotten into her hair
and in subsequent days she avoided mirrors for the face
reflected therein was a reproach and a rebuke to her sense
of herself that must be maintained in public at all costs.

Farce! But we must not let on that we know.

Several times she called the Stirk family—she tried to call them. On her presidential letterhead she wrote to the Stirks, a handwritten letter, which she didn't expect the Stirks to answer, as they did not. She understood that she was very likely defying Leonard Lockhardt by trying to contact these individuals who would sue her and the University for "criminal negligence" in the matter of their son's condition yet she felt almost desperate to contact them.

I am so sorry. Please accept my sympathy.

Did this constitute acknowledgment of "criminal liability"?—M.R. didn't dare to think.

It would be a matter of attorneys, exclusively. The University president need not be personally involved at all.

She'd been one of the hundred-odd recipients of course.

She'd thought it might be a personal message to M. R. Neukirchen but it was not.

Like a two-line poem, the boy's departing curse. An unrhyming couplet with the sting of an adder.

VENGEANCE IS MINE SAITH THE LORD
JUSTICE WILL PREVAILL

Was "prevaill" misspelled? She stared at the word, as it seemed to shift its meaning.

Mudgirl in "Foster Care."
Mudgirl Receives a Gift.

June 1965

"You are a very lucky girl, Jew-ell. Hope you know that!"

Where the Skedds lived at the edge of Carthage was a faraway place from the countryside where Momma had lived with her two little girls in hiding from Satan (as Momma had said). Never could Mudgirl have hoped to retrace those many miles in her memory nor could Mudgirl even recall the circuitous route that had brought her to this squat asphalt-sided house in a rubble-strewn field which was the *foster home of the Skedds.*

These were *Mr. and Mrs. Floyd Skedd.*

These were strangers of the kind Momma had cursed, and told her daughters they must not speak to, but Momma was not here now to see how Mudgirl disobeyed her.

Except Mudgirl could not speak at first. In the tight-shut throat was something like a thistle or a thorn and there was something like mud if mud could be sticky and clotty and no sound, no breath could penetrate it. No words could emerge from the child's throat or through the tight-shut mouth and tight-clenched little jaws.

Alone, Mudgirl would whisper this word that was strange to her—"Carr-th'ge."

Such meager syllables she uttered only when she believed no one could hear.

It was a word that was exciting to her, mysterious. For it was not a word that Momma would know. (She believed.) As "Skedd" was a new, strange name that Momma would not know.

And the name that was hers now—"Jewell." How surprised Momma would be!

In the way that, seeing a coin on the sidewalk, or a glittery little button that might be a coin, and nobody to claim it, you had the right to stoop down, and snatch it up in your fingers.

"Jew-elle"—that was, now, *her.*

In the hospital at Carthage where they had kept her for more days than she could count there came visitors—men, a woman—to ask her what was her name and many times she whispered *Jew-ell* before they comprehended. And so next they asked her where is your mother?—where is your sister Jedina?

These questions, the child could not answer. Or the child would not answer. Though many times she was asked. Where? Where? Did your mother take your sister away somewhere—where?

When your mother took you to the mudflats did she take your sister, too? Was your sister in the car with you then? Was there a man?

Often it was not clear if the child could comprehend these questions for the child's bruised eyelids were so heavy, she could barely keep awake for more than a few minutes soon after waking. Her skin was sallow and sickly as the underbelly of a mud-creature and her poor shaved head was pitiful to see, as fine dark hairs grew back amid a scribble of scratches, scabs, rashes and abrasions.

Her arms!—her poor arms!—stick-thin and discolored from numberless needles. For fluids came to her through tubes, dripping into her pallid veins.

The little skeleton pushed against the sallow skin like the wire insides of a doll crudely fashioned of papier-mâché.

Sharp little wrist-bones, ankle-bones, pelvis-bones, shoulder-bones.

Bruised and swollen little eyes in which the pupil was likely to be dilated.

The child's blood was drawn—many times. The child learned that to flinch or to resist the approaching needle was futile. The child was subjected to neurological tests, CAT scans. X-rays of the brain and spinal cord. There was no discernible reason that the child could not speak nor was her hearing impaired. She did not appear to be mentally retarded or autistic though she would have to relearn certain skills—"motor coordination"—walking, running—climbing stairs—that had faded from her brain like moisture evaporating in the sun.

After a while, the visitors ceased asking her where is your mother? where is your sister Jedina? It may have been that the original visitors ceased coming to the hospital and were replaced by others and the child could not distinguish between them for they were adults and interchangeable and they were strangers.

It was enough that not one of them—not one of the women—was Momma. Beyond that, the child had no real concern.

At this time, Mr. and Mrs. Skedd must have come to see *Jewell Kraeck*. For this would be explained to her later. Yet she did not remember them, really. Seeing that Mrs. Skedd was not Momma, and Mr. Skedd was not one of Momma's men-friends.

The nurses—the nice nurses!—who brought her food and coaxed her to eat—at first, just liquids—

hot soup, fruit juice—and then mashed food like baby food laced with sweetness—who bathed her battered and bruised little body, changed bedclothes and her soiled nightgowns—were careful never to ask her questions to make her clench and tremble. They did not ever ask her questions she could not answer. Brightly they spoke of *Jewell* and what a *good sweet girl* she was, and how she would be *well soon, and out of this place and in a new family where no one would hurt her.*

At the rear of the Skedds' property was a steep drainage ditch.

The Skedds' property was two acres of tall slovenly grasses, scrub trees and rusted hulks of abandoned vehicles and farm equipment the *foster children* were warned not to play in for they could injure themselves. The drainage ditch flooded in heavy rainstorms. In the shivery water windblown clouds were reflected like fleeting thoughts.

And beyond the ditch, a stretch of marshland where many birds gathered and of these birds the noisiest were crows.

Early morning you were wakened by shrill scratchy cries that entered your sleep like claws tearing into paper, or crinkly cloth.

The first morning waking in the new house—in her little bed which was a narrow cot with a flat, smelly mattress in a row of similar cots in the slant-ceiling room called the *girls' room*—before opening her eyes Jewell heard—the King of the Crows!

He had followed her here from the mudflats, to this faraway place amid strangers. He had not forgotten Mudgirl.

And so in the *foster home of the Skedds* she had reason to know, the King of the Crows would look after her if but at a distance.

At the Skedds' the child was shy in the presence of others.

The child was slow to speak and slow moving as if under a spell.

You would see that the child was listening to someone—something—in the distance beyond the house. You would see that the child often did not hear what was said to her from inches away.

"Jewell! Wake *up*."

Mrs. Skedd—"Livvie"—was determined to make a special effort with the little Kraeck girl. For Mrs. Skedd felt very sorry for poor Mudgirl and had vowed to County Services, she would protect the child from further harm. "You are a very lucky girl, Jewell," Mrs.

Skedd said often. "Very lucky to be found and rescued and brought to live *here*."

Mrs. Skedd was a good-natured woman except easily "frazzled"—as she acknowledged—for the Skedd household was a busy place, especially the Skedd kitchen was a busy place like a wasp-hive at the center of which Mrs. Skedd was obliged to raise her voice frequently. Mrs. Skedd's habitual expression was one of incredulity and exasperation as if, like a TV housewife, she was being tested and her Christian good nature stretched to the limit by the high-decibel noise of the household of four Skedd children—youngest seven, oldest fifteen—and a shifting number of *foster children*—youngest three or four, oldest eleven or twelve. And there was Mr. Skedd—"Floyd"—a burly man with oil-stained clothes—T-shirt, work-trousers—always in a rush, always tramping mud onto the God-damned linoleum floor that Livvie and the girls had just mopped—looking for the God-damned keys to the pickup, he'd dropped somewhere—flinging jackets down, kicking off running shoes and boots and barging into the refrigerator to eat whatever he could find by hand, and quickly; Mrs. Skedd had to shout at Mr. Skedd to make him listen to her, and even then Mr. Skedd paid the woman little heed—with a wink at whichever of the children was a witness, and a gat-toothed grin. Mrs. Skedd's throat was raw with shouting at Mr. Skedd and with shouting up the stairs at a stampede of feet overhead—for if you spoke in a "normal, nice" voice as Mrs. Skedd complained no one would pay the slightest attention.

In the midst of so much commotion, the younger girls—of whom Jewell was the youngest—cowered together in the kitchen. For in the interstices of the Skedds' shouts at one another there were moments of sudden calm, even tenderness—Mrs. Skedd liked to surprise her favorite girls with hot little kisses on the tops of their heads, fresh-baked gingerbread cookies, an invitation to ride with her in the pickup to the grocery store—"Just us. Not *them*."

Atop the refrigerator in the Skedds' kitchen was a red plastic radio which Mrs. Skedd kept on through the day turned up high—music, news, jingly advertisements. Momma too had had a radio—Momma had listened to religious programs predominantly—and so Jewell took comfort in Mrs. Skedd's radio for the radio voices were never rushed or confused or angry or mumbling—the radio voices were both female and male—clear and confident and sensible-seeming—so it was possible you could talk in that way, too.

"Jewell! What're you listening-at, so hard?"

Mrs. Skedd would recall how the little girl had a look—how to describe it—like someone much older than her age. An expression you don't see in a child's face of *listening, thinking.*

Mrs. Skedd liked it that, in her household, the little Mudgirl was making a recovery. To the neighbors, and to other foster-family people she knew, or anyone who'd listen—Mrs. Skedd was known to boast quietly what sounded like a fixed formula: "Broke-things not too bad-broke, we can fix. Floyd and me."

So it was little Jewell was learning to talk, and learning to eat—not quickly but by degrees. The color was coming back into her sallow face, and fine wavy hair was growing back on her head; she was learning to walk without lurching or scuttling—"like a little crab"; she was shy when the other, older children were present but relaxed and happy-seeming in the kitchen with Mrs. Skedd as "Momma's little helper"—happiest when Mrs. Skedd gave her small tasks to do that she could do, capably.

Scouring a heavy iron pan with steel-wool until her fingers stung. With wetted paper towels, wiping the Formica-topped counters that were always sticky.

Clearing out the old General Electric refrigerator that accumulated leftovers like proliferating mold, and a mix of smells—placing things in order on the shelves—tall bottles (milk, beer), dairy and smaller bottles, plastic containers of leftovers, fresh produce in twin drawers at the bottom. Setting the long table that seated as many as twelve people in a jumble of different sorts of chairs—helping to serve the meal that was brought directly from the stove in pots and frying pans—helping to clear the table—helping to wash dishes—carrying out garbage at the end of the day in a large colander to dump on Mrs. Skedd's "compost pile" in a field beyond the back door.

"Jewell! That's real nice."

Newspapers and magazines that came into the house, everything from throwaway flyers to Mr. Skedd's *True: The Man's Magazine* little Jewell examined with that expression of adult intensity—(could Mudgirl read? had she taught herself to read? so young?)—but if you called out, "Jewell! What the hell you reading so hard?" the child would back off as if she'd been caught doing something forbidden.

Once, Mrs. Skedd pulled a newspaper section out of Jewell's hand—it was the *Carthage Sun-Times*. On the front page was a photograph of a young Marine named Dewater Coldham, nineteen, of Keene, New York, who'd been killed "by enemy fire" in Vietnam. Seeing the frightened look in the child's eyes Mrs. Skedd quickly crumpled the paper saying, "Christ sake, girl, what's this to do with *us*?"

The child could not say. It did not seem that Jewell knew poor "Dewater Coldham" so far as Mrs. Skedd could determine, nor did Jewell seem to know what *Vietnam* might mean.

"Sure there's people in my family—some cousin, or two—that's over in Veet-nam—but there just ain't time to think about it, y'know?" Mrs. Skedd said, her voice rising with exasperation. "You get my age you learn there's more than enough evil in the God-damned world, that you have to deal with firsthand—you don't need to look out for any God-damned extra."

Such sudden vehemence, the child backed off like a frightened mouse and Mrs. Skedd made an involuntary movement as if to shove her, or to grab her, or touch her shoulder—Jewell cringed and shielded her head and now Mrs. Skedd was truly exasperated—"Christ! Nobody's going to fucking *hit you*—think I'm some crazy *mother of yours?*"

In utter silence—Mrs. Skedd would recall afterward, such silence did not seem normal—the child fled the kitchen, out of the house and somewhere into the field behind the house maybe to hide in one of the rusted cast-off vehicles or, though it was forbidden to the younger kids, the damn smelly drainage ditch beyond.

For she knew: the King of the Crows was watching over her.

Soon, the King of the Crows would come for her.

The Skedds—both Livvie and Floyd—were not hesitant to shout—scream—slap—punch—even kick and pummel if required to restore some semblance of order in the household. Especially at mealtimes when the fragile order of the house was most imperiled. For some of their *foster children* were near full-grown at age twelve and the only way to deal with them was *blunt force.*

Two of Floyd Skedd's brothers were prison guards up at Watertown.

Ask any prison guard he'll tell you—to keep peace it's *blunt force* that's required.

Except if it was getting serious, neither of the Skedds troubled to intervene when the children fought among themselves even when their own children were involved. The ten-year-old Skedd daughter Lizbeth was sulky and sullen and liked to pinch if you got in her way and in the crowded Skedd upstairs, seemed one or another of the younger children was always getting in someone's way. Mrs. Skedd might scream up the stairs till she was red-faced but suddenly then gave up, for what the hell—"You got to learn, you can't be a crybaby all your life."

It made her vexed as hell, but she couldn't be flying off the handle a dozen times a day, when older kids picked on younger, with no provocation. Out of meanness or idleness like the same older kids who would torment a frog, or a cat or dog. Like two girls—Ginny, who was eleven; Bobbie, who was twelve—would gang up on little Jewell calling her *Mudgirl! Mudgirl!* Like it was the funniest thing they'd ever heard.

At this, Mrs. Skedd did intervene if she was close by.

"Damn brats shut your mouths and keep them shut. Don't know what the God-damn hell you are talking about, fuckin brats."

It was so: Ginny and Bobbie didn't really know why Mudgirl was Mudgirl. Neither could have said where the strange, ugly name had come from.

In the Skedd household, nobody had last names except Floyd and Livvie. The children were just first names—Lizbeth, Ginny, Bobbie, Arlen, Mickey, Darren, Steve, Cheryl Ann and Jewell. And one of these—ten-year-old Darren—left a few weeks after Jewell arrived when some (male, middle-aged) relative arranged with the Beechum County Family Services to take Darren home with him to Nettle, Alaska.

Alaska! So far away, the road trip would require days, maybe weeks.

On the front porch of the Skedds' asphalt-sided house on Bear Mountain Road the entire family stood waving good-bye to Darren as uncle and nephew drove off in a minivan with Alaska plates. Jewell waved as she was instructed not sure why the others were so boisterous and cheery—for what did it mean really, to be *taken away to Alaska?*

The Skedds were feeling good about the uncle or whoever it was showing up, to "adopt" Darren.

"See? If you're God-damn good kids, good things will happen."

" 'Good things happen to good people.' That's a fact."

Whichever of the Skedds had uttered this cheery pronouncement, the other snorted in cheery derision.

"Fuck that's a *fact*. That's fuckin *hearsay*."

Sharp-eyed Mrs. Skedd observed that when the older children crept up behind Jewell to scare her by clapping their hands close beside her head, to make her jump, the little girl was learning to interpret their cruelty as just teasing, or as a joke—Jewell was learning the right response which was to giggle.

Not to run away in fright nor even to cringe and shield her head but just to giggle.

"See, sweetie-pie? Laugh, and the world laughs with you. Cry, and you cry alone."

Mrs. Skedd pronounced these words as if she'd just now invented them. So far as Jewell knew, Mrs. Skedd had.

Laugh you can laugh. Why cry if you can laugh.
Laugh, laugh! The God-damn face feels the same.

Though the Skedd house on Bear Mountain Road at the outskirts of Carthage was so faraway from Star Lake which was the last place they'd lived yet in the night sometimes there stood Momma at the foot of the cot staring at her so hard it was this that wakened Mudgirl from sleep. And the mouthing of her disgust. *In all that is done trust Him. You have not trusted Him.* Very still scarcely daring to breathe the child lay beneath the bedclothes until at last at dawn the crows in the marshland began their harsh jeering cries in ancient bemusement at the folly and futility of humankind. And Mudgirl listened for the King of the Crows amid the others. *These are sent by Satan* the mother said in raging disgust but the child kept her eyes shut and heard the mother's words less clearly as the morning light emerged. *You will be taken by Satan* the mother warned but the child lay cunning in stillness in relief that the mother did not seem to have the power to touch her as once she had had the power and now as the sun like a fiery eye slowly opened the only sound was the sound of crows in the marshland and in their midst louder than all the rest, shriller and more savage in triumph the King of the Crows.

One day in a faraway time which Mudgirl could have fathomed no more than Mudgirl could have fathomed any galaxy, any constellation in the night sky above the marshland she would confide in the Astronomer— *My life was saved by the King of the Crows. Don't laugh at me, I know that I am lucky. I am one of the lucky ones to be born and not to die after I was born.*

Out of the Skedds' kitchen one day she was summoned.

On the side stoop were Ginny and Bobbie yelling and laughing—

"Jew-ell! JEW-ELL!"

Jewell had not ever been summoned like this for any reason. Not ever her name shouted with such fervor.

And so she was in terror that (somehow) Momma had come for her after all.

Instead, in the driveway she saw a gangly-limbed young man in khaki jacket, work trousers and mud-splotched boots and a wool knit cap pulled low onto his forehead that was crisscrossed with lines like the forehead of an older man. A skimpy beard like thistles hid just part of his jaws.

Ginny and Bobbie leaned in the door pretending to be speaking in lowered voices—"There's a mountain-man out here! Hey Jewell—a mountain-man come to see you!"

You could not ever tell if these girls were serious, or teasing. Like Lizbeth too they had high wild laughs like screams and anything could set them off so they laughed like they were being tickled or killed. Jewell came to the door in deep embarrassment for the girls were so careless in their speech the man in the drive-way had to hear them. Then they went whistling and moaning in shameless hilarity—"In't he cute! Ohhhh man!"

Jewell had no choice but to step outside. A roaring came up in her ears like distant thunder.

"Here she is, mister! 'Jew-ell.' "

Giggling Bobbie pushed Jewell down the steps in the direction of the young man who was staring at Jewell, his soft-dark eyes snatching at her, as Jewell's snatched at him.

Did she know him? Did he know *her*?

The young man resembled a boy who has been made to grow up too fast—his skin was coarsened from sun, wind, cold and had a leathery look. He was slight-bodied with wiry arms and foreshortened legs and straggling hair to his shoulders. His facial features appeared just slightly mismatched but were not ugly, or alarming—his chin seemed to have melted away beneath the thistle-whiskers, and his mouth showed many small stained teeth like the teeth of a mink or a fox.

"Hi. H'lo . . ."

The straggle-haired young man and Jewell were of a similar shyness you could say like two creatures of the same litter though altogether different-looking and uncertain of each other. Though the rude girls on the door stoop snickered and snorted in explosive giggles neither the young man nor Jewell took notice.

"Guess you don't r-remember me. . . . I was the one who. . . ."

Staring at Jewell in a kind of startled wonder making an effort to smile with those stained little teeth. Saying his name which Jewell failed to hear in the way that children fail to hear adult-names as adult-faces too are likely to blend, blur, coalesce in a child's memory. And there was the roaring in Jewell's ears that drowned out all sound except the percussive and thrilling cries of crows on the far side of the drainage ditch.

"Guess you are 'Jew-ell'—I saw in the paper. . . ."

Sweating and tongue-tied the straggly-haired young man thrust at Jewell an object in a paper bag.

This ordinary brown-paper bag of the size that Mr. Skedd brought home his six-packs of beer in, or Mrs. Skedd brought home some small purchases from the store.

Unwitting Jewell took the paper bag from the young man. As soon as she accepted it the young man backed off relieved—"O.K. now. Take it easy."

Within minutes of arriving at the asphalt-sided house on Bear Mountain Road, the straggly-haired young man had departed.

He was driving a run-down pickup truck. Quickly he climbed back into the cab and backed out of the driveway and was gone up Bear Mountain Road before Jewell could remove what was inside the paper bag.

"What's it? A doll? Why'd the mountain-man give you a *doll*?"

"A *doll*? And Jew-ell's too damn dumb to say thank you."

Astonished Jewell stared at the doll. She had not ever had a doll—a nice doll—of her own. This was a blond doll of soft rubber colored to resemble flesh, just the size for a child to cradle in the crook of her arm.

It had a rosebud mouth and rosy circles on its cheeks and thick eyelashes framing wide-open plastic-blue eyes of the kind that shut when you lean the doll back to sleep.

Vividly Jewell recalled a naked rubber doll spinning arms and legs like a crazed wheel flying through the air then dropping into the marshy black muck.

The new doll was not naked but clothed in a pink satin party dress with lace collar, sequins and spangles. The new doll had not just painted-on ripply-rubber hair but soft silky pale-blond hair.

Ginny and Bobbie were curious, resentful. Plucking at the doll clutched in Jewell's hands.

"Why'd the mountain-man give *you* that? Why'd anybody give *you* a doll? Who's he s'posed to be—your daddy?"

"Mudgirl got a daddy! Mudgirl got a daddy!"

Jewell tried to run from the girls gripping the doll in both hands. She had not ever had a gift before except from the spiky-haired man and she had not ever really had a doll of her own before—the rubber doll tossed into the mud had not belonged to her but to her older sister, Jewell.

Mrs. Skedd had come outside, to see what the ruckus was.

"Jewell? What the hell? What's that? Who in hell gave you *that*?"

Mrs. Skedd snatched the doll from Jewell to examine. Weeks before when Jewell had come to live with her foster family they'd been given a box of secondhand clothing and a few toys from County Services, plus a few items from Goodwill, but Mrs. Skedd could see that this fancy blond doll hadn't come from any charity—it wasn't even slightly soiled, it looked *brand-new.*

Excitedly Ginny and Bobbie told Mrs. Skedd that a weird-looking *mountain-man* had parked in the driveway and asked for Jewell so he could give her something. "Why'n't you call me?" Mrs. Skedd asked, incensed. "I'm the adult on the premises."

All this while Mrs. Skedd was turning the doll in her hand, suspiciously. Jewell halfway expected her to sniff it. Jewell waited not daring to speak nor even to breathe until at last Mrs. Skedd handed the doll back to her with a faint wistful sneer—"Somebody who read about you in the paper, or saw you on TV. Somebody feels sorry for you and don't think we can provide enough, Floyd and me. Too bad the asshole didn't leave his name, maybe he's got other things he'd like to give away, too."

Mudwoman Makes a Promise. And Mudwoman Makes a Discovery.

April 2003

The sink! She had never seen any sink so—*sunken.*

It was a scallop-shaped hollow in the old worn faded-salmon marble counter. And the counter was far too high and too deep—to use the sink, so impracticably *sunken,* you had to stand on your toes, lean forward on your elbows and lift yourself, brace yourself, to bend above the sink, at a. broken-backed crouch; then you had to reach for the faucets which were antiquated and grotesquely large claw-shaped brass fixtures at least six inches apart so that, having managed to grip the left-hand faucet—(which emitted hot water)—you could not then very readily grip the right-hand faucet—(which emitted cold water)—for you needed the support of at least one arm/elbow in order to maintain your balance, and not slip back down from the counter.

"This God-damn sink."

It was Livvie Skedd's voice of utter contempt mixed with bemusement, incredulity.

There appeared to be no chair, no stool to drag into the high-ceilinged old bathroom, to kneel upon. Underfoot the floor was a duller salmon-marble dimmed with the grime of decades.

Was the hour day, or night? Dawn, or twilight? The single window was so narrow and its panes so opaque with dust no light was emitted nor did there appear to be a light in the bathroom, above the sink for instance, or recessed in the ceiling.

Yet there was light in the bathroom, of a kind. The pale-glowering light of a sunless day when a grudging sort of illumination seems to lift from all sides, sourceless.

"This God-damn *sink*."

Mrs. Skedd would have laughed at the "historic" marble sink in the oldest wing of Charters House, with her air of breathless snorting derision.

Though Mrs. Skedd would have been impressed, too—*Got to hand it to poor little Mudgirl come pretty God-damn far.*

At last, M.R. managed to turn the left-hand faucet on. She was panting, the effort had been considerable. Half-sprawled onto the marble countertop, her midriff aching from the strain. Hot water splashed into the deep-sunken sink but almost immediately it was scalding water, far too hot for her to use and so she had to grip the right-hand faucet to modulate the temperature which necessitated a good deal of strain as water— scalding-hot, splashing—continued to pour into the sink with maniacal abandon.

She was too short for the sink—was that the problem? Barefoot, straining to reach the faucets. Her legs were too short. The tendons in her knees ached with strain. And her hands trying to grip the claw-shaped faucets, too small.

From two floors below, at the foot of the front staircase there came the faint terrible words, that froze her heart:

"Ms. Neukirchen? Your guests are arriving. . . ."

One of the president's trusted staffers. One of the band of young women who adored M. R. Neukirchen even as they had begun to fear for her, and to fear her.

She'd asked them please to call her M.R. Why for God's sake could they not call her M.R.!

Of course, she knew—she was late. Somehow it had happened, though M.R. was never late, tonight she was late. In her own residence, late! For a social gathering she herself was hosting, she was late.

Nothing so terrible—so desperate!—as to be *late*.

To know that people are awaiting you—looking for you.

She could hear the doorbell ringing, downstairs. Horribly, she could hear it—ringing.

She could hear the door being opened. She could hear muffled greetings. Since M.R. wasn't yet present, very likely the dean of the faculty had taken up the role of host in her place.

When the president of the University was absent, other administrative officers would take her place. At this evening's dinner there was, in addition to the Dean of the Faculty, the University vice-provost in charge of research.

Both were prestigious administrative positions. Both were highly capable individuals, both men.

"God *damn*."

Mrs. Skedd's epithet halfway a curse, and a prayer for help.

Mudwoman could not go downstairs until she was ready to be seen. Mudwoman could not appear in public until she was *readied*.

So difficult to wash her face at this sink where she could barely reach the damned faucets!

A smell of drains lifted from the stained-porcelain toilet, and from the stained-porcelain claw-footed tub with its grimy urine-colored shower curtain. For some reason her private bathroom wasn't available and so she'd found her desperate way to the third floor of Charters House, up the spiral staircase at the rear to the airless upper floor of closed-off guest rooms, empty closets and alcoves where no one ventured for weeks, or months, at a time; where once, when Charters House had been a lived-in residence, in the days of University presidents with large families and numerous visiting relatives, these rooms had been in use.

Children had lived in Charters House, until recent times. Now, not even ghost-children trailed about the upper floors. Forlorn cries and calls were but the groans of antiquated plumbing, most distinct at night.

"God help me."

M.R. stared at her face in dismay. There appeared to be something wrong with the mirror above the sink— the glass was so old, it distorted all that was reflected therein, as if underwater. M.R.'s eyes were bloodshot, her lips appeared chafed, cracked. Above her right eyebrow was a prim little vertical wound that didn't appear to be entirely healed—red moisture gleamed at its edges. And the ugly bruise above the eyebrow had become unmoored, a lumpy little blood-sac that had been drifting down the right side of M.R.'s face for the past two weeks and was lodged now in her right cheek, below her eye.

Her face was still sore from the fall. Her shoulder, ribs, ankle and her skull at the right temple still throbbed with a reproachful pain.

"For once, help *me*."

In the rising steam her face had become luridly flushed. She managed to shut off the left-hand faucet and to turn the right-hand faucet on as far as she could—no hot water at all, only cold—so that she could lower her burning face into this water, to cool it.

However, the brass fixture was broken, that shut the drain. So as water splashed into the sink, which was an uncommonly large, low sink, water was draining out.

With the cunning of desperation M.R. fashioned a plug of tight-wadded tissues which she forced into the drain. So as water splashed into the sink it didn't drain out nearly so rapidly. Slowly then the deep sink filled with cold water until at last M.R. could lean over, and lower her face into it—what a relief!

She would be all right now, she believed. The lurid flush would fade from her face. And then with cosmetics, she would try to improve her appearance. All that was required was a few minutes.

Except downstairs, the voice lifted, polite, yet pleading:

"Ms. Neukirchen? Your guests are arriving. . . ."

Ms. Neukirchen! She was *Ms. Neukirchen!*

Faintly mocking the name seemed to her, and the title—*President.*

At the Skedds' long plank kitchen table that lurched and tilted at crowded mealtimes, an outburst of derisive merriment.

President Neukirchen! Who'n hell is Mudgirl kidding!

Blindly her fingers groped for the little jar of makeup on the sink counter. It was a putty-paste of a hue she'd thought would disguise her sallow skin and its deformities—*Honeyrose blush.*

Inexpertly, hurriedly, M.R. spread the putty-paste on her face. There was something so shameful in her desperation, she could not bring herself to observe the procedure closely, and could only hope that the makeup was more or less evenly spread, and would appear *natural.*

Her mother Agatha Neukirchen—this mother, the one of whom M.R. spoke easily and proudly to interviewers—the Quaker-mother, still living in Carthage, New York—had not ever used cosmetics of course. As her father Konrad Neukirchen had not troubled to shave, considering it a colossal waste of time, yet rarely trimmed his beard, that sprawled from his jaws like wires very oddly graying from the ends inward.

To the Quakers, what was unproven, insubstantial, false—was *notional.*

Far politer than the Skedds' *Bullshit!*

Where another might speak dogmatically, or say *I know this!* the Quaker would say, more provisionally, *I hope so.*

As a university president, M.R. was unusually soft-spoken, gracious. Never would she claim *I know this* but only—in a firm voice—*I hope so.*

Yet now, M.R. was not so clear-minded, or so hopeful. Her heart was beating in alarm as downstairs the voice lifted again, concerned:

"Ms. Neukirchen! Your guests . . ."

The president's staff would protect her. In fact, the president had two staffs—Charters House, Salvager Hall. There was not much exchange between the two staffs which were devoted to very different services for the president but increasingly, both were concerned with protecting the president from her own—possible—errors of judgment, mistakes.

She was late for the Conference dinner hosted at Charters House—but how late? Surely not more than ten minutes?

Frantically her fingers smeared makeup on her face, in upward swipes. The soft skin beneath her eyes had to be filled in, somehow—the bruises beneath her eyes made her appear cadaverous.

Or maybe it was just the light in the antiquated bathroom with its twelve-foot ceiling, low-wattage lightbulbs overhead. M.R. could not see her watch-face clearly.

Surely not more than—twenty minutes late?

Now came a deeper male voice—

"M.R.? Are you all right? Most of the Conference guests are here. . . ."

It was S___, her dean of faculty. M.R. had appointed S___ to his position, S___ had no right to speak sharply to her, when others might overhear.

And his voice unnervingly distinct, as if S___ had ascended the stairs to the first-floor landing.

Go away! Leave me alone! You have no right to come up here!

In the mirror, M.R.'s face did look distinctly improved. The blood-sac bruise in her cheek appeared to be hidden beneath makeup. And now—M.R. would pat loose powder on the makeup, with a powder puff made of some synthetic rubbery substance. Her fingers shook with—was it anticipation? Excitement?

Wanting to lean out the bathroom door and call down to S___ that she was on her way, she'd be downstairs within three minutes.

Wanting to call, for all to hear, in her cheery-confident M.R.-voice—"I'm fine! Thank you."

She would tell them—she would lie so very convincingly, as only a seasoned and trusted administrator might lie—that at the very last minute she'd had a "crucial" phone call—she'd been "unavoidably delayed."

She would apologize of course. M.R. always apologized when it seemed necessary. But she would not apologize profusely, like one who has good reason to apologize.

She would tell them she'd been delayed in such a way that no one, not even S——, who'd been M.R.'s friend, or friendly acquaintance, since she'd first come to the University, would feel that he might ask her what the "crucial" subject was, and if the emergency situation prevailed.

Her dinner guests would be sympathetic, of course, and respectful—though most of them were far more distinguished in their professions than M. R. Neukirchen was in hers—(that is, in academic philosophy)—yet not one of them could have been named president of this distinguished University, and not one of them would have been capable of doing M.R.'s work.

She was sure of this. Yes!

M.R. squinted at her watch-face, standing now at the window—still, she couldn't see the time. Drinks were scheduled for 6 P.M., dinner for 7 P.M.—she dreaded to think that the time was nearing 7 P.M. Surely—she wasn't more than twenty minutes late?

M.R. who was but partly clothed—in underwear, beneath a just-slightly-soiled flannel robe, and barefoot—would hurry back to her room, on the floor below. Her pale-gray light-cashmere suit from Bloomingdale's was laid out on the bed, just returned from the cleaners. She would wear a white silk shirt with it, with large pearl buttons, buttoned to the throat. And a pale-orange silk scarf, a gift from a colleague who'd bought it in Thailand—one of M.R.'s "trademark" silk scarves.

She had very nice leather shoes, with a low heel. Far more expensive shoes than M.R. would ever have bought for herself except in this role as President Neukirchen of whom a certain standard of dress, grooming, behavior was expected.

What a relief it would be, to be dressed! And her face *made up* to appear some semblance of normal.

Except—M.R.'s hair . . . She'd forgotten her hair, that was shapeless, limp, threaded with silver now at her hairline. . . . *Jesus! Like a God-damn haystack* Mrs. Skedd would sneer at her own reflection, running rough fingers through her carroty-colored hair.

Like Mrs. Skedd, M.R. would have to shrug and laugh.

"No time now. No time."

Hurriedly M.R. patted her hair down, tried to brush it, shape it, with her fingers. She'd meant to make an appointment to have her hair cut—styled—but hadn't had time, or had forgotten; as she'd forgotten, or canceled, appointments with her dentist, eye doctor, tax accountant. By brushing her hair back behind her ears, so that, seeing herself from the front, she saw relatively little hair, M.R. felt less obvious distress. However her hair looked would have to do.

President Neukirchen was not, frankly—*chic*. In some quarters, absence of *chic* suggested *sincerity*, *lack of vanity*.

Yet another time, maddeningly—just perceptibly closer:

"M.R.? Excuse me, but—"

God damn S___! Her dean of the faculty whom she'd appointed to his position of power—who surely talked behind M.R.'s back, complained of her—if but gently, fondly—had no right to take a single step on the stairs, to ascend to the president's private quarters.

M.R. stood at the (shut) door and spoke through it:

"I'm fine! I am fine! Thank you! I'm on the telephone, I have urgent business, I will be downstairs in five minutes!"

Not that S___ could hear her, two floors down.

Still M.R. called: "Just substitute for me! For five minutes for God's sake! Thank you! Thank you very much! *I am fine.*"

Except: S___'s voice so near, voices in the front hallway, doorbell ringing, late for her own social engagement—M.R. was feeling anxious, a little clutch—

twinge—of something curdled in her lower gut—a need to use the toilet, quickly.

"Oh God! Help me . . ."

In past weeks, she'd had some sort of intestinal flu, or diarrhea—not severe, and not chronic—but a flaring-up, a terrible clenching-pain sort of flaring-up in her lower bowel, in times of acute anxiety.

But—now? No worse time—than now.

Of the antiquated fixtures in the third-floor bathroom, none was older, less "modernized" than the toilet, which was positioned in an alcove of the room, out of sight of the sink; as if the very sight of the toilet, crude, oversized, dull-glaring-white, was likely to be distressing to genteel sensibilities. Yet M.R. had no choice but to hurry to the toilet, clutching her lower belly. Such pain! And so suddenly! The toilet was oversized like the sink, so that, trying to sit on it, M.R. could barely touch the floor with her toes; and how sticky damp the floor was, in the vicinity of the toilet. In the large rust-streaked tank attached to the toilet there was a perpetual melancholy trickling of water, like unacknowledged sorrow; the once-white porcelain toilet bowl was badly stained, no amount of scouring by any household staff could remove from it the feculent grime of decades. On this toilet seat, M.R. felt suddenly paralyzed; though needing badly to rid herself of the terrible scalding-hot diarrhea in her lower belly, she could not; nor could she urinate; her bladder ached, yet she could not urinate; a terrible pressure was building inside her, yet she could not release it for she feared a sudden pounding at the door—S___ having ascended the stairs not only to the (private) second floor, but to the (yet more private) third floor, now dared to knock on the bathroom door; or, more horrible still, grasp the doorknob and fling the door open, for there was no workable lock in this old door as, in the Skedd household, the children's bathroom door had no lock for—as the Skedds explained, numerous times—you couldn't risk having locks on the God-damn doors, some God-damn crazy kid would lock himself inside, or herself—Mr. Skedd would have to break the God-damn door down, that was the case.

Excitedly Mrs. Skedd spoke of this possibility—or maybe, it had already happened—a girl had barricaded herself inside the bathroom, slashed her wrists—what came next, Jewell never knew for Mr. Skedd interrupted his wife with a snarl: *Chrissake shut your mouth, woman. Nobody needs to know ancient history.*

On the ghastly toilet M.R. sat cringing, shivering. What her life had become was unfathomable to her yet she had no choice, this was the life she must live. Even as, from downstairs, in the front hall a virtual chorus of voices lifted:

"Ms. Neukirchen? It's almost 7 P.M., most of your guests have arrived . . ."

These were not mocking voices. She knew!

A tragedy, they were saying.

These grave-faced individuals. For of course their subject—the subject of their three-day Conference—was predicated upon the tragedy of others, precipitating the opportunity for intellectual speculation, ethical debate, the possibility of intervention.

" . . . beyond our most pessimistic predictions. And our demographics show it will worsen—unless we can intervene."

So it wasn't Alexander Stirk of whom they spoke.

In the high-ceilinged dining room of Charters House M.R. was seated at the head of the table, her back to the pantry door that swung open, and shut; open, and shut as servers brought food to the table to be presented to M.R.'s distinguished guests. M.R. smiled to think what Mrs. Skedd would say, Mudgirl waited upon like a queen! And Mudgirl's mother, who had filled her mouth with mud to silence all speech in her, forever.

M. R. Neukirchen at the head of the table. M. R. Neukirchen, president of the University.

Why was it happening, M.R. wondered, that, with passing weeks, ever more swiftly like a narrow stream rushing through a crack in rock, enlarging the crack, to rush more swiftly, these old—ancient— memories were rising in her, with the threat of drowning her?

Why, she wondered, wasn't she more frightened?

"Intervention isn't so easy. The U.S. must respect the rights of sovereign states. . . ."

" 'Sovereign states'! Liberia, Zimbabwe . . ."

" . . . remember Rwanda . . ."

" . . . Darfur will be next."

M.R. felt a small clutch of alarm: *Darfur?* She was moderately well informed on these other African states, but knew virtually nothing about *Darfur.*

She was moderately well informed in most subjects, or gave that impression. Like any successful administrator M.R. knew the questions to ask, to allow others to demonstrate their expertise.

What a relief, to be *here!* Downstairs, with her guests!

In her proper place at the head of the table. As if nothing were amiss or could possibly have been amiss, an hour before.

At the farther end of the table was S___, the dean of the faculty. S___ who'd cast glances of—concern? worry?—in M.R.'s direction, which M.R. seemed not to notice.

I am fine. I told you—I am fine! And now I am here, and I am the hostess.

M.R. hadn't been conspicuously late for her guests, who, as it turned out, had been directed into two rooms as they arrived—the larger of the living rooms, and the library—by the canny S___; the strategy being, M.R. supposed, a very clever one—guests in one room might plausibly assume that their hostess was in the other room, and not register that she was absent.

And then of course—M.R. had appeared in their midst—well before the hour scheduled for dinner.

Breathless and apologetic—"A telephone call! At first it seemed like a genuine emergency, but then—the situation is under control now, or nearly. . . ." Her gaze was direct and forceful, forthright.

They'd believed her of course—how could they not have believed M. R. Neukirchen.

Even S___ believed her. (She was sure!)

All that had happened to her upstairs, on the third floor, or almost happened—all that was rapidly fading now, like a bad dream exposed to the air.

This dinner! What a pleasure to be here, in the company of such distinguished individuals! Their earnest conversation eddied about her, avidly and sincerely she listened.

" . . . intervention isn't easy—of course. That's why bold steps are needed. Our current diplomacy . . ."

" . . . yes but there are religious principles at stake, as well. Not everyone wants to be 'saved' on our secular terms. . . ."

" 'Saved' from AIDS? Are you serious? Of course—sufferers want to be 'saved.' "

" . . . not always, and not in our secular terms."

" . . . not secular, *scientific.* There is a distinction."

As president of the University, M.R. was hosting a dinner at Charters House in conjunction with the University's annual Conference on Ethics and Economics—this year's theme was "First-World States and Third-World Relations"—with a special symposium on AIDS in Africa.

It was the third and final evening of the prestigious Conference that had been inaugurated in 1991 with a multi-million-dollar endowment from a University alum who'd had a distinguished career in the foreign service, as well as having inherited great wealth. Among the participants were the current chair of the National Committee on Bioethics, a Nobel Prize–winning economist with the World Bank, the executive director of the Rawling Institute for Advanced Study at the University of Chicago, and a (female) filmmaker who'd produced an award-winning documentary on the lives of girls and women in West Africa, which had been shown at the Conference.

Twenty-six guests and M. R. Neukirchen at the head of the long, elaborately set table and as the guests conversed animatedly—AIDS, famine, war, war atrocities—the responsibility of first-world nations— the responsibility of American universities to investigate moral, political, economic and medical issues—the wisdom/folly of the military intervention in Iraq, which had immediately unleashed an unexpected/inevitable insurgency against the American-led coalition forces— as in Afghanistan—and, oh!—the horrors of female circumcision in West Africa, of which the young woman filmmaker spoke in the most graphic and unsparing terms, even as (frozen-faced) servers brought plates of exquisitely prepared food to the table. Though M.R. listened with rapt attentiveness to the conversations nearest her yet with a part of her mind—again the image came to her, of a wild-rushing stream cutting through a rock facade—she found herself at another table altogether—the long plank table in the Skedds' kitchen amid a babble of voices—such a babble of voices!—in which Jewell's (small) voice was never heard—steeling her (small) body against being jostled, her (plastic, scummy) water-glass upset, bits of ketchup-drenched meat loaf on her plate slyly snatched from her by the gangling pubescent boy whose chair abutted hers; for always at mealtimes in the Skedd household there was what Mrs. Skedd called a *damn ruckus* precipitating flurries of pinches, slaps, shoves and profanities from both the Skedds that they might maintain some sort of (temporary) order; M.R. smiled to think of the sticky oilcloth covering on the plank table which it was her task to keep clean, between mealtimes; a task that was easy, with one of Mrs. Skedd's supply of gaily-colored kitchen sponges that darkened grimly with time; and the oilcloth covering in which, when she was feeling nervous, or anxious, she made faint marks with the prongs of her fork; as, in the years to come, in school classrooms she would contain the almost-uncontainable energy that thrummed through her body like electric currents by sitting very still, back straight and head straight and her eyes widened in utmost attentiveness and respect staring at the teacher at the front of the room—at the adult in the room—as at any adult in her presence—that the adult might sense the appeal *I am the one who listens, I am the one you can trust, I am the one who will excel.*

For it is the adults of the world who are the angels of the Lord.

For it is the adults of the world who will, if they wish, save you.

As the conversation swerved to the subject of female exploitation in Africa—the fact, as the filmmaker said passionately, that sex-relations are initiated by men almost universally in the African sub-continent, no matter if the man is AIDS-infected and his condition known, and no matter if the "sex-partner" is a child— (and suddenly it seemed an awkward fact, at M.R.'s dinner table there were only seven women amid the twenty-six guests, and four of these the spouses of distinguished men)—M.R. found herself thinking of the second floor of the Skedds' house where the girls slept in their cramped and often smelly dormer room, which was at least less cramped and less smelly than the boys' dormer room on the other side of the house; thinking of certain things the "big boys" did when no adult was near, still more the things the "big boys" said which were swear words and obscenities not to be repeated by any of the girls, at least not in the presence of adults; for there is the *child-world,* and there is the *adult-world,* which must be navigated with the utmost care. *And what was done to Jewell—was anything "done to" Jewell? Set beside the mudflat, no subsequent outrage could much matter.*

Infant mortality, AIDS-infected infants, infanticide—"Especially the killing of female infants no one wants, tossed away like trash into the underbrush"—

and M.R. seated at the head of the long, elaborately set candlelit table that seemed, with its large swath of antique Chinese carpeting beneath, to float upon a dark and unfathomable sea; thinking with a curious sort of tenderness of the doll—not the tossed-away rubber doll, ugly, naked, and very dirty but the other—the gift-doll—the pretty doll with the pale-blond hair, in the satin party dress—given to her by the "mountain-man" who was her friend. For there was the unspoken bond between them. *He is the one who pulled Mudgirl from the mud seeing that Mudgirl was not a rubber doll or any trash tossed into the mud—he is the one who loves Mudgirl.* Yet somehow, in her shyness Jewell could not acknowledge him, even as she could not stammer *Thank you for this gift* let alone *Thank you for saving my life.*

The doll! Jewell had loved her gift-doll! Even as she'd known that no love for the blond doll could keep the blond doll from being snatched from her by one of the older girls—Bobbie, or Ginny—or maybe it had been mean-hearted Lizbeth jealous of Mrs. Skedd fussing over Mudgirl when Mrs. Skedd had better have been fussing over *her.*

The mountain-man with the skimpy beard and beautiful dark-damp eyes M.R. could see so vividly, at the dining-room table in Charters House leaving her

weak with desire, yearning—all that she'd lost, that
had been taken from her; as the blond doll she had not
dared name, knowing instinctively that she had better
not name it, was stolen from her within a week, and
she'd never seen it again; whether one of the girls had
taken it, or one of the boys, she'd never known; out of
pure spite it must have been taken, since she'd never
glimpsed anyone playing with it. Her child-heart had
beat hard in hurt and resentment that Mrs. Skedd
hadn't seemed to care much that Jewell's doll had been
taken from her, finding Jewell in tears and saying,
shrugging, *Hell kid—easy come, easy go.*

This was a favored remark of both the Skedds. And
of their Carthage neighbors. Growing up, M.R. had
heard it often. *Easy come, easy go.*

What is easily acquired is easily lost.

What is easily acquired you deserve to lose.

"Ms. Neukirchen? Shall I take your plate away?"

Plates were being cleared away. M.R. stared down at
her plate—Chilean sea bass, barely touched—startled
that she was *here* and not *there.*

"Ms. Neukirchen—?"

The server—a sweet-faced Hispanic girl whose
name M.R. seemed not to recall—regarded M.R. with
concerned eyes. (Was it beginning to be known, among
the Charters House staff, that M.R. wasn't eating
much, lately? And wasn't taking time to talk with

them much, lately? When she'd been so very friendly, when she'd first come to live in Charters House, the staff had all adored her.)

"Yes. Please. Thank you."

Here was the irony: all that M.R. had accomplished, all that the world perceived as her achievements, had not been easily acquired. She had worked, worked. She had worked fiercely, single-mindedly, with an idealism born of desperation. Yet, it could be taken from her so easily—as if she hadn't worked, had not earned her position, at all.

"There is American poverty, too—and not just economic. A poverty of the spirit . . ."

So quietly M.R. spoke, amid the buzz and hum of talk at the table, few heard.

One of the stronger personalities at the table was the economist/philosopher E—— from Cambridge, currently a visiting professor at the University, whose (controversial) specialty was the "ethics" of killing; that afternoon, M.R. had rearranged several meetings so that she could attend a panel E—— had chaired— "The Ethics of Killing: Military Combat, Euthanasia, Abortion." Remarks E—— had made on the panel had offended K——, the young woman filmmaker, and now E—— and K—— were energetically discussing the distinction between "killing" and "abortion" which the filmmaker believed to be crucial and considerable while the economist/philosopher believed it to be "essentially a matter of vocabulary."

Around the table, other conversations subsided. For E____ was as strong-willed as K___, and K___ would not defer to E____. There followed now a vigorous general discussion of the specific/legal meanings of *fetus—infant—infanticide.* This would seem to be the sole issue about which there didn't appear to be near-unanimous agreement among the conferees, who were, on the whole, political liberals.

At what point does a *fetus* become a *human being;* does a fetus have *legal status?*

Such avid discussions had become, in contemporary America, the equivalent of the medieval Thomist quarrels about angels dancing on the "heads of pins"— except more emotion was involved.

In her head like a beating pulse M.R. heard the mocking rhyme in an insolently familiar boy's voice—

Free choice is a lie
Nobody's baby wants to die
FREE CHOICE IS A LIE
NOBODY'S BABY WANTS TO DIE

No one of the conferees had asked about, spoken of, nor even alluded to the *Stirk case,* that M.R. knew.

Very likely, in their highly specialized worlds, this sort of news—verging upon the tabloid, though reported zealously in the *New York Times*—did not qualify as significant. For that, M.R. was grateful!

Of course, M.R. had inherited from the previous president several drawn-out lawsuits against the University, on contractual/tenure issues, which were not of vital concern to M.R., and did not involve her personally; unlike the *Stirk case*, these were of little interest to the media.

Some of the University faculty had been interviewed on the subject—this was unavoidable. High-profile conservatives like Oliver Kroll and G. Leddy Heidemann who were often on cable news. M.R. had been relieved to read in the *New York Times* that Oliver Kroll had said that the University had behaved responsibly, in fact "admirably"; in the same article, Heidemann had said that the University with its "liberal bigotry" had behaved irresponsibly, allowing an "emotionally disturbed" young person to attempt suicide.

If only Heidemann would depart the University for another, more conservative institution! Or, if only the University could fire him.

How painful it was, to think of Alexander Stirk!—a subject of great distress to M.R.—for Stirk was said to be in an "unvarying" comatose state, neither alive nor dead on a life-support machine in Philadelphia.

The University was being sued by the Stirk family. Mr. Stirk had engaged a very expensive high-profile litigator to argue his charge of "criminal negligence" against the University and several administrators including the president Neukirchen. (M.R. thought it a blessing, Alexander Stirk hadn't singled her out as a particular enemy in his frantic blogs.) It would be months before the lawsuits erupted into public consciousness and during this interregnum M.R. was advised by the University's attorneys not only not to speak of it but not to think of it—for there was virtually nothing she could do, in any case.

Except, of course, in weak moments, she found herself thinking of Stirk. And when not consciously thinking of the comatose boy, yet she was thinking of him.

But I am not guilty—how am I guilty? Why am I guilty?

Stirk had hated her. Stirk had stuck his tongue out at *her*.

Yet: she could see his eyes. The woundedness in those eyes. The yearning in those eyes. Beautiful thick-lashed eyes glistening with hurt, fury. M.R. had failed Stirk, somehow. M.R. had failed to convince him to trust her.

Failed to convince him, to love her.

Suttis Coldham: that was the name.

He had looked at Jewell with eyes of—love? Such tenderness, in the whiskery mountain-man! Suttis Coldham who would love her to no purpose, in the way of the most pure and ineffable love—whom M.R. had rejected.

Would Coldham know her now? Would he recognize her—now?

A trickle on M.R.'s forehead—something coolly liquid, though it was blood. Unobtrusively M.R. took from her sleeve a folded tissue, to quickly dab against the cut. No one saw—she was sure.

By now, M.R.'s face should have healed. It was at least two weeks since she'd fallen so idiotically on the back stairs, and injured herself. (And no one knew. That was the sole consolation.) Yet still the ugly blood-sac bruise throbbed in her cheek, if she touched it; she was confident that with makeup she'd disguised the bruise; with makeup, her face was restored to some semblance of conventional attractiveness.

Without lipstick, M.R.'s mouth was pale, and doughy. Her eyebrows were heavy, brooding. She'd seen—(she'd thought she had seen)—quizzical glances in her direction, that evening. Her assistant Audrey, and another young woman-staffer named Felice. And S___.

If these individuals saw something amiss in M.R.'s face they did not dare speak of it.

For in recent weeks you could not speak lightly to the University president. Where once M.R. had been quick to laugh, in the interstices of her intense and protracted administrative work at Salvager Hall, now she was likely to be distracted, somber. She was likely to be impatient.

More distressing, the woman who'd once astonished her staff with her quite remarkable memory was beginning to forget or to muddle names.

Even swaggering Evander with his dreadlocked hair and his thrilling high-pitched laugh did not invariably capture the president's attention as he once had.

You could see the strain, in M.R.'s face. And how awkwardly—inexpertly—she'd applied makeup to her face, as a child might have done: uneven layers of beige foundation covered with loose powder.

If I can get through this evening. Just this.

Laugh, laugh! The God-damn face feels the same.

"What do you think, President Neukirchen? What's the consensus at this university?"

The question was put to her by a genial visitor from the University of Toronto whom M.R. knew only through his work in political theory; her thoughts had been so adrift, and so morbidly fascinating, she had no idea what the subject was, though reasoning that it had surely moved on from whatever it had been a few minutes previously. With a disarming smile, and not the slightest hint that she'd been thinking of other, far other things at the president's own dinner table, M.R. said, " 'Consensus'? Here? I wouldn't presume to say."

M.R. should have been embarrassed to realize, a moment later, that the Canadian political scientist had been asking about the Iraqi War—what sort of "public debate" had it stirred in the University community.

"And 'Operation Enduring Freedom'—your quaintly named military action in Afghanistan."

Quickly this subject was taken up, like a ball tossed into the air—everyone leapt for it, eager to speak. Of all the individuals at the table only one—or two—might have favored the wars, or some aspect of the wars, but remained silent in the face of others' vehemence.

M.R. said yes, they'd had several public debates on the subject. The largest had been attended by a standing-room-only crowd in a lecture hall seating eight hundred people, many from the community.

As soon as M.R. uttered these words—which seemed to her entirely reasonable, admirable words— she heard them as in an echo chamber, boastful, vain, and absurd; and Mrs. Skedd's jeering aside *Don't we think well of ourselves! Hot shit eh?*

From this subject, conversation moved to "bellicosity"—"irrationality." For without the irrational, there can't be the bellicose; bellicosity *was* irrationality. M.R. was moved to quote Nietzsche, as very likely she'd done often lately, since the start of the ill-advised Iraqi War—" 'Madness is rare in individuals, in nations—commonplace.' "

One of the guests objected, cleverly: "Except—madness in individuals isn't so rare, really. Individuals en masse are nations."

"Yes, but—there is certainly a 'crowd mentality.' A 'crowd hysteria.' A crowd is something more, and something less, than the sum of its individuals."

"It's sanity in individuals, as in nations, that is rare."

Everyone laughed. This was witty, and very likely true. M.R. thought, how good it is we can laugh together, secure in the knowledge that we are all sane.

For a while then, suicide bombings were discussed: 9/11, and after.

Then, suicide itself: the "pure, unmitigated and unpoliticized act."

Coolly it was debated: the ethical status of "self-murder" in its relationship to "murder"; how was it possible that such radically different values accrue to each?

Out of nowhere this disturbing subject seemed to have sprung. M.R. felt some resentment, it seemed so coolly—impersonally—debated.

The economist/philosopher from Cambridge said that suicide is volitional while murder, for the victim, is never volitional—"It isn't a helpful term, 'self-murder.'"

"Certainly it's a helpful term. Suicide *is* 'self-murder.'"

"But what *is* 'suicide'? There are degrees of volition—there are degrees of action. Suicide isn't always accomplished in a single act, but possibly in a series—a succession—over a period of time. . . ."

Like a volleyball game, this brisk discussion. The participants were so articulate, their opinions so glibly tossed into the air—you would not guess what it was, in the most literal sense, they were speaking.

"It's often been observed that very few people commit suicide in a state of civil unrest. Misery keeps us alive, if it's collective. We are engaged in a drama, and we want to see how the drama ends."

"Yes! In the Nazi death-camps, for instance. Individuals who'd been otherwise 'suicidal'—the most famous example is Primo Levi—are determined to keep alive."

M.R. listened, subtly repelled. How very like a game it was—words batted about. Did her guests know how close to the bone their remarks were right now, in this university community? She tried to speak calmly—of course, she had to be fair-minded—even as she was making sharp indentations in the linen tablecloth with the prong of her fork, and staring down at the table.

"The suicide thinks that he's in control—exercising 'volition.' But as soon as he acts, he has lost his 'volition.' He becomes matter—he becomes a body. And if he doesn't succeed in dying . . ."

M.R. was aware of her guests looking at her, surprised at her sudden emotion.

For M.R.'s public persona was such, her voice rarely lifted.

Rarely did she reveal—betray—what she might be feeling.

She didn't prevail. She would not continue. She was grateful that the subject was taken from her.

For nothing seemed to her more horrible than Alexander Stirk's fate. To be neither dead nor alive, only just *existing*.

In the mudflat, just *existing*.

Mud in eyes, nose. Mud in mouth so all speech is lost.

How many sufferers in the world—tossed away like trash, like living garbage. And so many females, mere *chattel*.

The wonder of her life, of which she dared not speak to anyone, was that the angel of the Lord had come for her, after all.

And in the hospital they had not let her die. Desperately she'd clutched at what she could grasp—*If I am Jewell, I will be older. I will be stronger.* For the smaller sister Jedina had been the one thrown away like trash.

There had been no birth certificates for either of the Kraeck girls. As if they had not ever been born, really.

M.R. thought *We must give birth to ourselves! I am strong enough.*

It was a fact, M.R. was strong enough. M.R. was suffused with pride, that she was strong enough. Saying, impulsively, as dessert plates were being cleared, and the subject of the oppression of women and girls in Africa was being taken up again, that she would like to extend to the filmmaker K___ and her associates—and to other filmmakers—and writers—who'd explored this subject—an invitation to a conference at the University on this subject, which might be scheduled for spring 2004.

"Will you come back? Better yet, will you chair the conference?"

The filmmaker—a handsome blunt-faced young woman with toffee-colored skin, densely curly hair trimmed to a half-inch on her exquisitely sculpted head—stared at M.R. with a startled smile—for this invitation from the president of the prestigious University, so spontaneously proffered, was certainly flattering, and unexpected. With a stammer of surprise she said yes of course—"What a wonderful idea!"

And M.R. said, "The University can fund an ambitious conference—we can pay generous fees. You wouldn't be expected to volunteer your time. In fact, you might consider coming here as a fellow of the Humanities—or maybe, in the Arts. . . . We can work out the details."

How boldly M.R. was speaking, as if she and the young woman filmmaker K—— were alone together in a private meeting. The other guests looked on not knowing what to think.

Pointedly, M.R. didn't cast a glance to the farther end of the table, where S——, the dean of the faculty, must have been listening to this exchange with surprised disapproval. How irregular this was! How awkward! M.R. wasn't behaving like a seasoned administrator, who had no right to make so impulsive and unilateral a decision, that would involve, if it were executed, many others at the University. With girlish enthusiasm she asked if K—— had a card—"Or—leave me your name and e-mail address, and we can write to each other."

"Yes. Of course . . ."

"In these matters—of ethics, 'policy'—it's most effective if there are striking visual images, I think. Documentary films. To change people's minds, you have to touch their emotions. Only the arts have that capacity—to touch emotions."

As the young woman removed a small notebook from a pocket, to write on, M.R. said, expansively, seeing how everyone was looking at her expectantly, "Please—I hope you will all come back to this conference! It can be a sort of continuation of our meeting this year. And if there aren't sufficient funds, somehow—which certainly there should be—I could provide it myself—funds for the conference, I mean—out of my salary. It's a needlessly high salary for a single woman, I never spend more than a fraction of it. . . ."

M.R. was speaking rapidly, almost gaily. Her guests were gazing at her with quizzical expressions while her University colleagues, who'd known her for years, were openly staring, speechless.

At last—dinner was over!

At last—M.R. could escape from her position at the head of the table, past whom servers moved more or less continuously through the lengthy meal, while a few yards behind M.R. the pantry door swung to, and fro; to, and fro; in a way that made her heartbeat accelerate.

M.R. rose to her feet. She'd drained her wineglass on a near-empty stomach and the wine had gone to her head but the sensation was a good one, a relief after so much strain.

Now, a discreet exodus of guests from Charters House. Some were clearly eager to leave—for the day had begun with breakfast at the faculty club, twelve hours before; others gathered around M.R., in the front hall, as if reluctant to depart, thanking her for the evening and shaking her hand. The genial visitor from Toronto observed that Charters House was a beautiful residence—"But it must be like living in a museum—yes?"

Yes. But no. M.R. considered how to reply.

"But of course I don't *live* . . . I mean, I don't exactly 'live' in these public rooms, but upstairs. There are rooms upstairs set aside for the president's private use."

How pretentious, to speak of herself as *the president*. Yet it seemed inaccurate to say *set aside for my use*.

The dean of the faculty, who knew much of the history of Charters House, said, as if in M.R.'s defense, that previous presidents had often spent time elsewhere, unofficially; when M.R.'s predecessor was president, he and his wife spent most of the time in their private house a mile away. "Leander's wife never moved in, really. But she assisted him in every ceremonial occasion in Charters House of course. He couldn't have managed without her."

"Couldn't he!"

M.R. laughed. This seemed to her very funny. And it was thrilling to her, it filled her with an illicit sort of elation, that she had gotten through the evening so successfully; she had taken up, with her old effortlessness, this skilled imposture; Mudwoman upstairs on the ghastly toilet, tears staining her battered face, and M. R. Neukirchen downstairs, in her proper place.

"My predecessors—dating back to the founding of the University, in the eighteenth century—had a distinct advantage which, I'm afraid, I don't have."

"What's that? Being male?"

"No. Having a wife."

There was genial laughter. M.R.'s guests were departing. A flurry of final farewells, and the door was shut.

Abruptly then M.R. was very tired.

Abruptly then M.R. could not bear another moment of the strain, of this imposture.

Saying, to whoever among her household staff was within earshot:

"Thank you! You've all been very—wonderful. And everything went very—very"—searching for a word, as one might search a pocket for a coin, and a very small coin—"well."

She hadn't the energy to go into the kitchen and thank them there. The cook, the servers—she would thank them, and praise them, in the way that M.R. always praised employees—but not right now. Next morning would be early enough.

Quickly turning, avoiding the (concerned? quizzical?) gazes of whoever might be in the front hallway, M.R. ascended the front stairs. She was determined not to falter on the stairs, not to lose her balance—sliding her hand up the banister. In the sleeve of her jacket that fitted her rather too loosely she'd secreted a wad of tissues that from time to time during dinner she'd pressed unobtrusively, or so she'd hoped, at her eyes that seemed too often to be brimming with moisture, and at her upper lip that felt chafed, cracked, as if the little wound of days before had not healed, and was leaking blood. And the damned cut in her forehead, that had turned out to be unexpectedly deep, and was so slow to heal . . .

Vigorously shaking hands with the last of her guests and out of her jacket sleeve fell the blood-stippled wad of tissues, onto the foyer floor.

No one saw. No one seemed to see. M.R. did not herself take note for already she'd turned, to hurry upstairs.

The bloodied tissues on the foyer floor would be taken up by one of the household staff, tossed away with the rest of the party debris.

Waking with a jolt.

Waking after an hour or so of sleep.

In the aftermath of the Conference dinner—that aura of excitement, nervous arousal that follows a stimulating exchange with others—with the thought that she'd misplaced the scrap of paper upon which the filmmaker K___ had written her name and e-mail address.

The promises she'd made to K___, in front of witnesses!

How unprofessional M.R. had been, and yet—how unrepentant.

Needing to look for the scrap of paper and in sudden distress that she might have lost it, carelessly—in the distraction of saying good-bye at the front door—and so, barefoot and in a flannel nightgown M.R. descended the stairs another time—the broad, curving front stairs—switching on a hall light—at once, shadows in the large public rooms leapt back—the chandelier in the front hall was massive, a dozen sparkling lights meant to simulate candles—M.R. glanced anxiously about seeing only just the polished surfaces of tables—how perfectly Charters House was preserved, and at what expense to the University!—for the historic old house was a national landmark and a showcase of course—it was not M.R. Neukirchen's residence except temporarily.

"I need a home. It's time—I need a home."

To K___ she might have explained this. To a sympathetic stranger, very likely another woman.

To Andre whom she loved, she could not explain this. She had only to hope that her lover would know, without being told.

In the long hallway there was nothing—no scrap of paper on any surface. In the library, at the back of the house, where guests had gathered before dinner but had not, M.R. recalled, returned after dinner, there was in fact something on the floor beside the fireplace—only just a cocktail toothpick with red-sauce stains—which M.R. picked up, to dispose of.

"I can't have lost it. I must have put it down somewhere. . . ."

In the library with its part-timbered ceiling there were a number of lights operated by wall switches and these lights M.R. tried to turn on without complete success. And then, on one of the leather chairs that resembled chess pieces, she saw a piece of paper, snatched it up eagerly, brought it to a light and tried to read—

How frustrating this was, and how strange! M.R. could have wept, she was determined to fulfill her promise to the young woman filmmaker . . .

In the library in Charters House in the aftermath of the Conference dinner. This would be a night in April 2003. This would be sometime in the week preceding the proclamation of the American president of the official end of combat operations in Iraq even as the Iraqi insurgency continued to grow and combat operations would yield to an abyss of a war. This night, too restless to return upstairs to her bed, M.R. discovered the Dikes Collection of Children's Literature in an alcove of the library, behind glass—a dozen shelves of rare editions of children's books that had been donated to Charters House by a well-to-do alum named Simon Dikes in 1959.

The glass doors had locks, but were not locked.

On the shelves were very old books—Latin texts that looked as if they might disintegrate if

opened—first editions in French, German, English—
Aesop's Fables—Fables of Fontaine—La Barbe
bleue—*French fairy tales collected by Charles Per-*
rault and German fairy tales collected by the broth-
*ers Grimm—*Stories of Christian Andersen—*several*
editions of Henrich Hoffmann's Der Struwwelpeter,
Charles and Mary Lamb's Tales from Shakespeare,
Kipling's Jungle Books—*Max Ernst's* Une Semaine
de bonté—*Frances Hodgson Burnett's* The Secret
Garden *and* Lewis Carroll's Alice's Adventures in
Wonderland, *and* Alice Through the Looking-Glass.

And there on a shelf amid American classics—
Washington Irving's Sketch Book, *Jack London's* The
Call of the Wild, *Mark Twain's* Huckleberry Finn,
Tom Sawyer, Innocents Abroad—*was an oversized il-*
lustrated book lacking an author's name, titled The
King of the Crows: Tales.

M.R. pulled this book from the shelf. It was old, and
looked weatherworn as if it had been left out in the rain;
the pages were brittle and smelled of mildew. Through-
out the crudely printed text were illustrations—pen-
and-ink, also rather crude—of a child fleeing through
a dark forest—in the background shadowy figures
of menace—wild animals, hunched human beings,
demons. The child was a young girl with long pale hair
that caught in thorns and tree-branches. The child's

face was delicate, heart-shaped—a face that betrayed no terror only faint surprise and alarm. The child fell down a stony incline, into a muddy ravine. The child would sink in quicksand except the King of the Crows—a handsome black-feathered bird the size of an eagle, with flamey eyes and outspread talons—flew to her aid.

Curled up in a window seat, having adjusted a floor lamp so that she could make out the faded and mildewed pages without squinting, M.R. turned the pages of The King of the Crows: Tales in fascination, through the remainder of this night in April 2003.

Mudgirl Has a New Home.
Mudgirl Has a New Name.

September 1965–September 1968

"You are a *damn lucky* girl, Jew-ell. Hope you *God-damn* know that!"

Sideways out of Mrs. Skedd's mouth came these hissing words for only Jewell to hear.

It was a surprise to Jewell—these "new parents"—out of nowhere they'd seemed to have stepped into the Skedds' house: *New-kitchens.*

This name was utterly mysterious to Jewell and would remain unpronounceable to her long after it became a name to which Jewell was attached.

The *New-kitchens* had been coming to visit Jewell at the Skedds' house through the summer. Long-ago now it seemed, the mudflats and Momma and the hospital. More recently, the mountain-man who'd come to stand in the Skedds' driveway staring at her and had brought for her the beautiful blond doll but this memory too was ebbing like water down a drain.

Even a clotted drain is not sufficient to retain water.

That is a solace, Mudgirl knew. Already, Mudgirl knew.

Though the *New-kitchens* had been coming to the Skedds' house on Bear Mountain Road for several months, usually on Sundays, and Jewell surely knew this, each time the child was summoned to meet the couple in the Skedds' living room Mrs. Skedd took the precaution of telling her their names as if for the first time: *New-kitchen.*

And their first names: *Ag-ath-a, Kon-rad.*

Smiling so you could see what a nice pretty girl she'd been, not so very long ago before she'd become Mrs. Floyd Skedd living out here in a squat old asphalt-sided house on Mountain Bear Road tending to a brood of spoiled brats of which several were not even her own God-damned blood-kin, Mrs. Skedd said, nudging the child, "Of course, you remember—Jewell—yes? You remember Mr. and Mrs. . . . ."

Shyly Jewell nodded *yes.* For *yes* was the required answer.

For *yes* was the only answer.

What a kindly smiling couple the *New-kitchens* were. It was like staring into the sun, the *New-kitchens.*

Though they were not-old they did not appear young, either—Mrs. *New-kitchen* wore a long full skirt to her ankles like a storybook woman from a long-ago time and Mr. *New-kitchen* wore a jacket that matched his trousers and a vest with buttons that strained against his middle. Because the *New-kitchens* were so smiling and so nice and because they asked questions of Jewell which they also answered and because they talked, talked, talked like TV people—not angry-loud TV people but the other kind, who were meant to be kindly, smiling, nice and good and your eyelids grew heavy listening to them, or not-listening to them, and also it was not possible for Jewell at this time to look too closely at these strangers—never would Jewell be a child to look closely at any adult for fear of what she might see—so not-seeing the *New-kitchens* as well as not-hearing the *New-kitchens* made her sleepy so it was all that she could do to keep her eyes open, and to keep *awake* except if Mrs. Skedd pinched her and cast her a sidelong glance like a scissor-flash. *God-damn you Jew-elle don't you fuck this up.*

Mrs. *New-kitchen* was a plump soft woman shaped like a melon and with a round melon-face and with a smell just slightly sweet like that of a melon that has been cut and left in the air without refrigeration. Often *Mrs. New-kitchen* was warm and perspiring and short of breath and her eyes were just slightly protuberant, direct and stark and seemingly lashless, if Jewell did glance at these eyes she was stricken with an emotion she could not name, that frightened her.

Mr. New-kitchen was not much taller than his wife and shaped like a pumpkin hefty and sturdy-fleshed and with a broad squinting stained-looking face like something left outside in the rain and sun and his eyes too were just slightly protuberant, direct and stark and seemingly lashless and these eyes too were startling to Jewell, to see too closely.

I could not know, it was love in their eyes.

Love for the little Mudgirl, shining in their eyes.

I could not bear this love! How could Mudgirl bear this love!

A strange thing too was that the *New-kitchens* so resembled each other you would think they were sister-and-brother and not wife-and-husband like the Skedds who were so different from each other, no one could ever mistake them for *blood-kin.*

Not just the shapes of their bodies nor their faces and eyes and manner of speaking and little ways in which they moved their mouths, their hands or their facial muscles—nervous little laughs, murmured asides—catches in their breaths—but also, which the Skedds thought was so very funny, the *New-kitchens* had a dog named Puddin' that resembled them, a mongrel-Labrador mix with a torso solid as that of a mature pig and a manner both shyly hesitant yet aggressively affectionate—all Puddin' seemed to require, for happiness, was being allowed to lick your hands, arms, legs with his soft limp damp tongue—and the near-identical lashless eyes, that look of yearning, hope and resolution that left Jewell stricken and confused for it was not a look that was familiar to her.

To know this love was to know how I had not ever known it, before.

Like being given food at last. After so long starving.

Strange, these unfailingly "nice" people! Yet more mysterious their reason for asking to see *Jewell Kraeck.*

Of the several foster children in the Skedd household—of the several "adoptable" children—it would not seem that Mudgirl would be the choice of any reasonable couple. Yet, when the Family Services woman first contacted the Skedds about the Neukirchens' interest in adopting a child it was only the poor little Kraeck girl they wished to see—"The one whose mother abandoned her."

(As if, Mrs. Skedd said afterward, incensed, anybody would have to identify Jewell so she'd know who the hell they were talking about!)

Then came the couple to visit with Jewell through that summer always regarding her with such strange staring smiles—speaking softly to her, and smiling encouragingly; at times squeezing her small limp unresisting hand and asking their familiar questions that were like caresses—"Oh how are you, Jewell?"—that in the next quickened breath they answered—"You're looking very good, Jewell! Very pretty, very—well . . ." Their voices trailing off in a quivering sort of emotion.

Mrs. Skedd was edgy and excited knowing that Agatha Neukirchen was a librarian at the Convent Street branch of the Carthage Public Library—(not that Livvie Skedd ever entered any public library, but such a position impressed her)—and Konrad Neukirchen worked at the Beechum County Courthouse. (Anything to do with the courthouse, or with the county, which oversaw Family Services, aroused wariness and apprehension in the Skedds who, like all foster parents, dreaded unannounced home visits from county inspectors or officials.)

All of the foster children were envious of Mudgirl, now! For the Neukirchens were known to be special, not like people you'd see in the neighborhood, or mostly anywhere in Carthage. Just to hear them talk—no matter if you could make sense of what they said—

was like being in school—where things were meant to be taken seriously.

Once, when the Neukirchens came to visit Jewell, and Mrs. Skedd had almost to pull Jewell down the stairs, and into the living room to be greeted by the smiling couple, Jewell stared at the floor as if the sight of the couple was blinding, and Mrs. Skedd exclaimed, "Jew-ell is just *shy*. Maybe just—a little—*slow*. You wouldn't want to say *retarded*, but—"

Quickly Mrs. Neukirchen said, "Of course not!" even as Mr. Neukirchen objected, "There's nothing wrong with *retarded*, Mrs. Skedd. Just so you know."

Abashed Mrs. Skedd said, "Oh yes—I know. Of course, I know. In our family we welcome all—any kind of . . . The children we take in are—equally— welcome." Not knowing what she was saying she paused, biting her lower lip. "And loved."

Mrs. Neukirchen said, wiping at her large damp lashless eyes, "We had, once—a long time ago when we were young—a child, a little girl, of our own—she was 'premature'—she 'failed to thrive'—her lungs, her heart . . ."

Mr. Neukirchen touched his wife's wrist. Side by side on a couch, that sagged beneath their combined weight, the Neukirchens appeared to be sharing a single melancholy thought that, in the next instant, was banished with the husband's happy smile—"We are all God's children, in a manner of speaking. And so— *retarded*—or not—does not matter to us."

All this while Jewell was tense with listening: but not to the adults' speech.

All that morning an agitation of crows in the marsh-land beyond the ravine and now the cries were louder at the edge of the Skedds' property but you could not know if these were cries of jubilation or protest nor could you discern the particular cry of the King of the Crows.

Is Momma gone away? Is Momma dead?—these were not questions Jewell thought to ask.

Is Momma waiting to take me back?—this was a more likely question, that Jewell did not ask, either.

"God will bless you now, Jewell. From this day forward."

There was no available birth date for *Jewell Kraeck,* as there was none for her younger sister *Jedina Kraeck,* so the child's birthday would be celebrated by her adoptive parents on the date when the adoption procedure was finalized in the Beechum County courthouse: September 21.

Presumed birth date: 1961.

Now, Jewell had a *new mother*, and a *new father*. The adoption procedure went smoothly once the Neukirchens had made their decision for all who knew of the abandoned child pitied her greatly and were happy that this very nice Quaker couple wished to adopt her.

"God-*damn*. That brat is *lucky*. Thanks to *us*!"

On that last day Mr. and Mrs. Skedd and their children and foster children filed out onto the front porch to say good-bye to Jewell being taken from them by the Neukirchens to live a few miles away in Carthage that might as well have been a thousand miles, for they would never see one another again. Her hand gripped by Mrs. Neukirchen's moist warm hand Jewell stared at them as if memorizing them—their strange livid smiling faces soon to sink into oblivion recalled if fleetingly in rapid hypnogogic images that flashed to M.R. on the brink of exhausted sleep but were lost in virtually the same instant. Yet at the time, as the child was being taken from them forever, how wildly they waved at her!—how happy they appeared, for her!—for any occasion for waving, hooting, whistling—what Mrs. Skedd called a *damn ruckus*—was a good one. All of their faces were split with smiles except for Mrs. Skedd whose face was stiff like something about to shatter and her eyes glistened with tears—"Oh shit! I am not going to bawl, this is a God-damn *happy time*."

Mrs. Skedd had to run after Jewell in the driveway to hug her so hard her ribs hurt. No matter that Mrs. Neukirchen was gripping the child's hand, Mrs. Skedd grabbed her away if but for a moment. And there was Mr. Skedd following them too, smirking and winking saying, "You ain't a good li'l girl, Jew-ell, these nice people're gonna bring you back here. Dump you in the driveway. See?"

And in the car in the backseat there was the Neukirchens' thick-bodied dog quivering and whimpering with excitement. Damp adoring eyes and a soft damp tickling tongue eager to lick Jewell's face, hands, arms and legs so she squealed with sudden startled laughter.

"Puddin' loves you too, Jewell! If you will let him."

" 'Meredith Ruth Neukirchen.' "

This was her new name. *Jewell* was no longer her name.

Only vaguely could she recall—*Jedina*.

(And where *Jedina* had gone, she could not recall. It was not possible for her to remember so far back in time as even at the time of what had happened she could not have said clearly, absolutely if much that had happened had truly happened to her or to the other; nor could she have said if *Jedina* had been her, or the other.)

(Enough to know that *Jedina* had vanished.)

" 'Meredith Ruth'—'Merry'—for you are meant to be *merry.*"

In the Neukirchens' house there was not the wild-rippling laughter of the Skedds' house but not the shouting, cuffing and slamming of doors, thumping feet on the stairs, either.

Nor the girls' cramped beds, the boys' pummeling hands.

When they'd come for her she'd had virtually nothing to bring with her. A frayed tote bag Mrs. Skedd filled with a few articles of clothing that were worn thin with many launderings. A pink plastic comb, some plastic barrettes. Mismatched colored shoelaces no one else wanted.

Mrs. Neukirchen shook these items out onto a bed, frowning.

"We'll get you some nice new things, dear! You're growing."

It was a good thing, to *grow.*

Perceiving, even as a child, that you must *grow,* or you will *vanish.*

Momma was fading now. Momma's anger and outrage. Momma's grip—her fingers like ice.

For now she was Meredith Ruth Neukirchen— "Merry"—and in a new and faraway place where

Momma could not follow. Not every night now did she lie awake in the night waiting for Momma to appear at the foot of the bed.

And in this new place there were fewer crows at dawn. Sometimes there were no crow-cries at all that Jewell—that is, "Merry"—could hear.

For the Neukirchens did not live in the country but in Carthage, in a *neighborhood*. They did not live on a road but on a street and strangely close to their neighbors' houses—(mostly brick houses of dark red, dark orange, beige with steep shingled roofs and narrow paved driveways leading back to single-car garages)—that so resembled the Neukirchens' house you could not have told them apart except for Mrs. Neukirchen's front-yard garden—a jumble of bright flowers and flowering shrubs of which some were "real" but others "store-bought—artificial." (Sometimes Mrs. Neukirchen planted real geraniums among the artificial whose vivid red blossoms never turned brown and fell off.) On Mt. Laurel Street there were tall shade trees and each property was far smaller than the Skedds' sprawling backyard and there was no ravine at the rear.

"This is your home now, dear child. 'Eighteen Mount Laurel Street, Carthage, New York'—you need never leave."

Mr. Neukirchen made this pronouncement in his rotund kindly voice that was like a radio voice, just slightly elevated, formal.

"Oh, Konrad! What a thing to say! Of course our daughter will leave—one day—not for many years we hope, but—one day—and if we're very fortunate, 'Merry' will return to live in Carthage, because she has been so happy there."

Mrs. Neukirchen spoke in a voice that was breathy, exclamatory. Though her movements were stately and studied often Mrs. Neukirchen sounded as if she'd just rushed up a flight of stairs.

"Please, dear child—will you memorize your new address? In case you are ever lost."

"Oh, Konrad! What a thing to say! It isn't very likely that our daughter will be *lost*—so quickly. . . ."

"I don't mean *quickly*, Agatha. I mean—well, what do I mean?—*in time*."

Time was a subject of unusual interest to Mr. Neukirchen who *timed* his walk to and from work each weekday morning—a "fast-walk" of precisely twenty-six minutes. (Except that Mr. Neukirchen's walk was hardly what you'd call "fast.")

Time was a subject in many of the paperback books—"sci-fi" novels—Mr. Neukirchen read in his easy chair beside the living room fireplace. *Time travel. Time paradoxes.*

"For instance, Meredith: if you travel back to the *time* before you were born, you would discover a world in which *you did not exist;* but if you travel back to the *time* after you'd been born, you would discover a world in which a *younger twin self of your own* existed! Only think."

If Mrs. Neukirchen happened to overhear, very likely Mrs. Neukirchen would cry, "Oh Konrad! Don't confuse our little girl with your ridiculous 'paradoxes'! Don't even listen to him, Meredith—'Merry.' It's just some brainteasers of his."

"If Puddin' returned to Puddin' of—say—just last week, imagine how Puddin' would sniff and whine! Dogs have much more sense than human beings do, in these matters."

In the kitchen, Mrs. Neukirchen dissolved into peals of laughter.

"A dog's olfactory sense is far, far more developed than a human being's olfactory sense." Mr. Neukirchen spoke gravely to his daughter, laying a finger beside his nose that was a large lumpy nose with wide, dark nostrils in which hairs bristled, like the bristling hairs in Mr. Neukirchen's ears. "D'you know what 'olfactory sense' is, Meredith?"

The child did not know. But the child guessed, *smelling*.

"Yes! One hundred percent correct!" Mr. Neukirchen called out to Mrs. Neukirchen in the kitchen: "Our little girl is *very smart*, Agatha."

Mrs. Neukirchen's breathy-girlish voice replied: "Of course she is, Konrad. And very pretty, too."

In the hallway, there came sudden silvery-sounding chimes—a clock?—Mr. Neukirchen's grandfather clock he had inherited from his parents. Always hearing these chimes—which were both delicate and singularly defined—Mr. Neukirchen would pause, stroking his whiskery chin. To his little daughter he said gravely, "You know, Meredith—'Time heals all wounds.'" He paused, frowning. "Well—modify to: 'Time does not heal all—but, significantly, *some*—wounds.' Dear child, that is a fact."

It was strange to the child—initially—how the Neukirchens spoke to each other in their special elevated language that was both playful/teasing and serious/urgent. Much of what Mr. Neukirchen said seemed to be with the intention of making Mrs. Neukirchen laugh—Mrs. Neukirchen's laughter was so quick and warm, and good to hear. Soon, their little adopted daughter would learn to laugh in mimicry of Mrs. Neukirchen's soft breathy-girlish laughter.

How unlike the Skedds, who aimed words at each other like flailing fists, and whose laughter hurt the ears. Never did the Neukirchens raise their voices to anyone—always they were polite in a way that would have made the Skedds hoot with laughter. For if Mr. Neukirchen asked a favor he would say, "Excuse me, may I trouble you—" and after you'd brought him what he had requested, graciously he would say, "Thank you *manifoldly.*" Mrs. Neukirchen behaved like a mirror-twin except often Mrs. Neukirchen would include a kiss on the cheek, also. "My darling husband"—"My darling wife"—"My dear little daughter": these were playful and meant to make you smile but were not jokes.

Where most things in the Skedds' household were jokes but not funny, many things in the Neukirchens' household were funny but not jokes.

Early each weekday morning Mr. Neukirchen walked in his slow-rolling but steady amble downtown to the Beechum County Courthouse where for "the past two hundred years" he'd been head of the "Department of Public Futilities"—which Mrs. Neukirchen would have to translate for a baffled listener: " 'Department of *Public Utilities.*' It's a very responsible job!"

"True: all the lights in Beechum County would go out, were it not for me. Plus all water would cease to flow—except sewage. But my job isn't nearly so responsible as yours, dear Agatha. You officiate in the realm of the most wondrous—*books*."

In the Neukirchens' house there was a great respect for books. By Mr. Neukirchen's estimate—(or was Mr. Neukirchen being playful?)—there were 11,677½ books scattered through the two storeys of the house as well as into the attic and into the basement. Books were crammed onto floor-to-ceiling shelves, some lying horizontally and some in double rows, books behind books, so you could not see their titles. Beside leather-bound sets of the *Iliad* and the *Odyssey*, *The Complete Works of Shakespeare* and volumes by such authors as Sir Walter Scott, Charles Dickens, Wilkie Collins, George Eliot, and Thomas Hardy were paperback books— shelves of mystery and detective fiction, science fiction with such titles as *The War of the Worlds, I, Robot, The Martian Chronicles* and *The Voyage of the Space Beagle*. There were reference books of all kinds—*The Book of the Year* for 1952, 1955, 1959, 1964; a set of the *Encyclopedia Britannica* and random copies of Time-Life Books; an entire wall given over to works of philosophy from *Abelard* to *Zoroaster*—volumes of Plato, Swedenborg, John Stuart Mill, Kant, Hegel, Descartes, Augustine, Aquinas, Jean-Jacques Rousseau. There was a shelf devoted to very old books that looked as if they had not been opened in decades—*Journal, Letters & Sermons of George Fox*—amid newer books with such titles as *A History of the Society of Friends, The Quaker Heritage, "Speaking Truth to Power."* At Mr. Neukirchen's easy chair, which had shaped itself to the contours of his hefty body, there were more stacks of books to be read, mostly works of philosophy, history, and what Mr. Neukirchen called *moral uplift,* with here and there something lighter-hearted—Mark Twain's *Library of Humor,* H. L. Mencken's *Damn: A Book of Calumny*—and paperback mysteries by Ellery Queen, Agatha Christie, Cornell Woolrich. At Mrs. Neukirchen's matching chair, on the other side of the fireplace, were biographies and novels mostly by women writers—Pearl Buck, Edna Ferber, Taylor Caldwell—gardening, sewing, and cooking books; and of course there were children's books, both new and secondhand as well as from the library where Agatha Neukirchen worked.

"Merry! Look what I've selected for us"—Mrs. Neukirchen would wave a book with an illustrated cover, excitedly—*The Wind in the Willows, The Tale of Peter Rabbit, Tales of Mother Goose, Heidi*—"for bedtime reading tonight."

Often, the child saw her "parents" kissing—not hard and messy on the mouth but lightly, smilingly, on the cheek; and if they saw her they would beckon to her, with wide-flung arms—"Merry! Come and *be kissed.*"

She would not: she did not want to be kissed.

She would hide her face. Run away, and hide. Back away staring and speechless and repelled— these strangers acting so silly and making so much of themselves.

I am not—Merry. I am Jewell.

"Merry, come! Hurry!"

"Better hurry, Merry—kisses are going fast!"

And so—somehow—with a breathy little laugh blindly she stumbled forward.

Ran to the Neukirchens who stooped to swaddle her in all their arms.

This was the way: blindly stumble forward, and *be kissed.*

"You will always be safe, Meredith—if you look within. For the 'light of the Lord dwells within us.'"

The Neukirchens spoke of themselves as "Friends"— of the "Society of Friends"—but there was no Friends' meetinghouse in Carthage. The closest meetinghouse was seventy miles away in Watertown.

Just too far! The Neukirchens did not like driving such a distance.

Especially, Agatha did not like driving. She'd had such a terrible time passing her driver's test—at age twenty-nine, after Konrad had taught her—that she had no confidence in her driving skills; she drove too slowly, so that other drivers honked their horns at her; if she had to sit behind the steering wheel for a while, arthritis pains began in her back, neck, and arms.

Nor did Agatha care for driving with Konrad who was, if anything, too good a driver—"He is so aggressive! It's shocking, what comes out of a good man behind the wheel."

In any case, the Neukirchens were not "going-to-Meeting" Friends. Making such a journey just to sit still—and not speak—(when Konrad dearly loved to speak)—wasn't worth the ordeal. They'd been married by a Quaker minister in the Keene Valley, in the Adirondacks in late summer, but that had been a unique occasion.

"The minister said just a few words—the Friends' service is not long. But he did ask if there was anyone 'to object to this union' and almost right away there was a terrible commotion—some Canada geese flying onto a lake nearby, all squawking and flapping their wings like crazed things. And everybody laughed, but sort of uneasily. And I was—I don't know why—so embarrassed."

Konrad laughed. "Well, I wasn't. Not in the slightest. If God had wanted to send a message, that He didn't approve of our union, you can be sure He'd have sent it some less comical way."

It was Konrad who'd been a Quaker first, and Agatha who had "converted." Their allegiance to the religion was in Quaker *ideals* and *ethics;* Konrad did not especially believe in "Christ Jesus"—of whom the Quaker founder George Fox had preached, and Agatha was "undecided" how much she believed.

Both agreed that the Society of Friends was the only religion they could cleave to, since it was a religion that didn't demand cleaving, and a religion in which "original sin"—in fact, any kind of "sin"—and Hell—did not figure greatly. Pacifism—which Konrad took to be a more human instinct than aggression—was only just, to them, "logical"—like the forswearing of vows to serve in the military. Konrad admired George Fox for his fearlessness in "speaking truth to power" in dangerous situations, and in accepting numerous imprisonments during his long campaign of preaching, often in risking death—but Konrad was not drawn to such displays of courage, and had no taste for martyrdom. Sincerely he believed that God was a vessel of "uncommon common sense" not to be found in slavish obedience to the state nor certainly in churches, rituals, or sacred sites: "God will come to *you* when you require Him. You do not have to travel a mile, to get to *God.*"

Adding: "God is already inside you, Meredith! God is the 'Merry' inside you—that little spark of being. Think of God in this way, and God will be your friend through life."

All religions were pathways seeking God, thus all religions were to be respected.

Though—Konrad had to add—some religions were more to be respected than others.

"All breeds of dogs, for instance, are of the species *Canis familiaris*—but not all dogs are equal. You see?"

Konrad winked at the little girl who gazed at him with a puzzled smile. If Konrad saw that the child was clutching—clenching—her hands in her lap, he pretended not to see; for Konrad was not the sort of father who wishes his child to see how much he knows of her innermost heart. Agatha, overhearing, said reprovingly, "Now Konrad! You don't want to confuse the child with your silly paradoxes."

"Don't I?"

"Of course you don't! Our little girl is very young, you know."

"How young is *very young*?"

Meredith laughed in the breathy way wondering was she expected to answer such a question?

She had no idea how old she was, really. It was believed that she was six years old for *Jewell Kraeck* would have been six years old. Yet even this alleged fact was not a certainty.

"Well—if we can't decide what is *very young*—can we assume that we know what is a *paradox?*"

Still the child stared smiling, wide-eyed glancing from her new father to her new mother. She knew, if she did not reply, both Neukirchens would answer their question for her; they would not pursue any topic that too obviously baffled her, nor would they continue to look at her when it became clear she was uncomfortable with their scrutiny.

"A 'paradox' is—what?—a 'pair of docks'—"

"Don't be silly, Konrad!"

"A 'paradox' is like a riddle—and the mistake is, people think they must solve riddles when the very essence of riddle is, *the riddle cannot be solved.*"

"Well, yes! Maybe."

"Agatha, *yes*. This is so. You don't have to solve the paradox, nor even understand what it is trying to tell you—you only have to live with the paradox. You *live*."

In the Neukirchen household, it was possible to live with *paradoxes*.

In the Neukirchen household, it was only possible to live with *paradoxes.*

Because she did not love them! Because she was lonely in the dark-brick house on Mt. Laurel Street despite the efforts of Agatha, and Konrad, and Puddin'—despite the shelves of books beckoning to her like shut-up little souls, as in some kind of mausoleum, inviting her *Open me! See what I am!*

Because—maybe—the woman who'd been Momma—the woman who was *still Momma*—had burrowed into her heart like a mean little worm that could not so easily be extricated. Just when she believed that Momma was faded and left behind that very night a dream would come to her leaving her sweaty and shivering for it was clear to her—it was meant to be clear to her—that her *new mother* and her *new father* were not Christians but emissaries of Satan like all city-people and courthouse people who had stolen Marit Kraeck's children from her forcing her to drastic measures to protect their souls. So very different from the Neukirchens who had not an idea what life *is.*

And Mrs. Skedd would sneer—the Neukirchens were fat homely—silly!—people. Maybe they lived in some fancy house—(Mrs. Skedd had never glimpsed the Neukirchens' house)—and had fancy jobs—

(Mrs. Skedd could only compare others' jobs with her own—foster-mother to a household of losers, rejects, retards, and brats). And all that sentimental fuss about love, and kissing, and being God-damn polite—like silly TV people. Mr. Skedd was no dope either, saw through that corny crap:

Bull-shit!

At the same time, she loved them. Of course, she loved them.

That Agatha and Konrad were silly, and sentimental, and always kissing, and kissing *her*—she loved them for this. Or badly wished she might love them.

They were kind, and funny, and smart; you could not see immediately how smart, just looking at them; and they would never shout, or push, even pinch, or sneer.

Even, disciplining Puddin', with his slovenly-dog manners tracking dirt into the house, and worse—they would not ever shout, push, pinch.

"Please! Try to call us 'Dad'—'Mommy'—if you can. Maybe not right now but—in time."

"Yes! All things *in time*."

And so she would try. Sometime soon.

For she had to know she was not *Jewell* really—she was *Meredith Ruth*. She was not *Kraeck* but *Neukirchen*. Soon, she would start school: first grade at the Convent Street School.

So very exciting, the prospect of starting school! The other *Jewell* had never gone to school because Momma did not trust any school as Momma did not trust anyone to do with the "government."

But she did not any longer live with this mother in the falling-down shanty behind the Gulf station in Star Lake, nor did she live in the squat asphalt-sided house of the Skedds on Bear Mountain Road: she lived now on Mt. Laurel Street, Carthage. She did not share a room with anyone, not even another girl—she did not share a bed. She had her own bedroom with white bunnies frolicking in pale green wallpaper and her own little bed with a white headboard and a bedspread of the cheery hue of sunshine Mrs. Neukirchen had herself crocheted. Here were books from which, at bedtime, Mrs. Neukirchen or Mr. Neukirchen read to her, and which she was learning to read for herself—picture books, talking-animal books, the most magical books! She had several dolls of which none was so special as the blond doll in the satin dress but she had stuffed toys and she had her own little shiny-maple dresser and in the drawers she had her own clothes newly purchased for her, and in a closet she had other, hanging clothes— dresses, skirts. She had her own flannel nightgown decorated with kittens that would never be mixed in with the laundry and worn by another girl. She had a child-sized desk, and she had a child-sized chair. As *Meredith Ruth* she seemed to know that there had once been, in this room, perhaps in this very bed, another *Meredith Ruth* who had passed from the Neukirchen household but whose spirit remained.

And with this spirit—this other, lost, cast-away child—she could live, too, as easily as she lived with herself. She would.

"Take my hand, Merry! Especially crossing the street."

Soon she would be six years old: so it was believed. Less seemingly developed than other six-year-olds yet already she could read, to a degree; already, with Mr. Neukirchen's tutoring, she'd learned to "do" arithmetic.

And so, with documents from the Beechum County Family Services and a "surrogate" birth certificate from the Beechum County Department of Records, Meredith began first grade at Convent Elementary School only four blocks from 18 Mt. Laurel Street, in fall 1968.

So conveniently, Agatha could walk with her on Agatha's way to the cobblestone library just a block farther. It was not at this small branch library but at the downtown Carthage library that Agatha had begun work as a librarian, a girl of twenty-two in 1955.

How happily Agatha told Meredith about how she and Mr. Neukirchen had met. How frequently, with the air of one who never tires of recounting happiness.

Eight months after Agatha had started work at the beautiful "limestone temple" downtown library, in the reference department, young fiery Konrad Neukirchen appeared with a request to see all the library's holdings in the special collections archives relating to the history of the Black Snake Valley from the 1600s to 1900— "Your father was *just so dashing*. And just so—as he is now—*bossy and commanding*."

At their first meeting, something seemed to have leapt between them—"Like sparks. But of course, I was shy . . . I'd hardly ever gone out with any boy or man before."

Three months, two weeks, and a single day afterward, Agatha and Konrad Neukirchen were married to the astonishment and (to a degree) disapproval of all who knew them.

Agatha had been a girl of twenty-three at this time! So inexperienced with men she'd had a notion she had to laugh—breathily, nervously—at virtually every remark the loquacious young man made, whether it was funny or forced; as Konrad had been so inexperienced with women, for all his pose of sophistication, he'd had a notion that he must not brush a hand against Agatha, however innocently, or accidentally, for fear of offending her. Of course, he would never have attempted to kiss her without asking her permission.

"How we ever managed to cast aside all that silliness, I don't know. One day we just woke up—I mean, in our separate residences—and I realized, 'Oh! I love him'—and Konrad realized, 'Oh! I love her.' It was that simple."

Except there were things about Konrad Neukirchen that puzzled Agatha.

The way he described himself as a "friend"—by which he meant "Friend"—that is, a Quaker.

And the way he told her, mysteriously, laying a finger alongside his nose as if in imitation of some elder in his family, that the Neukirchens had a "secret weakness"—each and every one of them.

"What kind of 'secret weakness,' I asked him, and he said—'What kind of a secret would it be, dear Agatha, if it was revealed?'"

Sometimes when she was alone with Meredith on these walks to Convent Elementary Agatha lowered her voice to speak tenderly and wistfully of the little girl who'd come into their lives who'd been *premature*—who'd *failed to thrive.*

"But Merry's soul is dwelling in light—somewhere. We can't know details of course but we can know this."

Meredith's mother squeezed her fingers, tight. Through parted lips she breathed damply.

Meredith did not look at the soft round woman beside her for fear of what she might see in the woman's face.

Meredith saw a blur of light—lights—and shadow-figures amid the lights—like white bunnies frolicking in a field of pale-green grass. One of these figures was *Merry* but you could not know which one.

Even for a young child it was exasperatingly slow to walk with Agatha. Like a naughty little girl Meredith would have liked to pull her hand from the panting woman's hand and run—run, and run—up one of the narrow paved driveways between the look-alike brick houses and through the backyards and into— where?—whatever was beyond. She was too nimble-footed to fall into a ravine and break her ankle or her damn neck—(this was Mrs. Skedd observing)—and if crows screamed at her, she wouldn't have been afraid. But of course Meredith would never do such a rude wild thing like the children she'd once known in the Skedds' house.

In new clothes that Mrs. Neukirchen had purchased for her, or sewed for her, in little white socks and black patent-leather shoes Meredith Ruth Neukirchen was not a rude child, not ever. Meredith Ruth was a quick smart child and very sweet if still somewhat over-quiet, chewing at her lower lip.

Nothing like any child she'd known in Star Lake. Nothing like any child in the foster home where sometimes suddenly one of them would run out of the house—run into the backyard, and along the ravine—could be anyone—a foster child, or one of the Skedd children who were noisy, profane, restless as cooped-up little animals.

Letting off steam for the hell of it. Can't take it!

Lighting matches, at the ravine. The big boys started it and younger children copied them but never Jewell of course. Stealing Mrs. Skedd's book of matches from behind the gas stove letting a lighted match fall twenty feet down into the ravine.

If flames took hold, in a panic Jewell ran. The others clambering about the ravine tossing rocks below, scarcely noticed her; nor did she tell Mrs. Skedd watching her TV programs sprawled on the living room sofa, a can of beer in her hand.

Who's that? Jew-elle? C'mere, honey—c'mon cuddle.

Meredith never remembered those days, now. She would not remember. Except how she'd wished that Mrs. Skedd would be as nice to Lizbeth as she was to Jewell saying *Damn bad you aren't my own*

*flesh-and-blood except shit, I spose if you were, you'd
be bratty like Lizbeth.*

Meredith was restless walking with Agatha but
Meredith was worried, too. For she knew—she'd overheard—Konrad worried about his dear wife who was
having trouble walking though still a young woman in
her early thirties—needing sometimes to use a cane,
there were such arthritic pains in her hips.

Meredith had seen: Agatha's legs were thick with
ropey veins. Her legs were encased in opaque stockings
like bandages and on her small feet were lace-up shoes
with crepe soles.

Though Agatha winced and moaned about *arth-ri-
tis* these remarks were couched in a cheery tone, as one
might complain about the weather. Nearly always Agatha
was in a cheery mood. This was just her "nature"—as
Puddin' had his cheery-dog nature—(though Puddin's
legs were losing their strength, too—Puddin' wasn't a
young dog, walked with a sort of sidelong lurch, and
shed dog hairs everywhere he brushed against). Agatha
loved her work at the Convent Street library. Though
she was not very well-paid—so Konrad claimed—yet
she loved the quiet of the old cobblestone library. She
loved checking out the same books year after year and
shelving these books and she loved the other librarians who were women of at least her age and girth and

something of her temperament and she loved chatting with library patrons who were mostly women as well except for a little platoon of retired men, all of them gentlemen, who adored Agatha Neukirchen.

Sometimes at the library when things were slow Agatha knitted, or crocheted, or even tried to sew. She had a quick dazzling way with a needle. She liked to sew her own clothes, which were large-sized, with ample waists and long, voluminous skirts, for she was made to feel uncomfortable in women's clothing stores. ("The fancier the store, the more they make you feel bad!") In public places Agatha wore ankle-length skirts that gave her an air of dignity and self-possession: Konrad called her *queenly*. She wore blouses with frills and lace and adorned with funny old brooches and necklaces Konrad gave her as surprise gifts. Her hair was a lovely chestnut brown lustrous as a girl's hair, she kept it in place back behind her ears and off her smooth clear forehead with tortoiseshell combs. In her daughter's bedroom she would sit on the edge of the bed that creaked beneath her weight brushing and combing the child's hair that seemed less lustrous than her own, a scrawny sort of hair susceptible to frizz and snarls.

"Oh! I'm sorry if I snagged your hair, Merry! I promise it won't happen again."

Afterward, she would read to the little girl. There was an endless supply of children's books and many of them wonderful she'd bought for Merry or had taken out of the library—Merry's favorites were the talking-animal books and books about little girls like Alice of *Alice's Adventures in Wonderland* whose straggly hair in the illustrations resembled Merry's own hair.

Agatha did not read scary passages from the *Alice* book. Agatha did not like scary passages in any books, children's or adults'.

"When you read a book you are *inside it*—and you are safe there."

Reading aloud to her daughter Agatha would run her forefinger along the large-type print just slow enough so that without quite knowing what she was doing, her daughter began reading with her, recognizing the familiar words because Agatha had read them before, or remembering them.

So easy to read, if you didn't try! If you just let the words come into your head.

Bedtime reading had to end at a certain time. In the first year she'd come to live with the Neukirchens, at 8:30 P.M.

In the downstairs hall beneath the child's room with the bunny-wallpaper and the bed with the white headboard was the tall beautiful old grandfather clock which Mr. Neukirchen described as a *Stickley clock.*

When she couldn't sleep Meredith lay listening to the calm ticking of this clock and to its chimes which were sweet and clear and soothing—the clock struck not just the hour but the quarter hour—(with a single chime)—which was beautiful to hear but scary too—sometimes—for the chimes came so often, and could not be stopped.

Here was a test: you heard the clock begin its chimes and counted with it—*one, two, three, four*—trying to guess when the chimes would stop—and often the chimes would continue—*five, six—seven, eight*—in rebuke.

In fascination Meredith examined the clock: the long brass pendulum swung slowly and languidly and once in a while slowed and ceased of its own volition. Mr. Neukirchen knew how to fix the clock, Mrs. Neukirchen professed utter ignorance of it, and would never touch it.

At the Skedds', such a big beautiful clock would have been broken within days. The workings so visible, almost taunting—you would naturally be drawn to jam your fingers into them. You would naturally be drawn to stopping the God-damn ticking/chiming.

But the Neukirchens loved the old grandfather clock—"It's like the ticktocking heart of this house," Agatha said, and Konrad said, with a wink to Meredith, "This clock is a genuine antique. It has come down through our family. And it makes me remember—even if I'd like to forget—that we Neukirchens have a secret weakness, that not a one of us has been spared."

Meredith smiled uneasily. Meredith clenched her hands together out of sight of her father's sharp eyes and smiled uneasily but did not ask what the *secret weakness* was; which seemed to surprise Konrad for he said, with the hint of a frown, "Hmm? Aren't you going to ask your dad, what the 'secret weakness' of the Neukirchens is?"

Meredith shook her head, *no.*

Meredith laughed at the look in Konrad's face.

"Really? You aren't going to ask?"

Again Meredith shook her head, *no.*

"My dear daughter is the only person, ever, to whom I've mentioned this secret, who hasn't asked about it! Amazing."

But Konrad would not let the subject go, and returned to it a short while later: "But why aren't you going to ask, Meredith? Aren't you the least bit curious about the secret weakness of the Neukirchens?"

Meredith shook her head, *no.*

"But"—Konrad was pretending to be exasperated now, plucking at his whiskery jaws—"why aren't you curious?"

"Because—it wouldn't be a secret, if it was told."

Konrad stared at the child. For a moment he was struck speechless.

"Why, then—of course—my dear daughter—you are correct."

Never again did Konrad bring up the subject to Meredith.

It was the morning after one of these nights—when Meredith was in third grade, and eight years old (if you counted her birthday as September 21, 1961)—spent listening to the grandfather clock in the downstairs hall wondering if her mother was alive and where if alive her mother was and if her mother could find her in this new place—that the terrible news was revealed, which Meredith was never to be told.

There are two kinds of news in a child's life: the news that is told, and the news that is not-told.

Yet somehow, Meredith would come to know.

It was the week of the Convent Elementary School spelling bee, June 1969. Though she was three years younger than a number of the "star spellers" competing in the spelling bee, Meredith Ruth Neukirchen became champion speller of the school with a correct spelling of *unicorn*. During this very week, news came of what newspapers and TV called a *grisly discovery*—the wizened and mummified corpse of a small child, a very young girl discovered in a junked refrigerator at the edge of a landfill, eleven miles west of Star Lake.

On local TV news came this ugly bulletin. In the Carthage newspaper.

Of course, the Neukirchens shielded their daughter from such an ugly story.

Yet somehow, Meredith knew.

. . . mummified remains believed to be those of three-year-old Jedina Kraeck, who disappeared in April 1965 from the Star Lake residence where she had lived with her mother Marit Kraeck and older sister Jewell.

Warrants had been issued for the arrest of Marit Kraeck in April 1965 on charges of child neglect, child abuse, and attempted homicide but these warrants had never been served.

A resident of Star Lake and his son fishing on the Black Snake River discovered the "mummified remains" in the refrigerator and reported the discovery to the Beechum County sheriff's department.

Detectives with the sheriff's department report that their investigation into the disappearance of Marit Kraeck is "ongoing."

Another time, several years later.

When Meredith Ruth Neukirchen was named "outstanding girl" in her seventh grade class at Carthage Middle School.

For often it happened in those years, Meredith made her adoptive parents proud of her, and happy for her.

Not that it was difficult to make the Neukirchens happy.

Never did they urge their daughter to study hard— never did they coerce her into behaving in any way other than the way she wished to behave. It was marvelous to them yet somehow not so very surprising for the miracle of their lives was that "Merry" had been returned to them—this was the profound miracle, beside which the child's high grades and sweet disposition were a secondary matter.

Very smart, and very sweet! From Konrad she seemed to have acquired a sharply inquisitive mind, if not a propensity to speak at length; from Agatha, a slight propensity for physical clumsiness. She was a quiet girl, everyone agreed—an "inward" sort of girl— "mature" for her age.

She did not want to hurt or offend her parents who so doted on her and so she never shut the door to her room quite all the way—but nearly so—spending time alone at the child-sized desk which within a few years she outgrew as she outgrew the child-bed with the white headboard and the handsewn clothes Agatha sewed for her with the cycle of seasons. There entered into her life at unpredictable times fugues of forgetfulness and entrancement when she appeared to be, to her adoptive parents, a mysterious being in their household as a fairy elf or luminescent light might appear in the most ordinary setting inviting you to touch it—to pass your hand through it. "She is God's gift to us, we have not deserved," Agatha said, with a shiver; provoking Konrad to say in reproach, "If God has given us this daughter, you can be sure we deserve her. God has never yet made a mistake—as Einstein noted: 'God does not play dice with the universe.'"

What seemed most fascinating to Meredith were books: printed pages: words. These were not mere school-texts or pastimes but might have been doorways into unknown regions. As the child seemed to have learned to read precociously with little conscious effort so she seemed to memorize with no effort—entire pages, long passages of texts were retained in her brain, vividly, thrillingly.

She was a good athlete, too—or usually; once she learned to mimic others. She hadn't a natural athlete's talent for improvisation nor had she a natural athlete's zest for competition, for *winning;* but she was a good team player, reliable, dogged, and uncomplaining. Though she was alert and attentive in school, in classes, at other times she seemed slightly disconnected, as if her own thoughts captivated her to the exclusion of the exterior world; casual conversations made little impression on her, and the names and faces of certain individuals whom she encountered numerous times—Agatha's bevy of women friends, and her less interesting school classmates. "Our daughter doesn't suffer fools gladly," Konrad said, "for which, though I can't claim genetic credit, I hope I can claim *influential credit.*"

"Oh but—Merry doesn't want to *insult* people—does she? Not remembering their faces, or names—"

" 'Insult' is in the eye of the beholder. Our daughter is cast in a higher mold."

What was important was the wisdom of the ages, the Neukirchens believed, and this wisdom was preserved in books. When you read, the book enters your soul, and you are inside the book; the book inside the soul is an aspect of the inner light, which is God.

The other, the vast sprawling cacophonous world— that would elude their daughter, they believed.

Meredith would become a teacher, probably—and if she taught high school, how wonderful it would be, if she returned to Carthage to teach!

"Or she might become a librarian, you know. She loves books."

"Yes. But no. Our Meredith loves books, but she loves even better thinking about them. Librarians, bless them, are the salt of the earth but, you know, they don't *think*—in the way I mean."

And so, how thrilled the Neukirchens were when Meredith was named "outstanding girl" in her seventh grade class. In the spring assembly at Carthage Middle School where, to her parents' delight, *Meredith Ruth Neukirchen* was summoned to the stage to be given a framed certificate and an illustrated gift-edition of *Little Women;* with other award-winning classmates her picture appeared in the Carthage newspaper the next morning.

Below the photograph on page six was the headline: CARTHAGE MIDDLE SCHOOL HONORS OUTSTANDING STUDENTS. And on the facing page seven another headline: BEAR MT. ROAD ARSON INVESTIGATION CONTINUES.

This was not new news. This was news of the previous week.

Meredith had not seen the original article. Very likely, that article had been hidden from her.

Nor would Meredith read this article in its entirety, seemingly.

A swift glance at the column of type, a skimming gaze as fast as a finger scrolling downward without a pause.

. . . home of Olivia and Floyd Skedd of Bear Mountain Road, burnt to the ground killing eight residents of the house in a nighttime flash-fire believed to have been arson. Mr. and Mrs. Skedd, forty-one and thirty-nine respectively, were foster parents "held in high regard" by Beechum County Family Services. Of the eight dead, four were foster children in the Skedds' care between the ages of three and thirteen. Two were the Skedds' children, aged eleven and fourteen. Traces of lighter fluid were found among the smoldering ruins of the ground floor. The only survivor of the blaze which drew fire trucks from three Beechum County districts is the Skedds' sixteen-year-old daughter Lizbeth, at the present time held in custody in Beechum County juvenile detention.

Though Meredith had time to scarcely run her eyes through this paragraph of newsprint—even as Agatha pulled the paper from her with a nervous little laugh, that she might show Konrad the wonderful picture on page six—yet the words were perfectly preserved in Meredith's memory. She would have no need to see the newspaper again.

That night, the Neukirchens celebrated their daughter's award with a special dinner: Agatha's Mexicali meat loaf with spicy ketchup baked on top, scalloped potatoes, and Agatha's pumpkin pie with whipped cream. They did not speak of the arson-article, or of the arson-news—the Neukirchens did not speak of such distressing matters, in any case. Their God was a God of light and not a God of darkness and of darkness, what is there to say?

When she'd been called to the stage that afternoon Meredith had been stricken with shyness, yet with pleasure; she'd been happy to have received the award, and all the happier that her parents were in the audience to applaud with the others. But she seemed embarrassed of the award and didn't really want to talk about it afterward; she hid away the framed certificate somewhere in her room. *Little Women* she'd already read, of course—she'd read it in fifth grade.

At the celebration-dinner the Neukirchens chattered happily while Meredith sat quietly between them; with her fork she made faint indentations in the sunflower-splotched tablecloth. There was no one to whom she might have said whatever it might have been she'd have had to say, if there'd been anyone to whom she might have spoken.

Her young life was beginning, had already begun. She would soar far from Carthage, from even this household in which, as in the most astonishing of fairy tales, she was beloved—whoever she was in this household, she was beloved. That she was Meredith Ruth— "Merry"—she would never want for love.

A very lucky girl, Jew-ell. Hope you know that!
She did. She knew.

The King of the Crows had departed from her life, she realized.

Badly she missed the King of the Crows. Mornings when she woke early it was not to the raw-yearning cries of crows somewhere beyond the walls and roof of a house but to the methodical ticking of Mr. Neukirchen's old grandfather clock, its steely-silvery chimes.

Mudwoman Mated.

April 2003

Readied she must be readied.

On this morning when they came for her without warning except such warning as even in her blindness she'd had to have known inescapably.

Must have fallen asleep, the heavy book fell from her hands and wakened her with a jolt.

Quickly she stood: what time was it? Where was she?

. . . in the library downstairs in Charters House. In the president's residence barefoot and shivering in a nightgown in one of the first-floor rooms and in leaded-glass windows a few yards away her ghost-figure hovered uncertainly faceless and bereft of identity as a dressmaker's dummy.

Without glancing at the cover of the awkward-sized book hurriedly she shelved it. One of the old rare-edition children's books from the nineteenth century perhaps, from out of the glass-front case—the Dikes Collection.

So many books in the president's house, and so rarely glanced-into!

Truly this was a museum/mausoleum. Not shelves of mummified and calcified dead, bundles of brittle old bones as in an ancient catacomb but hundreds of books and each with a proud title, a proud author's name stamped on the spine.

What was M.R. doing here, and at such a time! Barely clothed, barefoot!

Amid gleaming hardwood floors, crystalline chandeliers, faded Chinese carpets.

She'd long had an irrational fear—not a strong but a mild fear—a trivial fear—of which (of course) she'd joked—of nocturnal prowlers peering in the ground-floor windows of the elegant old mansion built at the top of a steep hill in a farther corner of the University campus.

Until 1919, the University president had lived in a Colonial residence near the chapel at the center of campus. Carousing undergraduates had long trespassed onto the president's private grounds and boldly peered in the windows and frightened residents until at last, after a scandalous incident, the presidential house had been moved a quarter mile away to Charters House.

Protected by a twelve-foot wrought-iron fence and (in theory at least, since it was never closed) a gate at the foot of the drive, Charters House was far less accessible than the previous residence.

Of course M.R. was perfectly safe here. No undergraduates had the slightest interest in trespassing here. The hill was densely wooded with conifers. The main house, carriage house, five-car garage were protected by surveillance cameras. There were motion detectors on the grounds monitored by campus security.

Still, it made her uneasy to be wandering about the first-floor rooms not fully clothed.

Why she'd come downstairs an hour or two earlier, she couldn't recall.

Insomnia is a shattering of the brain. Glittering puddles like slivers of broken glass in vast mudflats to the horizon.

"There—"

On a library shelf a few feet away, what appeared to be a folded note. M.R. snatched it up—but it wasn't a note, just another cocktail napkin smudged with cocktail sauce the household staff had carelessly overlooked.

A clock chimed the hour in the darkened front corridor—3 A.M.

Upstairs she tried to sleep until at last at 5:10 A.M. she gave up for the night. Throwing off bedclothes and hurriedly dressing and again returning downstairs and outside into the chill damp air with its fragrance of pine needles and moist earth that was a balm to what obscure hurt, what apprehension she could not have named.

Several times a week she swam at the University pool. More intensely, and more often in days of stress and always early so that she might be alone.

To be known, to be identified—how disagreeable this was to her, at such a time.

At this hour preceding dawn the campus was deserted. There were few lights and these blurred ghost-lights behind drawn shades or blinds. It was a quarter mile hike to the University gym and to the pool that opened at 5 A.M. and by the time she reached the building that housed the pool it was 5:25 A.M.

Initially she'd gone to the pool at 7 A.M. Most mornings she swam for forty-five minutes. But by the time she'd left there were a number of other swimmers in the pool and of these most would have recognized M. R. Neukirchen though few would have spoken to her without her having spoken to them first. Twice there had been Oliver Kroll just arriving at the pool as M.R. was leaving and his eyes moving onto her in a muted sort of surprise and so she'd arranged to arrive at the pool a half hour earlier. And a third time there had been Oliver Kroll arriving at the pool as M.R. was leaving and so she'd arranged to arrive at the pool another half hour earlier and since that time she hadn't seen Kroll.

Now at 5:30 A.M. there was no one in the pool. Within fifteen minutes a lone broad-shouldered boy would arrive, a solitary swimmer with sleek black hair whom M.R. saw often at this hour, but did not know nor did the boy, very likely an undergraduate, appear to recognize her in swimsuit, rubber swim cap. And another swimmer would arrive, and another as the hour of 6 A.M. approached and after 6 A.M. a steady succession of swimmers until the pool was no longer a desirable place for one who wished to be alone.

Now, it was still early. In her dark light-wool single-piece swimsuit and white rubber swim cap M.R. slipped into the water and began to swim laps in her customary lane to the far left of the pool facing the deep end, not fast, but steadily, feeling the pleasurable ache of arm-muscles and a tightness across her shoulders begin to relax. As a girl she'd thought it magical—the unexpected buoyancy of water, the ease with which her body that seemed heavy to her on land, and ungainly, could be propelled through water through an action of her arms and legs. And in the water too, she'd felt cloaked in invisibility.

Muffled echoes in the high-ceilinged room as of voices just out of earshot. High above were mosaics of sea-clouds. Swimming, M.R. half-shut her eyes. What a relief to be here, away from Charters House and her sleepless nights!

Almost, M.R. could think *Maybe I don't require sleep. Whatever it is inside me is so white-hot, incandescent.*

She would swim for forty-five minutes and she would return to the house and shower there and at 7:30 A.M. Evander would arrive to drive her to Philadelphia for a meeting with a prospective corporate donor.

One of the older and more powerful University trustees had arranged for the meeting. President Neukirchen had no choice but to comply at least initially to speaking with corporate representatives though all that she knew of the corporation—which was the third-largest natural gas supplier in the world—filled her with dismay and revulsion.

Was money from a (possibly) tainted source, tainted money?

Were those who received (possibly) tainted money, tainted themselves?

The prospective endowment might be as high as thirty-five million dollars, the University trustee had told M.R., in confidence.

Thirty-five million! Even for the University with its eighteen-billion-dollar endowment, this was considerable. Such an endowment alone would provide full tuition for all students who were admitted to the University, independent of their family's ability to pay.

Whether to pursue the endowment personally, or to assign it to her vice president for development, M.R. wasn't sure, as M.R. wasn't sure whether the endowment should be pursued at all.

It had been something of a scandal that the University was discovered to have had investments in South African companies during the era of apartheid, though the University lauded itself on being ultra-liberal in racial issues and a forerunner among Ivy League universities in implementing "affirmative action" in the 1960s; yet more of a scandal when a young historian on the faculty uncovered evidence that the University, that lauded itself on having been a stop on the Underground Railway in the 1850s and 1860s, had once profited, in the late 1700s, from the West African slave trade.

These minor scandals, heatedly debated at the University, had boiled over into the media, particularly into the pages of the *New York Times*.

These were legitimate ethical issues, M.R. believed. Though as a University administrator she was obliged to consider the matter of the natural-gas supplier an economic issue, too.

Months ago, M.R. would have felt anxiety about the upcoming meeting in Philadelphia: now, so very oddly, she felt a twinge of anticipation, excitement—the thrill of dropping a lighted match into a ravine for instance.

To see what flares up. To experiment.

Swimming was wakening her, ever more fully!

The 7:30 A.M. pickup at Charters House was not unusual. Often M.R. had breakfast meetings as well as luncheon and dinner meetings. Very often, the president's weekday was filled with meetings through the entire day as well as social events in the evening that were often, in effect, meetings as well, a kind of diplomacy by other means. Weekends, too, might be taken up with attending conferences, travel. If M.R. remained at home, invariably she was booked for dinner parties.

A tightly scheduled day was a day that redeemed itself. Where there were lacunae like patches of empty sky M.R. had come to feel herself unused, unmoored and adrift.

Once, new to administration, she'd yearned for more free time—to think, to ponder philosophical questions, to compose her meticulously organized, thoughtfully argued philosophical essays for which she'd been praised by her (mostly male) colleagues who were not otherwise lavish with praise. Now, the prospect of *free time* was not so inviting.

Agatha had not liked *free time* either. Even when she was reading, or watching TV, Agatha's plump hands moved with surprising swiftness knitting, crocheting, quilt-sewing.

Konrad was quite different. *I loaf and invite my soul*—Konrad had so many times uttered, it was a surprise to Meredith to discover, in high school, that the arresting line wasn't his but Walt Whitman's.

Her wonderful, loving parents! In interviews, M.R. praised them lavishly.

It was a mystery to M.R. why, as soon as she'd left Carthage—(first to attend Cornell, then graduate school at Harvard)—she'd seemed to forget the Neukirchens. Always she was meaning to telephone them, or to write; in those years before e-mail when letter-writing could be something of a pleasurable task. As if a mist were gathering at the back of her brain, chill and insidious.

And beyond these *wonderful Quaker parents* as she spoke of them in interviews, in the years preceding the dark-brick house on Mt. Laurel Street where she'd been so happy, and so beloved, the mist was yet more insidious, implacable. What was enveloped in it, what was lost to memory, M.R. had no idea.

Of those years, M.R. never spoke in interviews.

Forgetting! M.R. thought of the phenomenon as rather concentrating on the present, the headlong plunge of the present. As, shining a flashlight into the dark, your eyes follow the trajectory of the light, and ignore the penumbra beyond.

What was essential to her body, like, for instance, swimming—she wasn't likely to forget.

Often discovering when she searched among her papers—notes and sketches and early drafts of essays—that she didn't actually remember what she'd been working on, or why it had meant so much to her at one time.

Even her handwriting seemed to be changing for she so rarely wrote by hand any longer.

In our family there is a secret weakness. Not a one of us has been spared.

She'd never learned what Konrad's family secret was. Though, now she was an adult, she could guess.

Oh just some—riddle! Some brainteaser of your father's you know how that man is.

Laughing her quick breathless laugh. A glint of fear in Agatha's large limpid warm-brown eyes that the next moment dispelled.

"Ma'am?"

He was no one she knew: the sleek-black-haired young man, wide-shouldered, with dark twists of hair on his chest, shoulders, arms, legs, crudely squatting at the edge of the pool as M.R. was hauling herself out. His eyes lifted with her, as she stepped onto the wet tile floor streaming water down her legs in a way that made her feel intensely female suddenly, and intensely self-conscious.

The solitary swimmer she'd seen frequently in the pool—was this the same person? He didn't appear to be a University undergraduate after all.

Nor anyone in the University community.

"Yes? Are you talking to me?"

"Yes, ma'am. You."

He'd risen to his full height—inches taller than M.R. He, too, had only just emerged from the pool— his compactly-muscled body glittered with beads of water. He was older than M.R. had thought, in his mid- or late twenties, with a blunt coarse face, a head that resembled a seal's head, and dark shiny eyes like an animal's eyes; his sneering smile, teeth partly bared, reminded M.R. of a photograph, or a drawing—the head of a snarling dog from Charles Darwin's *The Expression of the Emotions in Man and Animals*.

M.R. was taken by surprise, in this University setting! That a stranger—an intruder—should speak to *her*.

And what an insult it was, that this stranger had no idea who she was.

M.R. was about to turn away annoyed when the young man gripped her arm at the elbow. "This way, ma'am."

She was too astonished to resist. So quickly he'd taken hold of her, in this quasi-public place, in this University setting in which she'd felt at home, she had no way of resisting but clumsily stumbled beside her abductor as briskly and without ceremony he force-walked her along the edge of the pool in the direction of the exit; he addressed her in a low muttering voice that was both soothing and coercive as one might address an animal being led into restraint—how tractable the mesmerized animal, in the clutch of terror! M.R. drew breath to protest, to scream—could not utter a sound—as in the vast pool with its gorgeous blue mosaics and overhead drifting sea-clouds the several swimmers continued to swim laps in their individual lanes like automatons oblivious of M. R. Neukirchen abducted from the pool area as they'd been oblivious of M. R. Neukirchen when she'd been swimming laps beside them.

Readied you must be readied. Ma'am.

Behind the University gym there was a paved parking area and beyond this a steep hill and—somehow—

unrecognizably—beyond this another paved area like a loading dock where the air smelled of creosote and oily water as by a polluted river and now in the astonishment of terror she was seeing others like herself—women—forced by their male captors to walk along a roadway beside the river like refugees pushed and shoved and spoken to harshly and yet with bemusement stumbling forward in dread of falling for to fall in such a place would be to perish—this was no place for weakness, any sort of vulnerability, female "sensitivity." M.R. saw that in the company of the sleek-seal-headed young man was another young man who resembled Evander—(but was not Evander)—and another, older man who resembled Carlos—(but was surely not Carlos)—and their eyes upon her were bluntly assessing and all but dismissive for she was no longer a young woman.

With the others like staggering cattle M.R. was forced past flares of manic flame along a sunken roadway and across a bridge of rust-corroded girders and beneath the bridge a sound of dark rushing water like the cries of the damned. None of the others were known to her as she was not known to them and none wished to reach out to her, to offer solace—as M.R. herself had no solace to offer, in the extremity of her terror. She seemed to know this place—this bridge—

the river—but could not recall their names for the names of places were lost to her and soon too she realized that she was bereft of her name and her identification of which she'd been so ludicrously proud—*M. R. Neukirchen.* No more than a lonely child's imaginary play-game her life was exposed as the unflattering white-rubber swim cap had been snatched from her head, the straps of the unflattering swimsuit yanked down and torn and tattered and her breasts partly exposed as beneath the bridge the rushing water called to her jeering *Did you think you could escape forever? Did you think you could escape this—forever?*

It was meant: her femaleness.

That she was a woman, in the body into which she'd been born.

She had known this—had she? She had not known this, she had cast the knowledge from her, repelled, disbelieving. She had not loved any man, really—she had not had any child nor had she ever been impregnated, the thought had filled her with anxiety, disdain. For that was not *her.* That was not *her wish.*

They had come for her and for other women who had been over-cautious of their lives, who had hoarded their bodies as they had hoarded their souls. Now it was time, now all was exposed, the comfort and deceit of their names—"identities"—the pathos of their lives.

For it was the way of nature, women were possessions of men—fathers, brothers, husbands. It was not
the way of nature, women were possessors of their
selves, their bodies. She would be mated—she would
be impregnated—too long had she escaped this life of
the (female) body—the profound and inevitable life of
the (female) body as at the foster home long ago the
boys had forced younger frightened girls to squirm
and squeal and kick and flail beneath them but Mudgirl had been spared, it was Mudgirl's wish to believe
that she had been spared, the sharp-elbowed boys,
loud-laughing boys, doglike, crude, cruel, blank-
eyed—afterward threatening to strangle the girls if
they "told"—though maybe it was a joke and not a
threat—all that happened, a joke and not a threat—and
not real—as much of childhood was (possibly) a joke
and not real and in any case lost to memory as when
Mrs. Skedd asked if those little fuckers had touched
her and she'd shook her head mutely and evasively and
Mrs. Skedd chose to believe her or in any case not to
further inquire and when she'd hidden—crawled into
the smelly dark space beneath the stairs—when the
man with the spiky hair pulled her out by the ankles
laughing—it was out of instinct as now out of instinct
she dared to pull away from the others, crouched and
cringing and to her relief she found herself beneath

the bridge somehow, or—this was later, farther along the roadway—this was hours later—crouched beneath a road in a drainage pipe, naked, shivering, yet eager with relief—eager to believe that she had escaped, and must now make her way back home—wherever "home" was—by cunning, like a wild animal; by night, that no one would see her; crouched in the filthy drainage pipe for how long until there came a scrabbling, a sudden flash of light, hooting and laughing and she'd been discovered hiding, in the pathos of hiding, but the men had tracked her down of course, hauled her out by the ankles so that her body was scraped, the skin broken and torn and bleeding *Did you think that you could escape—this?*

Along the river were warehouses and in one of these she was taken into a large barracks-type room with other staggering stunned exhausted and terrified women, blank-eyed women, broken women, their shame was such they could not bear to acknowledge one another, and she was one of them and not distinct from them or among them and in a place smelling of creosote and dirt she was thrown down and the remains of the ridiculous swimsuit torn from her and a male figure—a stranger—mulish, heavy—without a word forced himself upon her, grunting with effort, forcing her to lie still and her legs apart—with dry, brute force she was entered—her head struck against the floor—*Uh! uh! uh!* Trying to scream but again no sound came from her throat—trying to fight her assailant, her rapist, kicking, squirming, clawing at him until he knelt above her and slapped her, shut his hands into fists like rocks and struck her, the old cuts on her face sliced raw, her face lacerated and bleeding and yet she fought, in a frenzy of terror she fought, in terror of her life she fought, and somehow—later—when he'd finished with her, or had in disgust grunted lifting himself from her, to depart—she was crawling in an open field—she had escaped, had she?—or they had finished with her and so she was alone now crawling like a wounded animal her body racked with pain and her face bleeding yet there came to her ears the excited cries of crows—a flurry of black-feathered wings in the jungle-like trees at the edge of the field—and there, the King of the Crows flying above her flapping his wings in fury—whether protective of her, or punitive, in disgust of her like the others, she didn't know.

Hurry! Here! This way!

Crouched over making her way like a grotesque broken-backed creature pushing through grasses and into a marshy area where her feet sank into mud and insects hurtled themselves at her exposed face and skin and overhead the King of the Crows continued to shriek

Hurry! This way! This way! and she came upon an open area near a shallow stream in which countless bird-tracks were tamped into the mud like crazed and deafening languages warring with one another and it was her task to make sense of this, it was her task though the human brain could not make sense of so many languages, such vastness, as overhead birds called and mocked and the King of the Crows shrieked at her but she was too exhausted to continue so slept where she lay in the mud her hair caked with mud, mud in her nostrils, her mouth she thought *I will dream now of God. This is a place only God can redeem.* When she wakened she saw that the sun had a belated look in the sky as if this were a day out of some past-time now lost and recoverable in memory only by the most extreme effort of which in her weakened state she was not capable. And in this open space she was naked, terribly exposed, vulnerable and small and her breasts were aching and sensitive with wounds, bite-wounds, where her rapist had sunk his teeth into her—had he?—the nipples torn as if violently sucked-at, bitten. And in this too she was given to know *Not one thing that has happened to you has not happened to others before you.* In this way even her pain was a rebuke to her.

Yet there was beauty even here, that was a rebuke to her despair. On all sides the mudflats riddled with galaxies of flittering light-puddles—a vast broken mirror reflecting a broken sky.

On this mildly overcast day the sun was unnaturally strong. Even behind a scrim of clouds like half-shut eyes the sun was unnaturally strong.

Waking to the marsh-smell in her nostrils, her hair and mouth and the King of the Crows overhead in a tall spiking conifer bereft of nearly all needles and twisted like a misshapen spine yet here too there was a strange sort of beauty as in the sleek-black-feathered bird with the mad yellow eye and Mudwoman was given to know, she was impregnated; and what would come of the rapist's seed jammed up inside her, she had no idea.

"Oh. God."

She must have fallen asleep, the heavy book had fallen from her hands and wakened her with a jolt.

Quickly she stood: what time was it? Where was she?

. . . in the library downstairs at Charters House. Barefoot and but partially dressed and shivering convulsively like an inmate deranged and terrified in some corner of some mental asylum of long-ago in the aftermath of a dream so visceral it would seem to have had no visual or intellectual or even emotional content whatsoever but to have been the equivalent of having been trapped inside a clanging bell or dragged behind a speeding vehicle along a graveled roadway and yet she would not succumb, she would not give in to whatever this was, whatever vision, or whatever failure of vision, for she was strong and determined and she was M. R. Neukirchen—she remembered the name, in triumph—and it was a good strong respected name—it was *her name*—she would bear through this day as through the other days for as long as she was capable and so she would make her way back to the second floor of Charters House and try to sleep until it was time for her to get out of bed with the twittering of the first birds and make her solitary way to the University gym to the cavernous University pool which opened at 5 A.M. for solitary swimmers like herself and if this day was like M.R.'s other days she would arrive no later than 5:30 A.M.

This is my life now. I will live it!

Mudgirl, Cherished.

On the Convent Street bridge they were walking together. Though she was not really a little girl any longer
yet Mrs. Neukirchen held her hand firmly and warmly
and Mrs. Neukirchen was telling her a story as Mrs.
Neukirchen often did at such times when they were
alone together in her soft breathy-girlish voice that
made Meredith think the story had *really happened*
though this story was in fact a fairy tale—one of the
happy-ending fairy tales and so fit for a child to hear—
"Little Briar-Rose."

Such happiness! Mrs. Neukirchen and her little
daughter walking together close together, on the narrow
pedestrian walkway on the Convent Street bridge.

Though Mrs. Neukirchen had to walk slowly because of her swollen legs and ankles. And Meredith had

to walk slowly to keep pace with her mother though Mudgirl would have liked to break free and run, run— run across the Convent Street bridge like a restless little mongrel-dog, that wants only to shake off her mistress's grip and escape.

Escape where?

You have already been there. And there is nowhere.

"Little Briar-Rose" was—almost—a scary story because Little Briar-Rose was cast under a spell by a cruel witch and slept and slept and slept for a very long time until awakened by a king's son and Mrs. Neukirchen did not seem to comprehend that the story was scary for it ended with the words *And then the wedding of the king's son with Little Briar-Rose was celebrated with all splendor, and they lived contented to the end of their days.*

If you did not hear the ending of the story, it was a scary story. But the ending was meant to change the story as if you could change a story backward.

And uttered in Mrs. Neukirchen's special storytelling voice and in a trance of concentration Meredith was staring through the bridge railing at the water rushing below whispering and laughing quietly and a shivery sensation rose in her and she heard herself say as if it were the river speaking through her, "Did you find me somewhere—Momma—and bring me home?"

It had been a hard thing to learn, to say *Momma*. As she'd been instructed to say *Momma, Daddy* like a deaf-mute child instructed to mouth sounds she can't hear. And now, she had said a wrong thing. As Mudgirl should have known. As Mudgirl did know, in the startled and appalled aftermath of her question that so resembled a fairy-tale question naïvely put to a fairy-tale stepmother.

Mrs. Neukirchen stared at her horrified. Her soft raddled-pretty moon face flushed with blood and her eyes were damp with hurt and reproach.

" 'Find you!' 'Bring you home!' What on earth are you saying, Merry? You were always ours—God sent you to *us*. Out of all the world—you are our daughter."

Mrs. Neukirchen's voice quavered with hurt and indignation. For where a stepmother is hurt, there is indignation as well.

Mrs. Neukirchen did not release Meredith's fingers but squeezed them harder. Traffic was passing over the Convent Street bridge causing the old wrought-iron bridge to vibrate and shudder and the planks to rattle and beneath the bridge where Meredith was staring the river was swift and purposeful-seeming. Mrs. Neukirchen continued to speak but Meredith heard only these desperate repeated words—"You know that, Merry, don't you? Out of all of the world—God brought you to Mr. Neukirchen and me—you know that?"

Was this so? Mudgirl could not recall.

Confused with the whispery-laughing river-sound was a memory of—a house that wasn't the Neukirchens' house but a smaller house—a woman's nasal-sharp voice calling *Jew-ell!*

But really, this memory was lost. Smudged and faded like a weatherworn billboard. As poor wheezing Puddin' whose stumpy tail wagged so eagerly even in his last, elderly months had begun to fade—they had loved Puddin' so, and Puddin' had loved them so, but one day Puddin' was gone and it was not good— "healthy"—to brood upon Puddin'.

Tearful Mrs. Neukirchen stooped to hug her little girl. There was no escaping now, Mudgirl must stand still and unresisting in her mother's anxious arms.

And Mudgirl was a good girl, really. Mudgirl had learned to be a good girl in a trance of smiling terror stammering *Y-yes. Y-yes M-Momma don't cry.*

There is a day, an hour. When you understand that the swift-flowing river runs in one direction only, and nothing can reverse it.

"Did you find me somewhere, Daddy? And bring me home?"

Like little poison toads in a fairy tale these words leapt from the child's mouth.

Mr. Neukirchen drove—slowly, fussily—over the Convent Street bridge. For this was a narrow rattly old bridge and Daddy took care crossing any bridge as he said with any passenger on board and particularly his dear daughter. And how much nicer it was to drive—to be driven—over this bridge than to walk for inside the car you could shut your eyes and not have to see the slate-colored water rushing below or the iron railing close beside the car. And once they were on the far side of the bridge Meredith opened her eyes and there was no rushing water—no danger.

This day—a Saturday morning in June—was some weeks after the walk with Mrs. Neukirchen across the bridge when Meredith had asked her strange question that had so upset her mother and in this interlude both Mrs. Neukirchen and her daughter had forgotten the words they'd exchanged as if these words had never been and so it was a surprise to Meredith, and unexpected, how these shocking words came to her again when she was with Mr. Neukirchen—*Did you find me somewhere? And bring me home?*

For truly she could not recall. Only very faintly the names *Jew-ell—Jedina*—sounded in her memory like distant tolling bells.

But Daddy was not upset by his daughter's question as Momma had been. For Daddy rarely became upset as Momma did—it was his "phlegmatic soul" as Daddy said. For a moment not speaking sucking at his lower lip in a comical expression of hard-thinking and then he laughed and said, evenly, as if the child's question were the most natural question in the world, "Meredith, of course! Yes! We found you! But not just 'somewhere'—in a very special place. You wouldn't remember—you were *too little*—we found you beneath a toadstool in our backyard, by the garden gate—not one of those puny little toadstools that grow everywhere but a big toadstool the size of"—Daddy cast his thoughts about like a loose net, seeing what sweet silly thing he could snag—"a Rhode Island red hen. That big."

Meredith giggled, Daddy was always so funny. A toadstool! A red hen! Even when you had no idea what Daddy was talking about, Daddy was so very funny.

But Daddy squinched up his face in a frown. "What? What's so funny? It's the gospel truth—your mother and I discovered you, a *wee little thing the size of a baby chick*, beneath the toadstool by the garden gate. You wouldn't remember, you see—and now the toadstool has vanished."

Meredith knew what a *toadstool* was—a *stool* for a *toad*—Daddy had explained. She had never seen any actual toad sitting on a toadstool but this was the purpose of the strange gray growths that festooned near the garden in the early morning that shattered to powder if you didn't touch them very gently.

But it was silly—wasn't it?—to believe that her parents had found her beneath a toadstool. Even a big toadstool.

Daddy insisted, "Oh yes! We did find you there, that's exactly where you were when we first laid eyes on you."

Meredith giggled she was *not.*

Daddy insisted yes she *was.*

"Of course, we'd ordered you. The way we order pizza from Luigi's—over the phone. Instead of tomato-cheese-pepperoni pizza we ordered a *beautiful little baby girl the size of a baby chick*—wavy brown hair, brown eyes, long narrow feet—*Meredith Ruth*—*"Merry."*

By now Meredith was giggling so hard, she nearly wet her panties. There was rarely any time when she laughed except when Daddy teased in his funny-Daddy way going on and on—and on—lifting his hands from the steering wheel to gesture and making his beard bristle; there was no way to stop Daddy or even to question him for in such a state Daddy was a vortex sucking everything into it faster and faster so that whatever Meredith had asked him initially was lost and lost even to Meredith who was weak and breathless and jittery from giggling and Daddy, too, was laughing and then abruptly—for it was Daddy's way to be abrupt in such matters like switching off TV—Daddy was pressing his forefinger against his nose meaning *something secret*, that Momma need not know.

So this was a good ending, too. Meredith would never never never *never* ask her silly question again.

Mudwoman, Bereft.

April 2003

Please could you call me. I am in need of. . . .

In distant nebulae he was traveling. Through constellations whose very names meant nothing to her—Centaurus, Hydra. Light-years he was gone from her yet she called him, or tried to—the long-memorized numbers at Cambridge, and at the Kitt Peak National Observatory in Arizona—leaving terse and enigmatic messages in case the suspicious wife checked his voice mail.

Please Andre could you call me. I am in need of . . . verification of . . . something.

Her voice lifted in the cheery M.R. way for she could not help herself, M.R. must always assure the listener that beneath the raw plea was spiritual well-being, good common sense. Not any sort of *hysterical female.*

Beyond Earth, there is no day, and there is no night. All is illuminated by "starlight"—the most beautiful light of all. And all is silence—the most beautiful music.

At the University pool she'd become strangely exhausted swimming though she had not exerted herself in any uncommon way. A vigorous half hour swimming laps but soon her arms began to tire, her breath came short and ragged and her heart beat too quickly and staggering out onto the tile she'd found herself staring at a constellation of miniature bubbles in the water in the wake of the sleek-black-haired wide-shouldered undergraduate diver.

But this bubble of time! This rapidly shrinking bubble of time in which we exist together . . .

It was terror to her, this realization. That her life was passing swiftly and the time in which she might have loved and be loved in the intimate way of living with another person was passing yet more swiftly.

The wide-shouldered boy who had not seemed to recognize her—or was too shy, or too aloof, to acknowledge her. It was a university in which undergraduates took on the roles of adults with precocious zeal and capability and were not reluctant to shake the hands of their elders and yet there was this boy, very possibly on the varsity swim team, a champion in his high

school district in—where?—the Midwest, perhaps—
and this hour wasn't his practice time but additional
time for himself, alone; and the sinewy-snaky ease of
his body, his sculpted shoulders, narrow hips and the
bulge of his groin and water streaming down muscled
columnar legs and she felt again that thrill of terror, of
loss—sexual loss—as the bubbles emerged out of the
churning water and were gone in the next second. And
she thought *I am losing everything—am I? Why has
this happened, that I am losing everything?*

Mudgirl, Desired.

Those years Mudgirl moved among the others as if she were one of them.

Meredith Ruth Neukirchen: a dull-earnest name that suited her.

She was an athlete—but not a star athlete. On the girls' basketball team the lanky long-limbed reliable guard who passes the ball to her faster and more aggressive teammates, to sink baskets—*a great team-player.*

Of course, she was intelligent. Though shy and not inclined to speak readily in class yet she excelled in tests and written work and was so very "gifted"—at least as measured in the Carthage public schools—her more responsible teachers took care not to praise her excessively in the presence of her classmates, or even to her parents whom they recognized as hyper-vigilant parents who *cared too much* about their only child. The shrewder of these teachers were even sparing of their praise to Meredith herself, sensing something over-zealous and just slightly frantic in the girl that might effloresce to consume much of her life. By her senior year at Carthage High School Meredith had accumulated numerous academic prizes and distinctions and was regarded by her classmates with the sort of condescending pride one might feel for the achievements of a big sister who is also lame, has a withered arm or a cleft palate.

It was crucial to Mudgirl, that she not be *disliked*. That no one feel *envy*, *jealousy* of her. Only that, in the narrow Carthage High world, there was a place for *Meredith Ruth Neukirchen* that was hers, that would allow her to survive, and even to flourish.

With her high-A average she was named valedictorian of her class. But though she was co-chair of the senior prom committee and worked tireless hours stringing crepe paper streamers and paper lanterns around the gym, setting up tables and chairs and ordering food and soft drinks, no one thought to urge any boy to invite her to the prom as his "date"— and so Meredith had stayed at home on senior-prom weekend as she often did on such occasions, with her parents. If she was disappointed, hurt, embarrassed or humiliated—she was too good-natured—or too practiced in stoicism—to give any sign. Mr. Neukirchen joked of taking Meredith to the prom, himself—"If Dads who can only fox-trot and have one wooden leg are allowed"—but Mrs. Neukirchen objected, that was an utterly ridiculous idea—"Merry doesn't need their silly old 'prom' any more than she needs *them*. She has *us*."

Not in the late spring of Meredith's senior year of high school but in the previous fall, this happened.

Meredith was never to tell anyone. Certainly not the Neukirchens!

He was her math teacher Mr. Schneider. By far the least popular of teachers at Carthage High for the difficulty of his subject, his "blitz" quizzes and severe grading and his general air of barely concealed disdain for his students, colleagues, the city of Carthage itself. He was a somber-brooding man who might have been any age between thirty-five and fifty, with vertical frown-lines in his forehead, a beakish nose and one nostril larger than the other, like an empty eye socket. Hans Schneider was tall, and thin; his shoulders were sloped, like broken wings; his clothes fitted him loosely, and were always the same clothes—long-sleeved white cotton shirt, striped necktie, gabardine trousers shiny in the seat. His eyeglasses were heavy black plastic frames that were often crooked on his nose. He smelled of chalk dust, faintly rancid milk or butter—or garlic; his teeth were uneven, grayish and thin-looking as a child's teeth. Often he suffered from colds, or worse—in the midst of teaching he turned aside to sneeze, cough, snuffle, blow his nose in a succession of disgusting wadded tissues that accumulated on his desktop; at times, to the unease and embarrassment of his students, he was required to use some sort of plastic inhaler kept in a desk drawer.

It was said of him that he was a "freak"—a "fag"—a "Nazi"—but in math class, no one dared to behave other than respectfully toward Hans Schneider. He was acknowledged to be very smart—the smartest of Carthage High teachers by far. He was certainly a strict disciplinarian. When he slouched to the front of the room to strike chalk against the blackboard in a rapid pattern of geometric figures, equations and numerals that left many in the class baffled, Meredith took note that her teacher seemed to be compensating for a leg that gave him pain, or was slightly shorter than the other leg; his evasive manner, his habit of heavy sarcasm, was camouflage of a kind, like her own.

She'd begun reading "classics" in her father's library—one of them was the massive *Dialogues of Plato* —and there she'd read, amid much else that meant little to her, but excited her with dogmatic certainties and paradoxes, that *beauty is symmetry and exactness.* And so she saw that Mr. Schneider was *off balance* somehow.

Like her, Meredith thought.

For often in mirrors Meredith saw, to her dismay, that one of her eyes was larger than the other, or set at a different angle in her face; her eyebrows would grow together thickly above the bridge of her nose except, secretly, without her mother suspecting, she plucked them with tweezers borrowed from Mrs. Neukirchen's "vanity." And in gym class it seemed to Meredith that she sometimes ran *crookedly*—though in the confusion and excitement no one was likely to notice.

Though Mudgirl moved among the others as if she were one of them—though she'd learned, she had thought, to skillfully mimic their speech, their gestures, their ways of moving their bodies, the pitch of their laughter and their shifts of emotion rapid and seemingly random as the sudden flights of birds—of course she was readily detectable, by an observer shrewd as Hans Schneider, as an imposter, even apart from her high intelligence and classroom deportment.

He'd been seeing her, Meredith knew. *Seeing* her as not even the Neukirchens could see her.

And often staring at her, for no evident reason, during math class, with an intensity with which no other teacher stared at her.

"Well, Mere-dith! You seem to have gotten some things correct, eh?"

Handing back Meredith's neatly executed homework assignments, tests and quizzes, Mr. Schneider went out of his way to lean over Meredith's desk, just close enough that she could smell his body-odor, and his breath which other girls described as *garlic-breath,* or more cruelly, *mummy-breath.* He had a way of ignoring students as if their very existence annoyed him and here he was leaning over Meredith Neukirchen at her desk in the front row—squinting at her through crooked eyeglasses as if she were a rare species of being.

"Unless you have a father at home who helps you, this is very good work." His manner was awkwardly jovial—a crude imitation of the way he supposed other teachers at Carthage High spoke to make their students laugh. "And if you have a mother at home who is helping you, she is very good—for a Carthage, New York, housewife."

Meredith laughed uncomfortably. Was this meant to be funny? Meredith didn't quite dare to insist that she'd done her homework herself—of course, she did all her homework herself—for that would seem to be challenging her teacher.

He'd relented, finally. Seeing the look of alarm in Meredith's flushed face and the way in which the other students in the class were staring at him, in disbelief, as if a zombie had roused himself to life: not that the zombie can mimic a human being convincingly, but that the zombie can rouse himself to life at all.

Another time, when Mr. Schneider waylaid Meredith at the end of class as the others trooped out of the room.

"Mere-dith! Tell me—do you like geometry?"

Yes. Meredith did like geometry.

"And why do you 'like' geometry, Meredith?"

Because geometry involved drawings of figures as well as numbers—you could see the problems not just think them. And because—she thought—geometry was always the same.

"But how do you know that geometry is 'always the same,' Meredith? Have you experienced geometry in China? India? On Mars?"

Meredith had to admit, she had not.

"Then how can you be so certain that geometry is 'always the same'? There are 'laws' of nature that don't apply to distant galaxies, you know. Such regions where time doesn't exist or, if it does, befuddles us all by running backward—so that it is never bedtime no matter how tired and bored we are."

Meredith smiled uncertainly. She had no idea how to reply to this. She tried to think how Plato, or Socrates—or Isaac Asimov—might reply; but her mind was blank.

She did not say to her teacher *Because geometry is a game and nothing real—that's why I like it. Because there are rules you can learn to play this game.*

Though he must have seen that his student was stricken with shyness and self-consciousness, eager to slip away from him, yet Mr. Schneider persisted in the interrogation: "And—Mere-dith!— what of the singular year A.D. 1111?"

The singular year A.D. 1111? Was this too some sort of joke?

When Meredith's other teachers spoke with her the substance of what they had to say was immediate and accessible and there was no need to try to decode it—but whatever Mr. Schneider was talking about had little to do with the words he uttered in his forced-jovial voice.

Meredith murmured she had no idea about A.D. 1111.

"And what of the singular year A.D. 3011?"

And no idea about A.D. 3011.

"How can you be certain that geometry will 'be the same' then, as it is now?" Mr. Schneider chuckled, triumphantly.

Politely and gravely Meredith listened, for it was Mudgirl's way to placate her elders.

You did not want to think that your elders were deranged, ignorant, stupid, or malicious. You did not ever want to think such a thought for fear that one of these elders would read your mind, behind the polite grave good-girl smile.

"Mathematics is supposed to be always and forever—permanent—for that is its beauty. Yet how can one know—not think but *know*—that it is always and forever permanent? In quantum physics . . ."

Meredith understood that Mr. Schneider was teasing her schoolgirl sobriety, as her father often did. Though with Mr. Neukirchen you knew that his teasing was affectionate, and with Mr. Schneider you couldn't be certain for there was a coercive nature about him. An uneasy sense that, if Meredith made a break to leave the room, Mr. Schneider might speak harshly to her, or reach out to restrain her.

" . . . the impossible becomes necessary, to believe. Because the merely possible is inadequate."

Students were trooping noisily in, for the next math class. Meredith didn't run from the room but departed quickly.

"Mere-dith. Please see me after school."

More frequently then, in October of that year, Hans Schneider began to murmur these words to Meredith in a lowered voice, as if not wanting other students to hear.

This was crucial: the math teacher wasn't asking her to see him after class, as he often instructed others. But after school, at 3:15 P.M., when he was likely to be alone in his classroom, and Meredith would be his only visitor.

He wanted to establish some sort of relationship between them, Meredith knew. Since the start of the fall semester of her senior year she'd felt this—there was so distinct a difference between Mr. Schneider's interest in her and her other teachers' interest in her; she'd never had Mr. Schneider for any course until now, and was quite mystified by him. That he invariably gave her high grades on her tests—scrawled in his crabbed hand, in red ink—did not seem to shield her from his crudely jovial, coercive manner.

It was Mr. Schneider's technique to summon his better students to the blackboard, to work out homework problems for the rest of the class. There were several students he called upon but no one so frequently as "Mere-dith"—at first she'd been stricken with shyness and embarrassment as if she were being exposed naked to the stares of her classmates but gradually, over the weeks, she'd become accustomed to writing on the blackboard as she explained what she was doing. In Hans Schneider's classroom Meredith learned to "teach"—it was clear to her that Mr. Schneider knew his subject thoroughly but he couldn't relate to students; he assumed that each student knew more or less what all the others knew, and never took any notice of students left behind in utter bewilderment; he could not see that a student's sulkiness and resentment had anything to do with *him,* but only with the deficiencies of the student. Perhaps his habitual sarcasm was a kind of shyness, Meredith thought: a mask to hide behind.

As Mr. Schneider drawled and mumbled and sometimes spoke with his back to the class, indifferent to his audience, so Meredith learned to speak clearly, so that students in the back row could hear her. She who could not have spoken to a group of classmates with any sort of ease, in the cafeteria for instance, found it easy to speak to her classmates from the front of the room, for their attention, fixed upon her, gave her permission; more than permission, it was a sort of plea, for Meredith was their intermediary in math class, their only hope of understanding. Teaching a classroom of students was really just a way of talking to individuals singly, Meredith thought: you fixed your gaze upon them, you smiled, you spoke matter-of-factly and without any sort of humor or irony, which would only confuse them; if you could, you allowed them to think that what they were learning was only just common sense, and that they already knew it. Imparting knowledge was a pleasure—while Mr. Schneider seemed always to be begrudging students his knowledge of math, which they must extract from him, like squeezing a few drops of moisture from a rag.

As Meredith went through a typical homework problem, Mr. Schneider stood a few feet away observing her; ready to pounce upon her if she made a mistake; but Meredith did not make a mistake. If Mr. Schneider had given her problems beyond the homework assignments, very likely Meredith would have become confused; but Mr. Schneider never did this. Close by he stood dabbing at his nose with a wadded tissue, or fussing with chalk; he slouched, like a broke-backed crow; in fact, there was something crowlike about him, an uncanny yellow-eyed vigilance, that might have been a solace to Meredith if it had not made her so uneasy.

"I suppose you know, Mere-dith—among our Carthage students, you are someone special."

Was this meant to be a fact, or a kind of question? Was it *teasing*?

Meredith's face grew warm. The sensation was both pleasurable and disturbing.

A voice warned her *Mudgirl is not special! You know this.*

"Of course you have no natural 'gift' for math—I mean, a serious gift. You're a good high school math student—in college, you'll soon realize your limits. From what I've heard about you, you have 'talents' for other things—for writing—but math is very special, and few of us can live up to its demands." Mr. Schneider spoke flatly as if this were a truth that must be uttered though Meredith would surely be hurt, to hear it. "However—in you—quite apart from the 'math'—there is a kind of—depth"—now Hans Schneider spoke haltingly, blinking behind his oversized eyeglasses, as if he wasn't sure what he meant to say—"to your soul, that none of your Carthage classmates has. This—depth—is far more valuable than a—a gift—for. . . ." Mr. Schneider's voice trailed off like the voice of one groping his way in the dark.

Meredith, deeply embarrassed, stared blinking at the floor, at her feet. She was clutching textbooks and notebooks against her chest. What was this strange crow-man saying to her!

Depth?—soul? She was sure that Mudgirl had no soul.

Was he the one who'd pulled her from the mudflat, when she'd been a little little girl? Almost, she could see his face—the face of the one who'd grimaced and grunted, taking hold of her shoulder, tugging at her. Almost—that man had been Hans Schneider— had he?

"You are an adopted child, I believe. Your birth parents are—unknown?"

With astonishing matter-of-factness Mr. Schneider was addressing her. Meredith was so taken by surprise, she could not reply.

"I don't mean to pry. I would never betray your confidence. The facts of your life—your previous life—are not secret, you know—but a matter of 'public record.' Still, I would not—if you're uncomfortable talking of such things. . . ."

Meredith shook her head. No.

"No?—what?"

"No. That isn't right."

"It—isn't? You are not adopted?"

"I am not—'adopted.' "

"I see."

Mr. Schneider frowned. It was not like Meredith Neukirchen—it was not like any of Mr. Schneider's students—to so directly contradict him. But she would not back down. Her heart beat in anger like the heart of a small enraged creature and calmly she said, "You can ask my parents, Mr. Schneider. They will tell you."

"Yes—I see."

"I think you've met them—they met you—at PTA. You can ask them if I am adopted. . . ."

It was an awkward moment but Mr. Schneider did not want Meredith to leave, just yet. Clumsily he reverted to his previous subject—and what a "good, if not gifted" student of math Meredith was; in a sudden flurry of praise he told her that in his opinion she should certainly apply to college but not the New York State teachers' colleges—"Somewhere distinguished, like Cornell."

The Neukirchens had attended state schools: Agatha had graduated from the library school at Albany, Konrad from Buffalo State. Cornell was a private university and known to be very expensive and Meredith had no realistic hope of applying there for her parents couldn't afford the tuition and in any case expected her to attend one of the teachers' colleges, to train to be a high school teacher and return to Carthage.

Of course—there is no pressure on you dear Merry!

You will make your way into the world as you will— you are very very talented we are sure!

But teaching is natural for you—as the library is natural for me—and you could live on our street—

—could live in our house—

—could live right where you are living now—

—when we're old and lonely and needing our little girl. Pro-mise?

It was time for Meredith to leave Mr. Schneider's classroom with its five rows of desks, its chalk-cloudy blackboard and rancid smells. He hovered about her, uncertainly; in his fingers he fussed with pieces of chalk which in his nervousness he broke, without seeming to know what he did.

"I—I have basketball practice, Mr. Schneider. I have to leave now."

"In a minute! Surely your ridiculous 'sports teams' can wait."

"Practice begins at—"

"Look, Meredith: you are not like the others. Even the other good students—I swear, I can see through to the bottoms of their souls. But you . . ."

Meredith was becoming anxious. On the wall the clock read 3:49 P.M.—basketball practice had begun at 3:30 P.M. Younger than sixteen she'd become anxious about *being late.*

Urgently Mr. Schneider was saying, as if he'd read her thoughts, "You're sixteen, Meredith—are you? In five years, you'll be twenty-one. I am twenty-nine and in five years I will be thirty-four. The difference is not so profound. In some cultures, it is non-existent."

Twenty-nine! Meredith would have guessed that Hans Schneider was ten years older.

Numbly she stared at the floor. Her ears were ringing. She could not be certain she'd heard what she had heard.

"You're not a shallow girl, Meredith. You're not a pretty girl—not vain, childish. You did not live a child's life. Beyond these others, you are *mature*. You—like me—"

In Hans Schneider's face there was the defiant look of one who has spent a lifetime constructing an elaborate structure out of some flimsy material like paper and now, with a reckless gesture, he was intent upon destroying it. His dull-striped tie was loose at his neck as if he'd been tugging at it. His fingers were cloudy with chalk dust and there were chalk-smudges on his face. In a quavering voice he said:

"You could wait for me. There won't be other men—boys—not many—who would pursue you. The 'physical life' will not be easy for you—you can be sure. We—you and I—could have an agreement like a—contract."

If the Neukirchens knew of this exchange! Meredith must protect them.

"We have an understanding already, I think? From the first day you walked into this classroom? And then, when I sent you to the blackboard to demonstrate the properties of an isosceles triangle . . ."

Meredith remembered: after he'd met Hans Schneider at a PTA meeting at the school, Mr. Neukirchen had been so intrigued by his daughter's math teacher—"Such an original personality!"—he'd looked into Schneider's background and discovered that he'd gone to college in a most unusual place—Scotland! Hans Schneider had a B.A. degree from the University of St. Andrews. Though his grandparents lived in Watertown, less than two hundred miles away from Carthage, his parents lived in Boston, and he'd enrolled in Boston University to earn a master's degree in math; he'd supplemented these courses with a program at SUNY Albany that certified him as a high school math teacher. He'd come to Carthage in 1973 and during his first year he'd given failing grades to many students and was bitterly complained of by both students and their parents; he'd advised the Math Club whose membership, already small, soon vanished altogether; he had disagreements with colleagues and with the school principal. Yet, he'd remained on the staff, having learned to "adjust" his criteria to Carthage standards; for it was rare that any teacher in the Carthage public school system had a master's degree from a university as distinguished as Boston University, and the school board had not wanted to lose him.

Hans Schneider lived alone in a rented apartment on Midland Street, and walked or bicycled to school. He was seen at the local movie theater, always alone. He ate meals at a succession of inexpensive restaurants, always alone. He seemed to have no familial or personal life and when Konrad Neukirchen invited him to dinner one evening he'd seemed utterly "flummoxed"—(Mr. Neukirchen's description)—and declined.

There would seem to have been no connection between Mr. Neukirchen's invitation to Hans Schneider and the math teacher's interest in Mr. Neukirchen's daughter. Though in some way, Mr. Schneider might have misunderstood. Meredith recalled the way he'd summoned her to the blackboard on one of the first days of class—*"Mere-dith Neu-kirch-en come forward please"*—in his arch manner, all but snapping his fingers at her as you'd summon a dog. He had meant the class to laugh—a few students did laugh, uncertainly—but the joke, if it was a joke, had fallen flat. And yet, with each passing class-day, it had seemed as if Mr. Schneider and Meredith Neukirchen did have some connection and it may have been remarked upon, that Mr. Schneider called upon Meredith more often than he called upon other students, and that, within earshot of the others, he frequently asked her to see him after class and after school.

She thought *I can run out of the room. He can't stop me!*

She thought *But that is something only a child would do. I am not a child.*

She was not sixteen, as the records stated: but she was certainly not a child.

With seeming unconsciousness, a stick of chalk between his twitchy fingers, Hans Schneider had maneuvered himself between his frightened student and the classroom door. He was speaking in a disjointed manner, rambling, yet urgent; his forehead, creased with lines like downward-pointing arrows, was oily with perspiration. Meredith often found herself, in Mr. Schneider's class, watching his hands, his fingers, with a sort of appalled fascination: the math teacher fussed with chalk-sticks, choosing an unbroken stick at the start of each class and then, as minutes passed, breaking the stick into two; tossing the smaller piece onto his desktop, and continuing to fuss with the larger until it, too, was broken; and so on, through the fifty-minute class period. You could not easily calculate how many pieces of chalk Mr. Schneider broke because each broken piece did not yield two more broken pieces, and so there was no ready equation, that one with Meredith's limited grasp of mathematics could devise; yet it seemed to her, if Mr. Schneider were allowed to continue, if he were never interrupted by a ringing bell, he might break chalk-pieces to infinity; but if there were no witness to Mr. Schneider breaking chalk-pieces to infinity, was that an accurate description of what Mr. Schneider might do?

Meredith was intent upon the nervous chalky fingers, long, somehow talonlike, and the nails—discolored, very short, with reddened cuticles as if bitten-at. Mr. Schneider was explaining—as one might explain to an excitable, very young child—that he was "not lonely"—but "yes, alone"—he had "granted himself" six years to become "like the quotidian, outwardly"—and beyond that. . . . Somehow too he was speaking of the rotational movements of the stars and planets that were predictable as clockwork until—one day—some unique comet-incursion rendered them no longer predictable. Forces in equilibrium—centrifugal, centripetal—and the "human" at the core which was the true mystery.

Meredith could barely hear the math teacher's voice, through the ringing in her ears. She thought *He will never forgive me.*

"The essence of a brute life is—you can live alone, or not alone. If you chose to live alone, you must be far more resilient than some of us suppose. For if you are always alone, you will be thinking non-stop—your brain will never click off. It is not possible to live a life of thought continuously—this, I have discovered in this terrible place—'Carthage.' Oh aptly named! If you are amid others their chatter will put you to sleep—but that is not such a bad thing, truly. I could live with my parents of course—but no—that would be stressful for all of us. And I will not *beg*."

By slow almost imperceptible degrees Meredith was trying to ease past Mr. Schneider to the door. But like a tall lanky hyper-vigilant guard on the basketball court Mr. Schneider blocked her way.

Stupid she'd been, naïve—unseeing. Not wanting to think that the math teacher had been staring at her, thinking of her—so strangely, obsessively. For Meredith had had little experience in attracting the attention of boys, still less men. No one had ever seemed to "desire" her—no one had ever been mean to her. No one scrawled her name or initials in graffiti on the side of the Convent Street bridge, or on the water tower, or at the rear of the school building, as they did the names and initials of other girls. When she was alone and unobserved Meredith paused to examine these crude markings with the anxious hope that she might discover her name amid the others; for even to be insulted would be a sign that Mudgirl's imposture had not yet been detected.

As she worried, more generally, about *being normal*—as Mr. Schneider would say, *the quotidian*. Her life as a female—an adolescent—was fraught with small embarrassments and anxieties; what Mrs. Neukirchen called with quaint indirection *Your menstrell period* did not come to her normally—(every twenty-eight days?)—but at erratic intervals from which no reliable hypothesis could be drawn. And her body didn't seem to her a female body, exactly. Not as the bodies of her girl-classmates were female.

Her breasts were small and hard and unyielding unlike the softer, fuller breasts of girls she glimpsed in the locker room; she had virtually no hips, or buttocks; yet her shoulders were wide, her limbs long, her arm- and leg-muscles hard—the body of a skinny boy. In slacks and a windbreaker Meredith was often mistaken for a boy—her face, un-made-up like the faces of her girl-classmates, was shiny-pale, and plain; she hadn't yet acquired the mysterious word *androgynous*, that might have comforted her, or roused her to more anxiety. Despite the Neukirchens' wish to shield their daughter, and despite the spiritual solace of Quakerism, which was a benign-blinding light that swallowed up all shadowy crevices in which *hurt, harm, cruelty, sorrow, evil* might flourish, Meredith understood that the world was governed by crude raw forces—the striving for territory, and the striving to reproduce one's kind.

It was "biology" to which the clumsily drawn penises ("cocks") and vaginas ("cunts") of adolescent graffiti made obsessive reference. And how naïve of Mudgirl, to imagine herself in any way among these.

She did not want to believe that it was "biology" that had drawn her math teacher to her. To Mudgirl! For this had to be a terrible mistake.

"I—I have to leave now, Mr. Schneider. . . ."

"Why? Why must you leave?"

"Because—it's time."

" 'Time' for—what? Who?"

"B-basketball practice . . ."

Meredith's voice faltered like the voice of a guilty child.

In the math teacher's talon-fingers a stubby piece of chalk managed to break. Half fell to the floor, unnoticed. Mr. Schneider, now breathing harshly, as if his lungs were shutting down in a fury of distress, was standing less than eighteen inches from Meredith, and leaning forward; she could see oily globules on his forehead, and a fanatic look to his large blinking eyes. Coldly he said: "You know perfectly well that there is an understanding between us. You know this, and you knew it from the first, Mere-dith."

"I—I don't think so, Mr. Schneider. . . ."

"Yes. Of course—you knew. You are *not stupid.*"

Boldly Meredith stepped forward—blindly. She must take the risk, to escape from this strange quivering man.

It must have happened then—swiftly, and confusedly—that Mr. Schneider took hold of Meredith: her right shoulder, and then her right upper arm. How strong his fingers were, and how unexpected! Yet she twisted from him, at once. For it was Mudgirl's instinct to save herself, to flee her opponent. And how quick, strong, agile she was—her opponent was shocked for he'd expected a more docile girl.

"Meredith! I have not given you permission to leave—come back. . . ."

She fled. Flung open the door, ran into the hall. And in the hall lined with lockers, running.

She told no one. Never would she tell anyone. Her bruised upper right arm she hid beneath sleeves, until the talon-marks faded. To her basketball teammates that afternoon she apologized stammering and flush-faced so they stared at her in amazement—(had they even missed her?)—and to the Neukirchens she said nothing for she knew she must spare them at all costs.

And the next morning at school it was announced in all the homerooms that Hans Schneider had had an "accident" and would not be teaching his classes that day; a substitute would teach in his place.

And the following day, it was announced that Hans Schneider would not be teaching for the rest of the week. The same substitute, a middle-aged woman with a nervous smile, would continue to teach his classes.

And so finally, the following week, it was announced that Hans Schneider would not be returning to Carthage High for the "foreseeable" future.

Meredith didn't tell her parents about Mr. Schneider's behavior with her—certainly not that he'd tried to restrain her from running out of the room—but it was altogether natural for her to mention to them, that her math teacher had had some sort of accident and wasn't teaching any longer and that the woman who was substituting for him was "nice, but not nearly so smart" as Mr. Schneider.

And afterward Meredith overheard her parents discussing Mr. Schneider in their private, lowered voices which were not for "Merry" to hear.

Poor man! They said it was asthma medication. . . . And some sort of arthritis drug. Ster-oid? It was an overdose.

Only twenty-nine! He looked so much older. . . .

But he is alive, they said. In the hospital.

In Watertown, in the hospital. Not here.

I knew that there was something wrong with him, y'know.

You did? How on earth?

When he didn't come here for dinner, dear. When I invited him to one of my darling wife's delicious homecooked meals and he looked at me as if I'd invited him to swallow poison.

Mudwoman, Challenged.

Ready! She must be made ready.

In this shadowy place trying desperately to see into a mirror—to see her face—for there was something wrong with her face, that had betrayed her; something wrong with her face, that had to be remedied; something disfiguring, that had to be disguised and made ready.

For this event—this "meeting"—was crucial in her life. She had no idea who the individuals were or even where they were—(in a distant building? Was this the University campus?)—but she knew that they were sitting in judgment of her—and they were waiting for her—for she was late, already she was late and— desperate to disguise the singular ugliness of her face, where the blood-bruise-splotches had worked their way down her cheeks and into the soft tissue about her mouth like an accusing finger of God so she looked as if she'd been devouring something raw and bloody—she was going to be even later.

The end, when it came, came swiftly.

For M.R. it would not have seemed like *the end.* For M.R. it would have seemed at most a kind of *interruption, a minor mishap.*

An annoyance, a misunderstanding. Maybe even—a blunder.

But not—the end.

Like one who, amid an afternoon of pressing appointments, is told by her doctor that her condition is inoperable, untreatable—terminal: that she will die within a few weeks, unavoidably: yet seems not to hear, only just continues with the remainder of the afternoon of pressing appointments chiding herself *How busy I am! How important I must be.*

Late! In fact yes she was late.

The very word *late* thudding in her ears like a demented pulse.

Late you are late late—late.

A principle of Time: once you are *late,* you cannot be *not-late.*

Once you are *late* you cannot undo your *fate.*

Inexplicably, inexcusably—eighteen minutes late.

Eighteen minutes! For the trustees' meeting in Charters Hall. For this crucial May meeting for which M.R. had planned for countless hours.

Hours, days, weeks. President Neukirchen had planned!

Budget for the upcoming year, admissions issues, student aid proposal, "development" . . . And she was *late,* and there was not a thing she could do, breathless, eyes feverish, hands trembling—(but shrewdly like many afflicted with tremor she knew to keep her hands still, clenched or clutching something, to disguise the trembling which was new, this very morning)—to render herself *not-late.*

"Excuse me! So sorry! A—an emergency—phone call. . . ."

Did they believe her? Why would they not believe her?

(M. R. Neukirchen did not lie: why would they not believe her?)

(Had she used this explanation before? These words—had she stammered these words before? To this very gathering of people? She did not think so. She did not think so. She was sure, she had not. And yet— why did they stare at her, as if disbelieving? And the expression in their faces—alarm, surprise, concern? What did this mean? Because they were *trustees*—why did that mean M.R. must *trust* them?)

This May meeting. This crucial May meeting. An annual meeting, and a crucial meeting, and these were *trustees*.

These were *trustees* of the University, who had hired M. R. Neukirchen. They were her *employers*, you could say. They were her *overseers*. Her salary and contract were set by the *trustees*. The president is the hireling of the board of trustees and cannot disobey them, or offend them—cannot lose their *trust*.

Yet: eighteen minutes late! There was a record of this, M.R. supposed. Sessions of the Board of Trustees were meticulously recorded for legal as well as practical purposes.

Meetings of the distinguished Board of Trustees of the University took place, by tradition, in the Octagonal Room of Salvager Hall. A beautiful old rotunda with a stained-glass ceiling, ornately carved antique mahogany furnishings, an octagonal table and plush chairs and on the walls portraits of the University's earliest revered presidents and of these the most prominent was Reverend Ezechial Charters whose views of the female sex, children, Indian "savages" and "blacks" and all religious sects save his own Protestant sect were exactly antipathetic to President Neukirchen's views in fact repulsive to her, obscene. Yet, she and Reverend Charters were of a single—singular—lineage.

Smile, smile! The God-damn face is the same.

"President Neukirchen? Is something—wrong?"

Quickly she answered *No.*

No—of course!

Wanting to say how ironic it was, how—fitting?— that she'd inherited the presidency of the University, when, in the eyes of the first president Ezechial Charters, she'd have been dismissed as a mere female, worse yet a non-God-fearing female savage.

No—of course—not.

The only possible answer to so insulting a question.

These people—*trustees*—twenty-eight of them, around the octagonal table. One by one she counted them: she could not stop her brain from counting.

The governor of the State of New Jersey was an ex officio trustee of the University but the governor of the State of New Jersey embroiled in his own hazardous politicking in Trenton was not present today.

Other individuals at the octagonal table were M.R.'s advisers—director of the University Corporation, vice president for finance, vice president for development, provost of the University, president of the University Investment Company—names she knew very well—of course—as she knew their faces—but had forgotten, temporarily.

"I think—if we are all here—those of us who *are here*—the meeting will begin."

M.R.'s bright smile! Eighteen minutes behind schedule.

But now it had begun, and would continue until *the end*.

Never can you anticipate *the end*, from the perspective of *the beginning*.

For she would have thought—had wanted, desperately, to believe—that this was still the beginning for her, or nearly.

Her first year as president. Scarcely completing her first year.

First woman, first year. First president of the University who is a woman.

How grateful she was! Yet, how resentful.

First woman, first female. Why did it matter so much. Why did sex matter so much!

It was a classical paradox in philosophy: where is the *self*?

In the body, or in—the *soul*?

Is there in fact a *soul*?

Is there in fact a *self*?

Or rather—*selves*?

Or rather—(this horror the more probable contemplated in the stark bright sunshine following an
insomniac night)—*no self except brain-matter on the
perpetual verge of being extinguished.*

She was breathless and distracted and agitated like
one wakened abruptly from a dream. Her clothes
were—not disheveled exactly but somehow not *quite
right*—and her hair was certainly disheveled as if she'd
hardly had time to run a comb or a brush through it
and her face—M.R.'s poor ravaged face!—would
betray her after all for it was strangely swollen about
the mouth and hastily, bizarrely made-up with a pasty
sort of makeup that, drying, had darkened like mud.

Not a shining-faced girl-Valkyrie any longer but one
of those primitive mask-faces in Picasso's *Les Demoi-
selles d'Avignon.*

Yet President Neukirchen was speaking with unusual clarity like one enunciating words in a foreign
language whose meanings were not altogether clear to
her. And President Neukirchen was gracious welcom-
ing the *trustees* to the University, and thanking them
for having come. And in the midst of her welcom-
ing speech there came abruptly into her (left) field of
vision like a figure popping out of a box a gentleman
with a familiar face—an older gentleman, silvery-
haired, in an elegant suit, necktie—she knew his name:

Lockhardt?—only just not his first name—and chided him gently, to disguise the annoyance she felt at being interrupted in so clumsy a way: "Why Lockhardt! Are you sneaking up on me?"

It was a strange, strained moment. Leonard Lockhardt stared at M.R., speechless; then, murmuring an apology, taking his seat at the octagonal table.

M.R. had no time to wonder how her chief legal adviser had somehow appeared in the octagonal room out of nowhere, to sit with the others as if nothing were unusual.

She supposed then—it came to her in that instant, irrefutably—that her chief legal adviser had been meeting previously with the *trustees*, without her knowledge.

He is my enemy. My enemy here at home.

And her staff, too—some of them—were probably aware of the conspiracy.

Yet she would say nothing—of course. Her hurt and her indignation she would temper with cunning.

She was speaking with unusual clarity and so she meant to listen with unusual clarity as officers of the University gave their reports and questions were asked of the officers by individual trustees and answered and M.R. marveled that nothing was said—nothing was asked—of the boy who had tried to kill himself, not very far from Salvager Hall; she could not recall his name except the surname began with *S* but how vividly she could see him! The young aggrieved face, the wounded eyes, mouth!

His voice, defiant and anguished. As if accusing *her.*

He was alive, still. He was alive on a life-support machine in Florida. His brain had been extinguished, more or less. The *self* that had so unjustly accused President Neukirchen had been extinguished yet the undersized boy-body existed, still. This was a cruel, terrible fate. This was the *life* that awaited him.

The lawsuit hadn't yet been initiated, by the Stirks' attorney.

("Stirk": that was the name.)

Very likely, the Stirk case was in the trustees' minds but they were not speaking of it, just yet. The meeting had just begun, they had plenty of time. The University's chief legal counsel would confide in them *I'd warned her. Not to speak with the boy personally. The foolish woman didn't take my advice—of course. And now . . .*

Which of the *trustees* were her friends, M.R. wondered. And which her enemies.

Initially she'd been persuaded that all of the *trustees* were friends—supporters—of M. R. Neukirchen. All were enthusiastic about her—"admirers."

This naïve supposition she'd had to discard. For now they were sitting in judgment of her.

Certainly there had been an edge to their greetings. Not all had smiled at her as warmly as she'd wished. Not all had called her *Meredith!* in that special way that signals *I like you, I am your friend.*

For—(of course)—they'd been reading about the Stirk case, they'd seen coverage on TV—they did not think so highly of President Neukirchen any longer.

And how steely the look in the eyes of one of the older trustees—a wealthy businessman from the Midwest whom M.R. had inherited, as she'd inherited so many trustees, from her predecessor. She could not recall his name—the surname began with *D*—and the first name was deceptively affable, commonplace: Bob, Rob, Ron. A graduate of the University from the long-ago era before women were admitted and before more than a frail fraction of non-whites—(these would include Jews)—were to be seen on campus; and, if seen, were to be attributed to the protocol of the *quota.*

Here was a man whose appraisal of a woman was swift and blunt and unsentimental and who had been able to accept M. R. Neukirchen not as a woman but as a sort of honorary man, if an inferior sub-species.

Or maybe D___ wasn't from the Midwest, maybe M.R. was confusing the man with someone else. That brisk hard handshake that is both a greeting and a warning.

Don't think that you can put anything over on me. I am not one of your liberal lackey-assholes.

Still M.R.'s brain was counting figures at the table: twenty-nine, thirty, thirty-one, thirty-two. . . . A part of her brain counting even as another part of her brain, like a beacon shining into darkness, perceived the situation with heartstopping clarity.

That *no one had brought up the subject of Stirk!* This was significant.

That it had been planned, perhaps rehearsed, that D___ would surprise President Neukirchen with a prepared statement about Stirk—(you could see how D___ had something contentious to say: his bulldog jaws quivered)—but cunning President Neukirchen guided the meeting in another direction, skipping items on the agenda so that she might present to the trustees her ambitious new plan for student-aid reform: full-tuition scholarships for all students who are admitted to the University regardless of their family's economic status; with particular emphasis upon the children of lower-middle-income families who had been seriously neglected in the University's zeal for racial diversity.

For the University was very wealthy, as the trustees well knew—even with the downturn in the economy, the University's endowment was the highest per student in the country. Tuition provided a small fraction of the University's operating costs in any case.

As M.R. spoke, in even her somewhat distracted state she was aware that she wasn't receiving, from the individuals seated at the gleaming octagonal table, the sort of affirming smiles, nods, murmurs of approval to which she'd become accustomed at such meetings. Somehow it had ceased—the flow of *flattering attention* to which she'd become accustomed.

For few of the trustees were looking persuaded. M.R. had prepared for this presentation with charts, graphs—statistics. . . . It would be her strategy to wear down opposition, if no other strategy would prevail!

With a part of her brain trying desperately to recall D____'s name. It would be terribly embarrassing if this belligerent-looking individual, bald-bullet-headed, clench-jawed, a *Forbes* billionaire who'd endowed one of the new, lavish science buildings at the University, realized that M.R. had forgotten his name.

He is my enemy. One of my enemies.

Questions were put to M.R. about the practicability of her proposal.

For there was a fixed number of undergraduates at the University—it was the University "tradition" not to expand—the University was an "elite" institution and must remain "elite" and not succumb to pressures of "socialized education."

And there was the need to keep places open for legacies of course.

Children and grandchildren of alums.

Wealthy alums: donors.

Trustees.

(For this was the unspoken "tradition" at the University, as one of the most coveted of Ivy League universities: college-applicant relatives of the trustees were granted a special status by Admissions. *Legacies* was the term.)

"Excuse me. You haven't been listening, I think. This is not 'socialized education'—it's private education meeting its responsibility in a public sector. It is 'elite' education for anyone—anyone!—who merits it. Our nation is a meritocracy—not an aristocracy. Think of it as *noblesse oblige*—you can supply the *noblesse*, and we educators will supply the *oblige*."

Poison toads! These remarkable words leapt from President Neukirchen exactly like the little poison toads of yesteryear.

And once released, such delicious little poison-toads cannot be called back. That is the nature of the genus *Poison toad.*

Around the octagonal table, eyes were fixed upon M. R. Neukirchen with utter astonishment, and the fascination that follows astonishment.

Had her remarks been witty? Intended to be witty? Several individuals smiled, uncertainly. Several blinked and stared. No one laughed.

Twenty-eight, twenty-nine, thirty, thirty-one . . .

Live alone and you will be thinking non-stop. Your brain will never click off.

. . . thirty-two, thirty-three, thirty- . . .

Uncanny calm at the eye-of-the-hurricane! Despite the tremors in her hands (which she'd brought under control by gripping the edge of the shining mahogany table, hard with all her fingers) M.R. was feeling very good; M.R. was feeling assured; M.R. was feeling confident; M.R. was feeling very much the authority. Like the most patient, kindly, just-slightly-condescending high school science teacher she proceeded to lecture to this gathering of *elite individuals* on the subject of the phenomenon of plant succession.

"Consider: an outcropping of rock upon which there is no life but then—suddenly—'life' appears: air-borne spores take hold, and manage to survive; these are simple lichens that cultivate their kind, and reproduce, until they create a 'hospitable environment' for a successor, a more complex species of plant—eventually grasses. Each species cultivates its own kind but in so doing creates an environment hospitable for a more complex successor. After grasses come plants, ever-more complex plants, and eventually—after a hundred years, or more—trees! A tree-species will grow one day on the formerly blunt rock face that has been covered in 'soil'—depth and texture of a kind to support the 'climax' species. And so—you are looking at me with such bewildered expressions"—M.R. laughed, in the old M. R. Neukirchen-way of disarming critics with a smiling directness, oblivious of the fact that, in this setting, the old M. R. Neukirchen-way no longer prevailed—"because you are thinking *Where am I, where is my species, in this parable?* The mystery of 'succession' is that you can't predict, if you'd examined the original rock-face, all that would follow: particularly, you could not predict a beautiful pine forest. The start of such a parable can't suggest its ending for its ending is utterly at odds with its beginning. The succession of people—races, classes—must be similar, and inevitable. It is not 'tragic'—it is not 'socialized education'—for each species comes into existence at the expense of its predecessors and is, in nature, usually destroyed by its successors. But the human race—that is, the human agenda—'civilization'—is not inevitably determined by such principles. A liberal is an educator and must wish well for all, must wish to create the optimum environment *for all*. That is the liberal principle of our great University. . . ."

Little poison toads! Hopping about the gleaming mahogany table like creatures sprung to life out of a child's storybook.

On the bare rock we clung. Our kind will cling, desperate to survive. Why we are so dangerous!

Despite the startled silence of her audience and a look in the face of—for instance, Leonard Lockhardt—signaling intense alarm M.R. spoke warmly and without hesitation, indeed like an educator; despite the trembling within, which her fingers gripping the table-edge had precipitated, since they were prevented from trembling. And there was a sullen blood-heat about M.R.'s mouth, that was distracting to her though she thought—she wanted to think—that she had made up her face in such a way, the disfigurement was *disguised*.

Later she would discover, to her horror, that the thick theatrical makeup (she'd purchased at a drugstore in town, after some perusal of the cosmetics shelves) she'd applied in layers had dried erratically, to a much darker shade than she'd anticipated. In the mirror stared at her *Mudwoman!*

But now with an effort at charm she said, as if it were a casual afterthought: "The essence of the Quaker religion is, you know—not to sign any *vow*. Not to the state, to bear arms for instance. Not to surrender our moral integrity, to any state, or institution . . ." Her voice trailed off for she could not remember why she'd brought up the issue of Quakerism other than—wasn't it the case that Reverend Charters had been of a party to persecute Quakers? Or was she trying to define M. R. Neukirchen, whose *moral position* as a liberal educator was under attack?

Indeed now D___ leapt to the attack.

A bald-bullet-headed man with a bulldog face, glaring eyes. You'd have thought that M. R. Neukirchen had personally stamped REJECTED across his son's application to the University.

But the issue wasn't legacies. The issue was something M.R. had totally forgotten and for a confused moment could scarcely remember—the proposed contribution of thirty-five million dollars from the natural-gas supplier whose representative M.R. had declined to meet in Philadelphia.

The bulldog jaws clenched: for D___ had been grievously insulted, President Neukirchen had not only declined the gift of thirty-five million dollars which he'd had "a guiding hand" in cultivating but she'd declined the gift "unilaterally"—"without consulting anyone, it seems"—and worse yet, she'd declined even meeting the corporation officer to discuss the proposal.

Worse yet, she'd declined by e-mail.

" . . . tried to call you, President Neukirchen, several times in fact but you didn't return my calls. I'd hoped . . . expected . . . you would reply . . . explain . . ."

Barely could D___ speak, his dislike for M.R., and his outrage at having been treated disrespectfully, seemed to have stopped up his mouth.

Quickly M.R. apologized: for she had certainly meant to return D___'s call. She had asked her secretary to set a time for a conversation with the trustee, but—something had intervened.

"This is a gift we can't afford to 'decline'! If you want to expand student aid, President Neukirchen, you will need much more money—and in any case— Excellis has been a major contributor to research institutions, and no one has yet 'declined.' You owe this board an explanation of your extraordinary decision to act without consulting advisers—without consulting *us.*"

M.R. felt a slight chill—the man's pronunciation of *President Neukirchen* quavered with irony, hostility.

President Neukirchen! Don't think you can put anything over on me.

It was so: M.R. had canceled the breakfast meeting in Philadelphia the previous week, impulsively. She'd been suffused with such repugnance for her task—the task of representing the University, prostrating itself before the "third-largest natural-gas supplier in the world"—as if in total ignorance of the catastrophic consequences upon the environment, in the United States but yet more extremely in third-world countries, the absurdly named Excellis had wrought. So repelled had M.R. been by the prospect, she hadn't been able to bring herself even to rehearse the words she might have said face-to-face to the Excellis officer in charge of "gift-giving"; nor had she consulted anyone on her staff, not even her vice president in charge of development, or the University attorney. Instead of dictating a formal letter of apology to accompany her carefully chosen, tactful remarks, M.R. had sent the officer a terse e-mail, and deleted his reply without reading it.

Why was that so heinous? E-mail is the efficient administrator's way of saving time.

" . . . 'the University is grateful for the proposed contribution but, at this time, we find that we can't accept. Thank you very much for your interest in our institution.'" In his rage-thickened voice D___ read the very e-mail that M.R. had sent to the corporate officer, as if this were damning proof against M.R. "It's as if you're declining an invitation to a baby shower!"

Baby shower. Never had these innocent-innocuous words been uttered with such masculine contempt!

"I declined because it was the only possible—ethical—decision—to decline a 'gift' from this corporation which has had an unconscionable record of despoiling the environment. I did some research into this company—they allot millions of dollars annually to burnish their 'public image'—advertisements in high-quality print publications, sponsoring public-service TV, radio—a high school science project competition—it's all so very *transparent.* With so many more pressing things to do, I thought it an utter waste of time, and demeaning, even to begin a conversation with—is it Excellis—"

"Excuse me, President Neukirchen, this is outrageous! There isn't a university or a research institution that would turn down a gift of thirty-five million dollars from any corporation—let alone Excellis. The basic issue is, you had no mandate to behave unilaterally in this matter, this is an issue we should have planned to discuss today. . . ."

She had offended the gentleman-trustee irrevocably, she saw. For clearly, D__ was aligned with the criminal corporation; very likely, D__ was a major stockholder. But M.R. held firm.

"There isn't any 'issue.' You don't 'discuss' debasing the University's reputation by aligning it with a notorious environmental polluter in a kind of money-laundering scheme."

" 'Money-laundering'! That's an insult."

"Please! I don't mean to 'insult' anyone—certainly not anyone in this room." M.R. tried to speak calmly, seeing so many pairs of eyes fixed upon her in surprise, dislike, hostility; even the eyes of her University officers, who seemed to have abandoned her. " 'Money-laundering' is an unfortunate term—maybe I mean 'bribery'—good old-fashioned 'bribery'—a criminal enterprise seeks to associate itself with a great American institution celebrated for its ideals by paying it money—'bribes'—in this case, a 'corporate gift'—to enhance its tarnished reputation. Maybe one day the Excellis CEO will receive an honorary doctorate from the University—but only after I am no longer president." M.R. paused, like one who has boldly strode out to the edge of a high diving board, and has not yet glanced down at what awaits below.

She was agitated now. She was excited, and agitated, and suffused with adrenaline for she knew herself morally right—righteous; she knew herself *triumphant.*

"I see that you—most of you—are looking concerned—upset—and I'm very sorry that I didn't have time to consult with you but, from my perspective, there seemed to be no need. You did elect me your president, you know. You elected me to make such judgments, which are fundamentally moral, not merely financial. As the University divested its holdings in apartheid South Africa some years ago, and divested itself of all ties with the slave trade in the mid-nineteenth century, so the University has to maintain its independence from corporations that pollute the environment. We must take as a moral imperative Kant's ideal—'To behave as if the principle of our action were to become by our will a universal law of nature.'"

This was good! This was a way of *ending.*

" . . . our meeting adjourned, for the present time. If you don't mind. And we can reconvene. . . ."

She'd given them no time to protest. She was a skilled administrator and she knew when to end a meeting as she knew how to squelch opposition from an enemy.

"Till then, good-bye!"

Mudgirl: Betrayal.

You won't leave us—will you? When we are alone—to-gether—and you are grown up—I'm afraid . . .

Of course—there is no pressure on you dear Merry! Please understand.

Except if—if something were to happen to Konrad—and I was alone in this house . . .

Except if—we love you so . . .

High school teaching would suit you, absolutely. Not middle school, and not library-work. That would not be challenging for a girl as smart and independent-minded as our dear daughter!

It was like a storybook: her life was being written for her.

She did not have to write it, only just to read it.

The pages were being turned for her, too.

———

In this story, Mudgirl had faded, mostly. There was no Mudgirl living in the book-filled brick house at 18 Mt. Laurel Street, Carthage, New York.

Only just Meredith Ruth—"Merry."

For like geometry this was a game whose rules you could learn and if you played with skill, you would be rewarded. And so by the time Meredith was a senior in high school she scarcely had to reprimand herself

Mudgirl needs to do this. Mudgirl take care!

She was seventeen, she had a New York State driver's permit. She had passed the driver's education course at Carthage High School with a very high grade and the instructor's praise—*Here's a gal who drives like a man. Good!*

In acknowledgment of the "stellar" new driver in the family, Mr. Neukirchen had bought a new—used— automobile: a 1974 Oldsmobile sedan, cream-colored, with just-slightly-corroded fenders and just-slightly-stained beige plush seats. The battered old Dodge had been worth just $250 as a trade-in.

Now, Meredith could drive the family car if one of her parents accompanied her. It was something of a family joke that the daughter was an "infinitely better" driver than either of her parents—("Which is not meant to be faint praise," Konrad remarked)—yet poor Agatha flushed and laughing apologetically could not seem to resist flinching in the passenger's seat, drawing in her breath sharply and even making abortive braking motions with her right foot when Meredith drove—"Oh! I'm so sorry, dear! I just can't help it. You are a *child*."

A child! At five feet ten, weighing 135 pounds, Meredith—"Merry"—was hardly a child.

But Meredith always slowed the car at once, braking gently. She understood—her nervous mother had to be assured.

"It's just, well—I wouldn't want anything to happen to us, dear. To you, especially."

Ever more, Agatha was becoming edgy, fretful. Her ankles were swollen, her breath came quickly. Her long skirts, peasant dresses and shawls and rattling copper-coin-jewelry were not adequate to disguise her fleshy downward-sagging body, still not-old, yet very visibly not-young; even her girl's face with its tight, smooth-rosy skin was beginning to show signs of strain at the corners of her eyes. She'd cut back her workdays at the library to just Tuesdays and Thursdays. Always she seemed to be *on a diet*—rarely did she lose more than a few pounds, and at great effort: Konrad could not resist joking, to all who might hear, that his dear wife had lost, over a period of years, "somewhere in the range of six hundred thirty-six pounds." Poor Agatha made doctors' appointments but seemed somehow never to quite get to see a doctor—at the last minute she called to cancel, without telling Konrad.

"And please don't you tell him, Merry! Pro-mise."

"But I think—"

"Of course, I'll reschedule. I will reschedule the appointment *of course*. But don't tell Konrad, will you? Pro-mise?"

"But—"

Agatha clutched at Meredith and kissed her hotly on the cheek. Mischievously she giggled—they were girls together, sisters perhaps. And Meredith—"Merry"—was the elder, as she was the taller and the more *responsible*.

"Downtown, dear! There is research I must do at the 'big' library—Beechum County archives."

Saturdays were errand-days for Konrad. It was a pleasure for Meredith to drive her father as it had been to ride with him in the past—so long as fretful Agatha remained at home. Yet more loquacious in the passenger's seat than he'd been behind the wheel Konrad entertained his daughter with tales of the personal lives of "illustrious Americans"—George Washington, Alexander Hamilton, Benjamin Franklin, Andrew Jackson and "Stonewall" Jackson and Sojourner Truth;

his great fascination was with Abraham Lincoln who, he believed, possessed a soul "as deep, as capacious, and as profound" as the Grand Canyon yet, in this "TV-polluted" present-day America, would probably not be elected to the presidency since he lacked "a sunny-superficial disposition" and "photogenic features."

Ever the bright schoolgirl Meredith asked if Konrad thought that Abraham Lincoln had been justified in declaring war against the South, to prevent the South seceding—why not just let the Southern states go? Why was the preservation of the Union so very important, that thousands of young men should be killed for it?

In her high school history class Meredith had tried to ask this question of her teacher but had been met with a look of startled repugnance as if she'd uttered an obscenity or worse yet an outrageous anti-American sentiment.

But why? Why was the preservation of the Union so very important, that even a single soldier should be killed for it?

"What a good question, Meredith! A profound question, in fact."

Konrad was always pleased when his smart-schoolgirl-daughter asked what he believed to be *profound* questions, though often he could give no particularly *profound* answer.

"There is the fundamental question—whether an abstract principle is worth a single human life, let alone thousands of lives; yet there is the question—whether anything else in life is as significant as the 'abstract.' In other words—are individuals as consequential as principles? Would you wish to die to 'preserve the Union'—would you consent to the deaths, injuries, maimings of others?"

Meredith gripped the steering wheel tightly. Despite its corroded fenders and slightly-stained plush seats the cream-colored Oldsmobile was what Konrad called a "classy"—"swanky"—car. She felt a thrill driving it—a sense of elation particularly as she drove over one of Carthage's several bridges. *Away! Away from here! There is no stopping Mudgirl once she begins her journey,*

"I—I don't know, Daddy. I—would not want—to make such a decision. . . ."

"Well! If you had to, dear. If you were, for instance, not vice president of the esteemed Class of '79 of Carthage High School"—(for Meredith Neukirchen had recently been elected to this office)—"but our own President Harry Truman, in 1945, giving orders to drop atomic bombs on Japanese cities while knowing that most of the 'casualties' would be civilians—women and children. Yet, demoralizing the enemy would accelerate the end of the war, and would save the lives of American servicemen. How would you decide?"

"I—I would have a team to help me. I would have advisers—"

" 'The buck stops here,' Harry Truman famously said. And so with all of us, as moral individuals—the buck both 'starts' and 'stops' with us."

"Then I—I think that I could not—I could not make any decision that would harm another person . . ."

"Yes, but in this case you would be saving the lives of others—of Americans."

Meredith laughed nervously. It was like her father to befuddle her: one who had no clear answers himself to any question yet had many questions, and most of them paradoxical.

"I think that—I could not participate in any action that was related to *war.* I would declare myself a *pacifist*, and withdraw—"

"—and allow another to take your place, who might be less developed than you, spiritually? That isn't a very well-thought-out idea, is it!"

"But, Daddy—you're a pacifist, aren't you? Isn't that what a Quaker *is*?"

"Yes. But only in theory."

" 'Only in theory'—?"

"If you or Agatha were threatened, I would hardly remain a pacifist, Meredith! I would wish to inflict sufficient bodily harm upon anyone who threatened my beloved family, to prevent this individual from harming either of you; and I would act instinctively, and not regret it."

Konrad spoke vehemently. Meredith was both amused and touched by her father's words—for it didn't seem to occur to Mr. Neukirchen that in such a situation he himself might be threatened, and "harmed."

They were approaching the downtown public library. Meredith would park the Oldsmobile at the rear of the dignified old building resembling a Greek temple—easing the cream-colored car into a space equidistant between two other vehicles as precisely as if she'd measured it.

Mudgirl is not a pacifist. Mudgirl will fight for her life!

It was that Saturday morning in November when Meredith saw a man who closely resembled Konrad Neukirchen slip away from the library less than a half hour after they'd arrived.

She'd been working in the reference room—on a term paper for her American history course—when by chance she happened to look out the second-floor window to see a man—lumbering-tall, broad-backed, in an overcoat that resembled Mr. Neukirchen's overcoat and with Mr. Neukirchen's thick-tufted graying-brown hair—leave by the rear entrance below and cross hurriedly into the parking lot.

Meredith stared in astonishment. Where was her father headed? And why without telling her? Their plan had been to meet in the library foyer at 1 P.M.; it was 11:25 A.M. now. Konrad was so seemingly open with his daughter—as he was with virtually everyone—it was a shock to Meredith that he hadn't mentioned he would be away from the library, however briefly; and the way in which he was walking, with an air of purposefulness, was not at all characteristic of him.

Hurriedly Meredith put on her jacket, ran down the back stairs and followed Mr. Neukirchen.

She had never followed either of her parents before! She would never have thought of following them any more than she'd have thought of examining one of her old children's books—*Tales of Mother Goose,* for instance—*The Wind in the Willows*—to see if there was a passage, or an illustration, or entire pages she'd somehow missed.

It was a relief, Konrad hadn't returned to the Oldsmobile. It would have seemed to Meredith a double betrayal, if he'd driven away in the car so soon after Meredith had so carefully parked it.

The day was overcast, dull-cold, a gritty layer of snow on the ground like metal filings. Steam heat from clanging old radiators in the library had been making Meredith sleepy and so it felt good to be propelled outdoors so suddenly, and urgently. Mr. Neukirchen was almost out of sight moving with an agility surprising in one so stout–Meredith had to run to catch up with him—remaining then a little distance behind him taking care to keep something between her and him: a parked vehicle, a wall or a post, the corner of a building. It was like one of the strange rough "games" the older children had played at the Skedds'—you had to play without knowing the rules, or what might happen to you. You have no *choice*.

Along a narrow side street of small storefronts that ran parallel with Carthage's Main Street Mr. Neukirchen made his way at this quickened pace. It could not be an ordinary errand he was going on— these he did with Meredith—dry cleaners, drugstore, Mohawk Meats & Poultry—Army-Navy Surplus Store (where Konrad bought underwear, socks, pajamas)— this had to be something special, and secret. By this time, he must have been breathing hard; his breath must have been steaming. At least forty pounds overweight, Konrad argued that he was "fat but fit"—(in fact Konrad was not really fat, but not really fit, either). That he was walking so quickly and with such an air of purpose was a surprise to Meredith, who had probably never seen her father walk at such a pace before; it was a family joke, promulgated by Konrad himself, that he walked so slowly most of the time, if he'd been a bicycle he would have been in danger of falling over.

There was Konrad entering a store—a small florist's—and soon afterward he emerged with a plant in a clay pot covered in paper wrapping and encircled with a red bow.

Meredith observed from behind a parked car. She'd become heedless that other pedestrians were observing *her.*

"A present! Daddy is bringing someone a present. . . ."

It had not been easy for Meredith to acquire the usage—*Daddy.* And the usage—*Mom.* It was good for her to practice them—alone, murmuring aloud.

Maybe Konrad was visiting someone in the hospital? Maybe—he'd wanted to spare Meredith?

Now with mounting dread Meredith followed her father along another street—in the direction of the river, it seemed—and not in the direction of the Carthage hospital; she was reminded of those men in movies or

TV melodramas, seemingly devoted to their families, who had illicit liaisons with women, even second families; invariably it was said of these men *But he would never do anything like that! Not our Dad.*

Strangely, Mr. Neukirchen had not once glanced back over his shoulder. If he had, and if he'd sighted Meredith, how shocked—disapproving?—he'd have been. Meredith could not bear the possibility of being seen. Between her and Mr. Neukirchen—between her and Mrs. Neukirchen—was a bond of absolute trust, unsuspicion.

Cradling the large gaudily wrapped plant in his arms Mr. Neukirchen crossed through the asphalt parking lot of a Catholic grade school, and through the parking lot of an adjacent church; he entered Friendship Park, that ran along the Black River for several miles, where frequently in warm weather he'd driven his little family, on picnics and "outings"; Meredith had but to half-shut her eyes, to see poor fat Puddin' waddling after a stick tossed by his master in the picnic-area of this park. But after only a few minutes Mr. Neukirchen left the park by a wood chip path leading to Friendship Cemetery which was a municipal non-denominational cemetery adjacent to the park. By this time he must have walked more than a mile and his pace was slowing.

"Into the cemetery! But why. . . ."

Now Konrad was walking with his head bowed. His jovial manner seemed to have left him totally, as if he were a partly deflated balloon.

In a newer and relatively empty part of Friendship Cemetery, Konrad left the graveled path and approached one of the graves. From where Meredith stood it appeared to be a small grave—the marker was small, hardly more than a horizontal plaque in stone. Somberly he unwrapped the plant—a poinsettia?—artificial?—bright, garish-red, with the conspicuous red bow—and placed it at the gravesite like an offering.

"Someone has died. But who . . ."

From behind the thick gnarled trunk of an old oak Meredith watched. Fortunately there was no one else in this part of Friendship Cemetery on this melancholy November day. Everywhere the gritty layering of metallic snow cast objects in a cold pure neutral light, shadowless. The kind of light that pierces the heart, it is so very cold, pure, neutral, clinical—there is nothing human in it.

Meredith would recall this moment. Waking in the night twenty-five years later to the terrible realization that she had very likely ruined her career as a university president—in the way of a drunk stumbling and flailing about, smashing things, oblivious to the damage he has caused—she would recall this moment in Friendship Cemetery, Carthage, New York—her realization as a girl that she did not know Konrad Neukirchen, truly.

This sense of utter implacable ruin—the cold pure neutral light that is shadowless, soulless.

"Oh Daddy! Please come back."

By now Meredith was shaken, frightened. This was not a game—was it? She could see that there were numerous objects placed about the little grave—ceramic animals and birds, clay pots, desiccated floral displays, plastic bouquets. Most of the neighboring graves were adorned with far fewer objects and some had none at all.

This was not Meredith's first visit to a cemetery. But until now, there had been no connection between her and the cemetery, however oblique it was in this case.

It had not ever occurred to her until this moment—her sister must be buried, somewhere.

Jedina. Jewell?

Somewhere.

With care Konrad set the poinsettia at the center of the little grave—it was the care the man took, setting a heavy casserole dish onto a surface, having removed it from the oven for Agatha; the care he took in inserting and adjusting the ribbon in Meredith's manual typewriter, that had been a gift to her for a recent birthday.

For a long time he stood above the grave, staring down. His broad shoulders were hunched and his arms hung down apelike in a posture that could not have been comfortable. So rare was it that Konrad Neukirchen wasn't in a cheery ebullient mood, Meredith was incapable of imagining what his facial expression might be.

After what must have been ten minutes—(in a rising wind off the river, Meredith had begun to shiver)—her father went to sit on a stone bench nearby. His walk was slow now, shuffling. His head was bowed. In the stillness of absolute contemplation as if he had turned to stone he remained on the bench as snowflakes swirled and fell on his shoulders, his hands, his bare bowed head.

From behind the gnarled tree, Meredith stared with stark open eyes. Thinking how like figures in a movie, they were. One of those late-night mystery movies of the 1940s, in black and white. With mounting apprehension you watched, knowing that something would happen to one of the figures, or both—but what?

If Meredith had called to Konrad, and run to him—a distance of no more than thirty feet—how would he have reacted? Would his face have creased into its usual broad smile or would he have stared at her in a very different way, unsmiling, as if he didn't recognize her?

She realized that she was frightened of doing this: of his seeing her.

It might end, then. The masquerade.

Meredith retreated, to wait out her father's vigil, which lasted another twenty minutes. When finally he left, she came to the grave—saw the small stone marker:

MEREDITH RUTH NEUKIRCHEN
September 21, 1957–February 3, 1961
Beloved Daughter
Cherished Always

She saw that the poinsettia was large, lavish, beautiful—vivid-red—but not artificial: it was a living plant that would not long withstand the freezing November air.

At 1 P.M. they met as they'd planned in the library foyer.

Meredith saw that her father's overcoat was still slightly damp from the light-falling snow in the cemetery but his thick-tufted graying-brown hair appeared to have dried.

Konrad, who'd been perusing the bulletin board, called Meredith's attention to a flyer for free "Doberman-mix" puppies—"What d'you think your dear mother would say if we brought one or two of these home with us?"

Meredith laughed. He wasn't serious of course.

"My daughter will come with us. She will drive!"

So sweetly—naïvely—Agatha boasted of her beloved gawky-goose daughter, not one friend could possibly take offense.

"She is not just a 'passable' driver—Mr. Nash at the high school praised Merry as the only girl he'd ever taught who 'drives like a *man*.'"

And so to the unspeakably sad homes of the elderly, the reclusive, the mentally deranged in the ever-darkening days before Thanksgiving 1978.

For it had happened that an elderly woman who lived alone in Carthage had died and her body had gone undiscovered for a week in her trash-filled house hardly a mile from the proper brick houses of Mt. Laurel Street. In the Carthage newspaper there was a good deal of publicity—all of it lurid and recriminatory and upsetting. Agatha wept, seeing a photo of the deceased woman taken in 1934 when she'd been only just middle-aged, and had seemed healthy and happy; Konrad shook his head muttering—"Tragic! Very very sad"; Meredith stared in silence, feeling a thrill of something unnameable in her mouth—a taste as of cold oily muck.

And so Agatha gathered together several women friends, of whom one or two were Quakers, to visit the homes of individuals known to be solitary, reclusive, ailing, elderly—"at risk" in one way or another; and of course Meredith accompanied the women for Meredith too had been deeply moved by the news articles.

In all, the women visited a half-dozen homes: facades with peeling paint like psoriasis, cracked and carelessly mended windows, broken porches, broken roofs, broken steps, even broken floorboards. There were mangy dogs that barked hysterically; there were hissing cats that scrambled away underfoot; in one house, several filth-encrusted cages of bright-feathered canaries, too dispirited to sing. In each residence there lived a solitary woman, the eldest eighty-seven and the youngest just sixty-eight but clearly mentally impaired; it had to be just accidental—didn't it?—that these solitary individuals were women, in varying stages of distraction, melancholia, and dementia. "God doesn't want us to live alone!" Agatha said, shuddering. "It is just so *cruel,* these poor women have been *abandoned.* . . ."

In the midst of the nervous chattery visitors Meredith was a tall straight-backed girl with a quick sunny smile, quiet, unfailingly courteous, and *strong*—she could be depended upon to force open doors that had rotted into their frames, and she could be depended

upon to pack trash and raw garbage festering in kitch-
ens, to be hauled out to the curb; she did not shrink
from scouring sinks, tubs, even toilets with steel wool,
in filthy water, wearing rubber gloves that soon tore;
there were mattresses so terribly stained, you could not
have determined what color they'd originally been—
these, to be uprighted, and turned over onto sagging
bedsprings, revealing now the "clean" side; wielding a
rake she cleared pathways in rooms heaped with trash
as Agatha and her women friends followed timorously
in her wake. When the women were at a loss for words,
having gained entry into what were clearly hovels of
madness, that no amount of well-intentioned Christian
charity could exorcise, it was Meredith who spoke to
the resident, or tried to speak—"Hello! We are your
neighbors and we've come to say hello and to see if you
would like us to—to help out a bit."

It was not exactly true that they were *neighbors*. But
they were fellow residents of Carthage, New York.

The women were Carrie, Phyllis, Irene, and Agatha.
The girls were Meredith and Diane.

That is, Diane came on the "good-neighbor" ex-
cursion just once. Diane was Irene's twelve-year-old
daughter of whom Irene said with grim cheerfulness
that she was "strong as a baby ox"—a thick-set girl
with a low, broad forehead and glowering eyebrows

whom Meredith tried, in her tentative smiling way, to befriend, but was rudely rebuffed as if with a wayward elbow.

Diane was sulky, resentful; she showed little enthusiasm for the "errand of mercy" on which her mother had brought her, to the home of the sixty-eight-year-old woman who opened the door to her ramshackle house only after Agatha bravely rang the doorbell repeatedly and who lived—it was shortly revealed—in a hovel reeking of raw garbage, cat excrement, and a miscellany of dead, decomposed creatures beneath detritus that had accumulated to a height of several inches. "Jesus! I'm going to puke!" Diane whimpered, as her mother reprimanded her with a hiss.

This visit did not go well from the start. The elderly recluse—who refused to give her name—seemed to have no idea what her visitors wanted of her, or from her, and clearly resented their presence. Her skull was covered in wan wisps of hair like withered mosses on a rock and her face had a puckish corkscrew twist out of which small suspicious eyes peered. She was small, as if shrunken—a housecoat stiff with dirt hung on her skeletal body and on her feet were demented house-slippers with a spangle of beads. "Who? What? What're you saying?"—her voice was low, guttural.

Only begrudgingly did she accept bags of groceries
from her visitors, setting them on a filthy countertop;
these were mostly canned goods, but also a selection
of fresh vegetables—carrots with their long lacy-
green leaves still attached, red-skin potatoes smooth
as stones—and, appropriately for the season, a single
frozen turkey-breast in a cellophane wrapper, and a
box of turkey-stuffing mix. When Phyllis opened the
refrigerator door, thinking to put away the perish-
able things, it was to such filth, and such stench, that
she quickly shut it again.

"Oh. Oh, dear. I think that—maybe—a little house-
cleaning might be—something we could do. If . . ."

" . . . should be a caseworker assigned to this poor
woman! From the county."

" . . . we can report these conditions. The county
must not know how serious this is."

Meredith was stunned by all that she could see, and
smell. And it was obvious, the shrunken little woman
wanted her uninvited visitors gone—though deranged,
she was not a passive victim of circumstances; her life
in this squalor had its logic, however oblique and inaccessible to a stranger. "How long have you lived like
this? How long—have you lived alone?"—earnestly
Agatha tried to engage the woman in conversation but
the woman replied only in grunts and shrugs.

"For reasons of health, you know—'sanitary conditions'—it would be better if—if you would allow . . ."

Everywhere underfoot were discarded cartons, tin cans, plastic bags and bottles. Stacks of old newspapers, magazines. Rug-remnants like chewed tongues. It was evident that something had died—and decayed—on the premises. And on the walls—what you could see of the walls—were religious pictures—crucifixion, Blessed Virgin Mary—and plastic crosses, crooked.

Meredith was becoming light-headed holding her breath against the stench yet determined to "help"—if any sort of "help" was feasible here. "Christ sake!" Diane muttered. With the toe of her boot she poked at a pile of debris in a corner of the kitchen that had seemed to be quivering and out leapt a scrawny tiger cat panicked and hissing—as the women shrieked, the cat fled into the interior of the house. "This-here's a damn *pighouse*," Diane protested even as her mother sternly reprimanded her: "*Shhhh.*"

"People who live like pigs die like pigs. So what!"

"*Shhhh.* She can hear you."

"She can't! She's God-damn *deaf and dumb*."

Diane was one of those girls—not uncommon in the Carthage public schools—who had the look of stunted

women: sizable breasts and hips, "mature" facial features, foreshortened legs and large feet. Her hair had
been inexpertly but glamorously bleached—blond
with streaks of red, pale orange, purple. Her mouth
was fleshy and sullen and her smiles were mocking.
She exuded an air of peevish self-assurance that was
astonishing to Meredith for she could not have been
in more than seventh grade. Though several inches
shorter than tall straight-backed Meredith and several
years younger Diane seemed indifferent to Meredith,
disdainful.

"She isn't well, Diane. These people we visit—to
help—they need our help. They aren't—'well'—like
us."

Meredith spoke awkwardly. It had never been easy
for her to address girls like Diane who reminded her
of—of the girls who'd been sister-orphans, at the
Skedds'.

Years ago, at the Skedds'! Meredith did not care to
remember, just now.

Diane snorted, amused: " 'Like *us*'? Who the hell
is *us*?"

Meredith stared at the stocky twelve-year-old in
amazement. Why had Diane's mother brought her along,
when she was clearly so resentful of being here? The girl
made only the most desultory gestures at "helping"—

though strong, as strong as Meredith, she wasn't at all motivated; when she and Meredith were charged with dragging trash cans out to the curb Diane exerted very little effort, unapologetically.

Outdoors, in the startlingly fresh air, the girls paused to draw deep breaths. From the outside, the shrunken woman's house resembled a misshapen shoe, with a crumbling chimney, sagging gutters and rotted shingles. " 'There was an old woman who lived in a shoe—she had so many children she didn't know what to do.' " Meredith spoke whimsically, but Diane scarcely heard. In a childish aggrieved voice she was saying, "My mother is always bitching at me—'Di, watch your mouth'—'Di, your mouth is too damn *smart*'—why I'm here today, it's 'discipline.' 'Di is learning some *Christian charity* for once.' " The girl shocked Meredith by reaching into the pocket of her purple-satin jacket and taking out a pack of cigarettes.

" 'For once'? Like for twice, three damn times . . . Every God-damn time, I could count on both hands."

Meredith couldn't make sense of this, exactly. But she supposed she understood. It was both shocking to her, and amusing, that the twelve-year-old lit a cigarette and inhaled deeply, like an adult; she had not offered a cigarette to Meredith, as girls at the high school, who smoked, often did, as if slyly hoping to inveigle the good-girl Meredith into smoking, too.

Meredith thought *Why do I want her to like me? Why should Mudgirl give a damn, too?*

It was a prevailing mystery: what Mudgirl *gave a damn for.*

At the house, Irene leaned out the front door to call to the girls.

Diane yelled *Yah yah we're coming.*

To Meredith she said, like one imparting confidential wisdom, "My mother is some kind of Christian-nut. She really gets off on this bullshit. Fuck being 'good.' Everybody take care of himself."

Meredith laughed, startled. This was so crudely phrased, so cruel—"But the weak, those who need our help like this poor woman . . ."

"So what? 'Need' isn't 'want.' You see her glaring at us? Your silly mother trying to 'interview' her—what's she think she is, somebody on TV? People got a right to live how they want. So they live in garbage and dead crap, so what? It's the U. S. of A."

"But—she's mentally ill. She's probably physically ill. . . ."

"So what? Who gives a fuck?"

Meredith smiled, uncertainly. She wanted to think that Diane was joking—had to be joking. But there was Diane exhaling smoke through her nostrils, in turn regarding Meredith, who loomed over her, as if she didn't know what to make of her.

"Yah, your mom is pretty nice. She's O.K." Diane spoke grudgingly: Meredith understood that this was, to a girl like Diane, a very friendly gesture.

"My mom, Jesus! That bitch is always after me. Nothing I do is ever good enough, so fuck her."

Fuck her! Meredith was shocked.

Fuck her! Good. Meredith laughed.

In the Skedds' household, this was how you talked, sensibly. You did not *put on airs,* you did not pretend to be *something you were not.*

And in the long-ago house in—was it Star Lake?— where she'd lived with the woman who was said to be her mother—in the ramshackle house behind the gas station—(crosses on the walls! Meredith had not thought of these crosses in years)—memories like thunder at the horizon, ominous, not yet fully audible. She thought *But I am not Mudgirl, not now. This is proof.*

For Mudgirl had not been a "good" girl—Mudgirl would be contemptuous as Diane to think *You must help others. There is happiness only in helping others.*

Irene was calling from the door, louder—"Girls! Please come in here—we need you." Seeing that Diane

was smoking she cried, "Put that out! That cigarette—
damn you, put it out! Now!"

Yah yah fuck you Diane muttered under her breath,
nudging Meredith in the ribs, a sister-accomplice.

Meredith thought *But I hate this, too! Except I have no
choice.*

It was shortly after this, on Thanksgiving eve, that
Meredith observed Agatha slowly turning the pages
of an album—it appeared to be a photo album, with
a gaily-colored cover like a quilt—while sitting in her
easy chair, in the living room. Since the visit to the
shrunken little woman—which had been the least re-
warding of any of the "good-neighbor" visits, and
was in fact to be the last of the visits—Agatha had
been preoccupied, weepy. She had thrown herself into
preparations for a "festive Thanksgiving"—in addition to the Neukirchen family, there would be nine
others at the big old table in the dining room, most of
them single, unattached—what Konrad called "odd-
ducks." (Which was exactly what he would be, Konrad said, if he hadn't met his dear Agatha, and their
dear little Meredith had not come into their lives just
in time—"the quintessential odd-duck.") But on the
night before the festive day, there was Agatha in her

comfortable old chair, that fitted the contours of her body like a mold, turning album pages, biting her lower lip as if on the verge of tears, entranced.

From time to time, Meredith had seen her mother looking through this album. Always in so intense and preoccupied a way, Meredith had sensed that her mother didn't want to be interrupted. For always when Agatha wanted Meredith to see a book she would call to her, excitedly—"Merry! Merry! Come look—oh, this is wonderful."

This evening, sensing Meredith's presence, if at a distance, Agatha didn't glance up but shut the album casually, and put it away beneath a pile of books on her table. And later, the album had vanished.

Though Meredith had never been the willful sort of child to behave, unobserved, in any way other than the "good" way she'd have behaved if adults were observing, yet that night, after the Neukirchens had gone to bed, and the house was darkened by 11 P.M., Meredith crept back downstairs to search for the album, which she located in a bureau drawer at the farther end of the living room. Breathlessly she lifted it out, and examined it by lamplight.

MY LIFE AS A BABY
Merry Neukirchen

Inside, the first page was shell-pink as the interior of a baby's tender ear. Beneath a photo of a red-flushed infant with black Eskimo-hair and flat features, mouth opened in a distended wail, were block letters lovingly printed in a wide-tipped black felt pen:

MEREDITH RUTH NEUKIRCHEN
"MERRY"
8 LBS. 3 OUNCES
BORN SEPTEMBER 21, 1957
CARTHAGE GENERAL HOSPITAL
CARTHAGE, NEW YORK
USA
PROUD PARENTS
AGATHA RUTH HINDLE
KONRAD ERNEST NEUKIRCHEN

In stunned silence Meredith turned the stiff pages of the bulging album. For here were not only dozens—hundreds—of snapshots of the infant girl but snapshots of a much-younger Agatha with braided brown-burnished hair, sweetly shy smile, and lovely large eyes; and there was handsome Konrad, without a beard—Konrad, younger than you could imagine he'd ever been! Sometimes a beaming Agatha held Baby Merry, sometimes a beaming Konrad held Baby Merry, and sometimes both Agatha and Konrad held Baby Merry, arms around each other's waist. But Baby Merry was in all the photographs without fail.

And how happy the proud parents were! Meredith felt that sliver of ice pierce her heart, she'd felt in Friendship Park. That sense of loss, isolation, aloneness.

No pictures of Mudgirl! Not one.

So many snapshots had been taken of the infant, you had to suppose the parents were tracking her day to day; but gradually the red-faced infant metamorphosed into a plump dimpled baby, and then a plump dimpled toddler, then a pretty child of three, or four—the flat Eskimo features vanished, replaced by a rosy-skinned snub-nosed face that was a likeness of Agatha's face with something in the quizzical slant of the eyes and eyebrows that replicated Konrad; the black hair vanished, replaced by fair, brown hair with a slight curl, very like Agatha's hair. There were birthday celebrations: *First Month— First Six Months—First Year—Second Year—Third Year—Fourth . . .* Birthday cakes, Christmas trees, gaily wrapped gifts—stuffed toys, dolls, tricycle, wagon—black patent leather shoes, little white socks—snowsuits, mittens, fuzzy caps—pajamas, slippers—fair-brown wavy hair in braids, like Mer-

edith's when she'd first come to live with the Neukirchens, and tied with the identical pink velvet bow.
And there were the storybooks from which beaming Agatha was reading to the rapt-listening little
Merry:

*Tales of Mother Goose, The Wind in the Willows,
The Tale of Peter Rabbit, Heidi . . .*

Meredith closed the album, carefully. Not a single
loose snapshot fell out.

In the bureau drawer she replaced the album exactly as it had been so no one would ever, ever know
that this book with its precious mementos had been
disturbed by any intruder.

Somewhere distinguished, like Cornell.

In secret she prepared her escape.

Preparing college applications Meredith would spend
a minimum amount of time on the forms for the State
University branches—Albany, Buffalo, Binghamton—
which trained teachers of the sort the Neukirchens
believed their daughter would be, one day; most of
the time she spent on the application for Cornell, that
loomed large in her imagination like the Alps in a
child's picturebook, more wonderful even than actual
photographs of the campus she'd studied in a brochure
in the high school guidance counsellor's office.

Not the teachers' colleges. Not you. Somewhere distinguished, like . . .

The Neukirchens had told Meredith—somewhat vaguely—that tuition to private universities was "too high"—and certainly the Cornell tuition was many times more than tuition at the state-run schools; in this way the Neukirchens had discouraged any discussion of Cornell, for Meredith would hardly have dared to oppose her loving parents. Now, applying in secret to Cornell, she instructed herself not to be disappointed, not to be hurt even as she urged herself to believe, to hope—*Maybe it will happen! A scholarship.*

She had taken the State Regents' exam. She didn't yet know her scores and had to hope that they were high enough to offset the poor reputation of the Carthage school.

Not even its administrators and faculty believed that Carthage High was a very good school. The most impressive teacher on the staff, Hans Schneider, had departed, hurriedly, and had been replaced by an affable middle-aged woman with a degree in "math education" from Buffalo State College; in her classes rowdier students were frequently out of control and A-students, like Meredith, sat coiled with embarrassment and boredom in their seats as the teacher stumbled through the more difficult math problems, squeaking chalk on the blackboard.

When the teacher was most desperate, Meredith raised her hand to help out—of course. But Meredith never came to the blackboard any longer—the new teacher had never once thought of asking her.

It was so—even the rowdy students missed Mr. Schneider. Even the poorer students who'd disliked him. Or so they allowed his bumbling substitute to know, out of adolescent cruelty.

Often now Meredith thought of Hans Schneider. He had vanished from Carthage, so far as she knew—none of the other teachers would comment when asked, or perhaps they didn't know.

She did recall, Konrad had mentioned he'd been hospitalized in Watertown. But that was more than a year ago.

Meredith could not believe that Hans Schneider had died—that was one of the rumors. Or that he'd been sent to a *mental hospital.*

Still less could she believe that he'd "fled to Germany"—this was another, ridiculous rumor.

In her most secret times alone in her room while downstairs her parents watched TV—she found it comforting to hear them laughing, Konrad's robust laughter in particular, but she wasn't drawn to joining them, any longer—vividly Meredith recalled the math teacher with his thin beaky face, his twitchy smile, his fierce gaze, fixed upon *her*. For it was rare, any man or boy fixed his gaze upon *her*. If she was very still she could summon back his voice—*You did not live a child's life. You could wait for me. We—you and I—could have an agreement like a—contract.*

At the time she'd been astonished, frightened. Now hearing the words she felt her bones turn molten, her breath come quickly. Now in solitude she tested the words *I love you Mr. Schneider.*

Like tasting a rare spice, that would sting her mouth belatedly, after she'd swallowed.

I love you, too.

In secret she'd saved money from after-school jobs and the small allowance the Neukirchens gave her, to send a money order for twenty-five dollars, for the Cornell admission fee. Twenty-five dollars was not a trivial amount of money for her, she was gambling to win, reckless. A toss of the dice, reckless! Her reasoning was that the Neukirchens would never know how she was betraying them—"Unless I win a scholarship."

Mudwoman in Extremis.

May 2003

Smiling in the new, tight way she welcomed them into Charters House. She knew—*They are the enemy. But I can befriend them, perhaps I can persuade them.*

Too late she would realize that he—the man who despised her, the man who was her *enemy*—must have organized this delegation of University colleagues, to hide himself among them. To be invited—"warmly welcomed"—to meet with the president of the University at this unorthodox hour—to discuss "urgent matters"—to "appeal, reason" with M. R. Neukirchen who had—allegedly—(for this was a rumor, solely)—declined even to discuss the possibility of accepting a contribution of *thirty-five million dollars!*—from a major American corporate sponsor—on *political grounds.*

"Not political. Moral."

More stridently she spoke than she'd intended. And more steely the stitched smile, that caused her (still somewhat bruised, swollen) lower face to pucker, not very becomingly.

Of course, they would point out that the moral is political. The political is moral. Every "major action" of M.R.'s presidency had been "steeped" in her political ideology that had become "increasingly non-negotiable, unilateral"—"dictatorial."

Dictatorial! M.R. laughed in surprise, of course this was a—joke.

Even for a conservative enemy—such an accusation had to be a joke.

The delegation of "concerned colleagues"—faces M.R. recognized of course—most of them—several were startling to her, she had not seen these friends in a very long time—(since her inauguration, possibly)—in such close quarters—wanted her to know that their appeal to her was "informal, improvised"—they were most eager for her to know this—as they wanted her to know that they were "concerned for her health, her well-being"—in the University community there were ever-proliferating rumors that M.R. was "over-worked, exhausted"—"under enormous stress"—that she'd had "health issues"—which made M.R. laugh also, for it was such a cliché, and such a slander! *You would not approach a man in my position, would you. Only that I am a woman—you would dare to approach me, but not a man.*

While a part of her sharp-flashing mind was registering, still, this mild shock—faces of individuals she'd believed to be her friends, friends among the faculty, supporters of M. R. Neukirchen, their presence among the others was upsetting to her, she did not want to think of it as *betrayal.*

And there was Kroll. Of course, Kroll.

(Had it happened, M.R. had lost her friends? One by one, lost her friends? Like a sack of gold-dust, and there's a small hole in the sack, and the gold-dust trails away, and is lost, at last and finally, terribly *lost.*)

M.R. was concerned: she hadn't asked the University's chief legal counsel if she should see these people. And now, too late!

Surely Lockhardt would have advised against this late-night meeting with its disarming air of ex officio. He'd have pointed out to M.R. that most of these self-styled "delegates" were the usual conservative faculty members of long standing and thus her opponents and not as they'd described themselves as *your loyal opposition*—to inveigle her into meeting with them, politely listening to them, and not rather telling them bluntly—

as M. R. Neukirchen never would, of course—to *go away, to go to Hell.*

At least, not one of them had brought up the issue of Alexander Stirk. M.R. wanted to think that it was beginning to be accepted, in the University community, that she had behaved responsibly and that it had not been her fault that the undergraduate had been more emotionally unstable than anyone had suspected.

But Leonard Lockhardt was no longer M.R.'s friend. Amid the vast University network of *trustees, billionaire donors, prestigious and influential alums* that constituted the true University, as distinct from the public's awareness of the University, Lockhardt was conspiring against her—she knew.

He'd wanted to be president, himself! Of course.

Everyone must have known this. Except naïve "M.R."

Whatever they were asking her—asking of her—whatever "appeal" making of her in this unconvincing display of collegiality—M.R. had no need to listen, as she'd blundered listening to, for instance, the undergraduate Stirk who'd come into her Salvager Hall office *wired.*

Instigated by Heidemann, very likely. And Heidemann's willing crony Kroll.

"You know—you can leave now. This insulting 'confrontation' is over."

Delicious little poison toads, leaping from M.R.'s mouth! But M.R. had not uttered them really for her throat was too dry.

Or if she had, no one heard. No one would acknowledge.

"Well—thank you! All of you! It's late, I have to get up early, you've made your point—points—thank you for your 'concern' for my 'well-being'—but—"

Maybe these harsh-rasping words, M.R. was speaking aloud. And altogether reasonably for the hour was late: near midnight.

Several of her visitors were women and these women smiled at M.R.—wanting M.R. to know *Please listen! We are your friends Meredith.*

And there was Kroll in their midst. Kroll who stalked and plagued M.R. with unwanted e-mails *You are making mistakes, Meredith! Please listen to me please may I see you, I am your friend.*

She'd taken the measure of blocking Kroll's e-mails. If his e-mail server registered such rebuffs, he would know.

She hated his politics. She was morally repelled by his politics.

Most of these "delegates" had political beliefs that were offensive to her—she'd gone beyond arguing with them as the wars in Iraq and Afghanistan were escalating—these defenders of the *war against terror.*

She wondered what cruel tales Kroll told of her, when she'd been emotionally vulnerable to him, foolishly involved with him in another lifetime it seemed—in M.R.'s youth.

Kroll and his older and yet more infamous colleague—Heidemann.

It was terrible, intolerable to her—G. Leddy Heidemann had entered her house. Beside Heidemann, Oliver Kroll was a *political centrist*.

But where—where was Heidemann? M.R. looked for him, alarmed.

She was certain she'd seen Heidemann enter Charters House with the others. He would be the eldest amid the contingent, as he was the most "renowned."

The University's most conspicuous right-wing faculty member—the "architect"/"moral conscience" of the misbegotten wars against "terror"—adviser to the secretary of defense and, it was boasted, or anyway rumored, now an intimate friend of the vice president.

A burly barrel-chested man of over six feet, now in his late sixties beginning to collapse like a balloon that is slowly deflating, yet vigorous still, tireless; consumed by a taste for fame, M.R. thought must be akin to a taste for blood—once acquired, it becomes an obsession.

She thought *Heidemann will use me to catapult himself yet higher. He will persecute me, he will make a shambles of a great university.*

And yet—was Heidemann here? With the others? Unless he was seated in such a way that M.R. couldn't see him—and considering Heidemann's heft, this was unlikely—he didn't appear to be in the room.

Yet: she was sure she'd shaken the man's big, bruising, somehow mocking hand—unavoidably.

"M.R."! How very kind of you to invite us. How very—liberal-minded.

Her brain worked like flashing blades. But the flashing was dazzling, blinding. Even as she was remembering that Heidemann had come with the others, but was not now visible to her, she was forgetting that Heidemann had come with the others, but was not now visible to her.

"I think—you've all been very kind, thoughtful—except that you're really not qualified to comment on these issues since they are confidential—only the board of trustees and a very few others—in the administration—are aware of . . . what you are suggesting. And so—I think—I think our meeting is over—thank you so very much."

These coolly poised words M.R. did speak aloud. She was certain!

Webs of fiery itching across her midriff, her back—between her shoulder blades—she wanted so very badly to tear at with her nails, but could not. For the *loyal opposition* stared at her like an audience dumbly transfixed by a reckless high-wire performer.

Walking with them—you might almost say, herding them—in the direction of the front foyer, and the door.

"Good night! Good-bye!"

She did not slam the door behind them. Quietly and calmly she shut the door behind them, and turned the bolt.

Vast waves of relief flooding over her, she'd gotten rid of her unwanted visitors who had stared at her so rudely, and had insulted her with their ignorant remarks.

Belatedly realizing—she was only partly dressed, and she was *barefoot*!

How silent the house was! The mausoleum—the *museum*.

It is an error to live alone. And to travel through the nebulae, alone.

For the heart hardens, like volcanic ore. So hard, so brittle and dry, the merest breath will crumple it to dust.

She was breathing quickly. Her hair was in her face, her eyelashes stuck together like glue. And the itching, now her nails could scratch, scratch and scratch, and what relief—to draw blood.

Yet—was she alone? She had an uneasy sense that she was not alone in Charters House.

The instinct to survive is the most basic of instincts and so she was thinking *I am in danger—I think. Someone is here.*

She'd counted twelve, thirteen people—at least. Uninvited and unwanted intruders of whom only eleven had left.

Heidemann had come with the others! G. Leddy Heidemann, she remembered now.

It seemed evident to M.R. that Heidemann had manipulated the others into forming this "delegation" to speak with her. In secret they had wanted to speak with M.R., in confidence, to "respect her privacy," and so they had not made an appointment to see M.R. during her office hours at Salvager Hall.

No one so hateful as Heidemann! From the first he'd disliked M. R. Neukirchen for being, it seemed, a woman; a woman on the University faculty, with a Harvard Ph.D.; a woman whose lecture course in the history of philosophy became unexpectedly popular, and drew students who might otherwise—(so Heidemann believed)—have enrolled in his (notoriously flamboyant, "popular") lecture course in the history of political philosophy. When Heidemann had been appointed to the University faculty in the early 1960s he'd been a liberal—an activist supporter of the Great Society—but after the tumultuous year 1968 he'd reacted against all civil disobedience, civil unrest—the "Greening of America." Generations of University undergraduates had passed through Heidemann's infamous lecture course extolling the wisdom of the "three Thomases"—Hobbes, Malthus, (Saint) Aquinas—as well as William Buckley and the late "martyred" senator Joseph McCarthy; for years he'd maintained an Internet site called MYTHBREAKERS, INC. with links to Holocaust-denial sites. Like a fat spider the man had sucked at the life's-blood of the young and naïve and in the process he'd become a University "character"— perversely admired even by students who thought his politics were fascistic and his moral absolutism quaintly irrelevant.

Since the early 1970s Heidemann had opposed every effort of the University to hire women, minority faculty, gay faculty. He'd opposed any extension of "University government"—psychological counseling, student aid and loans, free birth control, summer internship programs. He'd opposed smoking bans in public places on campus, he'd opposed the (anti-rape) Take Back the Night rallies, he'd opposed day care centers, he'd opposed even handicapped parking in University lots, that was mandated by New Jersey state law. He refused to define himself as a conservative, still less a reactionary—he was a *civil libertarian*.

Much of Heidemann's public behavior, M.R. thought, was flamboyant and exhibitionist—he couldn't believe most of the outlandish things he said, she was sure. In this, he resembled his alleged hero Joseph McCarthy. He had a wife—whom no one ever saw. He'd had children—who'd grown up, and moved away, and were rumored rarely to return. He was sixty-nine and had vowed never to retire—for, under federal law, there was no longer mandatory retirement at the University. In the chaotic and poisonous aftermath of 9/11 he'd leapt into the fray, with his Ivy League credentials, to publish Op-Ed pieces in the *New York Times* and articles in prominent journals arguing that the war against "Terrorist Islam" was a more urgent war than World War II had been because the Nazis were not in opposition to Christianity as the Muslims were. Heidemann's vision of a "Christian-crusader-nation" had been immensely appealing to conservatives in the Republican Party. He'd made himself famous on right-wing cable channels by translating the most extreme terms of the Cold War to contemporary times—as the "demonic" Soviet Union had plotted to destroy the Free Christian World, so the "demonic" Muslim world plotted to destroy the Free Christian World, beginning with the United States.

Heidemann's views on abortion, birth control, "sexual promiscuity" and the dangers of "secular progressivism" had surely had an injurious effect upon the impressionable Alexander Stirk.

M.R. thought *But I must not think of him. I must not make myself sick.*

"But I will. *I will do this.*"

Just before her unwanted visitors had come to the house, intermittently through much of that very busy day at Salvager Hall, M.R. had been revising "The Role of the University in an Era of 'Patriotism.'"

This impassioned speech would be M.R.'s cri de coeur. She would not be prevented from giving it—she would not be *censored.*

Two hundred years of tradition! The University president delivers the commencement address, not an invited speaker, certainly not a celebrity.

The academic year was a winding mountain road that ascended to its formal, ceremonial conclusion—commencement weekend. Like the great-sailed *Cutty Sark* that has made its way through choppy seas and is headed now to port—excitedly sighted, making its ostentatious way to port!—the University presented itself, at the end of the term, as a sequence of public events resembling a quasi-religious theatrical festival in which self-advertisement was cloaked in tradition.

Some traditions were of more marketing value than others but all were crucial and none more crucial than the president's commencement address that had been, at the start of the University's history, unabashed Christian sermons.

It was a more recent tradition, that the University as an institution defined itself as politically neutral. The University president was not supposed to be "political"—not pointedly.

But M.R. was sure that, during war-crisis eras through the decades, for instance before the outbreak of the Civil War, her distinguished president-predecessors had not avoided political statements.

" 'The moral is the political—the political is the moral.' "

Except, those to whom M.R. had shown a draft of the address the previous October, including her provost and the University attorney, had advised M.R. against publishing it in the official journal of the American Association of Learned Societies.

Gently they'd advised her. For they had not wanted to insult her judgment.

But this was the very "talk" M.R. had been cheated of giving, in October! The keynote address to the conference!

M.R.'s heart beat quickly, almost she felt exhilarated, dangerously excited, as at the prospect of combat.

"I will not be *censored*."

It was true—to a degree—that M.R. hadn't been altogether well lately—in fugue-states, somehow not fully *herself*.

The meeting with the trustees, for instance—M.R. had been feverish with excitement and had believed that the meeting had gone well except that reactions from University officers like Leonard Lockhardt had seemed to indicate otherwise. Then, M.R. regretted that she'd terminated the meeting so abruptly; for she had not known that it would not be resumed within a few hours. But, to her surprise, M.R. was informed by the chairman of the board of trustees that the meeting was postponed until June—after commencement.

She thought, stunned *Are they meeting without me? Will they give me a vote of no confidence?*

This could not happen. Not once in two hundred years, so far as M.R. knew, had University trustees voted to impeach a president.

Her provost, her academic dean, her vice president for development—they'd begun to suggest that M.R. take a rest, a break—a leave; at the very least, M.R. might check herself into a clinic, to have a "thorough" physical checkup. Though she'd been stung by such a suggestion M.R. had managed to laugh.

"Just three more weeks! Then the term will be over. Maybe then I can rest—for a while."

That had seemed to placate them. That had seemed to encourage them to speak further, daringly.

No reason for her to be embarrassed or ashamed, they said! She'd run herself down with overwork, this first year in office.

Embarrassed? *Ashamed?*

She left them, then. She was deeply wounded.

Yet she intended to follow their advice—to see a doctor. For surely there was no harm in this.

So she'd had her secretary make an appointment for her but then—on the morning of the appointment— she'd realized what a rent the appointment would make in her afternoon schedule, a gaping hole for such an indulgence, and so she'd canceled.

The appointment had been with a doctor who wasn't the highly regarded woman internist to whom M.R. had been going since she'd first come to the University but a new resident in the area, yet still a woman doctor, of course—for M.R. could not lately bear to be examined by anyone except a woman doctor; and then, it came over her suddenly, she could not bear to be examined by anyone, female or male, because she could not bear to be touched.

She could not bear to be *examined, diagnosed.*

Mysterious bruises, welts in her flesh—allergic reactions, rashes—a kind of violently itching psoriasis across her midriff, between her shoulder blades—such symptoms M.R. could hide easily beneath her clothes—(she believed)—for she knew them to be neurotic reactions and not "real" health issues. And there was the rather bad example of Agatha—M.R. frowned to recall—who'd blithely canceled doctors' appointments even as her blood pressure—and her blood-sugar count—were mounting.

Most doctors in the vicinity would know who M. R. Neukirchen was. And certainly any therapist, psychotherapist.

If she were prescribed sleeping pills, for instance. Or any sort of psychotropic drug.

The damned rashes were spreading, and quite painful. While the "delegates" were gazing solemnly at her the itching had escalated so she'd felt that she was going crazy. But she hadn't succumbed.

In any case no rash is a serious symptom and M.R. self-medicated with a mild cortisone cream from the drugstore.

Insomnia, loss of appetite, "night sweats"—these clichés, symptoms of a neurasthenic female, M.R. brushed away as you'd brush away flies.

And how ridiculous, even her toenails ached! M.R.'s very toenails turning against her . . .

Formal dinners where M.R. had to impersonate herself for hours—hours!—and dared not activate any of the itching, for fear it would rush out of control. And at such occasions, and receptions where she had to stand on her feet, she could hardly avoid wearing (expensive, tight-fitting) shoes and so it had happened gradually that the toenails of the large toes of both her feet had become weirdly slanted, ingrown, and lately a dull-maroon hue as if blood had collected beneath the nail, and grown rancid.

It was difficult not to see these ailments as signs of *moral weakness.*

It was difficult not to see these ailments as signs of what misogynists like G. Leddy Heidemann would deride as *female weakness.*

Still, M.R. would see a podiatrist, and an intern— soon. After she'd discharged the last, the very last, of her presidential duties for the academic year 2002–2003.

The end. The end when she'd believed it was the beginning.

" 'M.R.'! Are we alone, finally? Have your kindly visitors abandoned you?"

The voice was sneering, with a faint British intonation—G. Leddy Heidemann had degrees from Oxford.

For there the man was sprawled in one of the brown leather chairs in the library, waiting for M.R. to glance into the room, to switch off the light.

So he'd remained behind! M.R. had suspected so, though her heart was beating as quickly as if she'd been taken by surprise.

" 'M.R.'! I've always wondered if the initials were meant to suggest—inadvertently of course—'Mr.'— 'mister.' An awkward—unconvincing—sort of cross-dressing, eh?"

He was taunting her. He was laughing at her. In his laughter such contempt and such wish to harm M.R. felt light-headed, faint—the blunder she'd made.

Sprawled in one of the old leather chairs in the library where lamplight cast a flickering glow upon shining brass surfaces, the prim glass fronts of bookshelves and latticed windows made opaque by night. Heidemann was buffalo-shouldered, massive and sunken in the torso, with a large blunt head and features that, dim-lit, resembled fissures in rock. But no rock-ore so *alive, threatening.*

M.R. felt a rush of shame. Purely shame! For she was barefoot, and disheveled; and had probably been talking or murmuring to herself, chastising herself, as she'd begun to do frequently, when she was alone.

"Mr. Heidemann—I think you should leave. Please."

" 'Mister'! But *you* are 'mister'—I thought we'd settled that."

When M.R. stared at him in dismay Heidemann laughed, a sound as of foil being shaken, mirthless but percussive.

"We've never really talked, you know—'M.R.' Even when you've invited intimate friends of mine—like Oliver Kroll—to Charters House, you have conspicuously not invited G. Leddy Heidemann."

"I think—please—you should leave. It's late. . . ."

M.R.'s voice shook like leaves rattling on a tree—desiccated leaves, a late-autumn tree.

Slowly—belligerently—Heidemann heaved himself to his feet. He, too, was disheveled, in rumpled-looking trousers, a mismatched sport coat. He was breathing audibly, he smelled of whiskey. M.R. was surprised at the bitter reproach in his voice and wondered if he were speaking truthfully.

"I could never—in all conscience—invite to Charters House an individual who promulgates war—against a non-aggressive nation in the Middle East—as a 'preemptive strike.' Or one who aligns himself with 'Holocaust deniers'—to be controversial, to gain attention."

Heidemann stared at M.R., as if he hadn't expected such a response.

But M.R.'s speech left her weakened, faint—like a boxer with but one powerful blow, exhausted now in the effort of that blow.

She had insulted him—had she? Now Heidemann lurched toward her, to frighten her—and M.R. shrank back, instinctively. Her skin crawled with the horror of memory—the mocking query *Did you think that you could escape—this?*

The man would hurt her, she saw. He would humiliate her physically. He was fearless in the confidence that M.R. would never report him—would never dare risk such exposure, such ugly publicity for the University.

"No! Please . . ."

" 'Please'—what? Take pity on you?"

Heidemann was vastly amused. But he was angry, too. And he'd been drinking.

M.R. turned to run from the library and somehow the heavyset man was close behind her, seizing her in his arms—his Buddha-belly pressing against her back. She could smell the whiskey on his breath and she could

smell his body. Hands crude as welders' gloves closed
over her breasts, squeezing—"What a sorry specimen
of a woman! You have failed even at *that.*"

M.R. winced with pain. She opened her mouth to
scream but could not scream. The man's fingers were
tightening, horribly. It was as if he wanted to destroy
her, obliterate her; it wasn't enough just to hurt her,
or to humiliate her. She would have fallen to the floor
except he held her erect, mocking—"You knew that I'd
remained behind. You were fully aware, inviting me
into your house. After what you did to that poor boy,
Stirk—one of *my students*—you who have no children
of your own! You deserve to be punished."

In desperation M.R. thought *If he hurts me, maybe
it will be over. He will release me.* She would have
pleaded with the man except words of abnegation stuck
in her throat and instead, unable to help herself, instinctively she resisted the man, and it was his maleness
she outraged, fatally.

Though he outweighed her by eighty pounds and
was very strong M.R. wrenched herself free of his
grip and was running—barefoot, panicked. He had
stepped—stomped—on her bare feet, and hurt her,
yet she was able to run, limping—as behind her the
man stared after her, swaying on his feet; then, he lum-
bered after her, cursing her. M.R. found herself at the

rear of the house, in the darkened kitchen area—in the butler's pantry—barely she was able to see the basement door, ajar—quickly she ran to it, and descended the steps in the dark. Thinking *He will never follow me here. I will escape him here.*

Beneath cellar stairs long ago she'd hidden. Crouched and curled like a stepped-on little worm amid cobwebs and dustballs.

They had not found her then—had they?

But the man—Heidemann—was not to be deflected. In a whiskey-rage plunging into the dark, thunderous on the stairs, groping for a light—which by chance he switched on—seeing M.R. crouched at the foot of the stairs, white-faced and terrified, panting—almost you'd have thought the woman stripped naked, so vulnerable she seemed, hair in her face.

He cursed, and laughed, and descended the stairs to her. But clumsily, on legs that seemed bloated, and the bloated torso veering, so the man lost his balance on the narrow stairs, and fell—as M.R. lifted something, an object she'd grabbed with which to protect herself, a rod of some kind, about three feet in length and made of iron—desperately swinging as the man plunged forward, and down; and whether the iron rod struck his head a fatal blow cracking the skull, or whether, as he fell heavily, his head struck the sharp edge of a step, he shuddered and lay very still partway on the stairs and partway on the cellar floor where an inky liquid began to trickle from a head wound.

M.R. crouched beside him. The large body damp with sweat, the large head with its thinning hair and despoiled scalp, a distressingly shallow breath, the small eyes part-closed and unseeing. She was pleading with him—"No! Get up! You can't be hurt!" She understood that Heidemann was crafty and might be playing a trick—she would not have been surprised, if the man had come to Charters House *wired*.

"No. Get up. Wake up. . . ."

M.R. dared to touch Heidemann's shoulder. She shook his shoulder. She could feel the man sinking, drifting from her—she thought *He will blame me. He will accuse me.*

In desperation M.R. stumbled back upstairs. In the dim-lit kitchen she groped for the telephone, which was a wall phone—with panicked fingers she punched the numerals 911. But there was no ring—there appeared to be no dial tone. M.R. broke the connection, and tried again—and again there was no ring. Heidemann had yanked the phone out of the socket as he'd lurched past—had he?

M.R. listened—had she heard a cry? A man's cry, from the basement?

Except for blood pulsing in her ears, nothing. She thought *There is no one there!*

For it seemed to her utterly impossible, that one of her university colleagues had pursued her on the cellar steps, fallen and injured his head—this lurid incident had to be a dream, another of her dreams, for ever more frequently she was mired in dreams of surpassing ugliness like one mired in mud; her deeper, most inward life had become a concatenation of random and humiliating dreams that left her exhausted and broken. But she would not give in.

Almost eagerly she returned to the basement. And there, to her horror, at the foot of the stairs the massive fallen body of the man lay unmoving and now no longer breathing—no longer shuddering and twitching. A putrid smell lifted from the body as if it had already begun to decay, in mockery and spite of her.

"Wake up! You can't be serious! This isn't . . . funny. . . ."

By this time, the wounded head was covered in blood like tentacles. The face was part-collapsed like a mask that has come away from a face.

Gravity pulled at the heavy jowls, the loose rubbery lips that even now in death were jeering, lascivious.

"Please! Let me help you . . . sit up . . ."

M.R. was terrified of getting too close to Heidemann, of his grabbing her—a wrist, an ankle. She believed that his eyelids were fluttering—he was observing her every move. Her breasts throbbed with pain and with the insult of pain, the man's fingers squeezing squeezing squeezing as if wishing to squeeze the life out of her—what was most offensive in her, the female. She could not bear his assaulting her again, her stupidity in coming too close to her enemy.

But he'd ceased breathing. He had no pulse—that she could find with her groping fingers.

Long ago as one of the good-schoolgirls at Carthage High, Meredith—"Merry"—had taken an extracurricular course in emergency medical care and "life-saving"; she knew, she must try to restart the unconscious man's breathing, by placing her mouth against his—pushing against his chest; she must try to restart his wicked heart, that had to be a fat, discolored muscle the size of a large brute fist; or, more sensibly, she must run for help, from the house—she must summon help for the stricken man, if she could not herself provide it.

But she could not move, she was paralyzed with revulsion for him, and the utter horror of what had happened. She thought *He has destroyed me. This was his intention.*

Like one staring at newsreel footage of a long-ago catastrophe in which all participants are now dead

M.R. saw in her mind's addled eye not only the devastation of her career but of her life—what minimal life she'd harbored for herself—and for all hope of a life beyond that minimal life. Most painful was the knowledge it was not the hateful man who had destroyed her but M.R. who had destroyed herself.

And then, she had no choice. It was necessity acting through her like electric current jolting her limbs.

The lifeless body heavy as a sack of concrete she dragged gripping the ankles into the dank-smelling interior of the basement and to the ancient corroded sink that had not been used in decades. Overhead the light—from bare lightbulbs—was faint as a distant galaxy. And so she could not see clearly the collapsed flesh-face except to sense its jeering and in the part-open eyes, a look of contempt that was the more terrible for its being an intelligent and discerning and not mere brutal contempt. She feared—she was awaiting— the man's derisive laughter that had somehow translated itself into—she knew this, as clearly as if he'd boasted to her—a powerful stink of urine, feces, decay.

She was not a weak woman but oh!—she could not stop herself from gagging, vomiting. The spasm wracked her like a creature inside her frantic to escape and no escape except through her throat, her gasping mouth.

Then, the spasm passed. Her mouth reeked of vomit like acid, she dared not swallow to make herself sicker but spat, and spat, and wiped at her mouth, and spat again.

Oh!—she was so very sick, and so appalled and terrified. Yet she understood what she must do for she had no choice.

Always it was claimed of her, she was strong, and she was capable. You are not loved for being strong and capable if you are a female but if you are a female and you are strong and capable you will make your way without love. Even so, some of her strength had drained from her in recent weeks and in these recent hours and so it was the memory of her strength that allowed her to act as she had no choice but to act for survival demands strength where weakness is death. For what is courage but desperation. What is the indomitable but desperation. What is success, triumph, but desperation. Yet what difficulty for her to lift the lifeless body heavy as a sack of concrete into the ancient sink—for long crazed minutes she struggled trying first to lift the legs, and then the shoulders and head; giving up on the torso and then again repositioning the bloated legs that flailed about with a kind of spiteful playfulness; to make the legs less heavy, and her task less cumbersome, she thought to remove the shoes—unlacing shoes on the feet of a dead man is not easy!—tugging off the shoes of any other is not easy but how much more difficult, the shoes of the dead—this was an insight M.R. had not yet had in her lifetime, till now. And thinking of her astronomer-lover who'd requested of her several times to remove his shoes—or, rather, hiking boots—for he was too lazy to remove them himself he'd said—(jokingly)—(she'd guessed that in fact Andre's back had been hurting, he could not easily stoop over but did not want to confess such a weakness to the much-younger and -fitter girl who adored him)—there was pleasure in the intimacy of the gesture, and playfulness; and now, removing her enemy's shoes, there was only disgust, dismay. And horror.

Yet, the decision was a good one. For now she had less difficulty lifting the bloated legs, the thighs enormous as hams, the fatty lower part of the body she struggled to balance on the rim of the sink as she struggled then to lift the torso that seemed both bloated and sunken, and the arms that flailed about as in the rudiments of a mock embrace, and then the head—the head!—that lolled on the shoulders in a way to suggest languidness, even flirtatiousness.

What intimacy in the transaction! Like secret lovers bound together, irrevocably.

At last, the body was in the sink. Very awkwardly, fatly crumpled in upon itself, and the heavy head yet uplifted—fallen back upon the shoulders—so that he might observe her through his near-shut eyes, in all her misery. It was as if she stood naked before him, exposed to his judgment. A thrill of mirth rippled through him. A slack-jawed grin played about the lips.

She waited, but he did not speak. She was certain that he was observing her, however.

She had never seen a dead body before. Except the body of Mudgirl, perhaps. And that had been a small broken child's body of little consequence and not the body of an adult, acclaimed man.

She was very tired from dragging the body, lifting the body into the sink. Her arms, neck and back ached from the strain. And all that lay ahead—she felt a frisson of pure horror.

Her bare, pale feet were splattered with blood. The front of her clothing was smeared. Beneath her nails, she knew there must be more blood.

She would have to clean herself thoroughly, afterward.

"I will do it."

She returned upstairs to the kitchen where a single light burned overhead. Except for the dangling phone which she replaced immediately there was nothing to suggest the desperation of a few minutes before— nothing out of place.

She returned to the library where lamplight cast a warm romantic glow upon polished surfaces—mahogany, glass. She saw that the leather chair in which the heavyset man had sprawled was out of place and she repositioned the chair and glanced about seeing nothing else that would catch the eye of the housekeeper Mildred. She switched off the lights and retreated.

In the living room, too, lights were burning—there were several chairs pulled out of place, in which her uninvited guests had sat, to form a casual half-circle. These chairs she repositioned, as precisely as she could remember. She switched off the lights and retreated.

In the morning Mildred would discover nothing out of place.

"But I have not much time."

Beneath the kitchen sink on a shelf were several pairs of latex gloves of which she took one pair.

A pair of shears, out of a kitchen drawer; several of the large, razor-sharp chef's knives on a magnetized rack overhead. These she appropriated as if she'd known beforehand what she would do with them.

In a storage room adjacent to the kitchen were supplies—black plastic trash bags of which she took as many as a dozen.

In the garage attached to the house, that had been converted from a carriage-house decades before, she found a handsaw amid a wide selection of tools in a workman's bench.

She found another cache of trash bags larger than the kitchen bags.

It was 12:29 A.M. She would have to move quickly.

Returning then to the basement and to the laundry room where in the antique corroded sink the body lay in its clumsy posture. She wasn't sure that the body had not moved in her absence—she couldn't be sure if the cold shrewd eyes had blinked. But the loose jeering grin remained, and the backward angle of the head as if vertebrae at the top of the spine had broken.

With the shears she removed the man's clothing. And now it was a part-clothed body, and by degrees a naked body—flaccid, dense with wiry hairs, splotched and spotted and pitted and foul-smelling. The hot flesh had begun to cool, the surface of the skin was slick with oily sweat. The terror of the brute physical life was embodied here, she could not judge the man harshly who'd had to dwell in this body, though reasoning that he'd been young, once—a child, once. Some profound disappointment in life had wounded him deeply, he'd been sickened by the infection and had not recovered. She felt pity for him, in that instant—bile had consumed him from within.

Hatred was in the man stopped-up like pus. It was not personal, that this hatred had spilled over onto her.

It is not a personal thing, that a man will loathe a woman.

The genitals were swollen. The penis was of the shape and size of a slug.

What sorrow in the body! Almost, she could not hate him.

Then, she remembered the Iraqi war, and the "preemptive" crusade against imagined enemies, and the links to Holocaust-denial Web sites—the fact that G. Leddy Heidemann had conspired to commit war crimes, or to aid and abet others in the commission of war crimes. He had lent his name to the vicious enterprise of war in the Middle East and the killing and maiming of civilians and by his association he had tainted the University. And he'd said cruel, critical things about M. R. Neukirchen in the very first weeks of her presidency, from which passages had been reprinted in the campus newspaper. . . . That, M.R. had vowed to forget but could not forgive.

" 'Disarticulate.' "

It had never been more than an arcane term to her.

She tugged on the latex gloves that were already stained. Like a surgeon—rather, like a pathologist— she took up the handsaw, shakily at first, but by degrees with more strength, sawing through the man's thick wrists, ankles. What a shock it was, to strike bone! She had to find a way through bones, at their joints. This was the secret of disarticulation. After much effort she managed to detach both the hands, and both the feet. Next, she sawed through elbow joints: the long arms had to be halved. The basement of Charters House was chill as the deep interior of a well yet her face was covered in sweat by this time and rivulets of sweat ran down her chest and back inside her clothes.

She sawed through knee joints. She sawed through hip joints. Blood coursed from the mutilated body, into the drain of the ancient sink. She was becoming drunk— drugged—by the stench of blood but by degrees she ceased to smell it as in the mudflats she had ceased to smell as she had ceased to see and to hear and to feel.

The genitals she would leave intact. The bloated and sunken torso she would leave intact. She could not bear the prospect of sawing open the chest cavity, or the midriff; she could not bear the prospect of removing internal organs, stomach and intestines and all that lay within of utter foulness.

She recalled the beliefs of certain Eastern religions, that the human soul is located in the bowels.

All this while, the fallen-back head was hideous to her. She tried not to glance at the face. The eyes now accusing, astonished. The slack-jawed grin of sexual idiocy. She was very tired, and she was swaying on her feet, and she was not thinking clearly for it occurred to her only now—she must detach the head from the torso, to hide the face.

It was not easy to detach the head from the body. She used both the handsaw and one of the razor-sharp chef's knives. She shut her eyes for she could not bear to see the man's eyes. She shut her eyes appalled and dismayed for it had seemed to her—in just an instant, she did not dwell upon the possibility—that the face was not the face of her university colleague G. Leddy Heidemann but the face of a stranger. A ravaged face, the face of a stranger.

Here was a miscalculation: when she managed to sever the head from the body a sudden spillage of dark blood ensued—an artery of the thickness of a supple young snake had been cut, and gushed blood for several terrible seconds. As if the dead man had come alive again, in this final spasm of fury.

Another miscalculation: she'd failed to ensure that the head would fall inside the sink. Instead its very heaviness caused it to fall back, and outside the sink-rim, and onto the gritty concrete floor with a thud of surprise.

"Oh! Forgive me."

She forced herself to lift the head—both hands were required. Yet she did not quite look at it. Her vision was blurred, evasive. She could not have forced herself to peer closely at the face even to identify it. Quickly instead she dropped the head into one of the black plastic bags.

What relief—now the torso was anonymous, only just male.

For hours through the night she labored. She had ceased to think as she'd ceased to smell the corpse. An almost pleasurable work-rhythm came to her out of the very effort of her arms, shoulders, and back—out of her very genes, peasant-American stock bred to hard and futile and inevitable labor for a pittance. She was not a weak woman, nor had her mother been a weak woman—physically.

Handsaw, knives, shears. Hip joints, shoulder joints. Smiling to wonder if there'd been a butcher in her family—how many generations ago. Thick suety flesh oozing blood, globules of fat oozing and draining out of the sink, she hoped to God would not be stopped-up too quickly. When the saw blade or the knife blade struck bone, a tremor ran through her arm to the elbow like an electric shock.

In a dozen or more plastic bags the parts of the body were neatly placed and the bags tied shut, knotted. Soon, it would be concluded—the "disarticulation."

Out of instinct she had acted, and not choice. As one desperately sucking at air has no choice but to breathe.

She had not reasoned clearly—a single, singular body would be difficult to dispose of but body parts, each weighing no more than twenty or twenty-five pounds, would not be difficult.

She had not reasoned clearly but she had acted upon this reasoning and with each bag tied and knotted there came a measure of relief. For the man was no threat to her now. She had conquered him!

She carried the bags upstairs and through the kitchen and outside, to her car. She thought—how strange it would be, if her uninvited visitors were still in the living room, waiting for her to join them! And the one who had slipped away, to hide from her and to torment her.

She thought—but then this could not have happened. And this did happen.

Earth-time is irreversible. Earth-time runs in one direction only.

At her car she set the bags onto the asphalt driveway. A single floodlight burned at the corner of the garage. Carefully she sheared open several trash bags to smooth flat on the floor of the trunk of her car and on these she set the bags. No observer could have guessed what was inside the tidily knotted plastic bags.

Not a drop of blood—not a hair—would remain behind in the trunk of her car, to incriminate her.

She had always been the good schoolgirl. She had done tasks perfectly, she had been the reliable one whom others had taken for granted. Not often but sometimes, they had laughed at her for her plain scrubbed face and her plain scrubbed soul.

It was 3:53 A.M. A high pale moon shone in the sky. Soon, it would be dawn: she must act quickly, and she must make no mistakes.

She drove out of the University town. It seemed to her a banal impoverishment of imagination—virtually all of the houses were darkened and why?—only because it was night, and human beings must sleep at night.

There is the nocturnal soul, that comes alive at night. She was of this breed!

Her senses alert as if she'd only just now awakened after hours of restful sleep she drove north along the state highway past a succession of darkened storefronts, small businesses and houses, fields and forests and along the Interstate where there was very little traffic and the moon drifted overhead like a child's paper lantern. At rest stops illuminated by a single light on a tall lamppost she exited the Interstate and in the Dumpsters of these rest stops she disposed of the trash bags one by one. Behind a Shop-Rite on Route 11 she left a single bag in the Dumpster and in the Dumpster behind a CVS drugstore on that same highway she left a single bag. And in a Dumpster behind a Ramada Inn at exit 6 of the Interstate she left a single bag. And in a Dumpster behind a Taco Bell on North Hamilton Boulevard she left a single bag she had reason to believe contained the man's head—the eyes aghast in that look of utter astonishment, fury. For even as she could not quite believe what she had done—and would fail to recall it, in any detail, later—so too the man could not believe what had been done to him, against all expectations.

"It was not your fault, truly. It was not mine."

With each bag removed from the trunk of her car her car became just perceptibly lighter. With each bag removed from the trunk of her car her soul became just perceptibly lighter. She drove in a wavering circle the circumference of which was approximately forty miles. She did not drive above the speed limit. She did not venture out of the right-hand lane. She took care to dim her bright lights when another vehicle approached even as, in the case of locomotive-like trailer trucks careening through the night, the drivers of these vehicles failed to lower theirs.

And now she was reasoning more clearly. She was beginning to see the logic of the past several hours.

The body parts, widely scattered, would be picked up by local waste disposal trucks and carried to local land-fills. The body parts would be compacted in vast acres of trash. Never could the body be re-assembled, as in one of the horror tales of Grimm.

Never would the woman be accused, the perpetrator of such a deed.

By 5:18 A.M. she ascended the curving drive to Charters House. Within the pine trees surrounding the house it was still night. The housekeeper Mildred would arrive no earlier than 8 A.M.—M.R. had re-quested this for she valued her early-morning privacy. It was a warm, overcast May morning. The pale moon had vanished, a ceiling of pitted and granulated clouds like Styrofoam hid the sun. She was both very tired and exhilarated. She was nearing the end, now! Enter-ing the house by the rear, kitchen door she experienced a moment's fright for she heard—she was certain she heard—a clatter of voices; but when she stepped across the threshold there was silence.

She returned to the basement and with paper towels and sponges she cleaned all that she could see. She was relieved to discover that hot water gushed from one of the faucets.

She'd worked within the sink, mostly. She'd taken care. And so the basement floor wasn't so very dirty.

She opened the basement windows, she aired out the rooms. These were niggardly little windows thick with grime, that opened just a few inches, at a slant. Still, you could smell an odor of—something. An animal—raccoon, opossum—might have crawled into the basement, become trapped and died. This had happened numerous times in Charters House, she'd been told.

She did not clean the sink too thoroughly—she did not scour it—for it had been a filthy sink, and if it were clean, one of the household staff might notice.

As she ascended the stairs to the kitchen she cleaned the stairs with wetted paper towels. Upstairs in her private quarters she removed at last her sweaty stained clothing that had become repulsive to her. She dropped it into a bathroom sink to soak in hot water and Woolite.

Very hot water, and so much Woolite suds! She had no doubt, the stains would fade.

Then in water as hot as she could bear she showered for a half hour. She scrubbed herself vigorously. Between her breasts that were bruised and reddened she scrubbed herself and between her legs where short wiry hairs sprouted from her like the hardiest of weeds.

She shampooed her hair, she cleaned beneath her nails with a metal nail file.

In the drain of the shower at her feet, a fan of loose hairs.

She was forgetting something—was she?

Already the events of this terrible night were fading. As the high pale-glowering moon had vanished, by day.

They would call on her this evening—the "delegates." They would appeal to her, to see them and to listen to them ex officio.

If the man came with them, to slip away into the library and to torment her after the others had gone, she would be prepared—she would not be so frightened.

But what remained now? Was there—"evidence"?

She tried to think. She could not think.

Yet instinctively she returned to the kitchen and at the top of the basement stairs she stood gazing into the darkness. She heard nothing below—the man had ceased his struggles, his hoarse breathing had ceased. Yet she was uneasy, he was waiting for her somewhere. He might have slipped past her and would be waiting for her upstairs in her private quarters where few visitors ever came.

She remembered now: it had already happened.

In the library he'd awaited her. In the brown leather chair he'd appropriated as his own.

Returning to the library and switching on the light and the leather chair was empty but there on the hardwood floor she saw the prints—partial footprints, blood-prints. Her own.

She laughed, in nervous relief. For she had almost missed these!

And quickly now with wetted paper towels she cleaned away these prints, too.

And now there remained—"Nothing."

In the chill dawn out of tall trees surrounding the house came the soul-chilling cries of the King of the Crows.

Mudwoman Ex Officio.

May 2003

Earth-time is irreversible. Earth-time runs in one direction only.

Earth-time is a way of assuring that all things do not happen simultaneously.

" . . . must be something wrong. This isn't like her."

In the morning at Salvager Hall they were awaiting the University president.

By 10 A.M. the president had not yet arrived. Where ordinarily she was in her office before any of her staff (sometimes as early, it was rumored, as 7:30 A.M.) on this morning she had not been sighted in even the vicinity of Salvager Hall and already by mid-morning she had missed several appointments and a number of telephone calls and she had not replied to her assistants' increasingly concerned calls to her cell phone and to the landline at Charters House and e-mails flying to her computer in Charters House less than a mile away went unanswered. And her chief assistant spoke with her housekeeper who reported that she hadn't seen Mz. Neukirchen yet that morning, either—she'd assumed that Mz. Neukirchen had left for her office early.

"Can you go upstairs? Can you knock on her door? Please—can you see if she's there?"

And so the housekeeper went upstairs and knocked on the door to Mz. Neukirchen's quarters and there was no answer.

Again she knocked, hesitantly—"Mz. Neukirchen? Are you there?"—and there was no answer.

She reported back to Audrey Myles who asked her please to see if the president's car was in the garage. And yes, the president's car was in the garage.

So far as anyone knew, the president had had no appointment earlier that morning, off-campus. No university driver had driven her anywhere and her schedule for this weekday did not involve an off-campus appointment.

"Please—can you knock on her door again? And if she doesn't answer—could you go inside?"

Mildred agreed to knock again on the door. But Mildred refused to enter the president's quarters without being asked to come inside.

"But—she may be ill. She may need emergency aid. Please—at least open the door and look inside, from the hallway."

Sharply Mildred said no! she could not.

Within ten minutes Audrey Myles arrived at Charters House accompanied by two young-women staffers, in a vehicle driven by the chief security officer at the University.

At the front door the housekeeper awaited them speaking rapidly and excitedly saying that she hadn't seen Mz. Neukirchen since the previous day in the late afternoon but that Mz. Neukirchen had been "looking tired"—"like usual." Audrey Myles and the others ascended the stairs and at the door to the president's quarters Audrey knocked sharply and her voice was sharp, anxious—"Hello? M.R.? This is Audrey. . . ."

When there was no answer Audrey knocked a second time and again there was no answer and when Audrey turned the doorknob it was to discover that the door was locked.

"She's inside, then. And something has happened to her. We will have to remove the door."

The head of security made a call. You could see that the University was well prepared for such emergency situations: an individual who has failed to respond, a locked door.

Within a quarter hour hinges were unscrewed from the door and the door was removed.

Not Audrey Myles but the head of security entered the president's quarters first.

For you could see, the University was prepared for the worst.

They found her on the floor in the farther room which appeared to be both a bedroom and a workroom.

They could not rouse her, she was deeply unconscious.

She'd fallen with her legs twisted beneath her. She'd fallen and seemed to have struck her head on the hardwood floor. Her face was drained of all color except where it was bruised and swollen around her mouth and her lips were a faint blue.

Her breathing was shallow, erratic. It wasn't clear to Audrey Myles whether she was breathing at all.

At a distance they were calling her. The name that was her.

At a distance at the earth's surface they stood staring down into the deep muck-pit into which she'd fallen.

Calling—the name that was her.

She knew, she was expected to pull herself up, to daylight. Out of the loathsome muck-mud. To claw at the rough-rock sides of the pit and to haul herself up with broken and bleeding nails.

To stand with the others. As if her back were not broken.

She knew! Yet she was so very tired, she could not perform as they expected.

It was shameful to her, to betray so many!

But she was so very tired. What had entered her bloodstream in hot acid-swarms, she had not the strength to resist.

Mudwoman Amid the Nebulae.

May 2003

Take me with you she begged.

Not one to beg yet now in this time of crisis she was begging and no shame in such begging for she adored her astronomer-lover, she had given up her life as a woman for this man and she could not bear it that the man was not worthy of such adoration and so relenting then as a god might relent seeing the anguish in a mortal face he brought her with him on this voyage, he was a mariner in perpetual motion ever more fanatic and obsessive with the passage of years journeying continuously, restlessly, out of a fundamental metaphysical unease with the quotidian-life as with the particular domestic/marital/paternal life it was Andre Litovik's fate to live and out of contempt for humankind he journeyed amid the most distant nebulae and his journeys were into Time as well—ever backward into the terrible abyss of Time before Earth existed and mere clock-time began. And like a lonely child eager to speak the speech of her elders in mimicry of her lover she murmured such mystery-words as *redshift, quasar, light-years, Andromeda, Hubble constant, megaparsec, trigonometric parallax, Hydra and Centaurus. Cepheid variables, Ursa Major, Great Attractor, pulsars, black body, cold dark matter.* And when she asked him what these mystery-words meant he had not the patience to explain saying *Look them up. You can read.* Or he said *You wouldn't have time, dear Meredith. I've used up most of my life trying to learn the meanings and mostly I have failed. And that effort has been my life.*

Mudwoman Flung to Earth.

May–June 2003

"I want to die."

Or was it: "I need to die."

Shameful to her, to betray so many!

Three months, she would be away. Three months, banished.

This is not a *mental illness*, they assured her. This is a *physical illness*.

There is no shame in *physical illness*.

Three months' *medical leave*. More crudely phrased, *sick leave*.

For she was so very tired. She'd collapsed from exhaustion, malnutrition, anemia. Her lymph glands were painfully swollen. Her vision was blurred. Her blood contained an abnormal increase of mononuclear leukocytes, infections had entered her bloodstream.

Her skin was burning with fever yet she could not stop shivering.

Try! You must try! Try harder.

She had ceased trying. She hated those who wished such effort from her.

" . . . time to die."

This was ridiculous! Self-pity of the mewling sort M.R. most despised.

Konrad would be shocked at her, if he'd heard such words.

Poor Agatha! Agatha would be spared such words.

"I certainly *do not want to die.*"

Three months to rest, recover. To become *herself* again.

Three months banished from Charters House, Salvager Hall.

Those places she'd come to fear. The high pit sides, she must claw her way to daylight.

Those places she'd come to loathe.

"No! I've been very happy. . . . I want to return to work."

An infection of the left ear canal and the "inner" ear—so violent the throbbing, she'd thought it must be an infection of the brain. In the nineteenth-century Russian novels, *brain-fever.*

Equally virulent infections of the throat, the lungs.

Antibiotics were fed into her veins, to wage war against the enemy.

And in the hospital, another infection would enter her bloodstream.

Sickness, and convalescing. But first, the sickness had to be overcome.

She had lost nearly twenty pounds. How this had happened, she seemed not to know. She seemed not to have noticed.

Her bodily self, her *ontological being-in-the-world*—she had seemed not to notice its condition.

Or, she had noticed but wished not to see.

It was a time of shame. A season of shame. As in Carthage and the surrounding countryside there were seasons of bagworms—hideous writhing things in feathery pearl-colored cocoons, in trees.

Almost, you would think *How beautiful! Large white blossoms in the trees.*

These small shames surfaced in her consciousness, like raging bacteria.

For instance, that final meeting with the trustees! She could recall only flashes of it, like a broken mirror. She could recall a man's face contorted with dislike of her, repugnance. The shock, embarrassment, alarm of others. And the priggish self-righteousness of her daring to quote Kant to the captive audience—Kant, the German racist.

This individual was quite black from head to foot, a clear proof that what he said was stupid.

So much for the moral transcendentalism of Kant!

Shame, her Mudwoman dreams. Of which she could recall just fragments.

Most shameful, she was missing commencement.

The pinnacle of the University president's year—and M. R. Neukirchen was missing it.

So shameful to M.R., she could not tell anyone. Never would she tell anyone.

The glossy commencement program had been printed before—before the president's collapse. And so on the morning of June 1 there would be an insert in each of the programs, noting that the commencement address originally to be delivered by President Neukirchen would be given by the former president of the University, Leander Huddle.

The very person she'd imagined she was so superior to. *Way better than that cynical shameless old man!*

M.R. would not see this. M.R. would be spared this humiliation.

Three months—June, July, August—the University would provide for the convalescing president financially, during which time the provost would serve as acting president.

The great sailing ship, the *Cutty Sark* of Universities, would scarcely falter, in M.R.'s absence.

Three months! A terrible void in which she might drown.

Three months! It felt like the rest of her life.

He was incensed: by the sight of her in the hospital bed, and by her surprise at seeing him.

"Of course I'm here! Where the hell else would I be?"

Yes he'd known of her breakdown for bad news travels swiftly.

"*Schadenfreude's law*—the worst news of the best people travels most swiftly."

She'd tried to laugh, hearing this. It was not the first time Andre had made this joke but each time was funny to her, for *Schadenfreude's law* was so very true.

The distance between the University in quasi-rural New Jersey and Harvard University in Cambridge, Massachusetts, was no more than a nanosecond. Andre had known what had happened to her within hours— the rudiments, at least—and at once he'd left his home with what excuse to his suspicious wife M.R. was never to know, flew to Newark airport, rented a car and drove sixty miles to the hospital, to discover her in the Telemetry unit.

He hadn't been able to contact her, first. She had not made any attempt to contact him for she'd been too ill.

"Why are you so surprised? Of course I'm here, I love you."

I love you was not a phrase Andre Litovik uttered easily. You could see the man's jaw muscles straining, not to amend *I love you* with a joke.

You could see the man's eyes—thin-lashed, large and frantic and always just slightly bloodshot—filling with moisture, to be wiped away with the back of his hand.

Difficult for M.R. to keep her own eyes open. She was so very tired.

Better to be spared the shock in her lover's face, at the sight of her.

He will cease loving me now. Whatever love he'd imagined.

By her bedside he sat, but not quietly. It was not possible for Andre Litovik to sit quietly for more than a few minutes. When nurses entered M.R.'s room, he interrogated them. What medications, what quantities of medications. He was brusque, bossy, comical. At the nurses' station he learned the names of M.R.'s several doctors and these doctors he tried to contact for he had questions to ask them and he had much to say to them. And to M.R., whom he scolded as if she were, not an adult woman of forty-one, but a wayward and willful child: "This ridiculous job of yours! I warned you not to accept it! The University will grind you up as in a meat grinder, swallow you and excrete you and if you're as passive a patient here, as you've been as 'CEO,' or have not anyone informed to intercede for you, you, you will die. These places are teeming with infections and the staff—the doctors especially—are too God-damned lazy to wash their hands."

She was trying not to laugh at Andre's words, the slightest jolting of her body caused such pain.

She was trying to keep her eyes open. Not to sink into sleep lapping just below the bed's surface like black mud-muck.

She was trying to speak to him, to move her lips that were parched, and cracked—*Andre thank you for coming. Andre don't leave me. Andre I am so frightened, so . . . tired. I love you.*

Often when she spoke in such a way, Andre seemed simply not to hear.

This time, he squeezed her fingers in reply.

He told her that whoever had admitted her to the hospital had requested no visitors except relatives and so he'd identified himself as a relative—"Litovik, an older cousin. *Doctor* Litovik, from Harvard."

Now she did laugh, wincing with pain.

"D'you want me to contact your parents? Maybe they should know about this."

Numbly M.R. shook her head *No!*

"Aren't they Christian Scientists?—They could pray for you. The shape you're in, you could use all the help you can get."

M.R. tried to explain: not Christian Scientists, Quakers.

"Whatever—Christians. The belief is, the Messiah has come and gone."

He was joking but she understood that he was upset, by the way in which he stared at her. They had known each other for nearly twenty years and in all those years he had not looked at her quite like this.

Nor was it typical of Andre Litovik, to look at another person so closely, at close quarters. A chronic revulsion for his own species—a perverse sort of shyness, social awkwardness—had exiled him, he'd said, to the farthest reaches of the Universe, at an early age.

So long and so far had Andre traveled, on obsessive and solitary journeys in the nighttime sky, his presence in a singular place, his *physical being*, exuded an air of surprise, whimsy. No astronomer—cosmologist—astrophysicist—can take the immediate world seriously, Andre had told M.R., even as he'd held her in his arms, and rubbed his rough face against hers: it just feels so *fleeting*.

As if all things visible and tangible are but screens, or images on screens—if you reach out, your hand will go through them.

If you reach out, your hand will dissolve to bones, dissolving flesh and evaporating blood.

Andre's skin was roughened, ruddy as scraped brick, as if in fact he'd been a mariner, on the high seas. His teeth so often bared in a grimacing grin were uneven, the color of stained piano keys. In his heavy-browed broad forehead—(a clear genetic link, Andre said, to his Cro-Magnon ancestors)—were curious dents and puckers and his hair was coarse and stiff as the quills of a wild creature. His eyes were gray-green, chill with frost or suddenly, unexpectedly crinkled with warmth, passion—you could not predict. When they'd first met Andre had been careful to tell her, as if to define the perimeters of their relationship from the start, that he was married and the father of a "difficult" son—the consequence of a profound and irreversible mistake he'd made in believing that he could map his life as he'd set out to map the Universe; he'd told her that he was further disqualified for reasonably normal human relations by a numbing coldness—"like ether"—that ran in his veins.

Not 100 percent of the time, this "ether." But some of the time.

Naively she'd thought *But I will change that!*

And often afterward she'd thought, both ruefully and defiantly *I can love enough for both of us. More than enough.*

Nineteen years. In all that time he'd remained married, and a father—and a mariner in distant nebulae.

Regions to which M.R. could not follow him. Regions from which he might return, following some indecipherable logic of his own need, to her.

"Where the hell else did you think I'd be? Soon as I heard about my darling 'M.R.,' I'm *here.*"

He remained with her until the hospital closed for visitors at 11 P.M. He spent the night in a motel near the hospital and in the morning returned at 9 A.M. bringing with him the *New York Times* from which he read passages to her, with extended commentary.

How happy M.R. was, that Andre Litovik had come to her!

Though still very tired, and easily confused. For it had seemed to her—from time to time during this visit—that her astronomer-lover was but a film, near-transparent, for all his animation and the heat of his skin, the bristling steel-colored hairs on his head, the low wide lined forehead, the wide dark nostrils like eye sockets and the way in which, at her bedside, he sucked up much of the oxygen in the room.

Several times she opened her eyes—the man was still *there.*

Several times he assured her—he would remain with her until she was *out of the woods.*

They were walking together, in a forest—or rather, if you looked closely, they were walking in the idea or concept of a forest: for the trees were sparse and their foliage niggardly like a child's drawing of a forest. With his myopia for things that were immediate and tangible—the curse, Andre liked to say, boastfully—of the theorist as distinct from the empiricist/pragmatist, Andre put out his hand to touch the bark of one of the trees and seemed not to notice that his hand passed through it.

She laughed at him, the man so delighted and perplexed her.

He was telling her something very complicated, as often he did. If she asked him about his work he would usually shrug and say it was too abstruse for her, too abstruse for *him,* and in any case it wasn't going well; and in any case, if it were going well, it was probably misguided, misbegotten—he would wind up like one of his great cosmologist-mentors, who'd slipped so gradually into senile paranoid schizophrenia, it was "a very long time" before anyone noticed.

Funny! M.R. laughed and winced.

She opened her eyes. There was one of the nurses, rousing her—"This might pinch just a little, it's a little

little vein"—and whoever had been in the chair beside had gone.

Newspaper pages scattered about the floor. And the chair shoved close to the bed.

She was feeling better suddenly! She laughed, for how simple *life* was—she had only to *stop thinking* and her life would sweep back over her, buoy her aloft until she was safe onshore.

"That man who was here—was there a man here? Where—"

Barely could her parched lips manage these awkward words. Even as the nurse smiled at her asking please would she repeat her question there came Andre through the doorway—bull-necked, bull-shouldered, and his eyes fixed eagerly on her.

"Hey. You're awake. Damn time."

Definitely she was feeling better. Her fever had subsided, the jolting pain in her ear and the scraped/ scratched sensation in her throat had faded, or nearly; she was able to eat some of whatever meal this was which was so unappetizing to Andre, he didn't even taste it—which ordinarily Andre did, when they were eating together; sometimes eating off M.R.'s plate until there was very little remaining for her.

Hey! Sorry! Did I really eat all this?

And M.R. would laugh, for truly she didn't mind. Truly!

He'd harpooned her, he liked to say. Saw the strapping young Amazon with the braid down her back bicycling on Garden Street and he'd thought *That is the girl for me.*

Except he hadn't been young. Not as the girl was young. And he hadn't been free. As he'd needed to be free.

This tale so frequently told between them, the very words had worn smooth as stones. Nineteen years!

In Earth-time, a considerable span to live through.

In galactic-time, too minute to be measured.

And another time opening her eyes: the man was *not there.*

Yet still, the scattered newspapers, as well as a crumpled paper bag from a deli where Andre had bought sandwiches for himself, and the chair at an angle beside the bed; and there was the TV high on the wall, on mute, for he'd been watching closed-caption BBC news. And so she'd thought *He has just stepped out of the room. He will be back.*

In the interim: cards, flowers.

A continuous stream of *wishes for a speedy recovery* that made her frightened, so many knew.

Frightened and resentful and ashamed: so many knew.

But no visitors, for M.R. had a dread of visitors. Not even relatives—if she had relatives.

Her eyes stared and squinted at the cards, many of which were affixed to cheery tinsel-wrapped potted plants with crimson cluster-flowers—the names of these flowers, Agatha would know—would have known. *You have broken our hearts, I am not even sure if you are our daughter. Still we will always love you. That is God's wish and that is our vow.*

He'd had a call, she knew.

Or, he'd made a call. She knew.

(It was not the first time. Nineteen years!)

At the first he'd told her—he'd confided in her—in the way in which you might confide in someone whom you didn't—really—think would figure in your life. *I am married not to a woman but to a domestic situation. I am married to the child thus to the mother of the child.*

And, plaintively, or defensively: *You can't divorce a child. At least, I can't.*

After nineteen years the child was no longer a child but in fact thirty years old but in fact still a child—"difficult"—"brilliant"—"never satisfactorily diagnosed."

And there was the wife—also "difficult"—
"brilliant"—a Russian-born translator of Gorky,
Babel, Pasternak, Mandelstam—who suffered from
mysterious ailments to which tentative diagnoses were
affixed: chronic fatigue, anorexia/bulimia, bipolar disorder, intermittent rage and unremitting depression,
envy and jealousy of her (professionally, sexually) successful husband.

Because the husband isn't faithful?—M.R. could
never bring herself to ask.

*Because the husband is a prisoner of fidelity! A God-
damned fucking martyr*—Andre claimed.

And now he was saying—(was this what the man
was saying?)—(the woman sitting up in the hospital
bed had to listen through a sudden fast-pulsing in her
ears)—that he wasn't certain how long he could remain with her right now.

Right now.

At this time.

But maybe—another time . . .

He'd hoped—and maybe he still could do this, or at
least expedite it—to help her move from her on-campus
residence to—wherever she intended to live. . . . For
there were, in his life—obligations, commitments . . .
Not just his *domestic situation*—of which by custom

he rarely spoke—(and of which by custom M.R. had learned not to ask)—but he'd reserved observational time at Kitt Peak in early June, the plan had been to take two of his post-docs with him to Arizona for three weeks, this was the project he'd told M.R. about numerous times, he was sure—measuring distances via redshifts for twenty thousand bright galaxies. . . . Observatory time was very limited, and for the post-docs a crucial opportunity. . . .

The way in which Andre spoke, mildly stammering, in a rush of words, shoulders hunched as in a strong wind and the wide low brow furrowed above eyes fixed upon her with a look of pained sincerity and regret, M.R. understood that yes, he'd certainly had a call from home; or, guiltily, he'd called home; and the "difficult" wife, or the "difficult" son, was summoning him back.

Quickly M.R. said—as M.R. invariably said, at such times—(for M.R. could be relied upon to be gracious even when despondent, rash-ridden, and suicidal, the "good" woman in Andre Litovik's snarled life who would one day be suitably rewarded)—that he should leave of course. As soon as he felt he must leave.

She was not disappointed! She was not even surprised.

And it was true, M.R. was "out of the woods"—discharged from Telemetry that morning and moved via wheelchair, though she could certainly have walked, to the general hospital on a lower floor.

Released of his vow to remain with her Andre Litovik was both relieved and edgy, uneasy. You could see— (M.R. could see)—that his ears rang with the shrill percussive accusations of the wife—even as he seized her hand in a gesture meant to be playful and rubbed it between his two big hands.

His breath smelled of something raw—garlic?—and the frost-eyes, netted in tiny broken capillaries—were alert, antic.

"I don't want to give you up, Meredith. But you can—you should—give me up."

"Oh but why—why would I do that?"

She'd meant to be light, playful—but the words had come out wrong.

So often, the words came out wrong.

"It won't be forever, I think. Maybe not so much longer."

"What? What do you mean?"

Almost, M.R. was frightened. For did she want to live with Andre Litovik—really?

It was intimacy that was the great risk. Not passion, yearning, envy, even sorrow—but intimacy, with another person. Andre had lived intimately if not always happily with his mysterious wife and his mysterious son and he had not lived with M.R. in such a way, not ever.

And M.R. had not lived with any living person intimately since—she could not recall.

"Andre? What do you mean—'it won't be forever.'"

"Which words do you have difficulty comprehending, my dear? *It—won't—be*—or *forever?*"

Glaring at her, in a pretense of indignation that masked, M.R. knew well, a sudden unease, Andre took up his beloved *New York Times*, shook the pages and stared at columns of newsprint. The terrestrial life was so utterly foolish, vain, absurd and yet absorbing—no traveler to distant nebulae could resist.

He pretended to read—in fact, he was reading—and M.R. lay carefully back in the bed staring at the IV line dripping fluid into her bruised arm thinking *This too is a kind of marriage. This is not negligible.*

Though she was still very tired she felt elated, suddenly.

He had come to her, in the crisis. That was the important fact, *he'd come to her.*

Of course, he was going away again. But he would not remain in the house on Tremont Street for long. Rarely did Andre Litovik remain in one place for long. The wife might claim him, and the damaged son, but Andre couldn't quite be captured by them, either.

For hadn't he told her, he'd been obsessed with mapping the Universe since the age of sixteen. Hadn't he told her, nothing is so real for an individual accursed as he was as travel into the Universe—recording, calculating, mapping, predicting.

One of his less technical papers was titled "The Evolving Universe: Origin, Age & Fate."

She'd tried to read it. She'd understood virtually nothing.

She opened her eyes, the man was *gone*.

Oh yes—frankly, this was a relief!

Always a relief when the astronomer-lover departed. For now the woman could be *herself*—whatever diminished *self*.

For now the woman would have, at least, enough oxygen to breathe.

She'd forgotten to thank him, in her surprise that he'd come to see her—he'd brought flowers, very likely from the hospital gift shop.

A hydrangea plant with bright dyed-looking blue blossoms like paper—near-identical to the hydrangea plant that Oliver Kroll had once brought her, that had dropped its leaves, turned to sticks and died.

Though, if M.R. had known how to plant it correctly, and cultivate it, as Agatha might have done, the plant might be living still, and coming into blossom.

The room was filling up with flowers. *Speedy recovery* cards. Too many to count. One of the potted plants—not a hydrangea, in fact—was from Oliver Kroll: *Thinking of you & will try to see you soon. Oliver K.*

Another potted plant, which M.R. discovered belatedly, on the eve of her discharge from the hospital, was from her colleague G. Leddy Heidemann—exquisitely beautiful/sickly-smelling calla lilies.

Sorry to hear of your illness & will remember you in my prayers & hope for your speedy recovery.

Gordon H.

Gordon H.! M.R. wouldn't have known who this was except that there was, beneath the brief name, the man's more formal name as well as his (endowed) University title.

Was the card mocking? Were the calla lilies chosen for their sickly smell?

Who could know?

Mudwoman Bride.

June 2003

Because I am in love. Love is a slow bleed.

At last, Mudwoman was being married.

So many years in waiting! So many years in yearning.

Now when it was almost too late, Mudwoman had been chosen.

The bridegroom was one of the long-term patients in the Herkimer VA Hospital. He'd been a corporal in the U.S. Army in the Gulf War of the previous decade and had been terribly burnt and disfigured in the service of his country and his eyes—(if you could bear to look closely you could see from what remained that these were beautiful dark-hazel eyes threaded with blood-filaments)—had melted into his misshapen face.

In the second year of his deployment he'd been so maimed. Ninety percent of Corporal Coldham was grafted skin, metal pegs, very fine titanium wires, and aluminum-and-plastic. His right arm was truncated at the elbow and held a hook like a sickle. Both his legs were truncated at the knees and fitted with prostheses. In his manually operated wheelchair he was a proud figure in U.S. Army corporal's dress uniform and he was shorter than his bride by half but his shoulders were wide as those of a young ox.

His hair had been singed from his scalp that was still pink like not-quite-cooked meat. His manner was tense with hope. As a lover he was tentative, tender. The fingertips of his remaining hand were light and fluid as the rapid flowing of tiny silver fish and with these fingertips the bridegroom "read" the bride's face.

You are beautiful to me

The bridegroom did not speak in actual words but in a silvery flurry of sound. The bridegroom's mouth was scar tissue that moved stiffly like calcified glue.

The bride was eager to be wed. The bride was not a young girl any longer.

Shivering as the bridegroom ran his fingertips over her face. She had to stoop to the bridegroom in the wheelchair, that he might run his fingertips over her face.

I love you

His ears had melted away also and in their places at the side of the misshapen head were whorls of twisted flesh. Holes in the molten-looking head like nostrils, seemingly unprotected.

Mudwoman was shy. To speak into such ear-holes you must choose your words with care.

Mudwoman was a tall gawky bird-girl. A bride at six feet in high-heeled shoes that teetered beneath her though the heels were old-fashioned and thick—the toes were rounded. And her legs were bare—muscled calves, stubbled with coarse dark hairs.

How embarrassed Mudwoman was as a bride, without stockings!

Hoping no one would notice.

As in high school they'd noticed. *Hair-y legs! Hair-y legs!* came the hilarious muttered chant.

Nothing personal for there were other girls so afflicted.

Hair-y legs!

The bride was being fitted into a stiff article of clothing like armor—a corset?—tightly laced up behind. Over her narrow hips, flattening her breasts, ever tighter!—the bride could scarcely breathe.

The wedding dress slipped over her head—carefully!—was of a translucent papery material, that would easily tear, or burst into flames. Layers of impracticably long and flaring and lace-riddled skirts and a five-foot train of papery lace dragging behind.

The bride was being dressed by strangers with deft poking hands who behaved as if they were not strangers but had the right to touch her intimately. The name they called her was *M*—but it was not a name she knew.

Muffled laughter, ribaldry. The women were happy for one of their kind being married though their laughter was sharp-edged, for it was Mudwoman being married.

She believed that these women were supposed to be persons whom she'd known as girls but their faces too were melted and their names had long since vanished.

They laughed at her for being in love—was that it?

This wound that would not stop bleeding.

In the season of her disgrace she'd been a volunteer at the Herkimer VA Hospital. That was how she and the corporal had met, very likely.

She'd come to the VA hospital in the southern Adirondacks with her father Konrad who did volunteer work there and at the Carthage Vets Co-op. As a young man Konrad had been a conscientious objector in wartime for Konrad was a Quaker-pacifist and yet stricken with belated guilt, that other young men had gone in his place, out of ignorance and innocent enlisting in the military that he might be spared. And so, Konrad who was retired gave of his time and his spirit to the surviving-but-maimed vets in residence at the VA hospital and to the co-op in Carthage, on a cobblestone back street near the Beechum County Courthouse.

Such a decision of her pacifist-father's did not surprise Mudwoman who was beyond all surprise.

Each Saturday driving with Konrad to the VA hospital in Herkimer.

Some Saturdays, to the Herkimer County Psychiatric Facility which was just three miles farther.

It was a good life. It was a life of service.

It was the life that had happened.

It was the life that happens to some of us, for whom a richer life has not been possible.

It was a life in which you could sleep for ten, twelve, fourteen hours a night.

Because I am in love Mudwoman wanted to plead. *Love is a slow bleed.*

How it had happened precisely that Mudwoman was marrying Corporal Suttis Coldham she did not know but somehow, it had happened. And now Mudwoman was absolved at last of her desperate love for the other— the other man whose name she could not recall.

The astronomer-lover, who had passed out of her orbit into the farther ranges of the Universe and if they were ever to meet again, light-years would have passed.

A woman learns *I can love one of them. If one of them will love me.*

The bridegroom could hear, to a degree. But the bride could not think what words to say to him, that would not be misunderstood.

With his stiff-glue lips the corporal spoke.

The helicopter was shot out of the sky. I woke in the hospital—I guess. I'm not really awake now.

This is my dream, I guess.

Corporal Coldham was much kinder than the other. He did not speak with the swagger and humor and threat of the other. Too long had Mudwoman endured the strain of a man of such intensity and so incandescent a soul and so it was a relief to her, the corporal was a blind man in a wheelchair with a melted-away face and no neck who would not judge her.

This is my dream the corporal said. *I am sorry for the wicked things that I did, the many lives I have taken, to bring this punishment to me.*

Mudwoman protested no, she was sure that it was her responsibility and not his. Those citizens who remain at home, whether pacifists or otherwise, while others, called "soldiers," go to war in their place . . . All are responsible.

But the corporal began to tremble, and to stammer.

No. The many creatures I killed, in my traps and with my guns. The many creatures gutted with my knife. This is my punishment.

There came a gurney on rickety wheels, that was meant to be a portable altar. Very awkwardly the bridegroom in his wheelchair and the bride teetering beside him were presented at the altar.

There was a gathering of people, mostly in folding chairs though many were standing about in the aisles, smoking and laughing together as if they had wandered in from another place.

The bride was frightened of misstepping and tearing her papery white gown. She was scarcely able to breathe for the corset squeezing her like a python's grip. The bridegroom held himself erect as he could manage in the wheelchair in his U.S. Army corporal's dress uniform.

His eyes melting into the sides of his head gave an unnerving impression of a fish that can see in opposing directions simultaneously though in fact the corporal was blind.

Yet possessed of *blind-sight,* the bride saw. For if she drew her hand before his face, his reaction seemed to indicate that yes, he could see—something.

Shyly Mudwoman asked of the corporal *Do you love me?*

Tenderly the man with no face said *Yes. I am the one who loves you.*

It was kind of him not to have said *Yes. I am the only one who loves you.*

It was kind of him not to have said *Yes. I am the only one who dragged you from the mud, that was meant to have been your fate.*

It was time for Mudwoman to declare her love, too. But—the words stuck in her throat like mud.

I love I love

This was a life of service she'd embarked upon. Serving others does not involve love but only the availability of others to be served.

Like a small boat without a rudder, or an oar. Where the stream takes you, you are taken.

Not just stockings were missing from the bride, now the old-fashioned round-toed high-heeled shoes had vanished also.

Her long narrow feet were bare and exposed, caked with dirt. Grime in her toenails. Her underarms had sprouted coarse dark hairs.

Already the paper-gown had begun to tear. Already the elaborate lace train was torn and soiled.

In an adjacent room, a vast hall, another ceremony was being performed. A woman sang "God Bless America" in a bold quavering voice.

Now it was clear—someone was missing.

At the altar, there was no one to marry the couple.

Hurriedly to the altar there came the man—the father—to give away the bride. She saw Konrad's kindly creased face, his winking smile and his eyes that forgave her. With a little sob of gratitude she linked her arm through his arm.

It was Konrad who performed the wedding ceremony. Konrad in an old shiny-dark suit that hung on his shoulders, sizes too large. His silvery-white whiskers sprang from his jaws with a look of great dignity and pride.

Do you take this man?

Do you take this woman?

Richer or poorer, sickness and health till death do you part.

God bless this union.

For even in Hades there are such unions. And blessed by God.

The bridegroom was groping for the bride—his single hand was large as a club but the fingertips were gentle. He would pull blushing Mudwoman down to him, to mash his eager wet mouth against hers.

It is what must be done to marry, to mate. To prolong the species.

Happiness crept over her like paralysis.

Mudwoman Finds a Home.

June–July 2003

. . . a secret weakness. Not a one of us has been spared.

Often now he spoke to her. In places of solitude in which she hid herself like a wounded animal licking the poison-abscesses that have not—yet—killed it.

He winked, and lay a finger against his nose. He spoke in a playful lowered voice so that Agatha would not hear.

His voice—oh, she loved his voice!—so subtle the commingled tones of irony, teasing, solicitude and warmth fused together as in the notes of stringed instruments—violins, cellos—conjoined in a single bar of music.

As a girl, she hadn't asked. What is the *secret weakness.*

She had not wanted to be told the Neukirchens' secret weakness because of course, Mudgirl had always known.

"Daddy! Hello."

Or, more likely: "Konrad? Hello . . ."

On the Convent Street bridge she began to shake.

She saw that the bridge had been partly renovated: a new grid-floor, replacing the badly rusted old grid-floor; new steel supports shining in the sun like exposed nerves; the pedestrian walkway fortified by an inner railing . . . She was sure that this inner railing hadn't existed, years ago.

If you walked across the Convent Street bridge, traffic rushed past just inches away.

And the outer railing was shaky. You would not dare lean against the outer railing.

Below, the river was wide as she recalled, moving swiftly in little spasms of white froth and long rippling snaky currents over submerged boulders. Its origins high in the Adirondacks were mysterious to her—hundreds of small tributaries and streams hurtling together, into the Black Snake River.

"Konrad! I'm sorry, I'd meant to call . . ."

Her lips were dry, scarcely could she speak aloud. And often her sentences trailed off, since she so distrusted speech.

Since her collapse when a vivid display of Northern Lights had erupted inside her head and in the same instant were extinguished, she distrusted her own speech and the speech of others.

It is all so provisional. It is all so temporary.

Not information you can share with others, readily. Nor do others much want to hear from you such information.

We are all so provisional . . . Temporary.

She gripped the steering wheel firmly. She would overcome this sensation of shakiness, unease. For hadn't Mr. Nash said admiringly of Meredith Neukirchen that she drove *good as a man.*

Such small prides, like beads of a rosary recalled through a life.

Proof that there is a *life*—singular, "historic."

Andre had once said to her how utterly boring it was to be *in one place solely* and M.R. had wanted to say to him how precious it would be, to be *in one place solely.*

To be *one person solely.*

Of course she hadn't told him—of her life. If he'd asked—and he had not asked, much—she had replied with the quick bright evasiveness with which she'd learned to reply to interviewers' questions.

Her parents he believed to be the Neukirchens of Carthage, New York—whom he'd never met: her mother a librarian, her father a (non-elected) city government official.

She had not told him that she'd been adopted. The word *adopted* was not in M. R. Neukirchen's vocabulary.

Slowly on Convent Street she drove. How familiar everything was, yet how strange to her, as if seen through the wrong end of a telescope! Very little ever changed in Carthage, New York, where the economy had been "stagnant" for decades—preserving the past as in a kind of gaseous formaldehyde.

And there was the little cobblestone branch library where Agatha had worked—(though you would not have called it "work": Agatha had never called it "work")—as a librarian. At the checkout desk, quick-smiling plump-girlish Agatha Neukirchen in her billowing long skirts, knitted vests and ruffled blouses, long sleeves splotched with ink from the little ink-pad with which she struck the stamp bearing the due date of a book.

That was Agatha's single, deft and practiced gesture, that bore with it a benign air of authority—stamping the due date on the little card at the back of the book.

Oh—everyone knows Agatha. Such a friendly woman!

Such a pity, about Agatha . . . So young.

M.R. could not bring herself to park her car, and look into the library.

Maybe later—if there was later . . .

(Would anyone there have recognized her—"Meredith"—"Merry"? This was a possibility she didn't want to consider.)

(For, so many times Agatha had brought her little Merry to this library with her. All the librarians had known her—"Merry Neukirchen.")

And now, Mt. Laurel Street—where Konrad no longer lived, so far as M.R. knew; like Convent Street a neighborhood of small single-family dwellings, just slightly shabbier than M.R. recalled—very small front yards, narrow asphalt driveways close beside neighboring houses, at the curb stumps of the giant ghost-elms that had been razed in the wake of disease when Meredith had been a little girl.

"Daddy! I'm sorry that I couldn't—that I didn't. . . ."

She was thinking that she might have helped Konrad move out of the house when he'd sold it, the previous year. But the timing could not have been worse, in the week following her inauguration as president of the University. . . . And Konrad had insisted he didn't need any assistance, he knew how very busy she was and it would distress him, if she took time to come to Carthage for such a "trifle."

She had been a disappointment to them of course. Though officially her parents were "proud" of their accomplished daughter—as how, reasonably, could they not have been "proud"—yet she knew, she had hurt them, particularly she had hurt Agatha by not only failing to be the daughter Agatha had wanted her to be but by failing to acknowledge her betrayal. And then she had not tried very hard to mend the estrangement between them.

In interviews warmly exclaiming *Such wonderful people—such good people—models of sanity, kindness, generosity, intelligence, love . . . My parents are Quakers—my father was a conscientious objector during the Korean War—in upstate New York where the U.S. army services are revered—he taught me courage, but also the value of "stillness"—"holding in the Light." . . . My mother is a librarian who taught me a love of books . . . and my father a voracious reader. . . . It was always understood that I would go to college unlike most of my Carthage classmates.*

In fact it was the issue of college, going-away-to-college and not-returning-after-college, that had wounded Agatha, beyond all reason as M.R. had thought at the time.

Konrad had been more understanding though in his oblique way just slightly reproachful—*Of course our brainy daughter wants to associate with "brains"—there's no Harvard in the Adirondacks, last I noticed.*

There, the old house: 18 Mt. Laurel Street.

The dark-red-brick house was looking distinctly shabby, weatherworn. The sooty facade could have used a sandblasting to spruce it up and the black trim needed repainting; each of the shutters, facing the street, was crooked in its own way. In the front windows, venetian blinds hung lopsided. The new tenants, whoever they were, had kept the remains of Agatha's eccentric gardening, that made 18 Mt. Laurel Street conspicuous among its more conventional neighbors, like a satin party dress amid a party of mourners: a tangle of living plants—black-eyed Susans, wild rose—and pots of artificial mums and geraniums.

Who lived in this house now? In her old room, facing the street?

Once, a cloying-cute girl's room with candy-cane wallpaper, a fluffy white chenille bedspread. A lamp in the shape of a little white lamb. Maplewood dresser and bookcase filled with children's books, gifts from Merry's adoring parents.

In high school, she'd changed the room, a bit. She'd replaced the children's books with others. She'd outgrown the girl's bed, her feet had pushed out over the edge of the mattress but she'd told herself she didn't much mind—she would be leaving, soon.

She hadn't been equal to their love. It was that simple.

Unlike the well-to-do suburban neighborhoods near the University, where no one but lawn crews and delivery men were ever seen, the Neukirchens' old neighborhood was *lived-in*. Children on bicycles, young mothers pushing baby carriages, a man mowing his lawn—a man in baggy khaki shorts and a baseball cap walking with a cane, who resembled Konrad, but was too young to be Konrad, now seventy-two. And Konrad did not live in this neighborhood any longer.

M.R. observed the man, who did look familiar. But he was trimmer than Konrad had ever been, in her memory; and his walk, despite the cane, was surprisingly jaunty. Behind him trotted a dog, a red-setter mix with a long tail and large feet, sniffing eagerly at front stoops, shrubs and trees, and pausing to lift his leg and to urinate, quickly; you could see that the man was chiding the dog, and the dog, even as he continued to sniff about and lift his leg, was listening attentively.

"Solomon! Have you no shame!—stay at the curb."

As the man in the khaki shorts drew nearer, M.R. saw that his jaws were covered in bristling white whiskers—it was Konrad.

"Daddy? Hello? Is it—you?"

Through glasses the gentleman squinted at her. A wide startled smile softened the bewhiskered face.

"And if it's 'Daddy' then it's ipso facto 'Meredith'—yes?"

In this season of disgrace she'd been thinking often of Konrad and Agatha and their exemplary lives, she had not been able to emulate.

Of course, she understood: it had not been *disgrace* only just *hubris, error, correction.*

Physically, she'd been broken, ill. But it was her soul that had been most lacerated.

And her vanity—with which M. R. Neukirchen had not guessed she'd been so afflicted.

Of course, Konrad knew about M.R.'s "breakdown" and the "medical leave" from the University—she'd called him, to forestall his calling her, and she'd asked him please not to come see her.

"Not just yet."

For there was nowhere, that M.R. now *was.*

The official word was *traveling.*

The official description was *between residences.*

Unofficially it was said *Poor woman! She has crept away to hide.*

But no one quite knew, M.R. was *homeless.*

———

Hurriedly after being discharged from the hospital she'd moved out of Charters House. She was living provisionally in an apartment lent by a faculty friend, near the house on Echo Lake which had been sub-leased by other tenants and in which she'd left her furniture, and most of her possessions, in the care of others. For there was the assumption—(or pretense, or fiction)—that M.R. would be moving back into the president's house in September, when she would resume the presidency.

The trustees had not evicted her from Charters House—of course. But M.R. had insisted upon moving out.

Must get out. Get away. I am suffocating here.

In some sort of delirium she'd thought—half-thought—that maybe—at this juncture in her life—when (possibly) she might be leaving the University—or (possibly, in any case) leaving the presidency—*Andre will want to be with me. Andre will take care of me.*

From the observatory at Kitt Peak he'd sent her photos—this was frequently Andre's practice, when he was on-site at a telescope—for he'd become, in the service of mapping the Universe, an excellent amateur photographer. Nearly each day, with no message, an e-mail photo of astonishing beauty and mystery came to her as if out of the void: "Perseids storms"—"Kappa Crucis cluster"—"Medusa nebula"—"stellar nursery in the constellation Centaurus"—"moons beyond rings of Saturn"—the raging-molten-orange surface of Venus ("computer reconstruction")—"star clouds"—"crepuscular rays"—"Milky Way shadows." She understood that in these visions her lover was offering her his essential being, and that the other—the actual man, the man whose mouth she might kiss, and whose arms she might clutch at, whose laughter she might hear—was inessential.

Why isn't the beauty of the Universe enough for you, dear Meredith?

It is enough for many of us. For me.

Even philosophy was little solace to her. Words!

She could not concentrate, reading. Even rereading works she'd loved, she could not concentrate. She felt the now-familiar tinge of panic, a kind of nausea, at the prospect of teaching a graduate seminar in the fall as she'd so ambitiously planned.

Failed once, fail again. Never recover from a broken back.

She threw belongings into the rear of her car. She left no word behind, where she might be going.

Homeless but it felt good: appropriate.

North along the Hudson River and into the Catskills and by mid-afternoon of the following day entering Herkimer County, and then Beechum County, and along the Black Snake River west to Carthage—a river-city near the eastern shore of Lake Ontario that had been losing population steadily since the 1970s.

She'd returned two years before, for Agatha's funeral. She'd returned seven months before that, at the time of Agatha's first stroke.

Neither visit had gone well. Neither visit had made M.R. eager to return.

At the funeral, Konrad had been dazed and—so unlike Konrad!—near mute with grief, protected by a fierce band of Agatha's women friends who'd absorbed from Agatha a disapproval of her "ungrateful daughter" impossible to be overcome, had M.R. the patience and time to try to overcome it. And at the visit with Agatha, after the stroke, M.R. had been astonished to encounter her once-genial mother so profoundly altered, there seemed little between them except the woman's bizarre childish rancor at M.R.'s "ingratitude" and "selfishness."

Agatha had been sixty-seven at the time of the first stroke. In her circle of Carthage friends and neighbors, sixty-seven was considered *still quite young.*

She'd suffered from high blood pressure for years. She was overweight by many pounds. Long she'd entertained others with recitations of her many failed diets—"grapefruit"—"water"—"Dr. Atkins"—"Eaters Anonymous 12-Step"—but really it wasn't funny, as M.R. had known as a young girl, and so there should have been no great surprise at Agatha's collapse, though Konrad seemed not to have anticipated it.

"But, Daddy, how could you *not?*—she made appointments with doctors, she canceled. . . ."

"Please don't speak of your mother as 'she'—you owe her that respect at least."

This cutting remark was so uncharacteristic of Konrad, M.R. was struck dumb.

Agatha had fainted and fallen in the backyard amid a wild tangle of flowers and weeds, and had called to Konrad for help. But she had refused to see a doctor and a few days later she fainted again, and fell, this time on the stairs in the house, and had not recovered consciousness for twelve hours. The stroke was considered "mild"—but she'd lost sensation in her right leg, was more than ever dependent upon a cane, and even with a cane had difficulty walking. She became averse to reading—"nasty squiggly lines like spiders"—and even to watching TV with Konrad—"just flat pictures and people acting like fools." Her hair turned white in streaks giving her a savage look, that quite shocked M.R. when she saw her. Where Agatha had been girlish and tender and her trilling laughter delightful now Agatha was harridanish and harsh and never laughed but made irascible grunting sounds in mocking mimicry of laughter.

Konrad confided in M.R., it was his fault for not having forced Agatha to lose weight, and to keep her doctors' appointments. He felt such terrible guilt, he couldn't bear to think of it.

Privately M.R. had thought yes, this was partly Konrad's fault. The Neukirchens had drifted through the years and decades like infatuated honeymooners in a little boat lacking oars and a rudder.

She'd said, "Daddy, it isn't your fault. You know how stubborn she—Agatha—is."

But Konrad hadn't been placated. With a little snort of derision he'd said, " 'Daddy'—you're calling me? But you call your mother 'Agatha.' There is something wrong there."

M.R. had been speechless. Was her kindly Quaker father now turning against her, too?

"Something very wrong, your mother sensed long before I did. Our 'Merry' was not the daughter we'd believed her to be."

"But—of course I am not 'Merry.' I was never 'Merry.' You know perfectly well that I—I am not your biological daughter. . . . You have no right to expect of me that. . . ."

Articulate before large audiences, never at a loss for words in public, M.R. began to stammer in her father's angry presence.

The power of a parent to wound, to kill. The power of a parent is terrible.

But it was Agatha who was most unreasonable of course. Agatha sprawled on the living room sofa splotch-faced and sullen, her eyes swallowed in the fatty ridges of her face. Her mouth that had always been so soft and warm now resembled a carp's mouth. Her disapproval of M.R. had hardened into dislike.

M.R. was frightened in the woman's presence like a stepchild in a fairy tale that has unexpectedly turned malevolent.

"You. I know why you're here. Waiting for—I know what. S-s-s-so you can have your father all to your-s-s-self."

M.R. protested, she'd come to see *her*—Agatha. She'd heard that Agatha wasn't feeling well and she'd come quickly. . . .

"Heard I had a s-s-s-stroke. S-s-s-so you can have your father all to your-s-s-self."

Yet even before the stroke Agatha had grown ever more resentful of M.R.—whom she called, coolly,

"Meredith"—for having deceived her and Konrad. "Promising you would return to Carthage to teach, after Cornell. And then—Harvard! Why wasn't one of the state colleges good enough for you? That cost a fraction of that fancy tuition? Some worldly notion of yours—some blindness . . ."

Notion was a Quaker term roughly synonymous with *unfounded, illogical, delusional.*

"And you never made the slightest effort to get a job here—I know, I have friends at the high school. And you never told us your plans—your plotting."

"Of course I told you—I kept you informed. When I received a fellowship to Harvard—"

" 'Received a fellowship to Harvard'—do you hear how you sound? How vain, how—hollow? And plain silly."

M.R. wanted to say hotly *What is silly about Harvard?*

M.R. tried to point out that, apart from the state university at Plattsburgh, and St. Lawrence University in Canton, there were no colleges or universities within a reasonable distance of Carthage where she would have felt "comfortable"—an awkward way of saying that no college or university in the vicinity of Carthage was quite good enough for her Harvard Ph.D., or for her.

M.R.'s voice faltered and failed. Maybe it was all— *silly.*

The vanity of the intellectual life, or any kind of life at all—*silly.*

"Your first duty is to your parents who brought you into this world. And kept you in this world. Who cared for you, and made a place for you in their hearts."

Duty! M.R. had wanted to protest, she thought of her life as a life of duty, in fact.

"You've broken our hearts! I'm not even sure if you are our daughter! Still we will always love you. That is God's wish and that is our vow."

Agatha glared at M.R. with a look of such contempt, M.R. had to turn away.

She does see into my heart. She knows me. Mud-woman!

"I had every intention of selling this house, Meredith! I signed the contract with McIntosh Realtor in full awareness of what I was doing, and that I would have to pay a penalty if I backed out. And then, at the closing—I backed out."

Konrad spoke with an air of disbelief as if this admission were scandalous to him, even now.

"It isn't in my character, you know. To 'back out.' "

They were in Agatha's overgrown garden at the rear of the house. Konrad was sitting in a frayed lawn chair and M.R., too restless to sit still, in a flurry of emotion at being in such proximity to her father, was prowling about Agatha's abandoned garden.

Crimson peonies, purple phlox, pink cluster roses and stunted sunflowers amid a choking profusion of weeds.

In the high grass, weatherworn concrete statuary—miniature pig, owl, cat, deer, leering gargoyle with hands pressed against its pointed ears.

How strange, the gargoyle! M.R. remembered the animal statues—she thought—but not the gargoyle, which didn't seem at all like Agatha's taste.

"Then, I intended to rent the house. Neighbors have been suggesting that I rent out just a room or two but that doesn't appeal to me—living with strangers. I wouldn't inflict myself upon *them*—you know how I like to stay up late, and watch TV and now my ears aren't so sharp, the volume has to be turned up high. And my eating habits—since Agatha passed away—are what you'd call *improvised*." Konrad paused, peering at M.R. "You should get Agatha's gloves, if you're going to pull those spiky weeds, Meredith. You'll cut your hands."

M.R. went into the garage, to find Agatha's old, soiled gloves.

There in a corner, her old bicycle—badly rusted, with two flat tires. She'd forgotten the bicycle, totally—with a rush of emotion she recalling now how thrilled

she'd felt, such a sense of freedom, liberation, flight—
pedaling the bicycle up the Convent Street hill, toward
the outskirts of Carthage.

Sniffing suspiciously Konrad's dog came trotting after her. Konrad had insisted that Solomon was
a "friendly animal"—"if not a very well-trained
animal"—but Solomon didn't seem altogether wel-
coming of this tall young woman whom his master had
greeted with such mysterious effusion.

When she returned to Agatha's garden, with Solo-
mon close at her heels, Konrad said loudly, "Solo-mon!
Don't fuss over dear Meredith, you will scare her away.
And she has just arrived."

The red setter was an older dog, with coarse, lus-
terless fur and mournful eyes. He'd been a "rescue
dog"—county animal control officers had rescued him
from an abusive home and, on the eve of his scheduled
execution, Konrad had adopted him.

"It was just after Agatha had passed away. One
morning I woke up and there was Agatha instructing
me—'Go to the animal shelter on Platt Road, hurry
and bring him home!' And I said, 'Him? Who?'—and
Agatha said, 'You'll know when you see him.' And so it
was, I saw Solomon—and I knew."

M.R. laughed. This was Konrad being whimsical—
was it?

In the frayed lawn chair, in baggy khaki shorts exposing his pale, oddly hairless legs, Konrad was determined to entertain. His silvery-white whiskers bristled with static electricity. His eyes were shrewd and intelligent and crinkled at the corners as in a perpetual squint.

It had always been his way, M.R. recalled. To render experience into navigable anecdotes. To soften the sharp edges of things.

"Then, I'd fully intended to rent it—I mean, the entire house. And I planned to find a smaller place, an apartment or 'condo'—on the river perhaps—where other retirees live. So another time I listed the house with McIntosh Realtor, for I felt that I owed them that much, at least—even if it was only a rental. And this very nice young couple was shown the house, and asked intelligent questions about it, and went away and deliberated, and came back, and—and they were set to sign the contract—and I was set to sign—in the Realtor's office—just last week—and I got cold feet, again. I mean literally!—I said to them, my feet are numb—my fingers are numb—I am numb with horror at the prospect of leaving my house where my wife and I—and our little girl—were so happy. Forgive me, I just can't do it." Konrad paused, laughing. Out of his squinting eyes leaked tears that gathered in his bristling beard like little glistening gems. "They thought that I was utterly mad. And I thought, Good! Then maybe they won't charge me any penalty."

M.R. was laughing. "And did they?"

"Well, yes—they did. And now my name is on every Realtor's blacklist in Carthage."

By the end of her first afternoon in Carthage M.R. had yanked up dozens of spiky weeds and dumped them in a heap on the grass. The sun was hot and beat on her head and Konrad searched for a straw hat for her in the garage, he hadn't needed to tell her had belonged to Agatha.

Can I stay with you please. I am so lonely.
If I could sleep. Sleep!

For ten hours she slept, a deep dreamless uninterrupted sleep.

In the room that had been her girlhood room though not in the girl's bed—for the room had been converted to a guest room, the candy-cane wallpaper replaced by a pale green floral pattern, and the cramped little bed by a double bed—she slept for ten hours and wakened at dawn startled and not knowing at first where she was, and stumbling to use a bathroom, and returning, and sleeping again for two hours until sunshine warmed her face like molten flame and she was smiling in her sleep and there came a voice calling to her—gently, teasingly—"Meredith? Are you going to sleep away the entire day?"

And that night she could not keep her eyes open past 10:40 P.M.—she and Konrad were watching a movie of the 1940s on a classic-movie channel—and again she slept through the night—ten hours, twelve hours—like one sequestered at the bottom of the sea, gently rocked by the rhythm of the sea.

Through her time in Carthage, in her old room in the house at 18 Mt. Laurel Street, she would sleep in this way, as she had not slept in many years. And she thought *Maybe this was all that I required. Waiting for me here without my knowing.*

"Since Solomon has come into my life I've wondered—is a dog an individual in himself, or only in regard to his master? When I am not present, is Solomon a 'dog,' or is Solomon simply a wild creature? He has no name—not even a generic name. He simply *is*. As soon as he sees me—hears me—smells me—he reverts to 'Solomon, Konrad's dear companion.' What Solomon would be in a pack of wild dogs, I wouldn't want to contemplate." Konrad laughed, shuddering.

They were walking above the Black Snake River on a bluff in Friendship Park. The sky was threaded with clouds like vapor. The air was warm and fragrant with honeysuckle. Though from the river, or from a freight yard beside the river, came a faint odor of something like nitrogen.

Innocently the coarse-haired red setter trotted nearby. M.R. had the feeling that the dog was listening intently to their conversation even as he went about his doggy routine sniffing, lifting his leg, lunging at grass-hoppers, trotting blithely on.

She might have said *Don't be naïve, Daddy! Solomon is subordinate to his pack leader. A dog, or a man.*

She might have said *With his wild-dog pack he would tear out our throats. He is no "Solomon"!*

She said: "Solomon adores you, Daddy. You are the one who saved his life. He would give his life for *you*."

Konrad seemed touched to hear this.

And it was true, too.

Twice a day they walked Solomon!

Sometimes three times a day.

For Solomon was not an indoor sort of dog but bred to hunt, as Konrad wittily said—*A hunter mon-gre.*

Nothing so comfortable as *routine*.

And in the neighborhood, they were observed: wiry-white-whiskered Konrad Neukirchen in his usual rumpled shorts, parrot green T-shirt with the white letters CARTHAGE VETS CO-OP on the back, very worn Birkenstock sandals, walking with a cane; and beside him a straight-backed younger woman, in loose-fitting slacks, loose-fitting shirt, sandals, crimped-looking hair tied back by a carelessly knotted scarf.

Evident to any eye *A middle-aged daughter, probably unmarried. Visiting her dad.*

Was this—Konrad Neukirchen's esteemed daughter? The one whose photo used to run in the Carthage paper, on an inside page?

The daughter who'd left Carthage to become a professor? A university president? Who'd broken poor Agatha's heart, and had not ever once come to visit her in the final year of her life?

And the red setter mongrel trotting with them— ahead, behind, to the left, to the right—describing about the conspicuous couple an invisible and protective figure eight of which, absorbed in their intense conversation, they were totally oblivious.

As an athlete she'd thought *If you are going to walk upright at all, you must be straight-backed.*

"And then, I've often wondered—is a person a kind of superior animal, or a totally distinct being? Of course"—Konrad spoke hurriedly, to make sure that Meredith understood the subtlety of his argument— "I'm familiar with Darwin. All that—'descent of species.'"

"Yes."

"'Yes'—what?"

"I'm sure that you're familiar with—'all that.'"

In fact, M.R. very much doubted that her father, for all his cleverness, and the many eclectic books he'd read through his life, was "familiar" with Darwin.

To the extent to which he was, in some residual way, imbued with the beliefs of the Society of Friends—very likely, Konrad wasn't a Darwinian, even to a rudimentary degree.

She said: "Even Darwin didn't seem to think that all animals were just—'animals.' He may have believed that his own dog possessed some sort of moral core."

M.R. spoke slowly like one turning a heavy rock in her hands—was it just a heavy rock, or a mineral containing veins of precious ore? Strange and wonderful to her, she was befriending her father who was both the man she believed she knew, and an intriguing stranger.

"Well—of course! Each master has a dog who is 'moral' in regard to his master—like a compass with no choice but to point north."

"Some of my colleagues—at the University—argue that we have no 'core personalities' but exist only in contexts."

"But not so succinctly put, eh? If they are your colleagues—professors."

"It's a theory of mind. One theory of mind."

"And do they believe their theories?"

"Well—I wouldn't know. Very few of us know what we 'believe'—our brains are like the depths of the sea, adrift with all sorts of things—organic, inorganic—'real'—'not-real.'"

And here is the failure of philosophy, M.R. supposed. Words were a crude loose net through which all things—all people—all events—flowed, indefinably.

"I know that I am always who I am—Konrad Neukirchen. I have never not-been Konrad Neukirchen. And I believe that I am a veritable compass of consistency, rationality. Yet—other people!" Konrad stroked at his beard, laughing. "All I can know of other people with certainty is, they are not me."

"They are not-you—but they might be identical with you, in certain ways."

"Oh, no—I can't believe that, really. Humankind is wonderfully fickle, changeable—as I am not."

"This fickleness has helped us to evolve—to adapt. To survive."

"But is survival at any cost worth the cost?"

"Daddy, you have to survive, to ask such a question! The minimum of life is life itself."

She was thinking of the boy who'd tried to hang himself, or had imagined he would hang himself, and die: the verb *die* had had no context for him, he'd misunderstood.

And now he was alive—his body had "survived."

Sick with guilt she could not bear to think of him.

Nor could she bear to think of her sister Jewell who'd died a horrible death—locked in a refrigerator by their mother, suffocated by degrees. It would not have been a rapid or a merciful death.

Five years old! And the other sister, Jedina, two years younger, tossed away like trash too, and yet—by the purest chance, she had not died.

But only because she'd been rescued—"saved."

"The world survives," Konrad was saying, "because there are 'saviors.' We can't save ourselves, but sometimes—we can save others."

M.R. felt a chill, this was uncanny. As if her (adoptive) father had been reading her mind.

Though more likely, each knew the other's mind very well. Like these several walks in Carthage—to the Convent Street bridge, and the river; to Friendship Park, and the river; to downtown by way of Spruce

Street, and the river; or to downtown by way of Elm Ridge Avenue, the "long way" to the river.

Each walk was a different and distinct walk in the walkers' minds, and very likely in Solomon's mind, yet each had the same destination: the river.

For the Black Snake River, traversing the city of Carthage, was the very core of the city, its noisy rampaging soul.

Today they'd walked to the Convent Street bridge. This was the shortest of the walks. In Konrad's presence M.R. didn't feel her usual childish dread of crossing the bridge on the pedestrian walkway—though Konrad strode along so oblivious of trucks passing just a few inches from his elbow, M.R. could hardly relax.

From the bridge, and at shore, men were fishing. Tossing out long, very long lines. Most of the men were dark-skinned, and elderly. It seemed that Konrad knew them—*H'lo Dewitt! Hey there Byron!*—as they knew Konrad—*H'lo Mr. Neu-kitchen!*

Courtly Konrad paused to introduce the men to M.R. Mumbled greetings were exchanged. It was revealed—M.R. asked—that the men were fishing for black bass, catfish, and carp. She wondered if the fishermen were men she'd seen fishing on the river many years ago when she'd been a girl.

As soon as they'd passed beyond the last of the fishermen M.R. said, like one throwing herself from a height: "Daddy, did you know my m-mother? Or—anything about my—mother?"

Konrad's hand stroking his beard froze. Pointedly, he looked away.

"Your mother! Why, Meredith—what do you mean? Agatha is your mother."

M.R. said, pleading: "Daddy, don't. Don't do that. Just tell me the truth, please—I am more than forty years old. I am not a girl to be shielded from the facts of my own life."

She'd come close to saying, *My own ridiculous life.*

Konrad walked on. The fishermen's path was growing fainter. They'd entered a scrubby no-man's-land of prickly weeds, flowering thistles and willow-like trees with wood so soft, many of the branches had split. Wielding his cane Konrad was walking away from M.R., even Solomon had to trot to catch up with him.

M.R. saw with dismay that her father's face was splotched with emotion. He was frowning, resentful. She felt the injustice of his reaction to her—so like Agatha's!

She wondered, does he feel that he must be as un-reasonable as my mother, out of fidelity to her?

Even the most liberal-minded, intelligent, and *ratio-nal* of men behaved spitefully, when his authority was challenged.

And Andre, too. Believing himself utterly fair-minded, yet thrown into a rage if his will was opposed.

Konrad whistled and called: "Sol'mon! Hasten! This way."

For several minutes they walked single-file along the narrow path, in silence. Konrad and his dog-companion ahead, M.R. behind.

Was Konrad not going to say anything more?

Did Konrad intend to leave her in a state of anxious anticipation?

She thought, wounded *I will leave him, tonight. The hell with them both!*

She thought *I was never their God-damned "Merry." What did they want of me!*

It had been their plan to walk to a street that ran parallel with Convent Street and then turn around and come back. It had been their plan to ascend to the street to make a small purchase at a hardware store—M.R. had offered to screw in, more firmly, several kitchen and bathroom fixtures that had become loose—but Konrad seemed to have forgotten.

With a sudden bright-false smile turning to her, to say:

"Well, Meredith! It's a lovely surprise that you've come to visit us. I mean—me. Your visits are rare, and precious. And how long do you propose to stay?"

The casualness of this inquiry was staggering to M.R. Was Konrad suggesting that she leave, soon?

Hesitantly she said, "I—I'm not sure. I haven't been—altogether well. . . ." Her voice trailed off. The straight-backed daughter, taken by surprise.

Of course, Konrad knew that she hadn't been "well." It was a pleading sort of redundancy, to tell him this.

"I was thinking—I mean, I hadn't exactly been thinking—my future is uncertain—and my present is not"—M.R. laughed, this was so stumblingly and so pathetically put, for a Ph.D. in philosophy from Harvard—"is not a model of certainty, either. And so I've wondered—if I could stay with you for a—a while."

"Of course. You need hardly to ask, Meredith."

Konrad spoke quickly, in a lowered voice. As if his daughter's pleading had shamed him.

She said, flailing about: "I can help you—I mean, I can pay my share, or—whatever. I can help you financially, Daddy. If you need help."

Now, had she insulted him? Konrad was staring at a point just past her head, blinking rapidly.

It was a problematic issue: did Konrad need money? The brick house wasn't nearly so shabby as some in the neighborhood but the shingled roof needed repair, the front and back steps needed repair, though Konrad claimed to enjoy vacuuming, the rooms were in need of a thorough cleaning, washing, scrubbing; organdy curtains Agatha had sewn thirty years before were still hanging, limp with dust, faded to a bleary no-color, in the living room. Very likely, however, this was a consequence of Konrad's bachelor indifference, not his financial situation.

Since her arrival several days before, M.R. had purchased groceries, household supplies. She'd gone shopping at a new mall—a quite adequate mall, with a Shop-Rite and a Home Depot—while Konrad had occupied himself at the Carthage Vets Co-op where, it seemed, he was director "by default"—the "qualified" director, the one who'd managed to channel a fraction of the co-op's meager funds into his own bank account, had had to resign hurriedly.

Konrad laughed, regaining his composure: "Oh, my dear—I'm very well off! I thought you must know. Our Carthage city government is so steeped in corruption, it's a tradition in Beechum County—our government workers have an excellent pension fund, even better than custodians and sanitation workers. Much better than public school teachers and officials, too! And I have Social Security, of course. Agatha never had cause to worry about the financial state of our household, not for a moment, and you have no need, either. I am quite prosperous in my retirement, my dear."

M.R. knew, Konrad made out checks to the Veterans Co-op, to the local no-kill animal shelter from which he'd adopted Solomon, and one or two other non-profits including something called "Rotunda"— she'd seen the check lying on a kitchen counter before Konrad had mailed it.

"What is 'Rotunda,' Daddy? I'm just curious."

"Rotunda! You will see, Friday night, if you are still here. Summertime concerts in Friendship Park, in the 'rotunda.' I only give them about one hundred dollars a summer, the concerts are free and sometimes not bad."

As if a dangerous path had been avoided they returned home by way of the parallel street—Hill Street—another, slightly newer bridge.

" 'I loaf and invite my soul.' "

" *You* do? Really?"

"Daddy, it's a line from a poem—Whitman."

"Is it?"

"Daddy, you've quoted it yourself."

"I did? Well, that was clever of me."

Still she was sleeping through the night. Sleep like the most exquisite blanketing of snow—powder-snow, feather-snow, Milky Way stardust-snow. Sleep that was soundless, speechless. Sleep of the kind she'd so envied in her astronomer-lover, the few times they had slept together through a night.

Even when he'd been stirred and disturbed by dreams, Andre never waked.

And in the morning, Andre never remembered.

Ten hours or more, she slept. Especially if rain drummed against the roof and the windows—the most blissful sleep. Sometimes it was the red-setter "rescue dog" who nudged the door of her bedroom open, trotting to her as she slept her heavy stuporous sleep and touching his chill damp nose against her face to wake her, concerned that she might not be able to wake otherwise.

"How lazy I'm becoming! I scarcely know myself."

For it was so, like one in an oarless and rudderless boat borne by a gentle current downstream, M.R. had entered a new region of the soul, scarcely contiguous with her old life, where her heartbeat seemed slower, and more measured; where she found herself, for minutes at a time, gazing into space—unlike her astronomer-lover who was searching restlessly for something in the Universe, M.R. had no object for scrutiny; where she could remain seated for minutes at a time without being active, and without even thinking much except in the most immediately expedient of ways: which vegetables—eggplant, broccoli, zucchini—to prepare for dinner while Konrad grilled hamburgers on the rear, brick terrace; whether to take Konrad's car to the garage for the soon-due state inspection, or assume that Konrad would do this himself, eventually; what to take as an appropriate gift—("Wine is out of the question, don't even ask")—when she and Konrad went to visit one of Konrad's several widow-friends who'd invited them to dinner.

M.R. had learned that her bachelor-father was a very popular man in Carthage. From his years at the county courthouse he'd made seemingly hundreds of friends, there were neighbors eager to invite him to outdoor barbecues, there was a small persistent band of Agatha's women-friends eager to feed him, clean house for him, enlist him as an escort—("Marry me! That's what they all want, poor girls. But Agatha would be so terribly hurt"). And there was the Carthage Vets Co-op where he was rapidly becoming an essential figure, instead of a once-weekly volunteer who picked up curbside donations in his car to bring to the co-op store, or sorted and labeled, in the company of other retirees of whom most were widows of Vietnam vets, every sort of article of clothing, household items and plain junk. And there was—this, M.R. was particularly surprised to discover, for Konrad hadn't mentioned it previously—his trips to the Herkimer VA Hospital where he was a volunteer-helper as well.

These activities were new, M.R. thought. Since Agatha had passed away.

"You're looking puzzled, dear Meredith! But Agatha is the spirit behind all this effort, you know. She had a truly charitable heart—I'd always been too lazy. But now—I am living for us both, I suppose."

Konrad paused, smiling. "You might come with me one day, Meredith. This very nice if hopelessly garrulous woman who runs the volunteers—the widow of a classmate of mine, who died in that very hospital a few years ago, a Korean War vet—is always looking for, as she says, 'fresh blood.'"

"I have a friend . . ."

So casually M.R. began, it might have been the recounting of a droll and entertaining story.

". . . he and his wife have a 'mentally disabled' son. Their lives revolve around this son, they are obsessed with him. Of course, my friend—he's an astronomer, a quite distinguished astronomer, at Harvard—doesn't use the term 'obsessed'—he doesn't use the term 'mentally disabled.' I'd met the son—Mikhal—just once, when he was eleven—he hadn't seemed so very strange to me, then—just distracted, dreamy. . . . That was nineteen years ago. Now he's in his early thirties—'an accursed Peter Pan' my friend—his father—calls him. He has violent temper tantrums, migraine headaches. Except Mikhal is very gifted—a virtuoso musician—pianist, violinist. He can't read music but plays by ear. He's a remarkable composer, too. The music he writes is staccato and dissonant but acoustic—supposedly, everything he writes has some reference to Bach. Mikhal could never work with any music teacher, though my friend and his wife tried to find a teacher for him for years. He can only listen, obsessively, hour after hour, to CDs on his headphones, saturating himself with the musical techniques of others. Mikhal's mother is a Russian-born translator of classic texts who has devoted herself to the son—much of it, trying to find a niche for the son in the music world in Boston. And my astronomer-friend seems to know that this is probably hopeless but at the same time he has hope—he can't not have hope—that Mikhal will improve, that some new drug or therapy will be discovered, and the beautiful boy—did I say that he was beautiful?—like his mother?—of course."

M.R. had been speaking slowly, even calmly. Again, she was like one who turns a heavy chunk of mineral in her fingers, trying to discern the precious streaks, or whether there are any precious streaks. Konrad, flicking a stick for panting Solomon to fetch, only just murmured to indicate that yes, he was listening.

"If Andre—that's my astronomer-friend's name: Andre—is traveling, and he's often away, at observatories, he has to speak with Mikhal every day. If Andre fails to speak with his son every day, Mikhal becomes very difficult to control. If Mikhal senses that Andre is drifting out of the range of the mother and son, some crisis will occur—a relapse in the son, a suicide attempt, admission to an emergency room; or the wife, who seems to be extremely manipulative, while also quite legitimately 'unwell,' might collapse and wind up in the emergency room, too. When Andre received a distinguished award from the National Society of Astronomers, in Washington, D.C., the wife—Erika is the wife's name: I've never met her—had to be hospitalized with some sort of tachycardia seizure."

Konrad listened quietly, stroking his beard. He did not look at M.R. as she spoke in her determined calm manner and he did not look at her when her voice trailed off in a way both bemused and plaintive.

"Andre is a—an unusual man. He has enemies, I think. But he has many friends. He's the kind of man—it occurs to me that you, Daddy, somewhat resemble him—I'd never thought of this until now—you

never truly complain, even when you're 'complain-
ing'—you're being funny. And you see the absurdity of
things, like a gift for seeing cubes where other people
see just flat squares. He has a kind of—well, maybe this
isn't you, Daddy, exactly—kingly manner. You imagine gold coins spilling from his pockets—he wouldn't
notice. There's a high-energy feel about him, you want
always to please him, so he's something of a dictator—
a benign dictator, I mean." She laughed. She wiped
at her eyes, laughing. More and more rapidly she was
speaking, out of control like a truck careening down a
steep grade; more pointedly, Konrad did not look at her
but continued tossing the now wet and gnawed stick for
the red-setter rescue dog to fetch.

She'd spoken to Konrad far too openly. She felt a
pang of regret, she could not retract her heedless words.

Konrad said, not looking at her, but with a pained
smile, "Well! Your astronomer-friend is very special,
I can see. But you, too, are very special, Meredith—
don't forget. And don't forget, the future doesn't have
to be a repetition of the past. Even in the cosmos, there
is nothing merely clockwork or predictable. A comet
plunges out of its orbit, a meteorite plunges to Earth.
Knowing what this man's life has been, you can't know
what his life will be." So strangely then, as M.R. would
recall afterward, he added: "When a man gets older,

his health isn't so very predictable, in fact. Unhappy wives take their revenge then. The 'difficult' wife—the estranged wife—may not continue to love your astronomer-friend then. If, as you said, she's younger than he is—"

"Did I say that?"

"I think you did, yes."

M.R. didn't think so. Though it was true, Erika was younger than Andre but not nearly so much younger than Andre as M.R.

"—she may tire of him. She may rid herself of him. He may find himself suddenly adrift in the cosmos, and needing a friend. These things can happen."

M.R. was astonished. What was her father saying?—suggesting?

And how did he come by such occult knowledge, like a sage in a children's fairy tale?

"These insights, dear, aren't mine—they are Agatha's. Based upon her close observation of certain marriages here in Carthage—the 'wandering' husband, the 'betrayed' wife—the revenge such wives will take when they can."

"Andre Litovik isn't ill. So far as I know, he's—he is not ill."

This wasn't true of course. Andre had numerous ailments, very likely more than M.R. knew. High blood pressure, for which he was medicated; stabbing back-pains, and muscle seizures; he was unusually suscep-tible to respiratory infections, and he'd injured both his knees mountain climbing and would soon need knee replacements, a surgical procedure the anticipation of which filled him with terror yet of which he spoke slightingly, laughingly.

M.R. bit her lower lip. Already she had said more than she'd meant to say—she had not meant to speak so unguardedly.

Konrad said: "All that I mean, my dear sweet daughter, is that things change. And we change with them. And sometimes that works for the best, though we can't think so ahead of time."

Later M.R. would recall that her kindly father had not asked her what Andre Litovik meant to her, that she knew so much about the man, and seemed to care so very much.

Don't want to give you up, darling.

But you can—you should—give me up.

(In her hospital bed M.R. had heard these words of Andre's, spoken with unusual sobriety. Of course, she'd heard. And the genuine solicitude beneath the words. As if even the predator male felt obliged to caution the female, sometimes. And the female smiling, unheeding. In the deepest sense, unhearing.)

(Recalling that morning almost two years ago when the phone had rung in M.R.'s house on Echo Lake. Early-mid-morning and she'd been preparing a brief introduction for a visiting philosophy colleague who would be speaking at a colloquium that afternoon. And so unexpectedly, it was Andre. But Andre urgent and harried as M.R. had rarely heard him—"Turn on your TV, Meredith. Now!" And M.R. had walked without hesitation carrying the portable phone into the other room, to switch on the TV, plaintively asking, "But which channel, Andre?" and impatiently Andre had said, "Any channel! Hurry!" And M.R. had stared at the screen seeing a news footage of some kind, tall buildings issuing smoke, the twin towers of the World Trade Center afire, she was shocked, stunned, confused having no idea what she was watching and Andre had no time to fill her in—"Just know that there has been a major terrorist attack. And there will probably be more. And along with a planeful of other luckless bastards I am stranded in the airport at fucking Cleveland and have no idea when we'll be cleared to fly back to Logan. G'bye!"

"Andre, wait—"

But the line had gone dead.

And so alone in the house on Echo Lake for the next twelve hours riveted to the TV set M.R. had scarcely moved from her chair staring and trying to comprehend what she was seeing—its horror, magnitude, and meaning—even as her eyes spilled tears for what had to be the unspeakable suffering of others as much as her own sorrow and self-pity.)

Konrad's specialty was breakfast: oatmeal with brown sugar, raisins, and skim milk—"The prime meal of the day."

M.R.'s specialty was dinner: lightly steamed vegetables of all kinds, in every kind of combination and with rice, pasta, or couscous.

Except for breakfast M.R. did most of the cooking. Konrad did most of the kitchen cleanup.

They bought groceries together at Shop-Rite. M.R. was fresh produce and dairy, Konrad was all the rest. Invariably, Konrad was the first at the checkout counter where he waited skimming *People*.

In the evenings they read, and watched TV. Sometimes they read while they watched TV—their favorite channel was the classic-movie channel where they saw Ingrid Bergman, Gregory Peck, Greer Garson, Robert Mitchum, Humphrey Bogart, Clark Gable, Ginger

Rogers and Fred Astaire. . . . "Agatha used to say, 'It's reassuring to see that they are all with us, still,'" Konrad said.

As if by mutual consent they did not watch TV news. They did not follow the news of carnage in Iraq, and in Afghanistan. They did not study the inch-high "Faces of the Fallen" published at intervals in the *New York Times*—sixteen photos vertically, sixteen photos horizontally—an entire newspaper page allotted to the mostly young, heartrendingly young and virtually all-male U.S. military dead.

(The *New York Times* was M.R.'s sole concession to the life she'd left behind in north central New Jersey: she could not buy the newspaper in Carthage, nor could the paper be delivered to her father's house except by U.S. mail, days late. She read it daily, online.)

At first, the many books crammed into the Neukirchens' bookcases had filled M.R. with a terrible unease. For she felt that her preoccupation with books—with a life driven by *words*—must have begun here, in this place where books were both revered and treated with the casual familiarity and affection of old friends.

On the shelves, the very same books in the very same order she recalled from her girlhood. Nothing was out of place, and little seemed to have been added. How many books, had Konrad boasted? Eleven thousand six hundred seventy-seven and one half!—of course, Konrad had been joking. At the time, the child Meredith had had no conception of what *joking* meant.

There, the books of her childhood, scarcely altered. How like the library at Charters House—except these books were not rare, and most were not in very good condition. And so many paperbacks, dog-eared, yellowed. Their collective significance confounded her. She pulled out a volume and opened to read—

One sunny autumn afternoon a child strayed away from its rude home in a small field and entered a forest unobserved. It was happy in a new sense of freedom. . . .

How strange, the pronoun *it* in reference to a child! The story was by Ambrose Bierce, whom M.R. had never read—"Chickamauga." The title was in reference, a footnote indicated, to the Civil War Battle of Chickamauga Creek (Tennessee) in 1863: thirty-four thousand casualties, one of the bloodiest battles of the Civil War.

She was filled with a childlike yearning to know more—to read the story, and the entire volume of stories by Bierce. But she returned the book to the shelf, for now.

A pile of books beside Agatha's chair was touching to see. These were Agatha's usual novels by women writers, gardening books, and a slender volume—*Ariel*, poems by Sylvia Plath.

She understood Konrad's reluctance to put these books away.

She wondered: was the full-to-bursting album MY LIFE AS A BABY still in the bureau drawer? But she made no effort to find it.

"Come with me, dear! I am going to visit Agatha."

She went with him. She knew that Agatha's grave would be beside the lost child's grave in Friendship Cemetery and so was prepared.

M.R. had to remember, little MEREDITH RUTH NEU-KIRCHEN—"MERRY"—SEPTEMBER 21, 1957–FEBRUARY 3, 1961 had not been her.

Thinking of Konrad's *paradoxes*. How he'd teased and perplexed her as a little girl speculating about *time travel*—as if, as a child, she could have known what *time travel* meant. He'd joked about returning in time to confront a younger twin—how strange that would be!

She wondered if her beloved father had been the source of her fascination with philosophy—its riddles, its pretense of wisdom and its perennial hope.

In Friendship Cemetery Konrad was unusually quiet. This was a relief—or was it? Even Solomon, trotting and sniffing between rows of grave markers, lifting his leg to urinate, seemed less exuberant, doggy. When Konrad snapped his fingers at him, the setter shrank back abashed.

"Solomon, bad manners! That is not what we do in a *cemetery*."

It was a windy day in midsummer. Bright patches of sunshine were blown about in the sky, and from the direction of Lake Ontario, in the west, a flotilla of storm-clouds approached. M.R. stared at the little grave marker beside the larger grave marker—AGATHA RUTH NEUKIRCHEN APRIL 7, 1934—NOVEMBER 19, 2001. CHERISHED WIFE AND MOTHER. Both markers were made of the same pale pink limestone.

Konrad busied himself tidying the graves. Konrad kept his face turned from M.R., that she would not see his tears.

M.R. helped him, pulling at weeds. How fast-growing weeds are, and some of them so prickly! At both the graves were clay pots that held, or had once held, living flowers, as well as ceramic pots containing artificial flowers. Konrad had stopped at a florist's to buy flowers—a pot of live, bright yellow day lilies—which he and M.R. set now between the two graves, steadying it amid tufts of grass. And, in the florist's, M.R. had purchased a curious artificial grapevine adorned with clusters of purple, dark-red, and green-streaked grapes, the very sort of thing that would have caught Agatha's eye, which she now twined about both the grave markers.

Konrad was deeply moved. "Why, Meredith—that's beautiful!"

And: "Just the sort of thing that would have caught Agatha's eye."

For some time they sat, gripping hands. Sensing their solemn mood Solomon ceased his trotting and sniffing and with a shuddery sigh stretched out between them in the grass, and shut his eyes. Very gradually, his long tail ceased twitching.

"Agatha loved you very much, Meredith. Until the end, when she wasn't Agatha."

"I know, Daddy. I understand."

"At the end most of us are not 'ourselves'—probably. We shouldn't be judged by our final words. You should remember us at our best."

"I do! I will."

"That is God in us, to remember us at our best. The clear light within."

She held Konrad's hand in hers. He had a broad hand, stumpy fingers. He'd lost weight since Agatha's

death, his features had sharpened in his face. Cheek-
bones long hidden by a layer of fat were now visible.
His flyaway grizzly hair had turned white, his gruff
eyebrows and bristly beard were white, in his seventies
he'd become, as if by default, a striking figure of a man.

How like a professor he looked. A professor *mongre*.

"Daddy! I could make inquiries at St. Lawrence
University, or—there's a Catholic college in Watertown,
I think. And the state university at Plattsburgh . . ."

"No."

" 'No'—what? What do you mean?"

"Don't be ridiculous, Meredith. You're not going to
stay here."

"I'm not?"

"Of course you're not. Not Carthage."

Still, she felt a small flurry of enthusiasm, hope—
she might reinvent her life in this part of the world,
if she could find a place—a position. If anyone would
have her, here. If—a person with her credentials, background, experience . . .

Adamantly Konrad repeated: "Not Carthage."

Like a baby bird that has ventured too soon out of its
nest, unfledged, her hope plummeted to earth.

Konrad squeezed her hand. Whether in a gentle
reprimand, or to bolster her spirits, M.R. didn't know.
Unless it was to prepare her for what he said next.

"Your mother, Meredith. Your—'birth mother'—as it's called . . ."

"Yes?"

"So far as I know, she's been institutionalized at the Herkimer State Psychiatric Facility since the early 1970s. Her name is 'Marit Kraeck' and she isn't old—not from my perspective—younger than I am, I think. She would be about seventy years old. If she's still alive."

M.R. listened in astonishment. These words, at last, so casually uttered!

"She was never tried for what she did to you or— what she did to your little sister. She was found 'not guilty by reason of insanity' and sent to the Herkimer facility and that's all that I know."

"My mother is—alive?"

"Well, I don't know that. I can't say if she's alive or not. It's been years since I have heard anything of her."

"But—you know where she is, if she's alive."

"Agatha never wanted to know, and of course I never told her. But when we adopted you, I was avid to know your birth mother's fate. For she was a troubled soul, a terribly maimed soul, and not the 'monster' depicted in the media—this, I believed. I have connections with local lawyers and judges and county-state law enforcement—I knew about the search for her and how, eventually, a mentally ill homeless woman in a shelter in Port Oriskany turned out to be her—'Marit Kraeck.' When she was apprehended, and brought back to Herkimer County, I hid the newspapers from Agatha, and from you—you were still very young at the time. And so she was never tried but sent to the Herkimer facility."

"Do you think she's still there? And I could see her?"

"Well, she may have 'recovered' and been released—but I doubt it. I don't think that, judging from what she'd done, the woman would ever 'recover,' still less be released." Konrad paused, breathing audibly. It was clear now that the conversation was upsetting to him. "I suppose you could see her—if that is your wish."

If that is your wish. How like a fairy-tale warning this was!

Yet, as in a fairy tale this is the abandoned child's wish.

" 'Marit Kraeck.' "

Thursday morning, Konrad was working at the veterans' co-op and so without telling him M.R. drove to the Herkimer State Psychiatric Facility seventy miles away in the adjoining county. Among Carthage schoolchildren the name "Herkimer State" signaled insanity, incarceration. There were many grim jokes about

"Herkimer State" that, at the time, Meredith had not found funny.

" 'Marit Kraeck.' I have come to visit her. . . ."

She was very excited. She could not have said with hope, or with fear—a sick sort of dread. She could not have said what she hoped to discover. Andre would have been astonished, and appalled. *A homicidal madwoman mother! No wonder you haven't wanted children.*

The psychiatric facility was a prison, it seemed. On a state highway north of Herkimer Falls, in a hilly, desolate landscape of felled trees, excavated earth, abandoned quarries. In the distance, the peaks of the Adirondacks were hazy as if evaporating into the horizon. M.R. felt a stab of terror, she was making a mistake to have come here and what would this mistake be but one of a concatenation of mistakes, foolish blunders that had ruined her life.

The prison—the facility—was surrounded by a twelve-foot fence topped with razor wire. There was a gate, through which M.R. was allowed to enter after showing the security guard her identification and explaining the nature of her visit.

" 'Marit Kraeck.' I have come to visit her, if I can."

And inside, to a frowning woman at a front desk whom you would not have called a "receptionist" exactly—rather more a combination of prison guard, nurse—in a not-clean uniform, stubby fingers adorned with cheap rings: " 'Marit Kraeck.' I have come to visit her, if I can."

"And you are—?"

"Her daughter."

Typing into a computer the woman scarcely paused at M.R.'s strained reply. It was amazing to M.R., the woman didn't stare at her in astonishment—*You? Her daughter?*

But Marit Kraeck was but one of many hundreds of patients—inmates—in the Herkimer facility. And M.R., showing the receptionist her identification— driver's license, University ID—with shaking hands was but one of many visitors.

There was solace in that, surely: one of many.

She and I. Mother and daughter. Sick, incarcerated mother, daughter adopted and now adult. Come to visit, if I can.

"Yesss. 'Marit Kraeck.' She's on third. I'll get some- one to escort you there. It's a locked ward."

"Is it! Thank you."

"Haven't you been here before? Is this your first visit?"

Now the woman eyed M.R. doubtfully. For what sort of daughter has not visited her mother in thirty years.

"I—I'm her adopted daughter. I mean—" M.R. paused, in confusion. The woman listened patiently to her as she fumbled for words.

"—I am her daughter, who was given out for adoption. I haven't seen her since I was three years old. . . ."

Lucky daughter! For it was "visitation time" quite by chance, and M.R. was escorted into an elevator with several other visitors, all of them women. Second floor, most of the visitors got out. Third floor, just M.R. and the attendant who was escorting her.

The woman, short, stocky, big-breasted, friendly and garrulous, led M.R. along a corridor to a security door in which she briskly typed in a code: not a very complicated code for M.R. easily read and memorized it: 2003.

"This-here is a locked ward, see. But there's no danger or anything, nobody has hurt anybody in a long time. The doctors keep them all pretty much under control—'medicated.' We'll go into the visitors' lounge and I'll see if Mar-ritt will want to see you. Nobody ever comes to see Mar-ritt, not since I've been here."

The smell! Smells . . .

M.R. felt faint. M.R. wanted to clutch at the attendant's arm, in desperation.

"Ma'am? You O.K.?"

In a gesture that touched M.R., so exquisitely sensitive, so unexpectedly solicitous, the woman gripped
M.R.'s arm by the elbow, to steady her.

"Yes. Of course. I'm . . . O.K. I am fine."

Dazed she sat in a vinyl chair. Her lips had gone
cold, her tongue had gone cold, numb. A ringing in her
ears, had to be a pulsebeat gone berserk . . . *Oh Andre!*
If you could help me.

But this was not reasonable, was it. More likely, it
was Konrad who would help her.

Oh Daddy you were right. This is not a good idea.

There was a wait. M.R. was alone in the visitors'
lounge. In the near distance, the drone of voices.
Animated, mechanical—TV voices. She was becoming more accustomed to the smells. She was determined not to succumb to her own weakness, anxiety.
She forced herself to sit straight in the uncomfortable
chair—straight-backed, head high. Addressing an audience, do not—do not ever—touch your face, or your
hair. If you are overcome by anxiety, clutch your hands
together beneath the podium.

Never show your fear. They will devour you.

"Hey! Sorry, ma'am! We're kinda slow-walking,
see . . ."

The stocky little big-breasted woman was leading
an older woman, not stocky but heavy, near-obese,

who made her way by painstaking inches, leaning on a walker. The woman was wearing a shapeless, badly stained dress, a kind of housedress, with a ragged hem that hid just part of her swollen, vein-ridden legs.

"Say h'lo to your visitor, Mar-ritt. Who'd you say you are, ma'am?"

"I—I'm— I am—"

The woman was easing herself, the bulk of her clearly pain-ridden body, onto a sofa, that sunk just perceptibly beneath her weight. Her face was spongy, her skin the color of rancid lard; her eyes were dull, so lacking in focus that you might think there were no pupils, no irises. A vacuous sort of half-smile played about her lips that looked rubbery, wormy.

"Mar-ritt's daughter? Are you?"

"Yes."

"Hey Mar-ritt—hear that? Your daughter's come to visit you—see? Say h'lo, can you? C'mon."

The woman's face contracted like a squeezed-together fist. The eyelids fluttered, but only briefly. The wormy lips did not move.

The woman looked much older than seventy. Her face was ancient, a ruin of creases and folds. Her head was near-bald like a rock that has been worn smooth, covered in wisps of gray hair. The smell emanating from her body was of dried sweat, urine, feces.

"M-Mother? It's . . . do you remember . . ."—
M.R. spoke shyly, gripping her hands together in her
lap—" . . . Jedina. Your daughter."

Except for the woman's labored breathing, and the
drone of the TV voices somewhere near, there was
silence.

The attendant nudged Marit, in a gesture that seemed
to M.R. familiar, even intimate. "Hey Mar-ritt—hear
that? 'Jed-in-ya.' She's come to see you, see? Try an' say
h'lo, c'mon."

But Marit Kraeck seemed not to hear. On the sofa
she sat with legs asprawl, the fatty folds of her thighs
uncomfortably visible to M.R. who was facing her.
Almost, M.R. wanted to hide her eyes, like a child in a
fairy tale exposed to a forbidden sight.

To M.R. the attendant said apologetically, "Well,
see!—Mar-ritt ain't used to socializing. We call it that—
'socializing.' I'm not a nurse—I never went to nurse-
school—but I know some things I picked up, and one of
them is—the brain kind of turns off if it ain't used, or
these kind of 'psycho-tropic' drugs they give them, like,
like a switch that's off, or a car ignition, that hasn't been
turned on in a long time—so, when you try to turn it on,
nothing happens. Nothing-the-fuck-happens."

This sympathetic recitation elicited no response
from the patient except a twitchy smile about the lips.

The eyes were dull as if a light had gone out behind them. The fat thighs sprawled farther apart, the soiled housedress was strained at the knees. M.R. saw to her horror that the woman's ankles were grotesquely swollen, more swollen than her legs, discolored as if tumorous.

"Well—maybe I should go an' leave you two? Sometimes that helps."

"No! Please don't go away."

M.R. spoke pleadingly. Marit Kraeck gave a little shudder, the bulk of her body quivered as if in anticipation of—something.

"I think it might be better—easier for her—for us—if you stay."

"O.K., ma'am. But you got to know, this is how they are. Mostly all of 'em. They are not dangerous—now. How you get to this ward, you have got to be some kind of 'danger to yourself or others' which Mar-ritt must've been, once. To be frank I don't know too much about her history. There's lots more interesting patients on the third floor, than Mar-ritt. More dangerous, too. Some of the men. You can see, she ain't well—she has got high blood pressure, something wrong with her heart, can't hardly walk without panting like a dog. Used to be, if you were a danger, they'd operate on your brain—this was a long time before I came here, but you hear about it." The attendant shivered, but she was laughing. "Now it's a whole lot better, with just drugs. They take their 'meds'—or they are injected— and everybody's life is easier."

As if roused by the attendant's chatter Marit Kraeck began to whimper, wanting to be returned to the ward. She stared at M.R. with widened eyes as if only now seeing her. The whimper grew louder, pleading tinged with rage.

"Uh-uh! Visit's over! C'mon, Mar-ritt—time to go back to your room." To M.R. she said: "This is kinda fast, I know. I'm sorry. Like I say they just ain't used to, like, 'socializing.' The idea of talking with your mouth like it's some kind of important thing to do, like eating, is just not clear to them. Also, their brains are not just turned off, some of 'em they've got Alzheimer's, see. You can't tell much, up here—there ain't that much difference between Alzheimer's and what they are anyway. They like their TV—she prob'ly wants to see TV. Maybe she thought you were some kind of fancy TV out here in the visitors' lounge."

Cheerily the attendant led Marit Kraeck away through another code-locked door. In horror M.R. watched her mother's broad straining back—the elephantine legs and ankles—the stooped shoulders. Very slowly and painstakingly the aluminum walker skidded forward on the badly worn linoleum floor.

"Good-bye . . ."

Belatedly, M.R. called after Marit Kraeck who took not the slightest notice of her.

How swiftly this had happened!

How swiftly, and now it was over. And nothing had happened—had it?

M.R. tried to stand, but could not. In the vinyl chair she sat stunned, uncertain what she'd seen, and what exactly had happened. Her mouth had gone entirely dry, she was trying compulsively to swallow. Her tongue felt numb as if paralyzed.

She thought *I have had a stroke. An aneurysm. Oh help me* . . .

But when the cheery attendant returned M.R. was able to rise to her feet as if nothing were wrong, or almost. "Ma'am—you O.K.?" the woman asked, peering at her. "S'got to be some kind of trauma, like—seeing the old woman like that. Nobody'd ever think she was your mother, if that's some consolation."

"I—I could come back another time, maybe."

"Sure! That's a good attitude."

"I'm not sure that she knew who I was. . . . Who I am."

"Prob'ly not. Prob'ly Mar-ritt can't hear too well."

"I'd hoped that she would remember me—to a degree. I mean—I wouldn't expect. . . ."

"Prob'ly she wouldn't remember you, ma'am. Like, she won't remember seeing you today, and kind-of, she don't remember me too well. Any of the attendants on the ward, or the nurses, the patients mostly can't tell us apart. And when I was new here, lots of them, the patients, I couldn't tell them apart."

M.R. allowed herself to be led by the arm, by the friendly attendant: back through the coded security door, into the corridor and to the elevator.

"Ma'am, I'm gonna escort you down to the ground floor, you're looking kind of white in the face. Like I said, you had a kind of trauma, eh? Seeing your mother like that?"

M.R. nodded weakly. The thought came to her— *That wasn't my mother.*

"People think sometimes, coming to visit, if they ain't seen the patient in a while—know what they think?—they think *It isn't my—mother, or father— or—whatever.*"

M.R. laughed. She was not such a fool, was she, to imagine that the obese idiot-woman was not her mother Marit Kraeck. Half-pleading she said:

"I thought—I might—just talk with her, a little. I thought that, if she remembered me, I would tell her about my life since—since she knew me. I thought. . . ." M.R. paused, feeling very strange.

I thought that I would forgive her. That is what I thought.

She laughed again. Her face was very cold, and her tongue felt like a stranger's tongue in her mouth, that would choke her.

In the elevator, there was a sound of sobbing, choking. Helpless as a child she hid her face.

"Oh hey, ma'am—don't feel bad. Mar-ritt is O.K. She's safe here. Outside, she'd be dead by now for sure. It ain't a bad life, they watch TV and they like to eat. It's pretty terrible crap they eat but they like it. Y'know, ma'am, you look kind of familiar to me. D'you know me, or anybody in my family? Di Plaksa."

M.R. shook her head no. She was feeling very weak and eager to get out of this terrible stifling place.

" 'Diane Plaksa.' I went to Carthage High, class of '84. You do look like somebody I used to know."

M.R. stared at the woman. Five foot three, heavyset and muscular, with enormous breasts, a pushed-in Kewpie-doll sort of middle-aged face—was this Diane, Irene's daughter? The girl who'd gone with Meredith and Agatha and Agatha's women friends, visiting elderly women on a "good-neighbor" mission?

"Diane! Yes, I do know you. I'm Meredith Neukirchen—Agatha's daughter."

" 'Meredith Neukirchen.' 'Agatha's daughter.' " Slowly Di Plaksa turned these words in her mouth, like pebbles. A dim sort of recognition came into her eyes. "Ohhh yes. I think so—yessss. 'Merry' they called you—my mom's friends. My mom is Irene Plaksa."

"Yes," M.R. said. "I remember her, and I remember you."

Yet, what a transformation in Di Plaksa! Hadn't she been the girl to speak with such contempt of doing good, helping the helpless—at the age of twelve, so hard-hearted she'd taken Meredith's breath away. And now, an attendant at Herkimer Psychiatric Hospital.

Who can understand such things, M.R. thought. Her life had been a cultivation of the intellect, the analytical mind—yet, she was constantly being confounded.

"Well—'Merry'! Or did you say—'Mer-deth.' It's real nice to see you after all these years. Weird how people are always meeting here, it happens all the time. You're looking real good—I guess you don't live here now, eh? You're some kind of teacher? I heard?" Di Plaksa peered at her, still very friendly, but with an air now of admiration. "I moved out of Carthage, I live in Herkimer Falls now. But that ain't far. None of us Plaksas go very far."

Di Plaksa followed M.R. to the front door where impulsively she hugged her, as if they were old friends after all.

"Hey—good to see you, Mer'deth! Y'come back again, will you? Maybe the visit will go better."

Like one stumbling on stilts M.R. escaped to her car, drove back to Carthage and fell onto her bed exhausted and slept for nine hours into the late evening and this time neither Konrad nor Solomon disturbed her sleep as if knowing exactly where she'd been.

That night this memory came to her.

When she'd been newly inaugurated: early June 2002.

When she hadn't yet taken residence in Charters House.

Though of course she'd begun working in the president's office in Salvager Hall.

When she'd been almost unbearably happy—hopeful . . .

And anxious. And grateful.

And very very busy. Never so busy in her life except she had a small team of assistants and she would learn—must learn—(so Leander Huddle advised, she would learn sooner or later and far better sooner)—to delegate authority.

Otherwise, Leander warned, she'd be eaten alive.

Invited to a gathering of what Leonard Lockhardt called *well-to-do activist alums* held on the fifty-foot yacht owned by the most wealthy of the alums, a balmy sundown cruise in the romantic-choppy waters off

Montauk Point. And smiling M.R. was introduced to the wife of the yachtsman, a beautiful woman in her early sixties who like her husband was renowned for philanthropy, who'd stared at M.R. with none of the warmth and admiration of the others saying suspiciously, "*You*? Who are *you*? I want to meet the new president of the University."

The woman's eyes were glassy, glazed. A terrible vacuity in those eyes. And the lipstick-mouth baring teeth in an expression of hostile uncertainty.

Fortunately, M.R. had been alerted beforehand—by Leonard Lockhardt, her escort for the evening—that Mrs. Huston had been recently diagnosed with early-onset Alzheimer's. And what a tragedy it was, for Mrs. Huston was so young still, and had always been so vivacious, so warm and generous and lovely. And so M.R. wasn't altogether surprised, or shocked by the confrontation—but she couldn't help feeling just slightly hurt.

And others were listening, and were uneasy on her account.

And so she recovered her composure and said, as graciously as she could manage, though inwardly (in fact) she was shaking, like any imposter who has been publicly exposed: "I'm so sorry, Mrs. Huston! But I am the new president of the University, and I'm delighted to be your guest on this beautiful yacht."

Next day—again without telling Konrad where she was going—M.R. drove to Bear Mountain Road on the outer edge of the city of Carthage. From this hilly prospect you could look down toward the city, and the snaky river—it was a surprise to M.R. how she hadn't known this, as a child.

Her perspective had been so truncated, so child-sized, she had not known that the Skedds lived on a hill!

But the Skedds' house was long-ago. After the fire no house had been rebuilt on the rubble-strewn property. It seemed as if no one owned it, or no one wanted it; to own it, one would have to pay taxes on it, and maybe that was the dilemma.

Or maybe it was believed, in Carthage, among those who knew of the terrible blaze that killed eight people, that there was a curse on the property.

Lizbeth had confessed, she'd set fire to the house. She'd hated them all she said.

Sixteen years old. But she'd been tried as an adult. Sent away to prison and not once had M.R. thought of her in the intervening years for there are some thoughts you need not think, as there are the most terrible poisons you need not taste.

M.R. pressed the palms of both hands against her eyes, and against her forehead. To calm herself. To still the pulses beating in her brain.

A long-ago time. And the pain, the shock and suffering—long-ago.

Remains of the asphalt-sided house that had seemed to her as a child so stocky-solid, like Floyd Skedd, were collapsed in ruins, scarcely recognizable. Boards and shingles burnt, rotted. And everywhere tall grasses, shrubs and trees had grown over it. M.R. stood in the tall grass brushing away insects. Her head was still ringing from the visit at Herkimer. Her head was still ringing from the sound of her mother's voice that was not a human voice but an animal whimper of alarm, rising rage. Now she shut her eyes seeing again Mrs. Skedd sharp-elbowed and frantic, swiping at one of the older children with a closed fist, screaming *Bastids! Nobody'd take you in in their right mind except dumb-ass us, and now look! Ingrates.*

M.R. smiled. So clearly she heard the woman's voice and the quaint surprising term *ingrates*.

And Mr. Skedd's nasal teasing. Mr. Skedd had had nicknames for them all but Jewell had not ever heard his name for her.

Mudgirl ain't she sad. That's Mudgirl that one.

See? That one. Sucking at her fingers.

And both Skedds would say *Don't let the bastids get your goat.* In the Skedd household this was considered a cheery sentiment. She remembered how Mrs. Skedd had run after her, in the front yard, to grab her away from Agatha Neukirchen. For just a moment, to hug her—tight. *God damn I'm not going to cry this is a God-damn happy time.*

In hot July sunshine M.R. stumbled in the ruins of the burnt-down house searching for evidence that she'd ever lived in this place. That the child who had lived here, as a foster child housed with Floyd and Livvie Skedd, had been her. Amid the burnt and rotted wood were chunks of broken cement, and these were sharp, and dangerous if you tripped on them.

Shattered glass, a badly burnt Formica-topped table, metal objects so rusted they were unidentifiable—the remains of a bed, bedsprings. At the edge of the rubble-littered property was a ravine and beyond the ravine a marshy area where denuded tree trunks emerged out of the algae-choked viscous liquid like a child's crayon drawings of trees—straight, featureless, lacking limbs and leaves. Acid rain that had plagued the Adirondacks for years had killed the trees.

In the marsh were isolated bird cries, unrecognizable. The King of the Crows had dwelt there once, but no longer.

She was deeply moved. But she would tell no one.

She thought *And here too Mudgirl was loved.*

Mudwoman Encounters
a Lost Love.

August 2003

In the bleak foyer of the Herkimer VA Hospital she first sighted him not knowing who he was. The startling-white shirt caught her eye, like floating wings.

A pristine white shirt—whiteness itself—seemed out of place here. The uniforms of the hospital staff were a grayish-soiled sort of white and the very air seemed tinged with melancholy dimness like a prevailing bad odor.

The man in the white shirt—no one M.R. had ever seen before, she was sure—was a visitor like Konrad and M.R., in the company of a fretful elderly woman who clutched at his arm as they moved with painstaking slowness toward the elevators. And was the man wearing a necktie with the long-sleeved white cotton dress shirt?—yes. And decent-looking trousers with

a crease. And, like Konrad, he wore Birkenstock sandals, but with black socks. On this hot, humid day
in late August! M.R. saw that the white-shirted man
walked beside the elderly woman with a quirky sort of
deliberation like one compensating for a mild impair-
ment of motor coordination, or poor vision; he wore
glasses with black plastic frames too large and too em-
phatic for his narrow face. He was lanky, and tall; his
shoulders were sloped; he might have been any age between forty and sixty, with wispy-thin hair like spent
dandelion seed, and a painstakingly courteous manner
that nonetheless suggested just barely concealed impatience. *Teacher, professor*—M.R. thought. Accustomed to authority if but a petty and inconsequential
authority.

M.R. hesitated, not wanting to take the elevator
into which the man in the white shirt and the elderly
woman were stepping. She was hoping that Konrad
hadn't sighted the Birkenstocks—the sandals were
enough for Konrad to strike up one of his animated
conversations with strangers that for all their warmth
sometimes lasted just a little too long and rang just
slightly too cheery.

But Konrad held back, too. For he and M.R. were
carrying clumsy-sized cardboard boxes filled with "donations" for veterans on the fifth floor, and the elevator,

which was the single elevator out of three in the lobby that appeared to be in operation, was crowded.

Konrad was in good spirits this morning, despite the depressing atmosphere of the veterans' hospital, or because of it—"The challenge is to rise above circumstances," Konrad liked to say. "The challenge is to resist circumstances. Any idiot can be happy in a *happy place*, but moral courage is required to be happy in a *hellhole*."

Happy! M.R. guessed her exuberant father must have been exaggerating.

He'd warned M.R. before her first visit that the long-term care VA hospital in the impoverished southern Adirondacks was clearly a dumping-ground for permanently disabled veterans whose families didn't want them or couldn't care for them, or who had no one. It was run-down, under-staffed and poorly staffed, notorious in the region, like the Herkimer State Psychiatric Facility just three miles away; yet, all the more need for volunteers to visit, and to bring cast-off clothing, shoes, toiletries, books and CDs and electronic equipment that ran the range of possibly-usable if ancient computers, cell phones, portable CD players and earphones. All the more need for *meaningful interaction* with the veteran-patients. "I know—there is something disagreeable about 'volunteerism.' Any sort of charitable act or contribution has an air of self-congratulation if not masochism. But—Agatha would like us to be here. I'm sure that—if she could see us—Agatha would be very happy for us to be here—I feel her spirit here—I mean, with us. In the car with us driving here to Herkimer—'I look at life from both sides now'—whoever that woman singer is—I've kept Agatha's CDs in the car as you've probably noticed."

M.R. was touched by such remarks but made uneasy as well. It was her wish to believe that really, Konrad wasn't serious when he said such things but was speaking, as he described it, "poetically—with a grain of salt."

When Agatha was alive, Konrad had teased her mercilessly about her taste in music—"Is it *soft-rock?* How is it possible, *rock* can be *soft?*" Konrad's musical tastes were classical-heroic: blustering nineteenth-century symphonies by Beethoven, Brahms, Mahler. And Shostakovich. Volume turned up, the very air tremulous with masculine drama, bravado. Konrad seemed truly to believe that there was no restrained way to suggest what was "profound" in life.

"Unfortunately, the shelf-life of 'volunteerism' is about the shelf life of clotted cream—finite. I've been coming here for almost two years—and hope that I can continue for a long time more—but in that short period I've seen the most enthusiastic volunteers, female and male, appear and—abruptly, without explanation—

disappear. The effort of service can be wearing. 'Good deeds are a needle in the heart.'"

"Who said that, Daddy?"

"I did."

M.R. laughed. The damned cardboard box was slipping from her grasp, a sharp edge nudging the soft skin below her waist.

And her ankles and feet were itching—from flea bites. Poor Solomon had had an unlucky encounter with a clumsily amorous husky in Friendship Park though both dogs were male, and both large—the result was an infestation of fleas. Over-zealous in treating him with a ghastly white powder, Konrad and M.R. had succeeded in ridding Solomon of fleas that had leapt from his fur onto their bare, lower legs and feet. What a nightmare of itching bites! Repeatedly they'd rubbed an anti-itch gel into their skin but its potency, like the shelf life of volunteerism, was very finite.

M.R. grasped the cardboard box in her arms more firmly. Fresh-laundered secondhand clothes neatly folded—flannel shirts, polyester trousers, frayed sweaters, tent-sized pajamas, underwear and socks. A jumble of mismatched socks. And always at least one pair of unaccountably new and shiny men's dress shoes as if whoever had purchased the shoes had keeled over dead before he'd had a chance to scuff them.

In the airless elevator they ascended to the fifth floor—Neurology.

Along with Burn Unit, Neurology contained the most devastated individuals. If the brain is injured, scrambled—the body's parts lack coordination like a puppet without strings.

Of course, there are happy endings—there was successful neurosurgery. But successful patients weren't hospitalized, still less were they hospitalized in Herkimer, New York.

M.R. steeled herself for meeting—remeeting— the dozen or so veterans who were able to communicate with visitors, or at least to respond to visitors; the men ranged in age from mid-twenties to somewhere beyond seventy. Most were in wheelchairs with permanent injuries—"deficits"—that might be visible or invisible, and a few, victims of unspeakable violence to their bodies, were missing limbs, or were disfigured.

Some were blind, deaf. Some were mute. Some were partly paralyzed. All had grown ashen-skinned in the hospital's relentless fluorescent lighting and all appeared older than their ages.

M.R. had to resolve not to betray the uneasiness she felt. How sick with shame and guilt, she who had never gone to war.

It seemed astonishing to her, that ex-soldiers could forgive those who'd been spared suffering as they had suffered. That they could smile at their able-bodied visitors with unscarred faces, unshattered spines.

For so many of them, their youth had been consumed by the military, if not by war. Their precious life's blood drained from them, to what obscure, cynical, and short-lived political end, they could not grasp nor in the circumstances of their suffering could not wish to grasp.

Konrad had cautioned M.R. not to bring up the subject of politics—not ever.

Not to bring up the subject of the current wars in Afghanistan and Iraq—not ever.

"They need to believe that their ruined lives make some sense. We are here to minister to them, not to our own political convictions."

Yes, M.R. murmured. Yes, of course.

She was accustomed to her father's admonitions that eased over her sensitive, smarting skin like warm water.

"In the VA hospital, 'politics' are too late."

Konrad continued, in a lowered voice: "Unfortunately, most of what we know comes too late. It was Goethe who said—'The owl of Minerva flies at dusk.'"

In fact, Hegel, M.R. thought. But she wouldn't dream of correcting her father.

This was her fourth visit to the VA hospital. The first time had been arduous, draining—yet exhilarating, to a degree. The second time had been less arduous and draining—yet less exhilarating too. The third time had given her a terrible pounding headache, that near-unbearable sensation of a heightened pulsebeat in her ears.

This visit, she'd been dreading. No appetite for breakfast that morning for already she'd been smelling the hospital-odor that was in part a rancid food-smell, yeasty and garbagey.

Agatha would be so proud.

Agatha always spoke of how you'd driven her and her women-friends when you were in high school.

The clear light within. God in our hearts and our hearts one with God.

Each visit to the hospital M.R. worried might be her last visit, and Konrad would be disappointed. (Agatha would be disappointed!) For M.R. would be leaving Carthage to return to the University at the end of August— would she?—or, less admirably, M.R. would decline to return to the hospital out of a loss of resolve, courage.

Tacitly it had worked out, M.R. drove herself and her father to Herkimer, and Konrad drove them home again. After an hour and a half in the Neurology ward M.R. was too exhausted to drive and was inclined to fall asleep in the passenger's seat even as Agatha's soft-rock CDs played and replayed.

Konrad must have been tired, too—he was over seventy years old. But Konrad was too gallant to betray any weakness that would impact upon others.

At the start she'd been eager to accompany Konrad to Herkimer, as she'd been eager to work with him at the Carthage Vets Co-op. Like one who has been starved for human companionship she would have accompanied her father virtually anywhere—she'd discovered since her collapse and hospitalization that she dreaded being alone.

A true Quaker is never alone. God abides in our hearts.

Still, her father's house was almost unbearably empty when Konrad was out.

If you are always alone, you will be thinking non-stop—your brain will never click off.

It is not possible to live a life of thought continuously. . . .

He'd warned her. She could not see his face though almost, she could hear his voice.

A faceless man. A man of authority. But not Konrad, and not—obviously—her astronomer-lover who craved aloneness and yet was rarely alone.

(Just as well, M.R. told herself, that she and Andre had never been together in any quasi-permanent way—Andre wouldn't have been faithful to her, any more than he'd been faithful to his wife.)

Serving others, you were spared brooding about yourself. Or anyway, that was the theory.

As they entered the long-term neurology ward, M.R. remembered—not just that she'd been here several times previously but also she'd dreamt of the ward in the most curious and intimate of ways.

In a recent dream she'd found herself here—that is, the dream-setting was supposed to have been the Herkimer County Veterans Administration Hospital though in fact it bore little resemblance to the hospital—and M.R. was supposed to have been—a bride?

In some sort of bizarre paper bridal-gown. And high-heeled shoes, and bare legs. And—who was the bridegroom?

She'd been strangely happy, in the dream. Or rather, she had not been unhappy. A warm sensation had suffused her chest, in the region of her heart. *Mudwoman is loved. At last.* It was absurd, the most pathetic sort of wish-fulfillment, clearly compensatory for her deprived life as a woman; the sort of raw shameless fantasy which, if she'd been in therapy, she could not ever have brought herself to relate to any therapist, her pride wouldn't have allowed it.

And her fear of being exposed, talked-of. Laughed-at, and pitied.

"Konrad, hello! And—is it Margaret?"

In an aggressively cheery voice the floor supervisor (female, middle-aged) greeted them. M.R. wouldn't have troubled to correct the woman but Konrad said curtly, " 'Meredith'—my daughter's name is 'Meredith Neukirchen.' "

The supervisor squinted at Konrad as if thinking it some sort of wonderful novelty, the feisty old white-whiskered gent took his adult daughter's name so seriously.

"Well—hello and welcome!—'Konrad' and 'Mer'dith.' As you can see there are familiar faces in the lounge this morning—old friends of Konrad's—and two new faces. I know, you can introduce yourselves, but this gentleman has a little trouble speaking, that's an 'electro larynx' you're hearing—Sergeant Hercules Kropav from Castle Rock—a veteran of Vietnam—one of our longtime residents—and this gentleman is Corp'ral Shawn Barnburger—excuse me: 'Barnbarger'—from Tupper Lake—veteran of the Gulf War—'Operation Desert Storm'—1991?—1993? (Now it's a video game, I am told—'Operation Desert Storm'—the favorite of all of the younger men, here at Herkimer.) Corp'ral Shawn trained for the Special

Olympics when he first came to us, he'll tell you about his challenges I'm sure. . . ."

Blindly shaking hands. Konrad was boisterous, clearly enjoying himself. In his wake M.R. followed not quite so emphatically but sensing that, as a woman, she had an advantage—amid so much *maleness,* the novelty of *femaleness.*

She heard herself talking. She heard herself laughing. The men did seem happy to see her, those who could see. And the others—they too seemed happy, intrigued and enlivened by a female presence.

Awkward, though, to be on her feet—towering over the wheelchair patients.

A sensation of déjà vu swept over her like nausea.

And pinpricks of itching on her skin, particularly the skin around her ankles, she had to resist an impulse to scratch violently with her nails and draw blood.

"Excuse me, is it—Meredith?"

She glanced around, and there he stood—the man in the white shirt.

She'd forgotten him. She had not given him a second thought since he and his elderly companion had stepped into the elevator what seemed a very long time ago.

And now, he was approaching her, alone—staring at her quizzically, eagerly. The elderly woman was nowhere in sight. In these drab surroundings the long-sleeved white shirt caught the eye like a daub of glimmering white paint.

M.R. had the impression that he'd been watching her, from across the lobby. When she'd hurried into the first-floor restroom, in distress.

(A bout of diarrhea, a swirl of nausea, and a tentative recovery, she thought. Running tepid water at the splotched sink and splashing it onto her face that was flushed, yet not unattractive, oddly—as usual, M.R. could imagine that no one was likely to guess her misery.)

"You do remember me, I hope?—You were one of my star math students at Carthage High in the late 1970s."

Hans Schneider! M.R. had not seen the man nor scarcely recalled him in more than twenty years.

"Oh yes—of course—'Mr. Schneider.'"

"And you are—'Meredith'?"

"Yes. 'Meredith Neukirchen.'"

"I thought that I'd seen you earlier today in the foyer, Meredith—I mean, I saw you but wasn't altogether certain that—it was *you*. After so many years . . ."

Clumsily Schneider extended his hand to M.R—she wasn't sure if he meant to clasp her hand, or to shake it;

instead, he gripped it between both his hands, pulling her off balance so that she nearly stumbled into him.

"Oh, excuse me—"

"Excuse *me*—"

They were staring at each other, astonished. M.R. could not believe how her former high school teacher stood before her, and so altered—in middle age Hans Schneider looked more youthful than he'd looked as a young man. His face she'd recalled as narrow and unattractive had filled out—his forehead was less severely creased—his nose less prominent—though his eyes fixed upon her face were no less intense. His manner that had been so aggressive had softened. His smile that had been a sneer had vanished. And why had she ever thought he'd resembled a *crow*?

Through the prism of derisive adolescent eyes the math teacher had been dismissed as *Freaky, ugly.* M.R. felt the injustice, in which she'd unthinkingly participated.

Though it did seem clear, her former teacher was ill-accustomed to sudden gestures of intimacy. Perhaps to any kind of intimacy.

"You aren't—married? Or—?"

How bluntly, blunderingly Hans Schneider spoke. His gaze dropped to M.R.'s left hand—her ringless fingers. She felt the absurdity of her predicament: she was in love with a man who was almost entirely absent from her life.

"No. I'm not married."

"And I also—not married. Not now."

M.R. understood the murmured qualification— *Now.*

M.R. understood the intensity in her former teacher's face. She had not forgotten the bizarre proposal he'd made to her when she'd been a girl of sixteen and he'd been an adult man of twenty-nine. *Contract. You could wait for me. We have an understanding.*

How shocked she'd been at the time! Yet, in her innermost heart, how deeply moved, flattered.

"You changed my life, Mr. Schneider. You made my life possible."

"Did I!"

"You encouraged me to apply to Cornell and not just to teachers' colleges. 'Somewhere distinguished'—you said. And so I did apply, and Cornell gave me a scholarship. . . ." M.R. heard the plaintive boastfulness in her voice. She hoped that Hans Schneider wouldn't ask her what she'd done after Cornell, where her career had brought her: for she'd have had no idea how to reply.

He smiled, uncertainly. As if he too were calculating what he might ask her, and what he had better not ask her. Some instinct urged him to step back, to return to the deeper past of Carthage High School which was their shared history.

"I seem to remember that you were ill, Meredith? In the spring of your senior year?"

M.R. was taken aback by the question, and by the undisguised tenderness with which it was framed.

"No. Certainly not."

"You had to stay out of school for several weeks. . . ."

M.R. laughed, protesting: "No! I wasn't ever ill, and I was certainly never out of school for several weeks. I graduated with my class—'79. In fact, I was class valedictorian."

Again, this plaintive boastfulness. Flea bites ringing M.R.'s ankles and feet were making her want to scratch violently.

As if trying to recall this extraordinary bit of information Hans Schneider frowned thoughtfully. But of course he couldn't recall Meredith Neukirchen as valedictorian because by the spring of 1979 he'd vanished from Carthage.

By the spring of 1979 he'd been presumed dead.

"Well. I must be thinking of someone else. . . ."

Schneider spoke apologetically yet with an air of just perceptible stubbornness as if he believed M.R. mistaken, but wasn't going to press the issue.

M.R. wondered if it was possible—Hans Schneider didn't remember what had happened to him in

Carthage? His "breakdown"—"physical and mental collapse"—so like her own recent breakdown.

"Well! I do remember, Meredith, you were an excellent math student."

"Actually you told me, Mr. Schneider, that I was only just a 'good' student—I hadn't any 'natural gift for math.' "

A hot flush rose into M.R.'s face as if she were sixteen years old again and vulnerable to the man's judgment.

Schneider protested: "Surely not! I'm sure that—I didn't say *that*."

"You did. And of course you were right, Mr. Schneider. I was capable of high school math including elementary calculus but—I had no 'natural gift for math.' " M.R. had intended her previous remark to be a rebuke but the mood between her and Schneider was edgy, giddy; their words were a kind of magical banter; she felt her heart beating with an absurd anticipation and childlike wonder—*Can this be happening? After twenty years—this?*

Schneider protested: "Please don't call me 'Mister,' Meredith—my name is 'Hans.' "

Hans! M.R. pressed the knuckles of her hand against her mouth, trying not to laugh.

"But—what is so funny?"

"I—I'm not sure. I don't know."

"It's a kind of—miracle—or maybe that's too strong a word: coincidence? Though not a coincidence, either. I mean, our meeting each other like this, in this terrible place. . . . I did think of you from time to time, Meredith, after I left Carthage, but—I didn't think it would be appropriate for me to contact you. And then, as time passed—I suppose I 'forgot' you. I mean—another life intervened."

You fell in love again. More appropriately. Of course.

M.R. spoke more soberly now. She had to resist an impulse to touch Hans Schneider's wrist.

"What I remember about our math class was how you taught me to 'teach'—Hans. You sent me to the blackboard to work out problems in front of the class. I was very shy—at first . . . I felt so clumsy and self-conscious! But you gave me faith in myself. You forced me to see that I could do something I would never have imagined I could do, and that I could enjoy it."

"Well—did I! Really! I suppose . . . I'd hoped it might have that effect. You seemed somehow to require 'affirmation'—some sort of infusion of strength. Did you become a teacher? Are you a teacher now?"

Schneider was smiling at M.R. as if he hoped his question wasn't intrusive. That he hadn't blundered in asking it. M.R. murmured *yes* in a way to forestall further questioning.

That she had a Ph.D. in philosophy from Harvard was not information she wanted to provide Hans Schneider, just yet. Her history at the University she did not want to provide Hans Schneider just yet.

Though she was relieved—though also somewhat hurt—that Hans Schneider seemed totally oblivious of the public career of M. R. Neukirchen, its small triumphs and small disasters.

Maybe later. If I see him again. Inevitably, then.

"Where are you living now, Meredith?"

Hesitantly Schneider asked. As if sensing that something unfortunate had happened to M.R., painful to reveal.

"Now? Right now—for much of the summer—I've been living in Carthage, with my father."

"Carthage! Somehow I wouldn't have thought . . ." Schneider paused, as if the possibility of Carthage, the very sound of the word, was somehow incomprehensible. At close quarters, M.R. could see that the man's white cotton shirt wasn't so fresh any longer, damp with perspiration beneath the arms. A smell of his body—anxiety mixed with hope—mixed with the faintly urinous/disinfectant smell of the hospital, that was without hope. "I—I left Carthage—as maybe you know—and never returned . . . I broke off all contact with my 'colleagues. . . .' Secondary school teaching isn't for the fainthearted! I went back to graduate school at Boston University and got a Ph.D. in math—expanding on work I'd done for my M.A.—a year as a post-doc at Penn—then I taught at the SUNY branch at Potsdam—then to St. Lawrence, in Canton, where I've been for seventeen years—still an associate professor and still toiling away at my 'original' research, that I'd begun as a master's candidate in the early 1970s! (That has turned out to be a dead end, I'm afraid. But who could have predicted, when I'd begun? Not even my adviser, long since emeritus and deceased.) Sometimes I feel—especially here in this hospital—(to which I've been bringing a neighbor, a widow, to see her son since the poor woman hasn't anyone else to drive her to Herkimer)—that my life hasn't yet—really—*begun.* As if somehow my life had careened off course—taken a wrong turn—a detour—and any day now, if I am attentive and alert, and don't succumb to despair, it will revert to what it might have been." Schneider had been speaking ever more rapidly in a voice that sounded as if it hadn't been used, in such a way, in some time; he paused now, wiping at his face with a handkerchief. (M.R. took note: not a tissue to be tossed away but a cotton handkerchief.) (Oh, what did this mean about Hans Schneider? That he wasn't a careless throw-away sort of individual, but one inclined to permanence? Or that he was a fussy middle-aged bachelor fixed in insurmountable habits, unnavigable as a vehicle arthritic with rust?) Now he spoke earnestly, stepping so close that M.R. instinctively stepped back:

"I wonder, Meredith—could I call you? Maybe we could—if you're in Carthage—see each other sometime? I would drive down of course. . . ."

"I think—I don't think . . ."

"We have so much to say to each other! After so many years it can't be just a 'coincidence'—I mean, meeting here, today—even if it's this place of misery."

"Yes. I mean, no—"

M.R.'s ankles itched violently. Yet she could not stoop to scratch them, while Hans Schneider spoke so passionately. And she'd been distracted seeing Konrad observing them from across the lobby. Her father had emerged from the men's restroom but had stopped short sighting his daughter in what appeared to be an intense conversation with a stranger—or possibly not a stranger; canny Konrad, at times so blustery and intrusive, at other times so sensitive to the subterranean intricacies of situations.

"I'll give you my number, and you can call me, Meredith, if you wish. It will be your choice, if you call."

Graciously Hans Schneider spoke. His smile had become forced, fixed. Perspiration glimmered on his face highlighting the ghost-rivulets in his forehead, those odd vertical frown-lines descending from his hairline that had seemed to have faded but were now reappearing. M.R. was deeply moved, tears stung her eyes. She felt an impulse to clutch at her old teacher's hand, to kiss the knuckles in gratitude.

"I hope—I do hope—we can see each other again? Sooner than another twenty years? Yes?"

He gave her the little scrap of paper upon which he'd neatly printed crucial information. M.R. folded it and put it into her pocket quickly in the hope that her sharp-eyed father would not see.

"Yes! Thank you."

Blindly M.R. turned away. She had a dread of Hans Schneider clutching at her in a clumsy embrace—and how would she have responded, if he had?

Crossing the heat-sweltering parking lot to their car, Konrad observed to M.R.: "A suitor in Birkenstocks sandals is every dad's dream for his daughter. Even with socks, in August."

It was Konrad's provocatively terse wit calculated to surprise. For one naturally expected Konrad to be anything but terse.

M.R. laughed. A wild sort of laughter. Wiping at her eyes, and not daring to look at her father's face.

Ridiculous! You have already invested your adult life in one man.

Too late! Too late! Too late for another folly.

Next morning M.R. telephoned the University president's office.

Next morning M.R. spoke with the acting president for nearly ninety minutes.

By the end of which without being more than half-conscious of what she was doing M.R. had savagely scratched the damned flea bites ringing her ankles, bare feet and legs to the knee, so that she was bleeding from a dozen tiny wounds.

Mudwoman:
Moons beyond Rings of Saturn.

August 2003

Unexpectedly he called.

Saying calmly, bemused as one reporting a fact in a Universe of facts and no fact of more profundity or significance than the infinity of others *She has kicked me out at last. She has asked me to leave.*

And he said *I'm sick, Meredith darling. I'm damaged goods.*

She didn't ask what her astronomer-lover meant. She didn't ask if this sickness would be fatal, and how soon; she didn't ask if he was in pain, or even if he needed her; without hesitation she said *I'll come to you.*

And he said *No, darling. It will be better if I come to you, in some way we can reasonably work out, for now.*

Mudwoman Not Struck by Lightning. Mudwoman Saved from Nightmare.

August 2003

"Meredith! Come look."

Reluctantly she came. She'd always been fearful of lightning storms—cautious, rather. Thinking how ironic to be struck by lightning out of curiosity, how needless a death.

When fiercely you so want to live, how ironic such a death.

And so reluctantly she came to the rear porch, where Konrad stood just barely sheltered from warm pelting rain lashing against the porch roof, the porch-posts, what was visible of the backyard grass and Agatha's tangled garden. Her father rapt as a child riskily peering up into the night sky where miles away above the Adirondacks rain clouds were illuminated by lightning-flashes like severed nerves.

Sheets of rain and a noise as of shaken tin and M.R. winced at the deafening thunder-claps, and the silence that rushed in its wake like a stilled heart.

For some of the lightning-flashes weren't miles away it seemed, some were closer, in Carthage, in the hills above the Black Snake River.

No need to see the river which was less than a half-mile from where they stood to know that, after a day of rain and now in the exigency of this torrential down-pour, the river was rapidly rising.

A smell of sulphur in the air, like struck matches! And a smell of autumn, that made M.R.'s heart beat in apprehension.

She had not told Konrad about Andre's late-night call, of the night before.

She had told him—of course—of the lengthy conversation she'd had with her provost, who'd been acting as president of the University through the summer; and of another conversation with Leonard Lockhardt that had followed.

"Meredith, we're perfectly safe here! The lightning is miles away—mostly. And how beautiful, like Northern Lights . . ."

Beautiful! M.R. supposed yes, if you liked that sort of thing.

Manic detonations in the sky, pulsing arteries, raw nerves, neurons—shut your eyes and it's a brain aneurysm, such a display of light.

Sensibly, Solomon was hiding inside the house. Cowering somewhere, very likely in the basement.

"I don't recall you being frightened of electric storms, as a girl," Konrad said. "That isn't a recollection of mine."

M.R. tried to think: this wasn't a recollection of hers either.

"Nightmares, now. You did have nightmares."

A fissure erupted in the sky just directly above them, scarcely beyond the treeline at the end of their property. M.R. gave a little cry and leapt back toward the opened door even as deafening thunder rolled over them, almost immediately; Konrad blinked and stared and held his ground.

She hadn't had time to count. Scant seconds between the eruption of lightning and the aftermath of ear-splitting sound.

She felt Agatha's distress—when Konrad behaved in some way brash, risky, dangerous—"self-destructive" and (Agatha's reiterated charge) "immature." How disapproving Agatha would be seeing Konrad on the porch steps in such weather. His bare feet, his trouser-legs and his lower body were riddled with damp, he scarcely seemed to notice.

M.R. said: "Daddy, remember Agatha's librarian-friend Crystal—Crystal's husband—I think it was her husband—was watching a lightning storm from their back porch like this and lightning struck one of the porch posts a few inches from him and sent wood-slivers into his face. . . ."

Absorbed in the display of lightning in the sky, the illumination of gigantic cumulus clouds like frigates, Konrad paid no heed.

"Daddy, at least stand back by the door here! Some of these lightning-flashes are less than a mile away . . . Crystal's husband was badly injured, and might have been killed . . ."

"Oh, that never happened, I'm sure."

"What never happened, Daddy? Why do you say that?"

"Agatha's friends always exaggerated. And especially her librarian-friends. Their lives are over-quiet—'repressed'—and they're surrounded by books—'stories'—they begin to invent their own."

It was near midnight. The storm grew fiercer, louder. Gusts of wind whipped leaves from trees—old cedars, sycamores, birches that badly needed pruning, that M.R. had meant to prune. A good-sized tree limb fell heavily

onto the roof and down the shingled roof rain ran overflowing gutters choked with leaves. It was so, you did
feel a fascination with the rampaging storm—almost, an
expectation that chaos was about to be discharged, into
the human sphere. Shattering the roof, the house—the
human habitation and its carefully named things. And of
course, there were myriad leaks inside, upstairs. Already
Konrad and M.R. had set out pans into which globules
of water dropped noisily as flung pebbles.

Earlier that day—at the Carthage Vets Co-op fund-
raiser picnic, that Konrad and M.R. had organized,
in Friendship Park—the temperature had risen into
the mid-nineties Fahrenheit, now it had plummeted
thirty-five degrees.

For all the effort of the Neukirchens, father and
daughter—organizing the fund-raiser, working with
veterans' wives, widows, families and volunteers—the
sort of "leadership" effort M.R. did so well—the co-op
had netted less than five hundred dollars which was
less than M.R. herself had contributed to the organization on her father's behalf.

Still, the fund-raiser picnic had been worth it!
Konrad insisted, and M.R. wished to think so.

The end of August. End of summer. Between M.R.
and her father it was tacitly understood: she would soon
be leaving Carthage.

"When you return to your home, remember: you have been placed in this world for a distinct purpose, and at the University, you have found that purpose."

M.R. smiled wanly. M.R. was not going to contradict her beloved father.

"And remember: you must not overwork your body, or your soul. You must not enslave yourself, as you would not enslave any other person. You must be the custodian of your *self*."

Still M.R. smiled, silent. She was thinking that she could not bear to leave Carthage after all—she could not leave her father who was her newfound friend.

Yet of course, she must leave. She would leave.

Don't risk it! Not again.

The next time you break, you will not heal.

She would invite Konrad to visit her, to stay with her. She would insist.

Easier for you both to remain in Carthage. This is your home, you are not at risk here.

In Carthage she'd regained sleep. She'd regained some portion of her frayed soul. Quite frankly she was concerned—she was terrified—that, returning to the University, she would return to the madness she had so narrowly escaped.

It is very hard to prevail where you are not, in the deepest and most intimate and forgiving of ways, loved. It is very hard to prevail in any case but without this love, it is close to impossible.

Yet—*I will do it! I must.*

M.R. would not tell her father these doubts. She would not tell her father about the sudden turn in Andre Litovik's life suggesting that now, his life would be bound up more tightly with hers.

Astonishing that Konrad, echoing a notion of Agatha's, had seemed to foretell such a turn . . .

With maddening inquisitiveness Konrad had asked her about the man he'd seen her speaking with "earnestly"—"at length"—in the Herkimer hospital— "the mystery man in the Birkenstocks"—but M.R. answered with embarrassed evasiveness: "Oh Daddy! It was nothing really. Just a former high school teacher who thought he remembered me."

"*Thought* he remembered you? Or—*remembered* you?"

M.R. laughed. Though Konrad's teasing could be like nettles, or flea bites, rankling one's skin.

"Was that the teacher who'd had a nervous breakdown, your math teacher? The rumor was, the poor bastard killed himself?"

"Oh Daddy! No."

"What was his name?—'Steiner'—'Schneider.'"

How canny Konrad was—what a good memory! M.R. was rather shaken, her father remembered Hans Schneider's name.

"I—I'm not sure. I don't remember."

"Don't *remember*? How many math teachers were there at Carthage who tried to kill themselves? Some kind of crazy-wild place, was it? Hive of decadents?"

M.R. laughed but said nothing more. You could never win by responding to Konrad's teasing—to respond at all was analogous to stroking an aggressive porcupine, to soothe it. She reasoned that Konrad need never know about Hans Schneider: she had no intention of telephoning the man as he'd requested.

She wasn't certain that she had the telephone number, still. Possibly crumpled in a pocket of her khaki shorts.

Konrad reverted to the subject of Meredith's health. Now he was serious, somber. One did not need to be a Quaker to know that "holding in the light" was essential to survival, he told her.

"Remember, Meredith: you pushed yourself too hard even as a child. In elementary school! You ground your teeth in your sleep—you gave yourself nightmares—you were always anxious about being *tested*. You were anxious about crossing bridges, getting lost,

missing school and 'falling behind' . . . You had nightmares for years."

"I had nightmares? I don't remember."

"Agatha, a far lighter sleeper than I, heard you
crying out in your sleep, and woke me, and we hurried into your room and woke you—sometimes your
eyes were wide open but you didn't seem to be seeing
anything. You were very frightened, shivering—you
couldn't speak. But we hugged you, and told you little
stories, and told you that we loved you and nothing
would ever, ever happen to you because we loved you,
and finally you settled down again, and slept."

"I don't remember. . . ."

"Well, better not to remember, dear Meredith!
That's what growing up means."

In the morning, Konrad helped her pack her car for
the drive back to New Jersey.

Mudwoman at Star Lake.
Mudwoman at Lookout Point.

August 2003

By midmorning she'd crossed into Herkimer County on the old state highway heading south and east along the Black Snake River. Traffic was drawn to the interstate several miles to the south, that ran parallel with Route 41, leaving the highway relatively deserted.

In the aftermath of the previous night's storm the air was glaring-bright. The sky a fierce cobalt blue that pained the eyes.

And the river! Rampaging, spilling its banks, a churn of mad white froth and part-submerged storm debris like projectiles.

Sunshine like broken-mirror glass on the river, winking of a thousand eyes.

"Good-bye, darling! Love you."

And: "Drive carefully, promise? Give me a call when you get home."

These words Konrad had uttered in a tone of jovial ebullience masking what concern, what care, what melancholy, what paternal anxiety M.R. could not know.

She'd laughed. She'd wiped at her eyes.

"Daddy, of course. Love *you.*"

She would not abandon her father another time, she vowed.

For Konrad and Andre would like each other, very much—she was certain. *What a great guy* each would say of the other. Almost, M.R. could hear the men's uplifted voices.

Meredith darling! What a great guy . . .

. . . wonderful to meet him.

It had taken M.R. and Konrad scarcely twenty minutes to pack her car. For M.R. had brought very few things with her and had accumulated little during her stay in Carthage.

With a fussy sort of tenderness Konrad had hung M.R.'s clothes on wire hangers on the little hooks in the rear, which clothes M.R. would likely have flung down onto the seat. He'd found a canvas tote bag of Agatha's—CELEBRATE NATIONAL LIBRARY WEEK!—to fill with books M.R. was taking with her from the house, mostly from Agatha's shelves.

It seemed wrong, a flaw of character if not a tragic presentiment, that a woman of M.R.'s age had accumulated so little that was essential to her.

"Life small enough to fit into a thimble! Well."

She'd spoken aloud. Breathlessly she laughed, the remark seemed to her not only astute but witty.

In her mood of excited apprehension M.R. took care to drive at just the speed limit. Though traffic on Route 41 was sparse from time to time vehicles rushed past her—trucks, pickups, local cars. She would connect with the interstate eleven miles ahead and on I–81 she would drive most of the way home almost directly south, a drive of about seven hours.

Next morning, her new life would begin.

Her new life, that would be a transformation of her former life.

For now she was stronger. Now she was prepared, *readied.*

In the near distance were steep wooded hills. The Adirondack forest, that stretched to the horizon. As a girl M.R. had felt her heartbeat quicken at the sight of the mountains—dense-wooded slopes, the higher peaks shrouded in mist; massed evergreens with scattered veins of premature red, red-orange, bright dying deciduous leaves like red stars in a distant constellation. For the end of summer was abrupt in this region.

On one of Konrad's battered old road maps—(that Agatha had tried to re-fold, without success)—M.R. had located Canton, New York: surprised to see how small the town was, not a town but a village, and so far inland, nowhere near Lake Ontario as she'd imagined it was, or the spectacular St. Lawrence River; the nearest city was Ogdensburg, the size of Carthage.

St. Lawrence County extended to the Canadian border. One hundred miles north of Carthage.

Amid the distraction and upset of packing that morning she'd searched for the scrap of paper containing Hans Schneider's phone number but hadn't found it.

Thinking *If he wants to call Neukirchen, in Carthage, he will.*

Thinking *It is out of my control. It is not my choice to make.*

She had not heard from Andre Litovik since his astonishing call of the other day. She wondered if he had actually moved out of the house on Tremont Street in which he'd lived for so long—how difficult it would be, for one who'd routinely traveled in extragalactic space, to make so literal, so *physical* a move! The Litoviks lived in an old dark-lavender Victorian house with lilac shutters and trim, in need of repainting and repair yet still, to the stunned eye of the young Meredith bicycling past, more than once risking being seen by her (secret) lover, a mesmerizing sight that left her shaken. Here was a *family house,* a *home*—with bay windows, steep-pitched roofs, ornate gables, and a front porch partly hidden by wisteria. Meredith, who'd rented a small single-bedroom apartment for what seemed to her an excessively high rent, could only guess what such a property would cost in stylish Cambridge near Harvard University. Yet Andre dared to speak of this spectacu-lar period house in such vague and negligent terms, you might be led to think the man scarcely lived anywhere solid, or even visible; you might be led to think that the house was the province of the wife entirely.

Material things don't engage me. Sorry!

The sort of cavalier remark, M.R. thought, made by those who never have to think of *material things.*

For a moment, M.R. felt sympathy for the woman of that house. But only for a moment.

Even more beguiling, there'd been a garden beside the house, hidden behind a six-foot fieldstone wall cov-ered in tattered ivy; through a part-opened gate, you could glimpse inside—Meredith had seen a beautiful autumnal ruin of a garden.

M.R. had never stepped inside the house on Trem-ont Street. Never stepped inside the garden. . . .

She was thinking of Agatha's garden. How moved she'd been to enter it, in the aftermath of the previ-ous night's storm—beaten-down as if with mallets and shovels and yet still vivid with flowers, clumps of crimson phlox, black-eyed Susans, and frayed roses. And sunflower stalks broken like snapped spines, big round affable sunflower-faces hanging crooked. Several of the older trees had been devastated and their splintered wood whitely raw as marrow and when M.R. had suggested to Konrad that she stay another day, another day or two, she would help him with the storm cleanup, Konrad had laughed saying *Certainly not!*

Saying *It's time for you to leave. Take care! Love you.*

She hadn't told Konrad about Andre's call because she hadn't wanted to talk to him further about Andre. Already she'd revealed too much to her father, she'd pained Konrad allowing him a glimpse of his daughter's sexual vulnerability, naïveté.

How love had entered her veins, a virulent fever. How she'd never built up an immunity.

She wondered if Andre's wife had really asked him to leave—"kicked him out." She wondered how either Andre or the wife could break off their relationship of decades.

The wife, the son. The damaged son.

Obviously, Andre's deepest feelings lay with his family. These were not, likely, happy feelings any longer—but they lay deep.

For hadn't he said, once, in one of his curious ruminative moods, in which irony contended with a raw sort of sincerity, that though love can "wear out" over time, a marriage of decades is like tangled tree-roots: the trees may appear separate and distinct above-ground, but are entwined below-ground. His implication had been—(so M.R. had thought)—that his relationship with her was superficial, shallow, set beside his relationship with his wife.

They had virtually no roots grown together, no shared past.

Their pasts did not overlap. M.R. really knew very little of her (secret) lover's life, as he knew virtually nothing of hers.

M.R. was frightened suddenly: Andre Litovik would never be her husband. What an idea!

M.R. was frightened suddenly: the prospect of living with Andre Litovik!

The intimacy between them had never been put to a serious test. For always there was the knowledge that their time together was limited, bracketed by their very different lives.

Always the knowledge that each life was totally exclusive of the other—a place of refuge to which the other had no access.

Andre loved "Meredith"—as the young woman not his wife, and not the mother of his (damaged) son. He loved her—(M.R. wanted to concede this, out of fear that it was true)—as a way of revenge on the other woman.

But this was too crude, too reductive. Andre was capable of the most extravagant emotions, it wasn't possible for M.R. to fully comprehend him. Hadn't he said to her *Better if I come to you. In some way we can reasonably work out, for now.*

"I will believe that. I will have faith."

At a crossroads M.R. saw bullet-ridden road signs: ALEXANDRIA BAY, WATERTOWN, CASTORLAND.

Canton was not so far from Watertown. To the west of Watertown was Lake Ontario, the massive inland sea.

And here was a sign for smaller towns: HERKIMER JUNCTION, SLABTOWN, SPRAGG, STAR LAKE.

STAR LAKE 9 MILES.

Star Lake! Only nine miles away . . .

Gradually Route 41 had veered away from the Black Snake River. But if M.R. turned onto the Star Lake road, soon again she would be driving beside the river.

Reasoning *There will be another entrance to I–81, farther south.*

Reasoning *No one is waiting for me today. Tonight.*

Next morning, M.R. had a sequence of appointments in Salvager Hall starting at 8:30 A.M.

Next morning was the first of September and but thirteen days before the start of the fall semester at the University.

Later she would think *It was a decision. It was not impulse.*

And so, turning onto Star Lake Road which was a narrow blacktop road bringing her through stretches of densely wooded countryside alternating with farm-land, or the remains of farmland; long sweeping hills of surpassing beauty and strangeness as on a facing hill a quarter-mile away where the road ascended, a dark-swooping-winged shadow like a gigantic crow moved toward her—the shadow of a cloud.

M.R. ducked, as the shadow rushed toward her.

Nine miles to Star Lake. But the road was circu-itous, tortuous. In the foothills of the Adirondacks, no route is direct.

Strewn by the roadside and frequently in the road were broken tree limbs, storm debris from the previous night. No one seemed to have driven on this road since the storm. A ditch fraught with muddy water had over-flowed and puddles like leprous lesions had invaded the road.

Several times M.R. had to get out of her car to drag aside broken branches to make a space for her car to pass. Soon her hands were stinging from thistles, thorns. In the bright sunshine she felt both anxious and exhilarated, curious. There was a purpose in visiting Star Lake, she knew: the tar paper dwelling behind the Gulf station on the highway. Bare floorboards part-covered in loose patches of linoleum—"remnants"—and a Formica-topped kitchen table from Goodwill with mismatched vinyl chairs that could be made to skid across the floor, if the spike-haired man was provoked to kick. And the big deep stained bathtub in the closet-sized bathroom. And on all the walls of the little house "crosses"—"crucifixes"— "Jesus Our Savior"—which as a small child she'd seen without *seeing*—upon which her eyes moved without *knowing, identifying*—"crosses" and "crucifixes"—"Jesus Our Savior"—mysterious words that fluttered in her brain like nighttime moths drawn to lamplight. Yet the fact must have been that at the time, when she'd been Jedina—(so young! lacking all volition)—she had never heard such words as *crosses—crucifixes*—she was sure.

If her mother had identified these objects at all it would be to speak of them as *special signs of God.*

Paradox: how do we know what we have failed to see because we have no language to express it, thus cannot know that we have failed to see it.

That was the human predicament, was it?—the effort to remain human.

The blacktop road so twisted, so turned back on itself to accommodate the hilly landscape, M.R. lost her sense of how far she was from Star Lake knowing only that, practicably speaking, she could not turn back: the road was too narrow, the overflowing ditch too close to the road.

The effort to attain civilization. To resist delusion. Even as the very mud-muck beneath the floorboards of civilization is delusion.

Nervously M.R. smiled. It seemed to be so—M. R. Neukirchen had made an (academic) career out of such paradoxes.

She could not be lost of course—so long as she stayed on this poorly maintained road.

She calculated she was about four miles from Star Lake when she crossed a wood-plank bridge—(not over the Black Snake River, which had veered away from the road again)—but over a fast-running, swollen creek. And in her rearview mirror she saw—(she'd been seeing, without exactly registering the fact)—a vehicle approaching on the blacktop road.

A pickup truck, painted a bright royal blue. And with oversized tires, that lifted the truck-chassis to a daunting height.

M.R. slowed her car and moved as far to the right of the narrow road as she dared. Roadside grasses and underbrush scraped noisily against the fenders and underside of her car.

How like a child's crude painting of an adult vehicle, tank-sized, bright blue, looming large above the road!

The pickup was moving at a speed greater than M.R.'s, jolting and lurching in potholes, crashing through debris in the roadway without slowing. M.R. felt a frisson of panic, the bright-blue vehicle would collide with her smaller vehicle, crash and crush and run over it like a tank.

M.R. was driving at a slow speed, to allow the pickup to pass. But the bright-blue vehicle had slowed also and did not pass her looming so large in her rear-view mirror that she could see only a portion of it, a windshield blinding with sunshine, obscuring the driver within.

She thought *Why doesn't he pass me! What does he want of me!*

The front of the pickup was about eighteen inches from M.R.'s rear fender. Deliberately the driver was matching his speed to M.R.'s reduced speed. Was this— harassment? A kind of game? Did the driver know her, or believe he knew her?

Playful, in the rough careless way of the men of this region.

Or maybe it was a kind of gallantry?—the driver would accompany M.R., a solitary woman, along this poorly maintained route to Star Lake.

M.R. wished to think this. Though she'd begun to perspire with unease. Staring into the rearview mirror. She could make out a figure behind the windshield— not clearly—seemingly an adult man with a blurred face, thick dark hair.

Calmly she drove. She did not increase her speed, to try to escape.

Impossible to escape! You must have faith.

A tangle of underbrush had worked its way around her right-front tire, bringing her almost to a stop. Only by pressing down hard on the gas pedal—frantically hard—could M.R. force the tire to turn.

Her car was limping! But the driver behind her registered no sign of impatience, or derision. Rather there was the sense—M.R. felt, staring into the rearview mirror at the haze of bright-blue—that she was being protected.

A foolish mistake, to have taken this road. The driver of the pickup wants to make certain that nothing happens to my car—to me.

Someone who knows me? Recognizes me?

Someone who knows it is wrong for me to be here?

There came a strong smell of pine needles, wet rotting leaves and wet earth. Ditch-water leaked like pus into the road causing M.R.'s wheels to churn, slide and slip.

The pickup slowed, waiting for M.R.'s vehicle to recover the road.

M.R. saw the driver's face through the windshield—then, glaring sunlight intervened.

Mudwoman's bridegroom! He had followed her here.

Slowly and in tandem the vehicles moved along the narrow blacktop road, that had begun to descend to the lake. To her relief M.R. saw mailboxes at the side of the road—narrow lanes leading into the underbrush—and caught glimpses of log cabins, tar paper shanties, corroded-looking house trailers mounted on cement blocks. Cheery signs were affixed to trees: HAPPY HUNTIN CAMP—"MY BLUE HEAVEN"—DAISY & MAC—7TH HEAVEN—KAMP KOMFORT.

No people were visible. Only just parked vehicles. If M.R. had been in danger she could not have risked abandoning her car in the road, running back one of the lanes crying for help.

Thinking *But he does not want to hurt me. That is not his intention.*

Thinking *If that were his intention, he would have hurt me by now.*

Entering the village of Star Lake M.R. glanced into the rearview mirror and saw to her surprise—the bright-blue pickup had vanished from the road.

The driver must have turned off, onto a side road. Or, into one of the lanes.

Of course, the driver must live in Star Lake. In one or another of the dwellings in the woods. He had not been following M.R. but only just returning home.

M.R. felt both relief and disappointment. Her heartbeat had quickened with the prospect of—she didn't know.

STAR LAKE VILLAGE
POP. 475

The Gulf station had vanished and in its place was a U-Haul rental and behind the U-Haul rental, down a steep incline amid a carelessly mown field was a small simulated-cedar cabin that looked as if it had been shellacked, shiny as Glo-Coat. Strewn about the driveway were children's toys, a tricycle and a wagon. Directly in front of the house was a patch of top-heavy tomato plants, battered by the recent storm. M.R. parked at the top of the driveway uncertain what to do for clearly this dwelling wasn't the squat little tar paper house in which Marit Kraeck had lived in the early 1960s.

And so the *special signs of God* had vanished.

Polyurethane strips over the loose-fitting windows like flayed skin, flapping in the wind. From outside, the little house had looked like its insides were coming out.

The big stained claw-footed bathtub in the smelly bathroom. The game of tickle! M.R. only just remembered.

She smiled, confused. A vein had begun to beat in her forehead, a warning-beat as, on the back stairs of Charters House she'd known perfectly well that it was a mistake to proceed as she'd done—yet, like a dreamer locked in a script not her own, she'd proceeded.

The spike-haired man who'd played with Jewell, and with Jedina, the *game of tickle.*

Cherry pie, out of the wax-paper wrapping. Gluey sugary cherry filling, mealy pie-dough and so delicious, M.R.'s mouth began to water. She'd hidden beneath the steps in a sort of—closet? storage area?—her knees pressed against her chest.

Wrapped in something like a towel, or a bed-sheet . . .

He'd bathed her with such care—the spike-haired man. But maybe he had not been her father.

Strange how M.R. never thought of her father— never thought of the very concept *father*—as if such were a distant galaxy, beyond her power of imagining as beyond her power of comprehension.

"He might still be alive. And living here."

Awkwardly she'd been standing in the driveway clutching her car keys. A figure appeared behind a screen door in the cedar-cabin.

The voice was female, friendly-seeming yet wary.

"H'lo? You looking for someone?"

"Yes! Thank you. I'm looking for . . ."

M.R. could not think what name to provide. Her face was unpleasantly damp, her hair had come loose from the scarf in which, early that morning, she'd tied it. (For M.R.'s stylishly cut hair had grown out ragged in Carthage, she dared not cut it with a scissors as Konrad snipped at his hair.) For the long drive home she was wearing rumpled shorts, a parrot green Carthage Veterans Co-op T-shirt in need of laundering. She wondered if she resembled a madwoman, or a drunken woman, or a woman who has had a bad shock, who has been assaulted.

The woman behind the screen door was waiting for a reply. A smaller figure had joined her, a child.

With difficulty, like hauling a pail of water out of a deep well, M.R. said, " . . . a family named 'Kraeck.'"

"'Krae-chek'? I don't think I know anyone named 'Krae-chek.'"

"Maybe—I'm not pronouncing it correctly. It might just have one syllable—'Kraeck.'"

The woman called to someone inside. There came a shouted reply M.R. couldn't hear clearly.

"You can try around town. Out by the lake, there's lots of older places—people who live year-round, or been coming back thirty, even forty years. We're here year-round but only for about five years. 'Krae-chek'—'Krick'—isn't any name I know."

M.R. thanked the woman. The shiny cedar-cabin, children's toys in the driveway, raggedly-mowed grass and the steep driveway—only the steep driveway was known to M.R. but as a dirt driveway, not gravel.

M.R. returned to her car and drove through the village of Star Lake to the lakefront, past larger cabins and cottages and the Star Lake Inn & Marina. On the lake, a braying of outboard motors. Angry noises like maddened hornets. It was a shock to her, beautiful Star Lake should be *silent.*

And a shock to her, nothing looked familiar. Yet very likely, neither Jewell nor Jedina had ever seen the lake, living in a ramshackle house a mile away.

At a gas station adjacent to a convenience store M.R. stopped to have her car tank filled. The attendant was a burly boy of about eighteen with rabbity teeth, sleepy-lidded eyes. His brawny forearms were discolored with grease, he wore a mechanic's cap reversed on his head. Sensing in M.R. a woman in some indefinable distress, old enough to be his mother yet not his responsibility, he listened to her stammering query with a shrug—

"Maybe yeh, there's some 'Kray-chek' somewhere, but nobody I know. Nobody around here."

In the convenience store M.R. bought a can of lukewarm soda. She asked the young-woman clerk if she knew of a family—or anyone—named "Kraeck" and the woman said, frowning, "This is—who? A man?"

"Yes. It could be a man."

"How old?"

"He'd be in his seventies, maybe."

A glaze-look came into the woman's face: she was in her early thirties.

"Can't help you, ma'am. Maybe you could try. . . ."

M.R. thanked the woman and left the store. She was gripped by the possibility—the probability—of her biological father still alive and living in this area. If she could locate someone who'd known her mother in the 1960s . . . But that was more than forty years ago.

Star Lake, approximately sixteen miles in circumference, was one of the less developed of the Adirondack lakes, far less affluent than Lake Placid, Tupper Lake, Saranac. The village was at the southernmost point of the lake that appeared, on maps, to be less "star-shaped" than shaped like a vertical, upright flame. Its rough shore was mostly wilderness but there was a road of some kind that circled the lake and the mad thought came to M.R. in perfect calmness—she could drive around Star Lake stopping at each cabin, each cottage, each trailer, to ask about her father. (And yet—what had been her father's name? Not Kraeck.) She felt a touch of vertigo, excitement. Forever she could drive around Star Lake in the southern Adirondacks in search of her lost father for there is no end to the circumference of any geometrical figure.

Thinking *I am breaking into pieces now. I must save myself.*

"No more. Enough. I have a father."

She threw the can of lukewarm soda into a trash bin. She returned to her car and drove through Star Lake in the direction of Route 41 east, that would bring her to I-81 within a half hour.

Thinking *You don't have to understand why anything that has happened to you has happened nor do you even have to understand what it is that has happened. You have only to live with the remains.*

At Lookout Point on I-81 she stopped to use a restroom.

Lookout Point was an elevated peninsula of rocky land above the Black Snake River valley east of Sparta. Looking north M.R. could identify Mount Marcy, Mount Moriah, Thunder Bay Mountain—Adirondack peaks dissolving into mist. It was a striking view—you wanted to stare, and stare. You did not ever want to look away.

Below, nearer the highway was a small picnic area, weatherworn picnic tables and grills and trash bins overflowing with litter and on the trail leading to the lookout point litter had been blown into the underbrush in a filigree like dirty lace.

Somehow it was late—nearly 3 P.M. M.R. had lost precious time in Star Lake. Yet for a long time she leaned over the lookout point railing, shivering. Her hair whipped in the damp cool wind. The sky was mottled, marbled—patches of sunshine like struck matches, appearing and disappearing, a sudden flare of light that abruptly vanished. Already, the air was autumnal, the sun had shifted in the sky.

She felt a stir of half-pleasurable melancholy, yet of anticipation—she had made the right decision to leave Carthage. She did have faith in Andre Litovik who would come to her as he'd promised. She must resolve not to retreat from him, to be so diffident in the face of the man's powerful personality. She must tell him bluntly, frankly—she would choose *him*. It was not just a matter, as it had been for so many years, of his choosing *her*.

"Ma'am! Hi there."

The voice was low, unnervingly near, and familiar.

M.R. looked around, startled. She'd believed herself alone at the rest stop except for a family—young parents, two young children—in the picnic area below. She was sure she'd seen no other vehicles. But here stood a tall lanky dirty-skinned boy of some indeterminate age—mid-twenties?—or older—slouched less than ten feet behind her on the trail. *Ma'am! Hi there* had been a sly sort of murmur like a caress across the back and shoulders of the solitary woman.

So quietly the boy had come up behind her, it was as if he'd emerged out of the steep rocky path.

His hair was stiff with grease and looked dyed—an unnatural caramel color. His bloodshot eyes were alert with ironic merriment. He wore a faded black T-shirt from which the sleeves had been torn and on the front of the T-shirt was a faded cartoon figure—a "superhero." His well-worn jeans resembled the stylish designer jeans favored by University undergraduates, bleached at the knees, strategically torn and patched. On his feet were the rotted remains of what appeared to be expensive jogging shoes. On his left wrist, an American eagle tattoo that looked as if its inks had smudged.

A university dropout, M.R. thought. But of another era.

She saw in his eyes a glimmering light of recognition. But she had never seen the boy before in her life,
she was certain.

"Yah howdy, ma'am . . ."

With an air of mildly distracted dignity M.R. tried
to ignore the insolent greeting. She knew that it was a
good idea not to lock eyes with the dirty-skinned boy
as one is instructed not to lock eyes with threatening
wild creatures.

"Excuse me, please."

M.R. turned to walk back down the path to the
picnic area. But the dirty-skinned boy didn't step aside
to let her pass.

"Ma'am? Din't-ya hear me?"

Now it was difficult not to look at him. Though still,
M.R. tried to keep her gaze from locking with his.

She was thinking: the young family was below, at a
picnic table. She was not alone on this trail and not in
any real danger.

"Ma'am, you got a car? Maybe can I ride with you?"

"I don't think so. . . ."

"Where you headed so anxious-like, ma'am?"

His face was a young-old face. The skin appeared
to be not dirty so much as discolored, stained. M.R.
wondered if he was wearing—makeup? Or had lightly
layered his face with mud, as his arms, with mud, to

stave off insects? She felt dazed, disoriented. There was something very wrong here, she knew.

The boy's smile was mock-respectful, sincere.

"I can drive, ma'am. You look like you'd benefit from some chauffeur-like. I can help, you're driving some distance and alone and are gettin like anxious, being alone. And I work with cars, ma'am, I know engines. I know the fuckin' insides of things."

His smile deepened, with a terrible intimacy. His teeth were small, yellowish-gray, thin. And his eyes, so familiar. M.R. had been looking helplessly at him, just slightly up at him, not knowing what she did.

The dirty-skinned boy was taller than M.R. by several inches. His shoulders were broad like wings but his chest was sunken, his waist and hips narrow. You might have thought, glancing at him, that one of his legs was shorter or less developed than the other, though this didn't seem to be the case. He appeared stunted in some mysterious way, not evident to the eye.

"Ma'am? Where're you from?"

"I—I'm leaving now. Excuse me, please . . ."

"I'm from Massena. Know where Massena is?"

Yes, M.R. knew where Massena was.

"Fuckin' shithole. You can't appreciate till you been stuck there."

M.R. was trying to determine: could she push past the boy, and risk being touched by him? Accosted by him?

Or should she back away, climb over the guardrail and try to get back to the picnic area below, by sliding down a steep pebbly hill? A sign warned DANGER DO NOT APPROACH EDGE OF CLIFF but she could avoid the sheer drop-off by cleaving to the narrow incline to her left, that descended to the parking lot about forty feet below.

It was not a good idea to be in this remote "scenic" place from which one might be pushed by a stranger, on a whim.

"You look like a nice kind generous lady, ma'am. Not like some selfish *boowoisee* would pass by a hitch-hiker 'cause he's a different *ethnic-type* from you."

A hitchhiker! That was why she'd seen no second vehicle below.

"Here, too—'scenic' shithole. Fuck it matters if you're starving. Can't appreciate, ma'am, till you been stuck here like—a helluva long time."

He coughed hoarsely, yet theatrically, as if to punctuate his extravagant words.

M.R. smiled guardedly. It was her nature to feel sympathy—not to ignore another's request even when, as common sense might decree, she was in danger.

"Ma'am? You smiling at me? Ain't laughing at me are you? That wouldn't be kind."

"I—I'm not laughing . . ."

"Maybe you got some change you could spare?"

"No. I'm sorry."

"Sorry you don't have no change, or sorry you ain't gonna give it to me? Ma'am?"

The thought came to M.R. *But you can give him something! A few dollars.*

But no. That would be a mistake. He will accept what you give him and take the rest by force.

Foolishly M.R. was smiling. Trying to determine if possibly the young family was still there after all, down the hill. If there was another vehicle below, in the cinder parking lot, she'd failed to notice. Or just M.R.'s own.

Badly now she wanted to call her father. She wanted to call Andre.

It was a mistake, to be so often alone. So much easier to be obliterated from the face of the earth, to be extinguished, if one is alone.

As if reading M.R.'s confused thoughts the boy said, with sudden vehemence:

"Ma'am! You are not in any fuckin' danger! I will ride with you and be your friend. Looks like you're all alone and got no husband, eh?—or he run off, or got old and died. Happens all-the-time, ma'am." The dirty-skinned boy laughed as if he'd said something witty and risqué.

With an air of calm M.R. was considering the nearby guard railing which was about two feet high. If she could manage to climb over it, quickly, before the dirty-skinned boy grabbed her, she would risk the hill; not certain how steep the hill was but she would risk it; as a girl living with the Skedds she'd been led into such seemingly desperate adventures and had not been injured, at least not seriously. And if another vehicle had driven into the parking lot below, or the young family was still there, someone would hear her crying for help, the dirty-skinned boy wouldn't dare follow her . . .

"You could give me a few dollars, ma'am. Ain't like you're going to miss a few dollars. In fact you could give me all the money you have and the keys to your car, ma'am. No matter it's a piece-of-shit car—beggars can't be choosers. You could give me, ma'am, or I could take."

Though M.R. had been expecting the dirty-skinned boy to rush at her, she seemed to be taken wholly by surprise when he did. She screamed at him, fighting back, more furious than panicked; at the Skedds' she'd learned to defend herself, however ineffectually, for you had to know—to give up is the error, you must never give up. She smelled the wild sick smell of her assailant, a rank animal smell, as he pummeled her, tried to wrestle her bag from her; of course, if all he wanted was her bag, she should surrender it to him, but she did not; she would not; she kicked at him blindly as he wrenched her off-balance, tugging at the shoulder strap of the bag. When she turned to run he grabbed at her—her clothing, her right arm. M.R. thought—*Is it going to end here?—like this?*

"Fuckin' cunt! Goddam ugly fuckin' cunt! Why the fuck d'you think you should be alive, fuckin' bitch, when the rest of us ain't?"

M.R. half-fell over the guardrail. On her knees but managed to right herself, then she was running down the hill, slip-sliding down the hill, nearly turning her ankle, if only she were wearing sturdier shoes! She'd scraped her knee, torn her clothing, but felt no pain yet, not even wet blood in a thin trickle down her leg.

The hill was near-vertical. Only a young heedless child could half-run half-fall down it without injury. M.R. clutched at shrubs and small trees to impede her fall as above her, leaning over the guardrail, the dirty-skinned boy jeered—"Ma'am! That's real dangerous, ma'am! Gonna break your neck, ma'am! Crack your skull!"

A small avalanche of pebbles and dried mud accompanied M.R., sliding down the hill. The dirty-skinned boy was making his way along the path, which was winding, and not direct, for he didn't dare follow her; she was aware that, for all his boastfulness, he was stiff-legged, and carried himself with his shoulders hunched. In a burst of strength M.R. ran limping to her car which she'd left unlocked—fortunately!—though Andre often scolded her for leaving it unlocked, carelessly—now, it was the proper thing to have done. M.R. threw herself into the car—locked the doors—jammed her key into the ignition even as the dirty-skinned boy hobbled in her direction yelling and waving his arms. M.R. saw that the young family had departed leaving her alone and in desperation she pressed down hard on the gas pedal as the car leapt forward; the dirty-skinned boy continued to taunt her, cursing her standing spread-legged in the path of her car; he had time to get out of her way surely, but stood his ground, defiantly, refused to move as the left front fender struck him—not hard, but hard enough to knock him aside, as the car rushed past; his thin body was deflected and tossed aside as one might toss aside a rag doll and M.R. thought *Have I killed him? What have I done?*—but there was the dirty-skinned boy staggering to his feet trying to rush after M.R.'s car but lacking strength, his face uplifted, a mask of blood on his face where he must have struck the ground—his expression one of astonishment and fury and M.R. acted by instinct not hesitating but re-versing her car, swiftly reversing and turning the car in a series of deftly executed if jerky maneuvers, turned the car around and swiftly exited the Lookout Point rest stop and within seconds she was on I-81 panting and half-sobbing yet exhilarated thinking *No one will know. Not ever, no one.*

By dusk, she'd arrived at the University.

THE NEW LUXURY IN READING

We hope you enjoyed reading
our new, comfortable print size and found it
an experience you would like to repeat.

Well – you're in luck!

HarperLuxe offers the finest in fiction and
nonfiction books in this same larger print size and
paperback format. Light and easy to read, HarperLuxe
paperbacks are for book lovers who want to see
what they are reading without the strain.

For a full listing of titles and
new releases to come, please visit our website:

www.HarperLuxe.com